"A wonderful mystery" – *Booklist* (starred review)

"A well laid out plot with many twists and turns…
a perfect edition" – *New York Journal of Books*

"A well-plotted, intriguing mystery" – *Library Journal*

"A must for any Sherlock Holmes fan" – *Bookgasm*

"A stand-out mystery novel" – *Culturess*

"Readers will find plenty of reasons to celebrate
this latest Sherlockian adventure" – *BookPage*

"[Abdul-Jabbar & Waterhouse] can pull off the historical
setting and the well-known characters, but also put their
own unique spin on things" – *The Sherlock Holmes Journal*

"Without any kind of doubt the best Victorian
mystery novel of the year" – *Rising Shadow*

"Another phenomenal novel" – *CrimeReads*

Also by Kareem Abdul-Jabbar and Anna Waterhouse,
and available from Titan Books

Mycroft Holmes

Mycroft and Sherlock

Mycroft and Sherlock: The Empty Birdcage

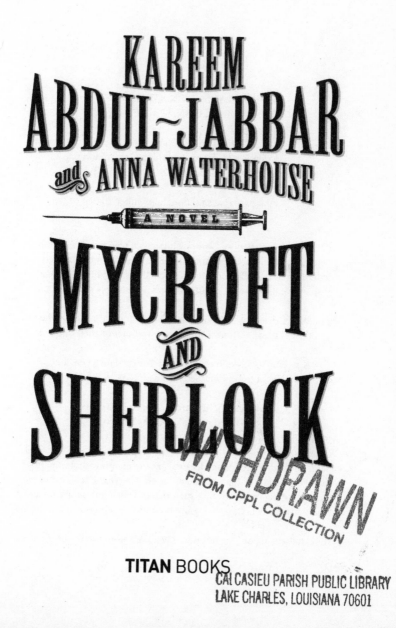

KAREEM ABDUL~JABBAR
and ANNA WATERHOUSE

A NOVEL

MYCROFT
AND
SHERLOCK

TITAN BOOKS

Mycroft and Sherlock
Paperback edition ISBN: 9781785659287
E-book edition ISBN: 9781785659270

Published by Titan Books
A division of Titan Publishing Group Ltd
144 Southwark Street, London SE1 0UP

First paperback edition: September 2019
10 9 8 7 6 5 4 3 2 1

A CIP catalogue record for this title is available from the British Library.

Printed and bound in the United States.

*This story is dedicated to
the many authors who've inspired me.*
KAJ

*For la famiglia, con affetto: Zia Mira, Zia Nana,
Zio Romano, Zia Maria, Susi, Paola, Marco, Tiziana.*
AW

MYCROFT
AND
SHERLOCK

1

London, England, 26 November 1872

MYCROFT HOLMES LEFT HIS TOWNHOUSE AT GREVILLE place in St. John's Wood and was opening his wrought-iron gate just as a passing neighbor called out a crisp good morning:

"No umbrella for you then, Mr. Holmes? You must be the adventurous sort: the papers predict a downpour!"

Mycroft politely bid him good day and glanced up at the eddying clouds, just as every Londoner had done every morning since time immemorial. But though the oatmeal-colored sky looked ominous, Mycroft was beholden neither to newsprint predictions nor to the common understanding of cloud formations, particularly as the average citizen could not tell cumulus from cumulonimbus. As for the volatile dance of wind and condensed water, he preferred other, surer markers.

His nose, for example.

With one whiff, he could gauge humidity to within

a percentage point, and discern certain fragrances that emitted from grasses and plants the moment that percentage point altered.

I could have been a perfumer, he thought wryly, *if duty and country had not intervened!*

There were other signs. The day before, he'd taken a constitutional in Regent's Park, a most serene location. Had its lofty pines discerned imminent rain, they would have shut up their giant cones against an eventual deluge so as to protect their seedlings. But they did not.

Now, would any sane man reckon on the inconstant atmosphere? The speculations of an overburdened newspaper reporter, sweating in a darkened cubicle and stinking of pomade, stale cigar smoke and printer's ink? Or would he rely instead on the sagacity of a pine tree, whose sole job it was to keep account of the weather?

No, it would not rain today.

As for his neighbor, errant waves of hair curling out from under his hat, crystals of sleep on the bottom lashes of his left eye, and a small spot of fresh jam on his waistcoat were all indications that his wife had once again departed in a torrent of tears for her mother's. Had she been home, she never would have permitted jam on her spouse's morning toast in such copious amounts that he could spill any portion thereof.

Her absence also explained why the family doctor, arriving promptly each evening with a new salve or patent medicine to combat fluid retention, insomnia or irritability, had not made an appearance since Friday last.

Beyond all that, it was a curiosity, but true nonetheless, that people were forever predicting their own worst fears or most fervent desires. A good drenching would be solace to a man like that, as he could be certain he wasn't the only poor wretch suffering.

Mycroft gazed down his street, at the handsome new houses set well back from the pavement, each one with its proper allotment of trees and greenery, and its languid, vacant air. The architect's aim was no doubt to create a tranquil atmosphere for the families who resided there, and, on the surface, it did just that. Mycroft's home was no more than an unmarried man four years from thirty, and of his station, would purchase. It boasted no remarkable possessions, and but a handful of servants to keep the hearths clean, dust off the shelves, and keep the plants watered. As he ate most of his meals out, there was not even a proper cook...

His thoughts were interrupted by his new carriage, which came around the corner and halted at the curb. Huan's dazzling smile was on full display as he waved from the sprung seat of a contraption so sparkling it all but glowed.

Before it stood a magnificent Irish Cob gelding, with a lustrous roan coat and snow-white mane and tail. However, Mycroft hadn't yet bonded to him as he had to his Hanoverian warmblood, his dear Abie.

"A most excellent morning, eh, Mr. Mycroft?" Huan said in his lilting, melodic voice.

From the moment Mycroft had persuaded Huan to leave his buggy-for-hire business and his beloved mule Nico in Trinidad and come work for him as driver and bodyguard, Huan had ceased calling him by his Christian name but had added the prefix "mister." Worse, when speaking about him to a third party, Mycroft would become "*the* mister."

It was insufferable, as in Port of Spain he and Huan had become friends, even brothers in arms. But no amount of threatening or cajoling would persuade Huan otherwise: *Mr. Mycroft* he was, and *Mr. Mycroft* he would remain.

"Let us hope so, Huan," Mycroft replied as he climbed aboard.

As for Huan's "most excellent morning," it wouldn't have mattered if the sun were baking bricks or if rain were falling down in sheets. Huan created his own contentment wherever he went.

From within the carriage, Mycroft heard him click his tongue, followed by the clattering of hoofbeats on the cobblestones, the gelding's rhythmical breath puffing in the morning chill as they proceeded on their way. What he had once found soporific was yet another reminder how much his life had changed—how different from whatever he had supposed it would be.

Of course, it *would* have been different, had Georgiana remained in his life. But then, what use was speculating? If one omitted Georgiana from his past, one omitted friendship, passion, adventure, heartbreak, and—in the end, he was forced to admit it—fortune.

No, had Georgiana lived, had he been blessed with the family he'd dreamt of, he would have remained what she had disdained: a rather dull government bureaucrat, grappling his way up the ladder one paltry rung at a time...

He glanced out the window and realized they were not heading to his bank (for that was always the first stop on a Tuesday) but towards Pall Mall.

He opened the trapdoor in the cab's roof. "Huan?" he called out.

"Ah, Mr. Mycroft!" Huan called back. "So you are now awake from your dream state? You see we are going to your place of business?"

"Yes, I do see that—but why?"

"You do not recall? The Mr. Cardwell, he is waiting for you. With a surprise!"

Mycroft closed the trap with a frustrated sigh. There was no work to call him to the office this day, nor for the rest of the week. Indeed, his promotion from assistant to special consul meant that he could come and go as he pleased. Unless of course his employer called upon him... whereupon he would be forced to drop all plans and hurry off to Cumberland House, as they were doing now.

A shameful waste of a morning. He would have to make some excuse so that he could be at the bank before noon, for a visit to Fleet Street and his private deposit had more import.

In the same way that he could smell the rain, he had developed an unerring nose for economic calamities, and one was coming upon Britain faster than anyone could stop it. He speculated that it would reduce the country's net worth, and that the underprivileged class would move from poor to destitute—which meant more abject misery in the streets.

Mycroft sometimes felt he would better serve his country in a post at the Treasury rather than the War Office. But as it was, without exposing his own wealth to scrutiny, he could not voice opinions in an official capacity—at least, none that anyone would take seriously. For what would a twenty-six-year-old special consul to the Secretary of State for War, with but one foray from his homeland, possibly know of international economies?

No, all he could do was to warn whoever would listen, and then shore up his own assets to at least ensure that those he cared for would never want for a thing.

He heard Huan open the trap.

"Mr. Mycroft?"

"Yes, Huan?" Mycroft replied, trying to keep the irritation out of his voice.

"Another body on Crutched Friars!"

It took Mycroft a moment. "Ah, yes. You are referring to the Savage Gardens Murders," he called back.

Thus far unsolved, the killings had been so baptized when the first three nude and mutilated corpses had turned up, one after the other, near or on the small street known as Savage Gardens.

"They find it just this morning," Huan added.

"Ah. And who is the 'they' who found it?" Mycroft asked.

"A publican," Huan replied. "Closing shop, two in the night it was, good working man, walking home, and he go falling over a body in the dark!"

"Dear, I hope he was not injured," Mycroft replied.

"Oh no, he was dead. Cut up in four pieces!"

"No, I meant the publican."

"Ah! No, he was fine. Just startled. But the corpse's face? No more nose. And below the waist, no more…"

When Huan hesitated out of propriety, Mycroft completed his sentence: "His reproductive organs had been cut off?"

"Yes!" Huan exclaimed. "Fancy way of putting it. Seven men now, murdered in same way."

"Truly, is it seven? I thought it was five. Must've missed a few," Mycroft replied. Truth be told, he was rather uninterested in the whole sordid affair.

"Not to worry, I let you know the next one!" Huan said cheerfully. "Number six, he was Chinese like the others. But number seven? A white man. Maybe now, they investigate."

To the present juncture, the victims had all been between twenty and forty years of age, sliced into four parts with near surgical precision, left to bleed to death, and then transported (by water, Mycroft wagered, as the river was nearby) to a poor but well-trafficked neighborhood so as to serve as a warning to others in the vicinity: *Cross us, and this too shall be your fate.*

In each case, given the small size of the Chinese community in London, the man's identity had been quickly confirmed. They had all been proprietors or heavy frequenters of opium dens, ne'er-do-wells whom society, Oriental or otherwise, would not mourn. As for the dead white man, he was doubtless in the same proverbial boat: a drug user who most likely owed money to a less-than-sympathetic lender.

"This not something for the War Office?" Huan called out to him.

"In what sense?" Mycroft asked.

"The Chinese, they are angry for the opium! For what it does to their land, they say it's *Britain's* fault—"

"That would be a strange message indeed," Mycroft countered, "for the Chinese to mangle their own people and display them in our poorer boroughs so as to, what? Protest the ugly consequence of the opium trade in their native land? Seems counterintuitive, does it not? I am hard-pressed to imagine they blame the working classes of Savage Gardens, Crutched Friars, Fenchurch and the like for China's addiction! No. If one wishes to protest the drug trade and Britain's substantial profit, best to do so before Parliament, where laws are birthed and enacted. In any event, one quarters a living body and cuts off nose and genitals to humiliate the *victim*, not the perpetrator."

"Ah! Make good sense, that. Was it also not your English custom as well?"

"It was," Mycroft admitted. "Hanging, drawing and quarter-ing, plus the removal of the 'privy parts'... Though in England's defense I hasten to add that we discontinued the practice several generations back." He heard the trap shut again, and sighed. What an ugly, burdensome affair this was.

His shoes felt suddenly tight. He wished he could hurl them off and wiggle his toes, much as he had when he was a child. Instead, he removed his hat, raked his fingers through his blond hair—getting rather long; time for a trim before someone mistook him for a dandy—and leaned back against the padded leather cushion.

He detested surprises. Especially as he always knew perfectly well what they were about.

2

CYRUS DOUGLAS WALKED BRISKLY. THIS WAS NOT SOLELY due to long, athletic limbs and equally long strides, or to the cloak of winter that had settled in the air with drab finality. Nor was it that a man of dark hue, a Negro from the isle of Trinidad, no matter how finely dressed, might be looked upon with suspicion in these nicer parts of the city. No, Douglas walked briskly because it was a brand-new morning, and he wished to get on with it.

He turned off Swallow Street (a suitable name for a timid flutter of a road) onto Regent Street, one of the finest thoroughfares in London. Its stone façades—not brick, as was most of the rest of the city—seemed cheery, in spite of a crackled sky overhead threatening to fracture into a downpour.

Early hour and fetid weather notwithstanding, humanity had turned out in all its ragged glory. Hansom cabs and workers' carts clogged the ample road, while the wretched and the well-to-do alike shared the pavements in a blur of moustaches, topcoats, skirts and bonnets.

By evening, young and old, rich and poor, would have had their fill of tribulations, of the wet air and the buffeting wind, and would make their ill-tempered way home, eyes averted and mouths set. But in the relative newness of morning, they still shared hope for a good outcome, a favorable return, a promise unexpectedly fulfilled; and each passed the other with a hearty good day, a smile, or a tip of the hat.

As he strode on with his head slightly bowed, as was his custom, Douglas heard itinerant vendors calling out the merits of prints and tassels, brocade and "rare" Spanish lace, along with the occasional entreaty to God or nature to keep their goods dry until all had been sold. But regardless whether a deity heard, they'd be there again tomorrow, and the day after that. Douglas was forever intrigued and humbled by that indomitable human spirit.

His first stop of the morning was to Regent Tobaccos. His little shop, which he had owned for nigh-on thirteen years, was in good hands. Gerard and Ava Pennywhistle, faithful employees, were now diligent and grateful partners, owning fifty percent of the business, which Douglas had ceded to them when his fortunes—or rather Mycroft's—had turned for the better.

Even so, he still felt a pang at having abandoned it and them for another enterprise altogether.

Can't be helped, he thought curtly. The children needed him more, and that was that.

He hurried up the steps that led to the familiar front door with its two arched windows, below a copper sign:

REGENT TOBACCOS
*Importateur de Cigares de la Havane,
de Manille, et du Continent*

The doorbell barely tinkled that Mr. Pennywhistle was already calling out from behind the counter: "Oho! Might that be you, Cyrus Douglas?" Then, over his shoulder, in volumes more fit for a seller of herring at Shooters Hill: "Mrs. P.! Come quick! You shall never guess in a hundred years who has come to see us!" Then, back to Douglas: "What'll you have, m'lad? Drink's on me!"

As he closed the door behind him, Douglas heard another voice, two octaves above the first, accompanied by hard, quick steps: "Don't be dotty, Mr. P.! What could our Cyrus possibly wish to imbibe at *this* hour? And what can you offer him that in't his already?"

Ava Pennywhistle, as broad as she was tall, hurried past her much shorter husband and made a beeline for Douglas, hands outstretched.

"Let me have a look at you, then!" She took him by the arms, angled him towards the hearth with its crackling fire, and then frowned as if she had just been presented with an inferior side of mutton. "Ah! And what have we done to ourself? Worked ourself to the very bone, says I! What the lad needs is sustenance, which any fool with two eyes can see! Thought that would exclude you, wun't it, Mr. P.?" she called over her shoulder with a chuckle, referring to her husband's myopia, presbyopia, and astigmatism.

"Cyrus!" Mr. Pennywhistle bellowed so as to drown out his wife's teasing. "A telegram come for you not a quarter-hour ago!"

"Oh? Who from?" Douglas asked, approaching the long mahogany counter.

If Mr. P. had been standing fully upright, its polished grain top would have reached his sternum. But bent over and peering through his tortoise-shell lorgnette as he scoured the under-counter for the telegram, he was very nearly invisible.

"The subject line said shipment! Or, perhaps ship!" he added brightly. "I placed it right here…"

As her husband scanned past bills and circulars, Mrs. P. hooked her arm through Douglas's.

"I was just making some tea, dearie, to warm the belly. Here, let me help you off with your topcoat, do rest your elbows a bit…"

"No time, I'm afraid," Douglas said, pulling away gently as she attempted to maneuver his coat off his shoulders. "I came only for a quick greeting and to ascertain that all is well. In one hour, I am to welcome two new boys, as two more have completed their first year's training and are now in full apprenticeships: one with a printer, the other at the City and Suburban Bank, both at a fine stipend."

"Well!" Mrs. P. beamed. "If your skin weren't the color of a clootie dumpling, I'd say you was blushing! You must be proud to bursting of 'em both!"

"I am, rather," Douglas said with a smile.

"It was right here…" Mr. P. mumbled again with less certainty.

"You *should* be proud," Mrs. P. reiterated. "But be careful out there, dearie, people is gettin' cut up! Noses alongside other more… masculine parts, if you get my meaning, tossed about like so much gristle! And this mornin' another one found quartered! Come fair by its name, Savitch Gardens, it does!"

"Mighty queer, this whole to-do," Mr. P. said, shaking his head, his voice grave. "You listen to me missus, Cyrus! 'Tis a bloody spot you're in!"

"That 'bloody spot' is nowhere *near* Savage Gardens," Douglas corrected soothingly. "You would have to cross the Thames to get close. Besides, I doubt they would be after me, Mr. P. From what I gather, all the victims thus far have been Chinese."

"Last one's white, I hear tell," Mr. P. corrected. "Though that still leaves you out, I'd say…"

"But just because they's Oriental don't mean their lives is worthless, do it?" harrumphed Mrs. P. "Hardly anyone botherin' to solve it's what *I* 'ear! We is all the same in God's eyes, says I! Surely they had mothers and fathers and brothers and sisters and——"

"Right you are, Mrs. P.," Douglas said quickly before she could make a list of every last family member of the poor unfortunate departed.

"But what is the goal in all of this choppin' up, d'you think?" Mr. P. persisted, glancing up from his search. "Nearly one a month it's been!"

"I assume," Douglas responded, "that someone is sending a rather stark message to the community of opium users—"

He was interrupted by a loud hammering on the front door knocker, and Mrs. P. let out a yelp.

"All but stopped me 'eart, it did," she muttered, adding, "Mr. P., tell 'em we ain't open yet!" as she hurried to the back before she could be seen: an upscale tobacconist was no place for a woman.

Before Mr. P. could intercept him, an older gentleman entered through the unlocked door. Douglas noticed the portmanteau in his hand, which he swung so easily it must have been empty. Anyone who entered an establishment with an empty suitcase was ready to buy.

Unfortunately, the man halted mid-step at the sight of Douglas, his eyes darting from the mahogany and polished interior back to the tall Negro in the middle of the room, as if he couldn't quite reconcile the setting with the subject. Before he could turn and bolt down the stairs again, Douglas pointed to a ledger on the under-counter and began to speak in a distinctive patois: "Nah nah, it de rot amont y'ia?"

Mr. P. turned to the wavering customer and smiled. "Doors open at ten, good sir, but seeing as how you have found your way in, kindly have a look round, seek your pleasure. I shall be with you in a twinkling." He peered at the ledger that Douglas was pointing to. Then he stood up to his full height, plus tiptoes, and attempted to look stern. "It'll serve *this* time, Cyrus," he said. "But the next time you bring us four crates of, er, Punch Habanas, the numbers must all be legible, do I make myself clear?"

"Yah, we fine, bredda, I gih ya! I goin' nah, yah?"

Bowing and waving, Douglas walked past the customer, opened the door and paused just long enough to hear the man say, "A workman so well attired? Never seen his like! Almost thought he was… but of course that'd be absurd, like a – a *jabberwocky*!" Delighted by his own cleverness, the customer set down his portmanteau while Douglas shut the door behind him and hurried down the stairs.

He hadn't felt the chill in the air before this. He looked up to see if the clouds had thickened or grown more ominous, but no. The sky was the same: all bark, no bite.

Douglas, you old fool, he remonstrated. *Forty-three years on this earth, and still so easily stung?*

He lifted up the collar of his topcoat and walked swiftly south down Regent Street, the handsomest thoroughfare in the metropolis, in the direction of Old Pye Street in the Devil's Acre, where no one would glance at him twice.

3

EDWARD CARDWELL, SECRETARY OF STATE FOR WAR, STARED glumly at the portrait of himself that hung above the desk of his Cumberland House office. If only he could change places with that rather bland likeness on the wall!

Although painted by George Richmond not a year before, it depicted a younger man with docile eyes and a luxuriant shock of copper-colored hair. In life, Cardwell's hair had been the color of steel wool for longer than he cared to remember, and his eyes were about as docile as a bull that had just been prodded in the gonads by the tip of a spear.

Birthday next, I shall be sixty, he thought as he appraised his own immortal likeness. Friends with better constitutions and less taxing positions had been keeling over like flies; how long could he possibly keep up his current schedule and its concomitant anxiety? One year? Perhaps two?

No more lollygagging. He could not guarantee ascendency, but he could sit at his desk, pick up his pen, and entreat and cajole the powers that be to select someone of his choosing!

Mycroft Holmes is twenty-six, in excellent health, and with notable accomplishments, he began.

It was he who insisted that one's financial resources should not dictate military advancement, a change that benefited our army to a great degree; he who devised a class of reserve soldiers who could be easily recalled in case of national emergency. Thanks to his ministrations, this office was also able to reduce the Army budget while nearly doubling its strength…

Yes, he would personally groom Holmes for the position, and he and Annie could retire to the seaside. Who would dare stand in the way of such advancement? And Holmes cut a good figure: a strapping lad with fine, perhaps even noble features, intelligent eyes (of an odd gray hue, yes—but surely that would not be held against him!), and a solid handshake. A faded scar from the top of his cheekbone to the tip of his chin gave him the slight aura of a jaunty buccaneer.

By all accounts, Cardwell had found his perfect successor… if he would but agree to "success." But Holmes was a strange bird. Plaudits and promotions did not move him. He had to see the wisdom of the decision.

Any man of ambition would leap at the opportunity, Cardwell grumbled to himself, *especially one with no family or other distractions*. But what did he know about Holmes in that regard? Precious little. A bit of gossip of an engagement gone sour, whisperings that something unfortunate had happened to the poor girl… dead, was she not?

Cardwell heard Holmes's voice in the hall as he greeted

young Parfitt, the junior clerk. He hastily covered the letter he had been writing with a blank piece of paper, tamped down his nest of hair, opened the door, and thundered: "Let us not stand about, gossiping like fishwives! Enter, Holmes! Parfitt, see to a cup of tea!"

Mycroft Holmes strode in.

This should be simple enough, Cardwell thought.

Mycroft could hear the *ding* of the front door bell, a signal from young Parfitt in the outer offices that he had two minutes to deflect Cardwell before the young clerk reappeared.

"Well, well, well!" Cardwell began with unfamiliar good humor as his fingers tormented the bristly hairs of his muttonchops. "So here you are at last!"

"Forgive me, am I late?"

"Not at all, not at all," Cardwell responded, gathering a stack of papers and books from the chair opposite his own, and placing them on the overburdened desk. "Sit! Sit!"

Mycroft did as instructed, removing his hat and placing it upon his knee while glancing at the older man's mouth. No blue splotches, not yet. Cardwell had not escalated to nervously tapping the nub of his fountain pen against his bottom teeth—though his cuticles were in a sorry state, as both temper and boredom caused him to gnaw at them.

He noticed a blank sheet of paper on Cardwell's desk, absorbing fresh ink from some document below. Cardwell had been careful not to stack anything atop it. It was obvious, too, that he had been composing something that required all his concentration, judging from the smudge of ink on his thumb, and the red mark below the first knuckle of the right index finger, where he'd been holding too tightly to the pen as he labored.

As he'd taken care to obscure the document, Mycroft assumed that it pertained to him. He kept another sigh at bay. Once upon a time, he could have conceived of nothing more glorious than to rise to the post of Secretary of State for War. Now it felt like a strait-jacket, a tedium of paperwork and interdepartmental bickering.

"Thought this would be as good a time as any for a little chat," Cardwell began.

"Happy to oblige, sir," Mycroft replied benignly. "And how is your dear Mrs. Cardwell faring?"

He saw from Cardwell's expression that he had caught him off guard. Not once in four years of working together had either man mentioned their home life. Mycroft could all but hear the gears in Cardwell's brain turning: they were men of business, after all!

"My… wife?" Cardwell repeated, as if he had misheard.

"Yes, sir. A touch under the weather, eh? 'Tis the season! Kindly give her my regards, along with my hope that the cough will improve quickly. And you are correct: sea air would do her a world of good."

"But how… That is…" Cardwell cleared his throat. "Regardless, that is not what I called you here to—"

A knock at the office door interrupted him.

"Who *is* it!?" Cardwell spit out.

"It is I, sir, P-Parfitt," came the meek response.

"Yes, damnation, Parfitt, I know it is you—what is it you want?"

The door opened and Charles Parfitt, nineteen, and as red-faced and damp as if he'd run a marathon, responded: "It's a message, sir, for Mr. Holmes. An urgent request, sir. Highly confidential."

"From whom?" Cardwell demanded, undeterred.

This was not a question that Parfitt seemed to have been expecting after declaring it highly confidential. Nor was he a liar of any notable worth. "Who from, sir? Why, it is from... Her M-Majesty the Queen!" he blurted out.

Mycroft felt his cheeks go a tad rosy. He stood and placed his hat upon his head before Cardwell could utter a sound. "Forgive me, sir," he said, "but may we continue this conversation at a later date?"

"Yes, yes, by all means!" Cardwell agreed, rising to his feet and motioning distractedly to the door, as if Holmes could perhaps not find it without assistance.

As Mycroft followed Parfitt out of the office, he reviewed the events of the last few minutes. That Annie Parker Cardwell had come down with a cough had been simple to discern. She and her husband had no progeny, yet in the jungle of items on Cardwell's desk he'd spied Mother Bailey's Quieting Syrup in its telltale cylindrical bottle, moniker etched in glass and partly visible. As he knew Mrs. Cardwell to be a teetotaler, she no doubt felt that a child's portion of opium and ethyl alcohol could do no harm; never mind that most people would then take a double dose, all the while admiring their own self-restraint.

The syrup had been placed beside a folder marked "Torquay," the lovely seaside town in Devon. Mycroft guessed that within were pamphlets and illustrations of the perfect spot in which to retire, something Cardwell would wish to take home with him as a distraction for his ailing wife.

Draped on the coat rack had been Cardwell's thickest winter scarf. Nothing like it to remind a man of his own fragility, to make him pause at every sniff and regard the slightest cough with foreboding. Given such watchfulness, it was a wonder his employer had managed to stave off his own infection for as long as he had. Mycroft assumed some minor influenza would strike Cardwell himself inside a week.

In any event, Cardwell's approaching birthday, combined with his wife's winter cold, underscored his need to settle on a successor: thus, the unfinished document—no doubt a letter to his superiors—and the formality of the meeting.

Discerning why Parfitt would blurt out that Mycroft had been called to an audience with the Queen, on the other hand, was not only more baffling but more troubling. Mycroft had grown to rely on Parfitt as an ally. The boy's loyalty was unequivocal, his research skills without peer. But that was of no account if his judgment was at issue.

"Of all the possible names you could come up with… the *Queen?*" Mycroft scolded as they retreated into the main hall.

"But, Mr. Holmes, that part be—*is*—true!" Parfitt

replied, amending his grammar. "Her Majesty the Queen sent an emissary with this note!"

The lad held it out to Mycroft, who took it, surprised. "It is sealed," Mycroft said, stating the obvious. "So how would you know she wished to see me?"

"That is the p-portion I invented. I thought you wouldn't mind, under the c-circumstances…"

"No…" Mycroft said absently as he broke the seal. He had asked Parfitt to "do his utmost" to get him away from Cardwell, and that was exactly what Parfitt had done.

As for the note, though the Queen's penmanship resembled smudged daggers, the content was brief and direct:

> *A nettling matter has come to our attention.*
> *Kindly discuss five this afternoon.*
>
> *Victoria R*

Mycroft glanced at his pocket watch. Nine thirty. The bank would have to wait.

As they passed Parfitt's desk, the lad grabbed a folder of documents, along with a stack of newspapers. "Here you are, sir," he said. "French reparations, the expansion of railways in the United States, specifically those funded by f-foreign investors, and of course your newspapers, all nice and p-pressed."

"You are a marvel, Parfitt. And how is Abie?"

"Right as rain, sir, and more than pleased for a visit. As would my aunt be, sir…"

"Yes, well, I shall certainly try, Parfitt. Give Mrs. Hudson my best."

Tucking the newspapers and the folder under his arm, Mycroft bolted out the door and back toward his carriage to pick up Sherlock.

4

HUAN AND THE CARRIAGE WERE WAITING OUTSIDE Cumberland House. Huan's face, as burnished and round as a penny, lit up with a smile the moment he saw Mycroft. He waved enthusiastically, as if the latter had been away for days rather than minutes. And though Mycroft thanked Providence for such faithful employees and friends as Parfitt and Huan, all he said as he crossed towards the carriage was: "To Shoreditch High Street, if you please. And kindly alert me to any more 'surprises' I may have forgotten."

"Of course, Mr. Mycroft," Huan replied pleasantly.

No one would ever guess what deadly skills he hides, thought Mycroft as he climbed into the cab.

"You do a bit of reading today?" Huan commented, as he swung into the driver's seat.

"The folder is mine," Mycroft said through the trap. "The newspapers are for Sherlock. He has begun collecting agony columns from various periodicals. He enjoys the personal advertisements, says that they reveal human nature.

He seems riveted by news stories of murder and mayhem."

The sorts of stories that Mycroft found distasteful were the latest in Sherlock's long string of obsessions.

"He is following the Savage Gardens Murders, yes?" Huan asked as they commenced their journey.

"I would consider it a perfect miracle if he weren't," Mycroft responded glumly.

"You are very good to the boy."

"I do my best," Mycroft said, not altogether convincingly.

"But young Sherlock, he cannot buy the papers for himself?"

"No, Huan, he cannot," Mycroft responded sourly.

"Ah. No money!" Huan said brightly.

"No, he *has* money. He simply chooses to misuse it." Mycroft shut the trap and lay back against the seat. He was generous with his brother, within reason, for he had not yet confided in Sherlock about his great fortune. A heady secret such as that would have been impossible to keep, were it not for Sherlock's utter lack of interest in the subject.

No, Sherlock's absence of ready cash stemmed solely from the fact that he did not understand the point of it. He would misplace it, or confuse a half crown for a halfpenny, leaving giddy vendors in his wake and himself insolvent. And paper currency was even worse. In the throes of some other pursuit entirely, he would pull a banknote from his pocket and clean out the horrid little briar pipe that he'd recently substituted for his hand-rolled cigarettes. Or, he would scribble upon it some equation or random thought, so that the denomination was all but obliterated.

And, as he had now trained Mycroft like a half-daft terrier to fetch whatever he deemed necessary, what need was there for him to change course?

As for his education, he had managed to graduate the upper sixth and was safely if unhappily ensconced at Downing College, Cambridge, Mycroft's alma mater. In exchange, Mycroft had promised that leisure time would be spent in London, rather than "abandoned to the intolerable doldrums of country life with our dreary progenitors," as Sherlock so charitably put it.

Mycroft stared down at the financial documents in his hands and frowned. Whatever it was the Queen required, could he perhaps find a moment to broach the subject of incipient economic collapse? If he could but get her ear on the matter…

Mycroft heard Huan's knuckles rap against the trap door. He looked up from his papers and tried to shake off the feeling of disorientation and nausea that seemed to plague him as of late.

From the window he spied the National Standard Theatre, where he and Sherlock had arranged to meet. The area was both down-at-heel shabby and oddly genteel, crowded with public houses, pleasure gardens, shops and bazaars.

"Your brother, he cares for theatre?" Huan called out.

"He is fond of it, in his manner," Mycroft said. "Although when I took him to see *The Bells* at the Lyceum, he mentioned neither the acting nor the writing, but went on about the costumes and makeup!"

As the carriage drew nearer and Huan fought for preeminence among cabs, carts and brewers' drays, Mycroft could see three figures underneath the theatre's great colonnade. One he recognized immediately: the profile reminiscent of a bird of prey, the tall, angular, even consumptive frame. If his identity had been in doubt, the instrument case that lay nearby—which Mycroft knew held a vielle, the five-string precursor of the violin, and Sherlock's latest passion—would have clinched it.

The two shorter, well-planted fellows were Sherlock's best and likely only friends, a strange set of twins named Eli and Asa Quince. They had longish hair the color of wet sand, and features so punctiliously carved that they could have been mistaken for ventriloquists' dummies.

Despite the frigid November morning, there they were—the three eccentrics of Downing College in their shirtsleeves—practicing a combat of their own design that incorporated boxing but which also involved a short staff. They were using the columns as obstacles and barricades. And although the theater would not open for several more hours, why the proprietor was not coming after the boys with the pointy end of a broom was a mystery to Mycroft.

Sherlock was beating the stuffing out of them.

His limbs might've recalled a scarecrow, had he been less subtle in his dealings and less deadly in his aim. At nearly nineteen, he had become a rather ferocious athlete.

Mycroft watched his brother, uncommonly pleased to

see how well he tucked his chin in and kept his wrists slightly bent to avoid injuring himself in a hit. Even his elbows were remaining closer to his body.

"Master Sherlock, he has gotten stronger, no?"

"Yes, Huan, it seems he has."

Sherlock must've distinguished the sound of the carriage from amongst all the others because he whisked round to look—just as one of the twins attempted to brain him with a short staff. But Sherlock was too quick. He ducked out of the way, pivoting to avoid a right hook, then with a side pass managed to land his own staff in the vicinity of the twin's spleen, while a left hook to the second twin's jutting chin sent him sprawling atop his brother.

"Ah! You see the jabs coming fast," Huan was declaring all the while. "Long reach, feet move, quick mix, good mind! Well done, Master Sherlock!" he bellowed upon the final blow, punctuating his praise with a round of applause.

Sherlock glanced blankly down at his vanquished friends. Then, instead of extending his hand in a sportsmanlike gesture—as Mycroft had dared to hope—he gathered up his vielle case, his short staff and his jacket, which lay on the ground along with the rest. Slipping it on, he removed the briar pipe from the pocket, packed and lit it.

At last, pipe between his teeth, and without a word of goodbye, he sprinted towards the waiting carriage.

5

"THERE THEY ARE!" SHERLOCK SAID BY WAY OF GREETING as he slid inside Mycroft's carriage. In one long move, he deposited instrument and short staff, reached across Mycroft, snatched the newspapers off the seat and propped them on his jutting knees.

"No farewells to friends?" Mycroft asked.

"No need," Sherlock said. "We meet Friday at Kensington to prepare for those dreary Latin orals. The language perished nearly two millennia ago—what need is there for *me* to resurrect it?"

"Now you are being a dunderhead," Mycroft exclaimed. "There are treatises of law, medicine and crime that you would do well to become familiar with, for surely they fall within your realm of interests—and they are most certainly in Latin."

"I follow the trail of my passions," Sherlock opined. "If said passions happen to lead back to Latin, I shall thank Providence that I learnt it once upon a bygone time. Until then, it occupies a necessary chamber of my brain, for which I thank neither it nor Providence, but simply wish it to go on its un-merry way."

With that, he lay back, opened up the *Daily Telegraph*, removed his pipe from between his teeth, and exhaled a long, bilious cloud of smoke.

Mycroft coughed. "It is even more acrid than those cheap cigarettes you used to smoke," he complained, waving a hand in front of his nose.

"A pipe is more efficient," Sherlock said, without taking his eyes off the newspaper. "Saves me an average of forty-seven seconds' preparation."

"We could stop at Regent Tobaccos. You will find many aromatic options from which to choose—"

"Dependent on some pretentious tobacconist? No thank you. My shag, I can pick up anywhere."

"A finer quality pipe, then."

"Briar has an inherent ability to absorb moisture, and a natural resistance to fire…"

"Now *there's* a shame," Mycroft said sourly. "But surely," he continued on a different tack, "as nearly every man smokes, being able to tell one scent from the other, possibly even one ash from the other, could be a helpful tool for someone keen to develop the art of deduction…"

When a concept penetrated, Sherlock would execute a hardly perceptible jerk of the head, as if he'd just thrown a thought into the uppermost drawer of his mind to be extracted when needed.

"So. What have we here," he murmured. "The *Daily*

Telegraph, *Daily News*, *Daily Chronicle*…" He turned to Mycroft. "Next time perhaps add *The Illustrated*, as well as *The Graphic*. Even a week old, it serves."

"Is that all?" Mycroft asked acerbically.

As Sherlock perused the crime column in the *Daily News*, he frowned. "Heard it, solved it, insipid, yet another theft in St. Giles, imagine that; some days are barely worth opening one's eyes for—wait, *there* is something!" he declared. "'Shocking discovery,' Russell Square, throat slit… promising!" He carefully tore the column out, pocketing it.

"I take it the Savage Gardens Murders do not interest you?" Mycroft asked.

Sherlock's expression was full of disdain. "The executions are altogether too overwrought. Someone has set out to make a point or to teach a lesson, which makes the motive pedestrian. And the only reason he, or most likely *they*, have not been apprehended as of yet is that no one much cares for the victims! Is it too much to ask that a motive be chock-full of intrigue, that killers show a modicum of finesse, and that victims be, if not noble, then at least somewhat worthy…?"

Mycroft sighed. He detested hearing his own unfiltered thoughts coming out of his brother's mouth. "You are not saying, because they are Oriental, that they have no value, I hope?" he reproved Sherlock.

"I am saying it probably has to do with lucre or some battle over territory and the like. In other words, a colossal bore." Sherlock was about to turn a page when something appeared to occur to him. He glanced out of the window. Then he looked over at Mycroft.

"We are not moving," Sherlock said.

"No," Mycroft replied. "We are not."

"Why?"

"Where is your overnight bag?"

Sherlock eyed him, perplexed. "To what purpose?"

"To the purpose of remaining ten days in the city!"

"But I have all I need. My music, my short staff, my hat, my shag…" He patted the waistcoat pocket that held his tobacco.

"An overcoat?" Mycroft asked, incredulous. "Latin texts? A change of clothing? An umbrella?"

"Mycroft, do not be histrionic. You know perfectly well that it will not rain today. After that, should it get a bit wet, surely the Quinces have all the umbrellas I might need, to say nothing of Latin textbooks, as each twin has his own…"

"Tell me you brought a shaving kit, at least."

"Whiskers have returned all the rage, and if need be, I can borrow yours, should you invite me to dinner—"

"No, you most certainly cannot. There," Mycroft indicated the sign of a shop just down the road. "Go purchase a small shaving kit. Or return to Downing."

The threat hit its mark. There would be no more arguing.

Sherlock opened the door of the cab and walked towards the shop, a ribbon of charcoal smoke trailing in his wake.

He is getting more difficult, Mycroft grumbled to himself. Perhaps he let Sherlock get away with too much. Perhaps instead of allowing him to lounge about with his nose buried in agony columns and tales of murder, his briar pipe polluting the rooms like a bad spell of winter fog, what he needed was a dose of how the other half lived. Being made to volunteer even a few hours at Cyrus Douglas's school might be the ticket.

I could take him to Douglas, make my appointment with the Queen, then have a bite to eat before retrieving him.

Mycroft was particularly fond of that last notion. Even breaking bread with Sherlock had become a chore. Either he ignored the food laid before him and said not a word, or else would criticize everything, from chewing to digestion, in minute detail.

The Albion might have an open spot, Mycroft mused. *I haven't dined there in a fortnight…*

He stared out of the window again. The twins had by that time picked themselves up and hobbled off. But just then, hurrying towards the Standard, Mycroft noticed a rather pinched and austere little man in a much-mended overcoat.

Mycroft knew him by sight: Sherlock's chemistry tutor, Professor John Cainborn, the only instructor that, to his knowledge, Sherlock admired. *When it comes to biologics,* Sherlock had once crowed, *the man is an alchemist!* It was Cainborn who had given Sherlock a new perception on the study of matter; Cainborn who allowed Sherlock the liberal use of the Cambridge chemistry laboratories; Cainborn who had suggested that he take up the vielle as a form of meditation so that his analytic brain might have the rest that sleep or lesser distractions could not give.

Cainborn who smoked a briar pipe, which had doubtless sparked Sherlock's own interest.

Cainborn and Sherlock passed one another on the street. Sherlock gestured towards his transport as a foray into polite conversation, and as he did, Mycroft witnessed a strange metamorphosis in his brother. Sherlock drew into himself, no doubt so as not to give offense by his greater height, his long body bent to greet the smaller man, his head nodding in agreement with whatever the professor was saying. And the handshake, when they parted, seemed genuine from both men.

A pang of jealousy took Mycroft unawares.

Both continued walking in their opposite directions, but then Cainborn turned his head to look back at Sherlock, almost as if he wished to be certain he was gone. Not a moment later, a Chinese gentleman of middle years approached the professor. He wore the traditional Han garb of green silk with deep blue brocade, decorated with Chinese dragons.

He and Cainborn shook hands as if their meeting was by happenstance, but their body language betrayed them. Mycroft could not help but notice how tense their limbs were, how strained their smiles, how white Cainborn's knuckles as he held his pipe aloft.

Why would two grown men in a casual encounter whisper to each other in a fractious back and forth upon a busy thoroughfare? And what business could a rich Han merchant possibly have with a university professor of chemistry?

It was Cainborn who seemed in charge, from the manner in which he leaned forward, insistent, while the other man leaned back like a recalcitrant dog on a leash.

Then Cainborn turned and looked directly at the cab and at Mycroft. The Chinese man followed suit, his expression suddenly fretful. He whispered something to Cainborn, who whispered back; then both men hurried off in opposite directions.

Mycroft watched the Chinese gentleman cross the road and climb aboard a canary-yellow landaulet. By the time Sherlock walked out of the shop, it had darted away.

Curious, Mycroft thought. Nonetheless, he determined that he would not inform Sherlock of what he had seen. He refused to undercut whatever his brother found to admire in education, even if it happened to be a strange little man in a much-mended overcoat.

6

THE DEVIL'S ACRE WAS A PATCH OF MALODOROUS SWAMPLAND off the River Thames that comprised Old Pye Street, Great St. Anne's Lane, and Duck Lane. Douglas had to admit that it was fit for nothing beyond "indescribable infamy and pollution," as Charles Dickens had once described it. The fact that it lay more or less between the three pillars of British society—Westminster Abbey representing the Church, Buckingham Palace the Crown, and the Houses of Parliament the State—did nothing to soften the blow of being born, raised, or forgotten in such a dismal place, this haunt of unimaginable squalor.

Yet Douglas loved it, as much as he loved Regent Street, albeit for different reasons. Regent Street was a place of possibilities, of striving. Its grand buildings and imposing promenade assured humanity that hope sprang eternal; that Providence could still be kind. The Devil's Acre offered no such assurances. There was nothing salubrious about its choleric streets. Its buildings, like its residents, tended to be hollow-eyed, grimy, and thin. But if one paid attention, from out its refuse-filled labyrinths one could pluck, here and there, a wildflower.

Hurrying to keep his appointment, Douglas stepped gingerly around horse dung, broken cobblestones, sleeping sots and stagnant pools of dubious origin as he recalled the first time he and Mycroft Holmes had spoken of this strange new fever dream of his.

Though summer, that day had been nothing of the kind: drizzly and cold, with wind gusts that set one's teeth on edge and that only London could concoct. They'd been back but a month from the stifling wet heat of Trinidad. With Regent Tobaccos closed on Sunday, he and Mycroft had made themselves at home. They had dragged their favorite leather chairs as close to the hearth as could be managed without setting themselves ablaze, and had opened an Armagnac, a twenty-year-old Favraud.

At the time, Douglas was still convalescing. He could feel, or imagine he felt, the bullets lodged near his heart: two tiny pellets that could mean instant death, should they shift one eighth of an inch to the left. And although he had kept up with his capoeira exercises, engaging in mock battles with Huan each day to remain flexible, his days of brute labor, of packing and unpacking heavy shipments of tobacco and spirits, even for his own little shop, were ended.

He and Mycroft Holmes had been discussing alternatives.

His first thought had been to open an orphanage for colored children, to be named after the four-year-old son he had lost. But in the final analysis it seemed statistically less helpful than aiding slightly older boys (of whatever hue) to secure the sort of apprenticeships that could care for them and their families for a lifetime.

"It is not enough to provide them with just *any* employment," he had told Mycroft. "We must keep them from the factory *and* the chimney *and* the mines and any other toil that destroys body and soul."

"How many boys would you take in?" Mycroft had asked mildly.

"Fifteen? Twenty?" he'd replied with a shrug.

He hadn't fully considered the logistics. It was still a dream fueled mostly by ideals and twenty-year-old Armagnac.

"There are thousands upon thousands in the city who are in need," Mycroft had countered. "Changing the fortunes of but twenty at a time seems a fool's errand—"

"Not to those twenty whose fortunes are changed," Douglas had retorted.

"Then why not more? Why not fifty? One hundred? Two hundred at a sitting? Surely I can afford it."

"But I cannot," Douglas had countered. "I cannot maintain two hundred boys, as well as a staff. Even if I could, I do not care for the institutional setting; it is not what I envision."

"The poetry in your soul may not envision it, Douglas, but I urge you to rethink for their sakes. If twenty boys 'whose fortunes are changed' are happy, surely two hundred would be happier still!"

But Douglas had been firm in his resolve. "We would need to ascertain that the boys were instructed properly and paid a decent stipend to boot."

"And what do their employers receive in exchange?"

"Intelligent, willing apprentices, along with a temporary subsidy for their upkeep—another expense I wish to take on myself."

"I see," Mycroft had said. "And where are we contemplating locating this establishment?"

Douglas told him.

"The Devil's Acre?" Mycroft had laughed. "All attempts at slum clearance have merely sloshed the poverty around like so much curdled milk. Even a stray dog knows better than to seek therein a scrap of food, lest he become someone's supper. And if you dare to build something," Mycroft had gone on, seemingly enjoying himself, "come first nightfall the Deserving Poor will cart off everything of value, down to the last nail!"

"Holmes, please," Douglas had protested—for he still called him *Holmes* then, as there was not yet the muddle of a younger Holmes to contend with. "You are sounding like a phlegmatic old country squire. Besides, I would not be alone in this. Urania Cottage is in Shepherd's Bush. And there are the ragged schools—"

"Yes," Mycroft cut in, "but let us not forget, in the consumptive heart of the place, the master classes in pickpocketing that your boys will most likely attend."

"They already reside in that 'consumptive heart,' as you

put it. They already know how to pick pockets, if that is their intent. We shall seek those who want more, as I did, as many do. I hope to use the promise of apprenticeships as an enticement to learn mathematics, science and grammar, at the very least…"

"You are an autodidact, Douglas. Why can they not be as you are?"

"Not everyone has the dubious privilege of being aboard ship for months at a time with nothing to do but read!" he responded. "Still, even I am forced to admit that "the blackest tide of moral turpitude," as Dickens had it, shall not be that simple to turn."

"Most do-gooders are simply caught in the undertow and drowned," Mycroft had concluded somberly. "I shall not be one of them."

"Nor would I ask it of you."

In spite of Mycroft's misgivings, Douglas had followed his heart. After a month of searching, he had secured an edifice at the center of the district. It was a plain, rawboned old thing with not an ounce of charm. But it had been built with adequate material, passable lighting and ventilation, plus good drainage, its own water closet and—if one accepted barrenness and muck in lieu of a garden—an outdoor space big enough for adolescent boys to blow off steam. The rooms were large and airy or would become so, once a few walls were torn down and windows replaced.

Mycroft had paid for the structure and the renovations in cash. From his Regent Tobacco earnings, Douglas had provided for the charges and salaries for a staff of eight: a supervisor, a teacher, two housemaids, a scullery maid and a cook, and two advocates to investigate possible apprenticeships for the boys, who were aged eleven to fifteen.

Granted, he had not much to live on after that; but then again, he did not need much.

Douglas christened it Nickolus House, Nickolus being the middle name of his dead son. In the whole of the building, that nameplate beside the front door was the only link to Douglas at all, and then only if one knew his history, which none but Mycroft did. Each time before he entered, he would pause and run his fingers over the engraved letters, in the hope that his long-gone family—and especially his boy—were proud of him. As he reached the front door he did so now, pausing for a moment.

He was shaken from his reverie by a carriage pulling up behind him; a fine one, from the sounds of it, or perhaps more accurately from the lack of sounds: no squeaking wheels or grinding brakes. He looked back and saw a pristine vehicle with Huan in the box seat, and Mycroft alighting from within.

Douglas smiled to see Mycroft cajoling someone inside to disembark. A moment later, Sherlock emerged, looking like a condor that had just realized, to its offended chagrin, that its wings had been clipped.

Douglas's smile disappeared. His patience was already wearing thin… and no one could rip away its remaining shreds more thoroughly than young Sherlock Holmes.

"Your newspapers?" he heard Mycroft ask, as Sherlock shut the carriage door behind him.

"I shall not be remaining long," the latter sniffed, a hint of warning in his tone.

As Douglas held open the front door of Nickolus House and the two brothers hurried towards the building, Douglas turned just in time to see another fine carriage—a canary-yellow landaulet—not a hundred yards away. It halted abruptly, turned within the narrow confines of the street, and bolted off again in the opposite direction.

Douglas caught Huan's eye: he'd noticed it too. Quite the coincidence, two fine carriages in a borough that often saw none at all.

Nevertheless, his visitors were already approaching, and if their demeanor had been any indication, they would need an arbiter or referee, perhaps even a jailer. Douglas put the landaulet out of his mind, wiped his feet on the mat, and walked inside.

7

AFTER DEPOSITING THEIR OUTERWEAR IN THE HALL, Douglas escorted Sherlock and Mycroft into a small drawing room while he went into the nearby kitchen to put the kettle on. He could hear Mycroft through the wall, trying to make the best of an awkward situation, his voice falsely cheerful.

"Generally, new boys await a 'feeble old gentleman' known to them only as Mr. Smythe," Mycroft was explaining. "They are told that he shall most likely not make an appearance this day but shall send his Negro secretary, one Cyrus Douglas, to report on their enthusiasm and general aptitude."

After that cheery introduction: silence. There seemed to be nothing forthcoming from Sherlock.

Douglas called out with his own forced bonhomie: "The cook is not about, but if you are famished, perhaps some hot rolls, fresh from breakfast…"

"After he settles the carriage," Mycroft called back, "Huan is free to indulge. But Sherlock and I are here on business."

Douglas left the kettle on the stove and poked his head into the drawing room, hoping he had misheard. "I beg your pardon?"

"We shall accompany you to meet the new children," Mycroft declared as if it were the most reasonable assumption in the world.

Douglas blanched. "For what reason, pray?" he asked.

"Sherlock is here to volunteer."

"In your *hat*!"

That last came from Sherlock.

"It is high time you learn compassion!" Mycroft turned to his brother, half furious and half pleading.

"Compassion," Sherlock countered icily, "is a useless emotion that goads people into doing good deeds for which they have no talent! Give me less compassionate workers and more efficient ones, if you please!"

"I confess I agree," Douglas interjected. "Regardless, neither of you may accompany me, for I will not have the boys examined like specimens."

"There is a classroom across from the supervisor's office, is there not?" Mycroft asked in an innocent tone that grated on Douglas's last nerve—for Mycroft well knew the building, as he had helped to choose it. "We shall wait there, if you would be kind enough to leave the door open so that we can see from across the corridor. Young boys are not keen to know what anonymous adults are about."

"Oh, bosh!" Sherlock exclaimed. "You have not dragged me here for compassion, but because you have an engagement with the Queen!" When Mycroft made no move to contradict him, he went on: "During the ride here, you eyed your pocket watch three times, a thoroughly unnecessary move, for you know perfectly well how long it takes to get from Shoreditch High Street to the Devil's Acre and can probably enumerate the number of times the wheels spun beneath our feet. You peered at a miniscule smudge of dirt on the tip of your shoe and flicked at it with your thumb, while nervously pressing the hem of your trousers with your fingertips, as if wielding an iron the size of a fruit fly. Your head was tilted forward and your eyes upraised, and you were staring into the middle distance, rehearsing what you intended to say."

"Is that all?" Mycroft asked crisply.

"No. There is a missive peeking from out of your coat pocket made from a strong and expensive stock called White Linen that the Queen tends to favor."

Douglas did his best not to laugh. Sherlock was certainly a handful, but it was rare to see Mycroft beaten at his own game. Douglas had to admit he was enjoying it just a little.

"And I am not an infant to be shuttled about then turned over into the waiting arms of an Ethiop nanny!" Sherlock concluded, snapping Douglas back to reality.

The impertinent ninny! Douglas thought. He fixed Sherlock with a searing look. "My arms are not 'waiting' in the least. And you are correct," he added, turning to Mycroft, "perhaps he has been too long between Cambridge and St. John's Wood and might do well to see how the other three-quarters live. Therefore, go. But do not permit *him*"—he indicated Sherlock again—"to utter one more word, or I shall personally escort him out, and I shall not be gentle about it."

"As if there were anything of remote interest to witness in a place like this," Sherlock sniffed.

"A keen example," Douglas added, "of the verbal vomitus to which I refer!"

Whereupon the two Holmes brothers (the determined older, and the unenthused younger) strode down the corridor while Douglas, with terrible misgivings, hurried back to the kitchen to turn off the kettle, and then went off to meet his new charges.

8

NO ONE STOOD WHEN DOUGLAS ENTERED THE SUPERVISOR'S office. Not the two boys squirming on stools; not the man seated behind his writing desk.

Harold Capps was a good-hearted fellow with black hair as coarse as a pig-bristle brush, which stood upright each time he removed his hat. Capps was aware that there was no such person as Smythe, that it was Douglas who paid the upkeep and salaries. But a white man of a certain age could not be seen rising to his feet when a colored man entered a room; it would create unnecessary confusion and perhaps even revolt among their charges. Therefore, the two had schemed from the start that Douglas would remain secretary to the never present, ever ailing Mr. Smythe.

"Ah, there you are, Douglas," Capps said when he entered. "This arrived for you not ten minutes ago."

Capps handed him a telegram. On the back was written one underlined word in Gerard Pennywhistle's large, block-like lettering:

FOUND!

Douglas tucked the telegram into his trouser pocket.

"Might I inquire as to the welfare of our dear benefactor?" Capps asked.

"A touch of influenza," Douglas replied, allowing his Trinidadian accent to surface a bit.

"Kindly give him our best. As sorry luck would have it, our teacher Mr. Undershaft has taken ill too, with enteritis. But *you* know something about mathematics!" he added as if it were a madcap notion. "Perhaps you will assist us?"

"I would be honored, Mr. Capps."

"Good. Our new lodgers come to us from Beeton."

Douglas was all too cognizant of Joseph Beeton. He owned a large chimney-sweeping business. It was the sort of business that Douglas would have gladly run out of England altogether. Chimney-sweep masters would take in the poorest, smallest lads, then feed them as little as possible so they could fit into coal flues, which were narrower than those that burned wood. Several boys at Nickolus House had been rescued from that sorry place and others like it.

"On your feet, young lads," Mr. Capps commanded jovially, coming around his desk. "Douglas, may I present Charles Fowler, aged thirteen, and his brother George, eleven."

Both boys were barefoot. But while the younger boy's clothes were in tatters, and he had not one square inch of visible flesh that was not caked with dirt, Charles—the older—was more polished. The greater part of his sooty covering had been scrubbed away, and his trousers, shirt and jacket, though picked-through rags, were not so threadbare as his brother's. But it was clear to Douglas that both boys' backs were already twisted, ankles chronically swollen. Through the rips in his trousers, Douglas could see that the knees of the younger boy were as gnarled as ancient oaks, and he assumed the same of the older.

"I am pleased to make your acquaintance," Douglas said, bending down so that he would not tower over them. Hunger and neglect had kept them both as small as eight-year-olds.

The younger boy, George, swallowed his greeting, scuffing a nervous toe back and forth across the floorboard with sidelong, slightly alarmed glances at Mr. Capps' lofty hairdo, while Charles squinted up at Douglas and reached out a calloused hand.

"Pleased to make *yours*! Thinkin' you a fair right speaker for a jimmy-grant, no offense…"

"None taken," Douglas said.

"An' so please tell yer lath-an'-plaster that me an' me bruvver are tickled to be 'ere!"

"Master. Not lath-and-plaster," Mr. Capps corrected, while George turned to Mr. Capps and added in a hoarse little voice:

"Does we get our new cloves nah, guv?"

"I am not 'guv.' I am Mr. Capps. And yes, this afternoon: a new set of clothes, along with a nightshirt for sleeping, and a good, solid pair of shoes. They shall be laid out for you after your bath."

Charles's little face scrunched in distaste. "A barf? *Mus'* we, gents?" he asked.

"Afraid so," Douglas said softly.

"But I's already *'ad* two!" George protested. "Once on Whitsuntide and one Christmas last!"

"Well then, this shall be your third of the twelve-month. So," Douglas continued, "your former home was with Mr Beeton?"

Both boys nodded.

"We was put wiv 'im cuz we're orphans," Charles Fowler explained somberly. "Quite alone in the world, we are. Our da was a pigeon fancier who took a tumble off a roof."

Douglas had heard that story before, from other urchins. There seemed a glut of pigeon-related deaths in the Devil's Acre. In truth, the parents might have been run over by a dray, or died from disease, or been disposed of. Or perhaps one or both had beaten the boys from one side of the wall to the other, until the streets and servitude seemed a fairer bargain than the brutality at home.

"And were you decently treated by him?" Douglas went on.

George stared at his wiggling toes. Charles thought on it a moment, then said brightly: "I grant you, 'e come by 'is name 'onest-like! A right good smackin' 'e could give! But I was beaten only twice, and li'l Georgie only once!"

George winced in remembrance. "Stung all the same…" he murmured.

"Mind, Georgie din't snivel one bit," his brother stated proudly, "but stood there an' took it like a man!"

"Now, boys," interjected Mr. Capps. "Tell Mr. Douglas what you wish to accomplish with your time on earth."

George's eyes darted about as if the Angel of Death were winging its way from Oblivion to drag him away, but the older one understood Capps' meaning and had an answer at the ready. With his stick-thin arms behind his back, he recited: "I wants to be a knocker-upper, Mr. Capps, cuz I already knows how to count to twelve. All I needs is to get me a fine used ticker, not nicked but purchased proper like, an' I'll make me a penny a month for every windah I knocks up! I'd be doin' workin' people a good turn, gettin' 'em to their jobs on time."

"Well," Douglas said, "while knocker-upper is certainly a fine ambition, perhaps we can do even better for you, eh?"

Charles eyed his brother and made a quick and subtle circle with his finger: he thought Douglas irredeemably daft.

Douglas grimaced. Now the boys looked upon him not merely as a "jimmy-grant"—an immigrant—but as someone whose sanity was in question. Nevertheless, he was determined to give them a decent future, one his own son had never had.

In the classroom opposite, Mycroft watched Sherlock become more and more entangled in the scene unfolding before them. He was leaning forward in his chair, the thumb and index fingers of his left hand stroking his chin. When Sherlock was intent on something, the involuntary reflex of blinking ceased completely, nor did he swallow. It was a wonder his heart still beat—although Mycroft debated if it was too much to hope that something in the woebegone little beings talking to Douglas had moved his brother.

As the boys followed Capps out, first for the dreaded bath and then for the undreamt-of set of clothes and shoes, plus a nightshirt, Sherlock sat back with a satisfied sigh.

"You seemed more interested than I expected," Mycroft began.

"Quite," Sherlock declared, rising to his feet and stretching. "The younger boy? Useless. But the older one, Charles, he is of note."

"Oh?" Mycroft looked at him hopefully. "In what way?"

"Why, he is an intravenous drug user!"

"Intravenous? Nonsense, Sherlock. If he does take opium, he smokes it, just like anyone of his caliber."

"I tell you I saw the mark of the needle on him. Now *that*, I should like to know more about, for he did not perform all those injections on himself. Someone is using him as an experimental subject. But why, and to what end? Rather intriguing, wouldn't you say?"

Mycroft leapt impatiently out of his seat. "Those agony columns have poisoned your brain! You cannot *possibly* see that he is an intravenous drug user. Even if you could, how does a boy like that afford injectable drugs? Or, let us say he can do so: then surely he could be injected by fellow users!

His small stature is most likely due to hard labor and near-starvation—"

"But that is my point, Mycroft," Sherlock declared. "A needle? At his age and station? With injections in unusual parts of his body? You shall find three punctures on his right foot, between the first and second digits, four on his right talus, three on the left clavicle, one between the index and middle finger of his left hand…"

As he walked in, Douglas queried: "And you saw it all underneath the dirt?"

Sherlock eyed Douglas with barely restrained disdain. "You have read Bernard Palissy?" he asked. "Olivier de Serres? As it so happens, I have begun a study of pedology and hydrology. My starting point was Palissy, and then de Serres for his quite adequate cataloguing of soil formations. Dirt, like nature, abhors a vacuum and will fill in each little rivulet and crack it finds. Now holes made by the hypodermic syringe are particular in that—unlike cuts or piercings with nails—they are perfectly cylindrical."

"Because of course you have done a study of hypodermic marks," Douglas posited, while Mycroft stared at his younger brother with increasing rage, mingled with fading hope.

"Not as thoroughly as I have dirt," Sherlock replied. "Dirt is omnipresent: on footwear, on clothing, under fingernails…"

"Spare us a list!" Mycroft exclaimed. "Yes, I suppose in retrospect the boy had signs of drug use, but then again, many do. And, again, the notion that he could purchase a syringe is absurd at its core."

"Again, you make my argument for me," Sherlock grumbled. "Go off to the Queen, or what have you. I shall wait for the boy to have his bath, after which I wish to examine him. It may be that a few hours among these young derelicts will be advantageous after all!"

"Forgive me, Douglas," Mycroft said, "this was a horrid notion. I shall of course remove Sherlock immediately; you shall not be burdened with him any further."

Douglas glanced at his friend, his eyes vacant. He was holding a telegram he had just taken from his trouser pocket. Then he looked at Sherlock as if struggling to place him.

"In truth," he said, "I… I could use him. Our teacher is ill and as it turns out, I cannot substitute, for I am called elsewhere. If he could teach the boys mathematics for a few days—"

"A few *days*?" Sherlock sputtered back, indignant. "Has the world taken leave of its senses? No indeed, Douglas, I categorically refuse!"

"Sherlock!" Mycroft said. "You will *not* speak to him in that manner! He is your elder; you are to address him as *Mr.* Douglas!"

"The entire concept of compulsory learning is daft," Sherlock shot back. "And I shall not be abandoned here, wasting my breath on ruffians while Douglas goes off gallivanting!"

"You will do as you are told," Mycroft responded stonily. "Or Huan shall take you back to the country and leave you there to rot. And if you think you shall find shelter at

Downing think again. I shall demand a full restitution of tuition. You can go scrub floors at Ye Olde Cheshire Cheese, for all I care!"

Mycroft turned. "Forgive his insolence, Douglas——" he added, but it was said to empty air, for Douglas had left.

9

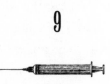

MYCROFT FOUND DOUGLAS IN THE HALLWAY, COAT buttoned and slipping on his gloves.

"There is a problem with a shipment?" Mycroft inquired.

"How did you know?"

Mycroft shrugged. "It cannot involve Nickolus House, for the note came from Mr. P. As you were reading the telegram, I noticed his distinct handwriting on the back. Mr. P. would not have written about his own troubles or his wife's, for I smelled the heady aroma of Regent Tobaccos on your coat, which tells me you saw them earlier this morning. And he surely would not have written "FOUND" on his own missive, so it had to come from elsewhere, albeit sent to Regent Tobaccos—which means it had to do with your business. And did you not send a rather large shipment to Sydney in the last several days? So there is not much else that could cause you such distress that you would leave your pupils in the hands of my brother."

Douglas nodded. "The *Royal Adelaide* was on its way from

London to Sydney with a full cargo of whiskey, gin and brandy, a good deal of it mine," he confirmed in a haunted tone. "Last night, it ran aground on Chesil Beach in Dorset…"

"Were lives lost?" Mycroft asked.

"The telegram does not say. But without the funds from my business, Nickolus House cannot remain open. I must leave immediately to see what can be salvaged."

"I would offer to help, Douglas," Mycroft ventured. "But we are at a terrible economic crossroads in Britain at this moment. What if my prognostications are correct and you and I must make do for ten years or more? Collectively speaking, we are in this maelstrom to begin with because we have thrown too much capital at projects that show no quick returns; surely it would not do to continue in that vein. And however admirable this house, it burns money…"

"I said that it would live or die by my efforts, and so it shall," Douglas replied firmly.

"On the other hand——" Mycroft began.

"No. Kindly do not make an exception on my behalf. For if I believe that Nickolus House exists solely on the basis of your rather reluctant charity, sooner or later I *will* despise myself and resent you—or you, me. And I cannot allow that to happen." He went to the front door, then paused. "Goodbye, Mycroft," he said. "Pray for me."

Douglas rode an omnibus to Paddington Station and from there to Bristol to board a Somerset & Dorset train, all the while wondering how this calamity could have occurred. The *Royal Adelaide* was not some ancient plug but a well-appointed iron vessel. Her masts were hardy, her wire rigging solid, and she was under a fine captain, a man named Hunter with whom Douglas was casually acquainted.

Douglas had counted on the *Royal Adelaide*'s strengths so that his Scotch and Irish whiskey, his brandy and Plymouth gin would make it to Australia and earn a tidy profit. And yet, she'd gone no more than one hundred and fifty nautical miles before meeting her watery end.

As for goods on grounded vessels… people would swarm like vultures until there was nothing left. He recalled Victor Hugo's words in *Les Miserables*: "If the soul is left in darkness, sins will be committed. The guilty one is not he who commits the sin, but he who causes the darkness."

No, rather than blame others, it was better to move forward. If he could but recover one half of his cargo, he might be able to go on.

If not, then Nickolus House would become another in a long line of failures littering London's slums.

With Charles Fowler and his younger brother George submitting to a good scrubbing and delousing, and two additional boys down with the croup, Sherlock found himself facing a classroom of sixteen undersized hooligans who eyed him with the sidelong glances of hyenas waiting to attack, and he cursed Mycroft under his breath for abandoning him to such a fate.

On the other hand, though he might not be able to outflank them, thankfully he could still outthink them. He simply needed their undivided attention—not difficult, considering all eyes were upon him.

He went to the window, holding his muscles loose but his posture upright, and let in a gust of air. Judging from the staleness of the classroom, this was a revolutionary move. Then he went back to the teacher's desk but did not sit. Just as one would do with an unfamiliar animal, he avoided eye contact, observing instead some point on the far wall above the boys' heads. Finally, he rapped his fingers lightly on the desktop to give them something to focus on, and to keep them slightly off balance.

"Wot've you done wiv ol' Undershaft?" one of their leaders called out, his tone impertinent. He was a hefty lad with thick black hair and the icy blue eyes of a husky.

"He is no affair of mine," Sherlock said with a shrug. "Care to see a magic trick? Simply shout out your names one at a time."

At first they were ill tempered, clearly despising this font of authority hardly older than they, yet infinitely more fortunate. Sherlock could see their minds work. Would they give up the fight so easily? But finally curiosity outflanked their bloodlust, and the boys spat out their names, daring him to deliver on his promise.

They had called them out randomly, but Sherlock tossed them back in alphabetical order; then in reverse; and finally in the order of the numbers of letters in each.

It took the boys a moment to realize what he had done, and with what speed. Slowly, the older ones began to chortle amongst themselves, while the younger ones gauged their elders' responses so as to calibrate their own.

"He knowed 'em afore!" argued the boy with the fierce blue eyes, while others argued back that even so, it was a neat trick.

While they were thus occupied, Sherlock observed their grins. French scientist Guillaume Duchenne de Boulogne had experimented with electricity on his subjects' faces to ascertain which muscles constricted involuntarily when smiling with genuine mirth, as opposed to a smile meant solely to disarm. While the large muscles on either side of the mouth—the zygomatic major—could be raised at will, people tended to forget the orbicularis oculi that encircle the eyes. When genuinely amused, those small muscles would tighten, pull down the brows and create crinkles at the corners of the eye sockets.

He was pleased to see that the orbicularis oculi of nearly every boy in the room was engaged.

"How high can you count?" Sherlock called out.

"A hunnerd!" the black-haired boy called back proudly. "Us older ones, the younger, not so much!"

"Thank you, Mr. McPeel," Sherlock replied—and he could tell from blue-eyed Joe McPeel's expression that he was not used to anyone recalling his name, much less referring to him as "mister."

Sherlock picked up his vielle and scraped at the strings, eliciting a sound like a yowling cat... then played a tune so pretty that all chatter ceased, and the boys stared at him, hypnotized.

"What is the difference between the first set of sounds and the second?" he asked and then answered: "*Mathematics.* There is a mathematical equivalent to every note that indicates the length of that note within the bar..."

A few more examples, and he let them discuss the revelations amongst themselves, something they'd clearly not been permitted by their Mr. Undershaft. Sherlock's purpose was not merely to put them at their ease but to waste time: he had but a half hour to go before he could dismiss the class and check on Charles Fowler.

"Has anyone heard of geometry?" he asked when the discussion turned to ribbing and threatened to get out of hand.

"Nah!" a big ruddy boy shouted out good-humoredly. "We is h'ignorant as h'asses, guv!"

Over the boys' braying laughter, Sherlock replied: "Then we're in luck, Ducasse. For ignorance is curable, while stupidity is not."

Picking up his short staff, he passed through a series of exercises that drew figures in the air, while naming the shapes' geometric equivalent. When he asked for a few volunteers, the boys grew shy. They had been around too many men with clubs, nearly none with noble intent. But finally, the big, ruddy boy, Alvey Ducasse, along with Joe McPeel, rose to their feet.

"Splendid. Now. If I were to strike Mr. Ducasse on his solar plexus, here…"

"We calls that a *gut*, sir," a boy named Baldwin shouted out.

"The gut, then," Sherlock replied. "Thank you, Mr. Baldwin. Now. What geometric shape would I use if Mr. Ducasse's body were turned in this manner, and I wished to strike him unawares?"

Alvey argued mightily that no one, ever, had struck him "unawares." But once the boys had ascertained that the word did not pertain to undergarments, they fell all over themselves, vying for an answer. For this, they agreed, was useful "fer life as we lives it!"

For the first time in their brief existence, they were eager to put pen to paper. Especially when Sherlock had them factor in how near to a victim's limbs, gut or head a swinging arc could get without turning said victim into pudding.

And so, the hour passed with but a few bruises, caused by Sherlock's dutiful revelation of the boys' errors in reckoning— though he kindly wielded the short staff at quarter speed, else there would have been infinitely more damage done.

"On the morrow, we shall go over momentum, a product of both mass and velocity, and how it pertains to street battles. And if we have time, we will cover chemical bonds. Just as males are partial to females, atoms are partial to each other. That is called chemistry. And, just as females are volatile and changeable, you will learn that chemistry is equally volatile and changeable, which makes it exciting, indeed. You are dismissed."

The boys sat silent as tombs, mouths set to catch flies. Sherlock eyed them curiously. "Did you not hear me?"

Alvey raised a tentative hand. "We was wundrin' if we could do some more, sir…"

"Your apprenticeships await!" Sherlock reminded them.

As the boys rose obediently and left the room, they'd been transformed from hooligans to frisky pups that had just bonded with a new keeper, and Sherlock wondered at his newly discovered power over adolescent boys. That he could outwit them was no surprise. The novelty was how quickly and how thoroughly it could be accomplished. His head jerked: the nervous tic that indicated he would mull it over at some future date, when necessity would perforce draw it out.

For the time being, he had but one goal: to inspect Charles and prove himself correct.

But when Sherlock reached the dormitory, he found only Charles's brother George admiring himself in the looking glass on the inside door of a good-sized armoire. He was staring at his reflection as if he half expected it to walk off, leaving behind his pitiful old self.

George was wearing his brand-new clothes. His hair, which anyone would have sworn was the color of ash and spent cinders, was in fact a fine strawberry blond, slicked back with pomade to show off a rather agreeable little face with bright green eyes, though lines of worry were already chiseled into the forehead.

"Where is Charles?" Sherlock inquired. When the boy said nothing he went on: "Your brother? Where is he?"

George scratched at the unfamiliar white skin of his wrist, then wiped his nose with the back of his hand carefully, the way he assumed a gentleman would.

"Gone, sir."

"Gone where? Don't tell me they found a post for him already!"

George shook his head. "'E likes 'is nice new cloves so much 'e went to make 'is mates' mugs go green with envy!"

As he spoke, George pointed to the window as the source of exit—then tore his eyes away from his own reflection long enough to turn and soberly assure Sherlock: "Not to worry, he'll be back, 'e *likes* it 'ere!"

"Can you direct me as to where he's gone?"

George shrugged. "Could be anywhere."

Sherlock sensed the boy was lying. It wasn't his tone or comportment; it was simply the boy's state of being. For what in his existence thus far might have encouraged him to trust anyone—much less a stranger—with the truth of the whereabouts of his sibling?

Sherlock could have pressed the matter and perhaps gotten to the truth, but the little ragamuffin was as spiky as a porcupine. Not only would he not break him, but he risked injuring a future collaborator. He'd have to bide his time.

As George removed his jacket and lay it carefully on his cot, the shirt underneath rose just enough for Sherlock to notice several scars on his back. Sherlock motioned to the cot next to George's. "Charles's?" he asked.

The boy nodded. As George opened the armoire and hung up his brand-new jacket, Sherlock knelt down before Charles's cot, not the least concerned that George was watching, and began to feel gingerly but methodically under the mattress.

"And your old clothes? Where are they?"

"Burnt, sir. Cuz a louses an' suchlike."

"I see. And tell me, what do you know of the punctures on your brother's body?"

"Punches?" George repeated.

"No, not punches, *punctures*. Little holes."

"Where, sir?"

"Well, between his toes, for example…" Sherlock replied, suddenly realizing that it would have been impossible for the boy to note any such thing.

Indeed, George replied, "I don't know nuffink about it. But sometimes Charles spirits off an 'e don't tell no one… but 'e always comes back," George added with a slight catch in his voice. "An 'e always cares fer me, sir. Always."

"Well. It is good to have a brother, is it not?" Sherlock said.

10

MYCROFT HOLMES COOLED HIS HEELS AT BUCKINGHAM
Palace, in one of the dingiest of several small reception
rooms located in the *piano nobile* and furnished in the Chinese
Regency style.

During the Queen's long mourning period for her
beloved Albert, most of the palace had been shuttered, with
entire wings left in disrepair. But he suspected that the general
decrepitude was not the sole reason he'd been relegated to
the least of the inner chambers. Two years before, he and
Cardwell had insisted on changes to the War Office, including
the basing of promotions on merit alone, rather than social
standing or a purchase by the highest bidder. These changes
had been bitterly opposed by high-ranking members of
Parliament and senior Army officers, as nearly all had bought
their way up the ladder and would thus no longer be able to
sell their promotions the moment they retired.

The most vocal opponent had been the Commander-
in-Chief of the Forces. Prince George, 2nd Duke of

Cambridge—who also happened to be the Queen's first cousin—had been set to keep matters as they were. And since Mycroft's presence at the palace would surely be noticed, it appeared that the Queen did not wish to rub salt into her cousin's still-open wound.

Mycroft sighed. From the time he had begun his professional life not four years before, he had already fallen on the wrong side of two cousins of the Queen.

That requires some skill, Holmes, even for you, he chastised himself, all the while hoping Her Majesty would run out of cousins before he ran out of royal toes to trample.

He looked at the play of gray light on the windowsill, the shadow drawing a vertical line down the red velvet flocked wallpaper. The bell in the tower of St. Stephen's chimed the quarter-hour.

Her Majesty was fifteen minutes late.

Why in the world did he feel so out of sorts? Perhaps it was the fire in the hearth. It was much too hot; fit for a monarch of middle years plagued by the first throes of arthritis, not for a twenty-six-year-old man in the bloom of health.

Just when he feared he would combust into flame at any moment, he heard a noise behind him. He turned quickly, lest he be found with his back to the monarch. Victoria Regina was dressed in black from head to toe, save for a bit of white lace peeking from her cap and framing her jowly features. She was stout, with the disapproving scowl of a pug dog. And, from the way she walked—as if trying to levitate off the hard floor—he could tell that rheumatism was beginning to claim her feet. But within the whitened folds of her flesh shone eyes of the most vivid and piercing blue.

With a wave of her hand she dismissed her attendant, who closed the door making nary a sound, leaving the two of them alone.

"Forgive us, Mr. Holmes," she said after Mycroft had bowed and kissed her proffered hand, "for not meeting with you in a more formal setting. But we cannot take the chance of being overheard, as what we are asking is of a delicate nature."

"I am all ears, Your Majesty."

"All in good time, Mr. Holmes. We are always glad for intelligent company and shall not let you go so soon as all that."

She planted herself into a tufted chair while motioning that he should do the same.

"Although you placed us in quite the precarious position some small time back, pitting us against our own cousin, not to mention half of Parliament, with the reforms you and Mr. Cardwell requested."

"Your Majesty signed them into law," Mycroft reminded her with a smile.

"Only because we recalled a small but pertinent favor you did for us at Ascot, one that you are much too well bred to ever bring up again," she murmured.

"I cannot recall it for the life of me, ma'am," Mycroft replied.

The Queen leaned in, appraising him, while he quietly appraised her.

Favors right arm. Still suffers the after-effects of quinsy a year ago.

Nails unkempt: has no patience for allowing herself to be groomed. Picks nervously at cuticles of right thumb. Grief still dulls her countenance, draws black circles under her eyes. Teeth worn at the edges, grinds them in her sleep…

"You are a fine-looking specimen, Mycroft Holmes," the Queen said. "What age might you be now?"

"Twenty-six, ma'am."

"A very good age. We were quite happy at twenty-six. We'd had four, no, five children by then," she mused. "Bertie, our second, is five years your senior but with not a third your wisdom. And handsome we cannot think him, with that painfully small and narrow head, those immense features and total want of chin. And yet, he has no lack of pliable women. As no doubt, you have. Falling at your feet, we take it?"

Mycroft laughed sadly. "If so, I have all but leapt over them…"

"Ah. You do not notice women, then?" she asked, amused.

"I notice falling in love. And when I do, I fear that one woman possesses my every thought."

"Well said. In that, we are birds of a feather. We must say that we prefer you unattached, as it allows you to be more available to us, should we desire it."

The Queen had hit a painful bull's-eye. Mycroft drew in a breath.

"Now to the topic at hand," the Queen said, either unaware or unconcerned. "Scotland and England are to play the first recognized international football match in history. And while we are forced to put a good face on it, it is ghastly news, occurring at a time of fierce animosity between our two lands. One extra point on either side could spark a national riot. We cannot have it, Mr. Holmes."

Mycroft wondered if he had heard correctly. A *football* match?

"I see the dilemma, ma'am," he said, "but surely you are not asking me to halt the match!"

"I wish you to arrange it so that *no one* will win."

Mycroft was stumped. It was one thing to provide a team with an advantage, as he had for the Cambridge crew a few years before; quite another to ensure a zero-sum game!

"The match is on Saturday," the Queen added. "Today is but Tuesday—surely you have time to think up something by then? Or have we perhaps been mistaken about the prowess of the great Mycroft Holmes?"

"Your confidence is gratifying," Mycroft replied, and the Queen rang a bell by her side. A mere blur of seconds later, one of the lord steward's men entered, a blank-faced assistant whose impeccable uniform boasted more personality than he did. He bowed to the Queen and presented her with a cloth folder tied in black ribbon. A barely perceptible nod of her head, and he disappeared again.

"Here you are," she said to Mycroft. "If you've need of more, simply inform our secretary, and he shall oblige you."

Mycroft opened the folder and peered inside, all the while feeling her keen blue gaze on him. It contained, among other things, a roster of prospective players.

"Ma'am," he said a moment later. "I can neither coerce

nor cajole grown men into abstaining from competition. But perhaps Your Majesty could assist."

"We would not know where to begin," the Queen grumbled. "If we did, we would not need *you*."

"You begin with Scotland, for it is the stronger team. It would serve us well if Your Majesty could persuade Arthur Kinnaird of the Wanderers to make himself unavailable. Also," he went on before she could object, "Henry Renny-Tailyour."

"Scotland may be ours," she replied, "but the Scottish are a notoriously stubborn, entrenched people…"

"Perhaps your servant John Brown might be of use," Mycroft suggested, "as he is beloved north of the border. But regardless, may I remind Your Majesty that Arthur Kinnaird's father has a seat in the House of Lords. I am certain you shall have no lack of sway with him, even without Mr. Brown's charismatic appeal. As for Renny-Tailyour, he is a lieutenant in the Royal Engineers and so might appreciate the wisdom of remaining at home for one day."

"I see," the Queen said. "Two changes on the Scotland side. What of England? Shall we do nothing with her?"

"No, ma'am. Charles Alcock is already hobbled by an injury. I have in mind one small adjustment that should balance the scales quite adequately."

"And what would that adjustment entail?"

"If Your Majesty can do her part," he responded, smiling, "I shall do mine. But if I may be permitted…"

Mycroft leaned forward, intent on using wisdom as well

as charm to communicate his next point: "I have pored over the economic forecasts and financial ledgers of 1868, 1862 and 1858 for guidance as to what is to come economically—"

"You have means, Mr. Holmes, but you are not an economist," the Queen said, interrupting him.

"No, ma'am. And yet, I know what I see. Within a year, prices shall plummet as much as forty percent. Shipbuilding and engineering—metal industries, in fact—will suffer terrible unemployment. Raw wool, cotton, wheat, tea, meat, beer and tobacco should be safe enough. But our investment in steel, those infinite railroads…"

The Queen's eyes grew hard. "No one else thinks so."

"You have been given predictions of milder weather, but they are wrong, do you see?" Mycroft said.

It was as if he had fired a shot across the bow. The Queen rose abruptly. "Thank you, that is all."

Mycroft rose, bowed, and kissed her hand.

Busy work! he thought furiously as he watched her go. *That is what I have been given!*

Nevertheless, he had an assignment, and he would perform it to his utmost.

If everything went according to plan—for he had already concocted one—he could be to Scotland and back within twenty-four hours.

11

BY THE TIME DOUGLAS ARRIVED IN DORSET, NIGHT HAD descended: a terrible time to discern loss of goods, especially if complicated by loss of life. At the station to meet him was an old square-jawed, square-headed salt by the name of Paleen whose days of sailing were well behind him. He now occasionally drove a cart for hire between the train station and the beach. Weather had twisted his hands and gouged wrinkles deep into his ancient face.

Douglas smiled when he saw him, for it had been some years since he had seen him last, and he well remembered that Paleen's natural scowl masked a friendly and honorable soul.

"Wot's the damage, Cyrus?" Paleen asked as Douglas took a seat beside him in the cart.

"Don't know as of yet," Douglas said. "The telegram contained only the bare facts. But gales and fog alone could not have brought her aground…"

"No indeed," Paleen agreed. "She come up through the Channel in fine fettle, but rumor has it Cap'n Hunter be thinking she's bound for Portland Roads when all along she's makin' fer Chesil."

"Wrong calculations, then," Douglas said, nodding. "And in the fog, he would not have gleaned that until it was too late."

Paleen nodded. "People on shore knowed she was in trouble. She burnt a blue light, but the sea was aboil; we could bare make 'er out past the flying scud. She drifted broadside, her anchors about as useful as a bone to a toothless dog, no ground to clamp onto, so she heaved and rolled. We lighted a tar barrel, worked through the night to save them poor souls aboard, but she split right in two afore our eyes."

Paleen swallowed hard, removed his cap, and dug his fingers through white hair as sparse as cobwebs while his other hand manned the reins.

"We were pullin' two to shore in a cradle when the rope brake. The surf swallowed 'em whole and they were seen no more." Paleen put his cap back on his head and went on in a monotone. "We got the second line up an' runnin', but now the poor souls on deck, women and children most of 'em, is cryin' to be saved while the ship splinters to bits and sheets of water careens over 'em. We gets the basket to workin'. A father with two children is beggin' for someone to take 'em, but a woman in the basket says, 'No indeed, I will take no one's child!' Milk of human kindness in that one!" Paleen exclaimed.

"How many deaths in all?" Douglas asked.

"Six we know of: two crew, four passengers. And four more on the shore."

"What do you mean, four on the shore?"

"The *Royal Adelaide* begun to disgorge her cargo of boxes and casks through her riven side. Four crewmen, they comes in safe but finds three bottles a whiskey washed up ashore; greedy cusses go and hide on the cliff, drinks 'em to the dregs, then pass out like happy sots. In the morning there they is, froze to death. Two of 'em local lads."

"May God have mercy upon their souls," Douglas said softly.

He did wonder, though, if the four had really died of exposure or something else. Deaths of crew at sea, or even ashore, needed careful investigation. Within the confines of a ship, an infectious disease could be fatal for all aboard.

Still, the first order of business was to salvage what he could. The thought of failing Nickolus House, and the memory of his dead son, was too much to bear.

Douglas presented himself to the coast guards and the soldiers of the 77th Regiment, and his request to recoup whatever he could was granted with weary consent.

Troops had been out in force through the day, but there was no stopping the rapacious and hollow-eyed humanity intent to haul off whatever their arms and skirts and pockets and kerchiefs could carry. All the law could do was to make its presence known, so that the people's assault on the ship would not mutate into an assault on each other.

Douglas and Paleen converted a few burly but good-natured marauders into well-paid workers, and together they pulled onto dry ground every floating crate and cask that they could find. Freezing-cold water helped to keep all but the most intrepid freebooters at bay. The few valiant thieves who did attempt to wrest a precious crate from Douglas's grasp quickly found themselves underwater, with a long, dexterous foot bracing their necks until their panicked and flapping hands assured Douglas of their noblest intentions towards him and his goods from that point on.

And all the while, he prayed that the bullets in his chest would stay lodged where they were one more time.

By Wednesday dawn, Douglas and his makeshift crew were done, and he was stunned to realize that nearly seventy percent of his cargo had been salvaged. It would be transported back to Regent Tobaccos to be shipped out again at a future date.

Relieved and feeling undeservedly blessed, Douglas's thoughts turned again to the four sailors whose lives had been cut short at the height of their merrymaking, thanks to his whiskey. In the chaos, their bodies had not yet been removed but had been left where they'd died on a cliff overlooking the sea, covered with tarpaulins.

Douglas made his way to the bodies and removed the tarps. All four had been dead a day, most likely perishing at first light, which often proved more chilling than even the darkest point of night. One of the men, a boy in fact, with long reddish-blond hair and a sprinkling of freckles across the bridge of his nose, still clenched an empty bottle of Irish whiskey in his right fist. Rigor mortis had cleaved boy and bottle together, and the freezing temperatures had made certain that he would not loosen that grip anytime soon.

Douglas, from his several decades aboard ship, was long practiced at deducing seaborne diseases of various kinds. He inspected the four men carefully for signs of infection. On the older two sailors, he found nothing. But the younger two, small and slender, whose age he estimated to be seventeen to nineteen, had what at first appeared to be insect bites. Upon closer scrutiny he realized that the bites were in actuality tiny holes made with a needle, along both arms, as well as between their fingers and toes, and even on the fleshy part of their triceps.

"I knowed these two," Paleen muttered by way of explanation, pointing to the young sailors. "Cuckney and Le Bone. So small, they was. And smaller still in death."

Douglas stated the obvious, though he framed it as a question. "Drug users?"

Paleen brought the light of his lantern closer, dropped to his knees and squinted. "Looks like it," he said gruffly. "But then, I don't know many seamen that ain't. You be cold and wet long enuff…"

"Had they been at sea for long?" Douglas asked. It was another obvious question, as he did not see the calluses of long months aboard ship.

"New hires both," Paleen confirmed. "First time out, I'd say."

And made it all of one hundred forty-four nautical miles, Douglas thought to himself, *only to die close to home.*

"But if they were local boys," he asked, "why have their families not come to claim them?"

"They ain't got none," Paleen said. "Bitty as they are, they went to the city and tried their 'ands at chimneyin', but they was already too up in years…"

Douglas picked up the hand of the boy still clutching the bottle and turned it so that the underside of the arm was visible. "Some of these injections," he said, "could not have been self-administered. He holds the bottle in his right hand, so he was right-handed, and yet the injections are here, in his right wrist."

Paleen grunted as if to say this was out of his frame of knowledge, nor did he care to pursue it.

Douglas sighed. "Could be that they injected each other," he said almost to himself, "but if so, why on the wrist? It seems a peculiar spot…"

"Cursed from birth, they was," Paleen concluded, wiping sand off his knees as Douglas pulled the tarpaulins back over the dead.

As the two men walked back to the cart, Douglas noticed a barefoot little girl protectively hugging a child-sized, sodden bisque doll, hurrying her treasure away lest anyone tell her no. It was a strange sight. To his knowledge, bisque dolls hailed from France and Germany and were therefore not the typical cargo of the *Royal Adelaide*, which did not make stops at ports in either country.

It must've belonged to a passenger's child, he mused.

Moments later, another discovery: long blond hair lulling like seaweed on the waves near the shore. Inebriated with chill and weariness, Douglas waded in. But instead of a child in distress, he pulled up a second doll, the space between its glass eyes and their sockets streaming with water. Within minutes, he was surrounded by six more: redheads, brunettes, blonds, their cloth bodies sodden, the hollow porcelain of their heads, hands and feet keeping them more or less afloat for a moment or two, before they sank under the waves again.

For a reason he could in no way discern, the vision of those sinking dolls, and two human beings barely into manhood dead underneath a tarpaulin, began to merge into the most disturbing image. As if a great evil were suddenly laying its cold and impenetrable blanket upon his little corner of the earth.

By the pricking of my thumbs, something wicked this way comes…

Enough, Douglas! he told himself as he made his way back out of the water. The second witch in *Macbeth* was certainly not referring to hypodermic needles!

12

BY EARLY EVENING, DOUGLAS HAD RETURNED TO NICKOLUS House. He had not yet bathed, had barely eaten, and his feet had not been dry for the last twenty-four hours. All he wanted was to remove his stinking boots and take a seat in the kitchen, where a nice cup of tea and a handful of biscuits to dip therein would set the world to rights.

Alas, he was still in the hall hanging up his coat and hat when Mr. Capps approached him. "*Mr.* Douglas," he said, hissing the first word.

Douglas turned, smiling wanly. He was about to say good evening and go about his business when he realized that Capps was distraught.

"The lad you left in charge of the tutelage? The brother of your friend Mr. Holmes, the one who was to teach the boys mathematics…?"

"Yes, Mr. Capps, I am aware of him. Did he not do as I asked?"

"Why, he most certainly did!" Capps cried. "And left

the boys bleeding and battered!"

Douglas stared at him, praying he had heard incorrectly. "What are you saying?"

"Battered! Battered!" Capps insisted.

"Steady, Mr. Capps. How do you know this?"

"Seen it with my own two eyes!" Capps exclaimed, his proper grammar evaporating with his equanimity. "This afternoon, I noticed that the boys were at their desks a good quarter-hour before class was to begin, scrubbed and eager. I had never seen them so enthused before, so I assumed they were in good hands. I left to go to the post office and when I came back, there they were, filing out to their work assignments, half of them sporting fresh nicks and bruises! And poor Alvey missing half an eyetooth!"

Douglas realized his arm was still raised to the coat hook. He dropped it to his side, hoping the blood would rush back up into his brain, where he obviously needed it most.

"Were the boys upset?" he asked.

"Upset!" Capps sputtered indignantly. "They were happy as larks!"

Douglas was not following any of this. He drew a breath and tried again: "Did you speak to them? What did they say?"

"Well of course I spoke to them! I demanded they tell me all that had transpired, but they refused to utter a word against him! Said they got the bruises elsewhere!"

"I see. And did you speak to Sherlock?"

"I most certainly did! He denied any knowledge and, I might add, in quite the grandiloquent way! I am a fairly well-educated man, Mr. Douglas, but I barely understood a word he said. But this I know: there is something very, very wrong with him!"

"Yes, I—I understand. Thank you, Mr. Capps."

Douglas left the hall and, cursing his grumbling stomach, took the back stairs two at a time. On the second floor, he followed the sound of the vielle to Sherlock's quarters, a small guestroom opposite the commodious dormitory.

Doing his best to repress burgeoning homicidal urges, Douglas knocked at the door and let himself in.

He noted that his current guest, unlike those who had come before him, seemed to prize neither air nor light. The curtains were drawn, in spite of a window that faced west. On the dresser beside the bed, three candles remained unlit. Over the room lay the smoky canopy of shag tobacco smoke.

Sherlock was sitting on the bed, facing away from the door. And though he must have heard it open above the squeal of catgut strings, he did not glance around to see who it could be, but continued to saw away mercilessly.

"Sherlock!" Douglas said.

The boy completed whatever measure was in his head, placed his vielle by his side, then turned and looked calmly at Douglas. "It is considered polite to knock," he said. "I shall, however, waive that nicety in exchange for clear and immediate reprieve, and I shall be on my way, for I have much to do."

When Douglas said nothing, Sherlock expounded: "Let me rephrase. May I assume that your presence means that

I am absolved of my chores? Dismissed? Might I collect me tuppence and go now, sir?"

Douglas narrowed his eyes and glared at Sherlock in a way that would have made most men shudder but that did not alter the other's countenance one whit. "You are lucky I do not throttle you to within an inch of your life," he growled.

Sherlock feigned surprise. "You wish to do me violence? I did only as you asked! I kept the little beggars amused, and I schooled them into the bargain."

"You *beat* them!" Douglas exclaimed, towering over him.

"In no manner!" Sherlock declared, offended. "I instructed them in geometry—a word they'd never heard, by the way. We covered trajectory, the arc of a weapon, where it lands and why, momentum—another word they'd never heard—and relative distance. We also conducted experiments in chemistry; basic, I must admit, but pertinent to their lives. They were taught as I would've liked to have been taught, had I been so fortunate as to have had myself for a—"

"*Children!*" Douglas spat out. "These are children, eleven to fifteen years of age! Here as our charges, we have a sacred duty to keep them safe!"

Sherlock looked up at him, nonplussed. "You of all people," he said, "prattling on about safety? From the endless stories that I've heard from my brother, is it not true that on the streets of Port of Spain you fought a band of Chinese ruffians and a boy half your age?"

"Yes! A boy trained in the Eastern arts from the time he

could barely toddle—not to mention that he was nineteen and not *eleven*!"

"Ah! And how young should one be when one learns to box?" Sherlock countered. "And when a blow lands, should one not feel it? And if one does *not* feel it, how can one be expected to learn to avoid it the next time?"

"They were not there for a boxing lesson, Sherlock!"

"No!" Sherlock declared, rising to his feet. "They were there to learn a thing or two about geometry and chemistry, which they did! Besides, your Mr. Capps was so busy blabbing to you about a welt or two that he quite forgot to mention, or perhaps is not even aware, that your new charge, young Charles Fowler, departed yesterday afternoon and has not been heard from since!"

Douglas felt all the air go out of him. He pushed the vielle aside and sat hard on the bed. He closed his weary eyes for a moment, trying to summon up the strength to speak.

"If he is gone," he said at last, "I must go after him…"

With his eyes closed and head bowed, Douglas heard Sherlock say, with uncommon enthusiasm: "That is the single most cogent phrase you have uttered since you first barged in here. For it is what I have been desiring all along!"

Douglas opened his eyes. "What are you going on about?" he asked wearily.

Sherlock had slipped shoes onto his stockinged feet and was measuring shag into his travel pouch. "I am coming with you, of course!"

"Thank you, no," Douglas replied.

"Mr. Douglas. You are fatigued and lack proper nourishment. You have also abused your tendons and muscles most unmercifully. And I can glean from how you sit that your lower back and right hip are in some distress. Not to mention that your left cornea has been scratched by sand—"

"Does this soliloquy have a point?" Douglas interrupted, inadvertently rubbing his injured left eye while hating himself for proving the smug little sot correct.

Sherlock said nothing but wrapped his scarf about his throat with a jaunty twirl, and was at the door, waiting for Douglas to follow.

"No," Douglas said, his voice hoarse. "You care for the boys not at all, or merely for your own conjecture…"

"And you care for them a great deal. Yet they do not even deign to speak to you. And why should they? They do not know you pay the accounts. They see you only as the Negro lackey of a rich and ailing man they have never met. Your kindness seems to them the condescension of one who should be beneath them, and yet has improbably achieved something they could never dream of. You fit into no category they can discern, which makes you despised."

Douglas winced.

"Whereas they have befriended *me* lock, stock, and rather wormy barrel," Sherlock went on. "As for my feelings, you cannot presume to know them. But we agreed beforehand, did we not, that compassion is overrated? Like it or not, Mr. Douglas, you need me," Sherlock concluded.

Douglas took a moment. Then he sprang from the bed

towards Sherlock. He saw Sherlock flinch, as if in fear that, rather than do his bidding, Douglas had decided to pummel him after all.

He is somewhat human, at least, Douglas thought.

"Do not forget your overcoat," he said to Sherlock.

"I have none," the latter responded gaily as he stepped across the threshold. "Might I perhaps borrow one of yours…?"

Douglas sighed. What was that Latin phrase? *Auribus teneo lupum.* He had a wolf by the ears. Whether he held on or let go—either choice could be equally injurious to his health.

13

GEORGE'S SOMBER LITTLE FACE WAS AS WRINKLED AS A partially made bed, his brow coated with sweat. For it seemed he was beginning to comprehend that the two men standing before him depended on his knowledge of the environs to find his runaway brother, and to allow them both to remain within Nickolus House. And so, he did his utmost to explain, though his directions relied less on bellwethers of the road and more on local personages of note: "You goes past the old crone wot stuffs dog turds in 'er bucket fer the tan'ry, ain't no missin' 'er stink. Then you looks fer Mr. Boil—I dunno as that's 'is name, but that's wot we calls 'im, an' 'e begs fer alms on the same street as the copperpot man, an' they bicker like two cocks on the same hen…"

With these and other vivid directions, little George instructed them out of Nickolus House and along the roadways, going from human marker to human marker.

An hour after twilight, the Devil's Acre was already sealed in an exhausted darkness. Worn-out costermongers were returning to their hovels, hauling baskets of eels and pigs' knuckles too far gone for anyone to purchase, even for a pittance.

Muck in the streets could no longer be sidestepped even via sense of smell, for the senses had been pummeled into submission by pungent, rancid, sour and putrefying odors of such variety that they would have made the greatest perfumer in Paris weep aloud.

Douglas knew the quarter well enough that they were not likely to run into a wall or an inconveniently parked cart. Still, the cobblestones were chipped and broken; one blundering step could pitch a pedestrian ankle-deep into a steaming mound of dung or a pile of rags, with the owner of said rags curled up inside, drunk, sick, or slumbering.

And somewhere in this unrelenting blackness was the charming but unwise Charles Fowler drawing unaccustomed notice in his new clothes and shoes: a titmouse dropped headfirst into a bevy of snakes.

Wind stung Douglas's exposed face. It felt like miniscule shards of glass as he and Sherlock trudged along in the dark. While Sherlock was swaddled—or perhaps swallowed—in Douglas's overcoat, he himself was making do with a jacket. It did not matter. It seemed that his nerves had finally given up and gone to sleep, waiting for the rest of him to join them.

Painfully aware of his own limitations, he laid his hand over his breast pocket, which held a pistol: his old Smith & Wesson, top break, single action Model 3. He could not imagine having to use it, but he could also not imagine traveling in the dark without it, tempting fate.

As for Sherlock, Douglas had expected him to complain, but he had done nothing of the kind. It was he, in fact, though not quite so tall as Douglas, who had set the pace from the first and kept on relentlessly, and with nary a word. There was no meandering through the labyrinthine streets. Sherlock would find a marker, then move on to the next like a hound on the hunt. For although visibility was almost nil, George's directions thus far had been remarkably on point. And there was but one left. Douglas recalled the boy's words: "I'm finkin' if it's early enuff, there's a rag-and-bone man, right full of 'isself cuz 'e owns an 'orse—'*alf* an 'orse," George had amended. "His bruvver-in-loss owns the uvver 'alf an' uses it fer uvver work. You'll hear 'im snorin' somethin' fierce. He'll have 'is cart out an' be sleepin' afore the door."

"So you are saying this man parks his cart in front of a door?" Douglas had repeated. "And then sleeps against it while his brother has use of the animal?"

George had nodded, eyeing Sherlock with pity for having to put up with the poor dim Negro at his side. When Douglas had dared to inquire, "Which door?" George had stared at him as if realizing that trusting this half-wit meant that all his labors had been in vain.

"The door where Charles is!" he'd blurted out impatiently.

"Yes, but where does it *lead*?" Douglas had insisted.

"Why, it don't lead to no place!" The boy had said as

if this were the most logical response in the world. "An old storrige room's wot it was," he'd said, turning to Sherlock, "naught but rats in it now. But we makes two beds of rags an' paper, cuz our soot blankets we 'as to leave wiv Mr. Beeton, cuz they's 'is. But Charles an' me, we were warm enuff!" Georgie declared as if daring anyone to say different, until his tone became suddenly plaintive, eyes pleading. "Douglas? You will tell Mr. Smythe I was of aid? Charles shouldn't 'ave took off, but we wants to be 'ere more than anyfing…"

When Douglas assured him that Mr. Smythe would be informed of George's honesty and helpfulness, one big tear squeezed out of the boy's eye before he could prevent it. He roughly wiped it away, planted his feet more firmly on the ground, and scowled up at Douglas as if to say no one alive had better feel sorry for him, or they'd learn what's what.

"*There* he is!"

Sherlock had managed to spot the rag-and-bone man on the other side of the street, which made Douglas wonder if he could see in the dark, like a cat.

The man was just as George had described him: wrapped in a greatcoat and leaning against his now-horseless cart, snoring. And though all they could see behind him was a crumbling building the color of pitch, George had been unerring to this juncture, so they quickly crossed the road to the old storehouse door.

But Charles was not sequestered behind it, as they'd

been assured he would be. Instead, they heard a terrified cry—"'Elp, guv'nor! 'Elp!"

Down an alley, a lad who looked very much like Charles was struggling to wrench himself free from three grown men in threadbare clothing.

14

SHERLOCK COULD NOT ASCERTAIN WHETHER IT WAS Charles. It could be any boy, crying out for assistance so that his chums could then assail the Samaritan, stripping him of goods and his pride. He turned to glance at Douglas to gauge his thoughts—only to see Douglas's hands planted flat on the empty horse cart, using it as a springboard to hoist himself aloft, then flying feet first into the man tugging the unseen boy by the arm and landing a blow squarely on the kidnapper's head.

The man crumpled to the ground, and his two startled friends attempted to strike the tall black shadow that had improbably materialized before them. But Douglas was no underweight lad with a twisted spine whom they could haul about. As the two lunged at him, he struck again. His right forearm protected his face and his right leg was braced behind him, while his large left hand darted out of the mist and wrapped itself around one man's throat so quickly that it seemed easier to witness in retrospect.

As that same hand dropped to the ground for balance, Douglas's right leg was already lifting into the air, the foot like a cudgel smacking the third ne'er-do-well between his jaw and ear, sending him sprawling.

In the tumult, the captive boy took off down the alley, with Douglas right behind him.

Sherlock looked down at Douglas's vanquished opponents. The man kicked in the face was not moving; nor was the second with the crushed windpipe. But the third—thinning hair, scarred, mid-twenties—staggered to his feet. He stared at Sherlock, then came at him with the toe-heel alignment, relaxed torso and slightly bent knees of a pugilist bent on revenge.

Sherlock, who until this juncture had only sparred with Mycroft or the Quince twins, wrenched his short staff from the interior pocket of Douglas's coat. As the man came at him, he let go a decent left jab that came primarily out of sudden fear.

Blood spurted from a freshly made gash on his opponent's forehead that sent him stumbling backwards into the cart. It shuddered with the weight of him, and elicited an indignant roar of outrage from the owner whose slumbers had been cut short.

The owner reached for the interloper but missed and snagged Sherlock's coat instead, holding him long enough that his assailant was able to deliver a businesslike punch to Sherlock's gut, making him double over. The owner—confused but out to punish *somebody*—kept his vice-like hold.

Sherlock was forced to drop his elbow and jab it into the man's ribs until he let go.

As his nemesis came for him again, Sherlock delivered a well-placed knee to his groin that sent him crumpling to the ground near his two friends.

He tried to regain his spent breath. Now what?

"*Sherlock!*"

It was Douglas, bellowing out of the darkness.

He shook off his reverie and ran towards the sound, catching up with Douglas just as the latter managed to lay a hand on the fleeing boy, who tried to take one more step, only to collapse onto the street. As Douglas scooped him up in his arms like a rag doll, Charles vomited a viscous substance of indeterminate color across Douglas's shoulder but did not return to consciousness.

"What of the men?" Sherlock asked, looking behind him.

"Forget them, they are of no consequence," Douglas said.

Sherlock listened for the sound of footsteps coming towards them, but all was quiet. "Should we not discern why they were after him?"

"Hush." Douglas felt Charles's chest and mouth for a heartbeat and breath. "Feeble but present," he said. "We must get him home."

"Yes, by all means," Sherlock agreed, following somberly behind. "He cannot die, not when there is so much to discover!"

Charles's brother George, hiccupping back tears, was allowed to ascertain for himself that Charles was still, however tenuously, amongst the living. Then he was shunted back to the dormitory for whatever night's sleep he could muster.

He took off his clothes most reluctantly, hiding them under his very own pillow, another unheard-of luxury, lest anyone should ferret them away while his eyes were closed.

As for the nightshirt, he eyed it with misgivings. He confessed to Douglas that he did not recognize it as any proper clothing for a male of the species. He suspected it only fit for kings and the like. But because the cotton was finer than any he'd ever felt, Douglas watched him smooth it ever so carefully underneath him so that it would not crease as he slipped under the bedcovers.

Upstairs in the attic, Charles Fowler lay in *his* new nightshirt, in the little cot that Douglas had dragged up there for that very purpose. It would allow him to rest free of the prying eyes of his fellow residents.

As they waited by the light of a hissing gas lamp for the doctor to arrive, Douglas and Sherlock inspected the numerous bruises and cuts on the boy's body. The lad had the sign of the whip across his thin shoulder blades. There were at least ten scars, though none were fresh.

"I am disturbed by these," Sherlock said.

"You ought to be. The fact that employers can beat their charges with impunity—"

"No," Sherlock said impatiently. "I meant that Beeton appears to have ceased 'disciplining' the boy. Whatever for? He and George still worked as sweeps until a few days ago— why the reprieve? And it seemed to me that the stripes on George's back are as old as his brother's. I am no physician—"

"No, you are not," Douglas underscored.

"—but even so, every one of the gashes had scarred over."

Sherlock scratched the tip of his long, sharp nose and stared into the middle distance. "How'd they come to you?" he asked. "The brothers?"

"Through do-gooders, as Mycroft would call them," Douglas replied. "Sometimes they see a child that is more intelligent, more skilled, or simply needier than the rest. They alert Nickolus House, and we pay the parents, or the master, to take him off their hands. A wealthy patroness by the name of Adele de Matalin ferreted out these two."

"And I was correct that the boy is an inveterate dope fiend, as he has overdosed. But on what? Tincture of opium? Laudanum? Morphine? My guess is the latter, but it would take quite a bit to kill a boy with this large a habit."

"I am no physician…" Douglas began, his tone slightly mocking.

"No, you are not," Sherlock replied.

"…but the only drug we can rule out for certain is a coca derivative, as that would have raised his heartbeat, not slowed it down to almost nothing."

"Opium and its derivatives can be smoked or eaten without censure," Sherlock ruminated. "Why go to the trouble of a syringe, which costs money and is difficult for boys like this to procure? And as to the locations of the injections themselves," he continued, "it appears I have missed only three on the back of his neck, hidden by his hair, plus two fresh ones on his right triceps."

"So, he went out to flaunt his new clothes, and someone injected him—" Douglas began.

Sherlock shook his head. "I believe that was the tale he told his brother, if indeed he told it at all. For it sounds more like an eleven-year-old hard pressed for a story. No, he went out to *be* injected, for his own reasons or someone else's. He is almost absurdly right-handed. Judging by the left-hand pocket in his jacket and trousers, he does not use his left hand to put so much as a sou in there. The hole in his right triceps is too clean and precise for Charles to have done it himself. Even if he could, why would he? He can easily inject himself in the usual places, such as the crook of the elbow or the biceps, and no one would be bothered by the aesthetics of such an act, much less be the wiser."

Douglas thought back to the young sailors on the beach, and their own improbable punctures. The two lads and Charles had a handful of things in common: they were small; they had been, or had been around, chimney sweeps; and they were apparently addicted to injectable substances that had been administered in out-of-the-way regions of their bodies. He considered mentioning all of this to Sherlock, but he did not think he could bear his enthusiasm—nay, his unbridled glee—at being on the precipice of a very definite mystery.

Besides, he himself had passed his own precipice: he could no longer keep his eyes open, much less adequately gauge which side of an ethical dilemma to choose, without sustenance and rest.

"Enough for now," Douglas said, rising. "Let us wait to see what the doctor has to say."

"The doctor?" Sherlock sneered. "What could the doctor possibly tell us besides 'drug user'? And what relevance would that hold? No, what *is* relevant," he went on as he inspected the punctures on the boy's triceps with his spider-like fingers, "is who may have been injecting him, and why. Look here," he said, pointing. "Based on the degree of healing, these older injections have been administered with some regularity; if not day by day, then certainly every few days."

"You would now be an expert on how long wounds take to heal?" Douglas asked, to which Sherlock replied decidedly:

"Not yet. But I shall be. Sooner rather than later, I'd say. And when Charles ran off, he was wearing new clothing, and was found in same the following evening. Why were they not stolen? He must've known they would not be, for he took no precautions, had no weapon or spare set of clothes…"

Douglas had to admit that his first thought when defending Charles from the men in the alley was that they were after his belongings. The streets were such that nothing was safe, certainly not a scrawny lad in a new suit and shoes. That Charles might be somehow inured from such thievery never crossed his mind. But, thinking back on it, George had not been worried about Charles's physical welfare over the past twenty-four hours, only about their being banished from Nickolus House for Charles's transgression.

Was he under someone's protection?

If so, why then had he not been safe from those hooligans? Did they not realize that Charles was not to be molested?

"Then, when we undressed him and put him to bed," Sherlock was saying, "we found nothing that indicated drug use beyond the holes in his body."

"What do you mean?" Douglas asked, feeling slightly lightheaded.

"Those rags the boys owned were destroyed for lice," Sherlock clarified. "Do you not think a drug fiend of his caliber would keep a hypodermic syringe upon his person? And do not bother to tell me that he could have stashed it somewhere. The moment I realized he had left, I carefully inspected every inch where he could have set foot, from bedroom to classroom to bath. I found nothing."

The young sailors! Douglas thought once again. It never occurred to him to ascertain if one or both had carried a syringe upon their person. Now of course it was too late.

But too late for what? Was he truly being carried away by Sherlock's imaginings of a great mystery, of a conspiracy involving former or aspiring chimney sweeps?

Just then on the bed, Charles's shallow but steady breathing became a wheezing rasp. He half sat up and opened his eyes like a trout wrenched from the water and gulping oxygen.

Douglas slipped a hand behind his back. "Easy, lad, easy…"

Charles looked from one to the other with his wide-eyed, drowning gaze and sputtered one word: "Baker."

He attempted to draw one more breath, then he was gone.

15

AFTER AN EXQUISITE DINNER OF FRESH SQUAB AND MASH, followed by a peaceful night's sleep, Mycroft sat in his carriage on the way to catch the Special Scotch Express. It was the first morning in a long while that he had felt perfectly well. It was as if a fog in his brain had lifted, and he wondered— not for the first time—if the responsibility of caring for Sherlock somehow contributed to his muddleheaded state.

He picked up the *Daily Telegraph* and turned to the international news, a segment that Sherlock would never have deigned to peruse, for his brother's interest in worldly affairs was only slightly more than his interest in cosmology, which was to say none at all.

He bypassed all the news he already knew until he spotted a story whose subject matter he was unaware of: an American by the name of Susan B. Anthony and fifty other women had attempted to cast their vote for U.S. president, whereupon she and several others had been arrested.

He could hear Georgiana's plaintive tone, its sweet

melody in stark contrast to her terrible words: *And what of me? Am I to do nothing while former slaves are given more rights in England than I, as a woman, will ever hope to achieve? The right to vote, Mycroft! How long have I been dreaming of that?*

At that juncture, she was no longer Georgiana the quintessential English rose, the woman he had sworn to marry, but a specter the color of tombstone.

At that moment the carriage halted abruptly. He heard Huan mutter a few choice words in his Trinidadian patois. Mycroft glanced out the window.

Gliding across the street, with two brawny bodyguards at her heels, was the most beautiful Chinese woman he'd ever seen, though this was damning her with faint praise, as there were but a handful of Chinese women in all of London. *No*, he amended. She was easily the most beautiful woman of any race that he had ever seen. Her nose was rather elongated but fine, her eyes large and almond-shaped, and the color of tourmaline. Her mouth was small but full, her face a perfect oval. Her ebony hair had been combed into a two-coned chignon, each side interwoven with vivid purple flowers that matched the flowers on her silk skirt, over-blouse and Qing jacket. She was dressed sumptuously but was, Mycroft thought, the sort who would look every bit as regal if she were covered in rags.

As for her two companions, their vocation was rendered clear from their musculature, the way they carried themselves, and their steely glare.

As the woman made her way across the street towards

the carriage, Mycroft could not help but gape at her. This was not typical behavior on his part. He had no use for conventional standards of feminine desirability, paragons of soap-tin prettiness with mincing steps and eyes coquettishly downcast. This woman's gait was delicate yet purposeful, her gaze direct without seeming intrusive.

Early twenties, he thought, *upper class Han.* The last was clear by her bearing and attire. Yet she walked freely, her feet unbound. As ninety-eight percent of Han women kept the tradition of foot binding, the odds were better that she belonged to the Hakka subset that did not bind, and that emphasized education, even for women.

I can only hope that is what she is, he sighed. *For her sake*, he added primly.

The woman acknowledged Huan's kindness at letting her by with a gracious bow of her head. Mycroft gazed at her until she and her bodyguards had passed by his window and disappeared from view. Then he sat stunned and slightly chagrined at his own untoward behavior.

Oh, for pity's sake, he thought, defending himself against mute accusers, *Georgiana has been gone two years! I cannot remain a monk forever!*

Finally, he forsook all propriety; as the carriage commenced its journey, he turned to glance out of the opposite window, and saw her enter a herbalist's shop, her companions following behind, as if her small, perfect silhouette were casting not one but three shadows.

He marveled at the coincidence of the past few days.

Not taking into account the passel of Chinese sailors who came and went with the cargo ships, there were little more than two hundred Chinese in the whole of Britain. The odds of Mycroft having seen *two* upper class Han Chinese in the span of twenty-four hours was absurdly low. And the odds that the two were not in some way related?

Lower still.

Which meant the elegant Chinese woman was very likely linked to the Chinese gentleman of the same caste who had met with Cainborn outside the National Standard Theatre. Mycroft mentally compared her exquisite face to that of the man, as well as their relative age, height, weight, style of movement, and mannerisms. The older man had the same elongated nose, the same large, symmetrical almond shape to his eyes, though his were black. They had the same forehead, though a different chin—hers being a good deal daintier. And they both carried themselves like aristocrats.

Uncle and niece? Perhaps. But father and daughter was the most likely scenario, for their commonalities appeared unadulterated. *And what of it?* he reprimanded himself irritably. *What on earth could any of it have to do with me?*

Besides, he could be mistaken about the Chinese population in Britain. He knocked on the trap. "Huan?"

"Mr. Mycroft!"

Mycroft grimaced. "I believe there to be only some two hundred Chinese in the whole of Britain," he said. "Does that ring true?"

"I do not know," Huan said. "But it is a small number.

All my Chinese friends here know each other. The girl was beautiful, no?"

"Beautiful, yes," Mycroft responded rather crossly. "But she has nothing whatever to do with us."

"True," Huan responded. "Though to see two Han Chinese in two days, that is many, no? It is the Year of the Water Monkey. We are apt to see many tricks, many tricks," Huan concluded ominously before shutting the trap again.

Tricks or no, the further the herbalist's shop receded, the more Mycroft's anxiety grew. A touch of curiosity about this strangest of coincidences was surely healthy and worth pursuing, was it not?

"Huan?" he called, opening the trap. "Turn back!"

"Turning, Mr. Mycroft!" Huan called out gaily.

16

MYCROFT ENTERED THE TINY SHOP, SQUEEZING PAST THE two bodyguards, who stood on either side of the door. On the far wall, in floor-to-ceiling wooden shelving behind glass apertures, was an array of remedies and potions in multicolored bottles, from butternut and carnelian to jade and deep-water blue. Below were dozens and dozens of small wooden drawers with shiny copper pulls, each herb therein carefully labeled.

The Chinese woman stood at the counter, her back to Mycroft. She was turning the pages of a large book faded with age and wear, while an older man—perhaps the owner of the establishment—waited patiently to assist her, his sparse blond hair slicked back with pomade, the skin on his face and neck as soft as a baby's; a testament to his wares, Mycroft assumed.

As Mycroft approached the counter, the woman ran her finger down a page, paused a moment, and then closed the book.

He eyed the spine and cover. Though its characters were Chinese, its title was written out phonetically in the Latin alphabet: *Shen-nung Pen Ts'ao Ching.*

"*Ma huang,*" the woman said. "Twelve ounces please, and twelve ounces of monkshood. And a small bag of aniseed."

She had a slight accent. Her voice was melodious but lower than Mycroft had expected: a mezzo, as opposed to a soprano.

"Oh, and *Marrubium vulgare*, three bunches," she said, pointing towards a drawer of herbs while holding her little finger slightly aloft.

"No paregoric?" the herbalist asked.

"No," she said, her tone firm.

"You might try *natrii calcii edetas,*" Mycroft suggested.

She turned towards him with a start, as did the man.

"Calcium disodium edetate?" he translated. "Why would Madame wish for that?"

"It serves as an antidote for arsenic," Mycroft said, looking directly at the woman. The moment he did so, he noticed in his peripheral vision her bodyguards making a move towards him.

She raised her hand and halted them midstride. It was an impressive display of power and restraint, and it made Mycroft so giddy that he nearly laughed aloud.

"And what makes you believe I need an antidote for arsenic?" she said evenly, betraying the smallest smile that told him he was on the right track.

"The page you were on," he replied, nodding at the

tome on the counter, "concerned bronchial distress."

"Ah, so you read Mandarin," she said as if it were a statement of fact.

"No," he admitted. "But I recognize inflamed bronchi when I see an illustration."

Her smile was now full, and it was glorious. "Stunning, are they not?" she said. "The illustrations. I have studied this book since I was a child, yet they never fail to impress me. Still, it seems a leap from *ma huang*, anise, horehound, and inflamed bronchi to arsenic poisoning."

"It would seem so, yes. But there is a dye that clothiers and artificial-flower makers use to create a brilliant green hue," he continued, daring to draw a bit closer, the tension in the room rising even as he did so. Mycroft was temporarily distracted by her scent. Though subtle, he could still pick up hints of lavender, chamomile, and Marseilles soap, with its mixture of olive oil, sea salt and ash.

"Unfortunately," he continued, pulling himself together, "in order to achieve it, one must mix copper and arsenic trioxide, or white arsenic, a highly toxic cocktail. Much has been written on it of late. You must be familiar with it, for you carry a small green stain of it on the little finger of your right hand."

She lifted her finger to see, her expression part wonder, part horror. The herbalist quickly drizzled calendula oil onto a ball of cotton wool and passed it to her.

"Ah," she said as she rubbed off the telltale mark. "And, as you realize that I am neither a clothier nor a maker of artificial flowers, you assume I am here to seek a remedy for one thus afflicted. And so I am, for it is a gruesome way to die," she concluded, placing the soiled cotton ball back on the counter with a nod of thanks to the shopkeeper. "But since it is bad form for women to study medicine, and an abomination if one is not only female but Chinese, I pray you let this be our little secret, Mr.…"

"Holmes," Mycroft replied, doffing his hat with a slight bow.

Her eyes opened wide. "*Holmes?*" she repeated. "Are you perchance related to a *Sherlock* Holmes?"

"He… he is my brother," Mycroft said, truly thrown.

"Oh, but I have been hearing that name for months!" she said with enthusiasm. "Sherlock Holmes! He is quite the adept fighter, is he not? A boxer, I believe?"

"Yes, he is, but—"

"My younger brother Dai en-Lai is at Cambridge at Downing, and has seen him in combat with his friends! He is all in awe. Dai brings me home medical journals, which I devour, and risks the wrath of our father to do so!

"I am Ai Lin," she said, extending her hand. "I should like to extend to you and Master Sherlock an invitation to dinner next Wednesday. I would consider it an honor, and a proper recompense from me to my brother, were you to accept!"

When no answer was forthcoming but Mycroft had not released her hand, she laughed lightly. "Mr. Holmes, I seem to have caught you at a loss for words. Forgive me, my family often comment on my impulsivity, and not in flattering terms. I realize a 'proper' dinner party requires more notice than one week—"

"No, no, no, it is quite all right," Mycroft managed to stutter, letting go of her hand and recovering his wits. "I would be more than pleased to accept on our behalf."

"Wonderful!" she exclaimed, smiling. "We are confirmed, then!"

"Though, due to my post in government," he improvised, "I fear I must be accompanied by a bodyguard."

"As you can see, we have no shortage of those," Ai Lin replied wryly. "By all means. We shall provide sustenance to anyone you care to bring."

The door opened, and Huan peered inside.

"Mr. Mycroft?" he said. "You are to catch a train, yes?"

"Yes, Huan, I am coming," Mycroft replied. He handed Ai Lin his calling card.

"Mr. Mycroft Holmes," she declared staring down at it, and then at him. "I shall follow up with a more formal invitation and look forward to seeing you on Wednesday!"

Mycroft turned and walked out in a daze, past the burly guards with their steel-eyed glares and through the door that Huan was thankfully holding open for him, else he might have blundered directly through the glass.

17

ON THURSDAY MORNING, CHARLES FOWLER LAY ON THE
third floor, dead; on the floors below him, gossip was running
rampant, threatening to burst through the walls and spill
out into the narrow, twisted streets of the Devil's Acre.

Those boys who'd been at Nickolus House the shortest
time were the most suspicious, murmuring under their
collective breaths that anything too good to be true certainly
was, and that their new abode was "none other than an
'ouse of 'orrors" where terrible rituals were performed on
innocent young lads in the wee hours.

Those who had been in residence longer took great
umbrage at the scurrilous whisperings, arguing that if any
"'orrors" were about, they had hitched a ride on the louse-
filled rags of the newest recruits!

According to his brother George, Charles Fowler had
not been sick a day in his life. So if no one had murdered
him, then he had taken his own life, and was therefore not
fit to be buried proper, and would be going straight to hell so

that room in heaven could be saved for decent folk.

Douglas was devastated. He felt thoroughly responsible, for it was he who had set up the dominos to fall. After all, if he hadn't gone to Dorset, leaving Capps in charge without informing him of Sherlock's odd and occasionally misanthropic behavior, perhaps Capps would not have been taken so unawares, and would have noticed that a boy was missing.

Douglas was standing at the open door of Nickolus House, staring out into the yellowish morning fog and allowing it to cool him when he heard Sherlock's voice behind him.

"I have not had the chance yet to compliment you. That was fine combat. Capoeira is similar to ju-jitsu, then?"

"What do you know of ju-jitsu?" Douglas asked, turning around and facing him.

Sherlock's gray eyes were a similar shade to his brother's but less brilliant, and made more severe by his darker brows.

"Only that it is Japanese," he replied. "And that it involves utilizing your enemy's momentum against him. The twins and I have borrowed elements in our own combat."

"I see," Douglas said. "No, there are substantial differences in form and content. *Capoeira* hails from Brazil and is much in favor in Trinidad. And though it is used as a method of self-defense, its base is dance, not combat. It is also thought of as a *jogo*, a game, so it can be cooperative and playful. Although you are correct that it features momentum. What do you want, Sherlock? For I know you did not come downstairs solely to compliment me."

"We need to find out what the boys know, Mr. Douglas—"

"Sherlock, please. Call me Douglas. It will make me less prone to do something I might later regret."

"I must speak to them, Douglas. I am the only one who can."

Douglas sighed. "If you can promise to treat them like human beings and not subjects in an experiment."

"Done."

With that, Sherlock turned on his heel. Douglas watched him walk through the hall and wondered what he had just consented to.

Early that afternoon, Mycroft finally arrived by rented brougham at his destination: West of Scotland Cricket Club's home ground of Hamilton Crescent in Glasgow. The Queen's Park Football Club was on the field. They were just completing one of two back-to-back practices, while other members of the club, along with the odd spectator, watched from the stands.

Mycroft alighted and sniffed the air. The weather was certainly proving favorable, at least in terms of his plan.

From far afield, he set his sights on the Queen's Park team captain Robert Gardner. The forward, at twenty-five, was but a year younger than he, though Mycroft could never hope to grow a beard that lush. Nor could he compete with Gardner on the athletic field, for he was, without a doubt, the best footballer on Scotland's side.

A shame that Mycroft would have to undo all that good work.

He watched Gardner pat the sweat from his brow with the back of his hand, walk off the field, take a seat and pull out his pipe. Before he had a chance to fill it, Mycroft chose a spot upwind of him, pulled out his own pipe, packed it, and took a long and leisurely puff, blowing the smoke into the crisp morning air, which dispersed it as an aromatic mist.

A moment later, Gardner tilted his head and stared directly at Mycroft. "What is that blend?" he called out.

"Virginia!" Mycroft called back politely, all the while feigning interest in two lads kicking the ball back and forth.

"Cannot be!" Gardner exclaimed. "For that is what I smoke, but it never smells like that!"

"It is not the tobacco," Mycroft called back once more, "but the pipe!" *Even Sherlock's shag tobacco would taste passable, nestled within this bowl,* he thought. He held up the pipe, and Gardner, now as curious as Mycroft knew he would be, rose and walked over to where Mycroft stood.

Gardner's own clay pipe had teeth marks on the tip and burn marks on either side. *Impatient,* Mycroft thought, *and chockablock with anxiety.*

Gardner stashed his pipe in his trouser pocket and eagerly took Mycroft's in his right hand, staring down at it pensively while stroking his lavish beard with his left.

"Never seen its like," he said, marveling.

"I had it made for me," Mycroft lied. In fact it had been a thank you from the Queen for the "Ascot incident," as she referred to it. From Prince Albert's own collection: gold grade, made of virgin acorn, with a thick ivory band around its stem. One of a kind and obscenely expensive.

But Gardner did not need to know that.

"Try it," Mycroft offered.

"Why, so I can mourn it all my days?" the other man laughed.

"Perhaps you can have one made," Mycroft suggested.

"A year's salary would not be sufficient," Gardner replied.

"Be my guest," Mycroft offered again. "I insist."

As Gardner eagerly packed his borrowed treasure, Mycroft motioned toward the field, where Gardner's teammates were completing their practice. "Were I a gambling man, on whom should I wager?" he asked, altering his cadence and timbre to better match Gardner's own. Nothing like a familiar sound to put one off one's guard.

Gardner lit the bowl, took a satisfied pull and said on the exhale: "Marvelous, never had its equal." Then: "Always on Scotland, Mr...."

"Holmes. Aye, it is the stronger team," Mycroft agreed.

"Though I admit we came together with some difficulty," Gardner amended. "At the last moment, some of our best men abdicated."

Mycroft silently congratulated the Queen on her success.

"I ask," Mycroft said aloud, "because I was of course prepared to *bet* on Scotland. A goodly sum, in fact."

Gardner, admiring the pipe in his hand, said: "Yes, I would have imagined."

"And the weather *shall* favor you…" Mycroft continued. Gardner stared dubiously skyward.

"Oh, it is not raining yet," Mycroft explained, "but by tomorrow morning a drizzle will become a storm. There will be no respite for the next three days. By the time you take the field, your team— lighter and smaller than England's— will have the clear advantage. For the first half, at least. Until England regains her sea legs, as it were."

Gardner grinned. "You made your fortune predicting the weather?"

"Something like that. International shipments demand that one know when and where storms are likely to hit. But, as I said, I *was* prepared to bet on Scotland."

"What put you off?" Gardner asked, for the first time curious about something besides the pipe, though his gaze was reluctant to leave it.

"To be frank? Your goalkeeper," Mycroft said with an appreciable sigh. "Oh, he has talent, no doubt. But he knows only how to work the goal line. I never once saw him narrow the angle. Does he ever attempt it, I wonder?"

"I have pled with him repeatedly to do so!" Gardner exclaimed. "But players form patterns, Mr. Holmes, and he has formed bad ones…" Gardner took a worried pull off the pipe and stared out at the field.

"Aye. A shame that he, and not you, is tasked with keeping the ball out of the net," Mycroft added. "And your being ambidextrous is a great aid at the goal line, for you are equally strong on both sides. Whereas in your current position, it is not much of an advantage."

"How do you know I am ambidextrous?" Gardner asked, frowning. "Is it that I stroke my beard with my left hand?"

"No. Because you sometimes light your pipe with lamps; it is clear from the scorch marks. But whereas a right-handed fellow would most often light it on the left, and a left-handed fellow on the right, your pipe is burned equally on both sides. Now. You will have been given a natural advantage by the rain," Mycroft went on. "But you must take the whip hand and claim a position that, judging by your dimensions and maneuverability, will greatly benefit the team. If not, that natural advantage will go to waste."

Mycroft could see in Gardner's eyes that he had thought of the move before, almost to distraction. But Gardner had made his bones as the best forward in football.

Would the goal line serve him as nobly and as well?

"The goal line," Mycroft said quietly, "could be your best legacy."

Gardner stared at him the way people often did when they thought he had read their minds, instead of simply deducing their needs and motives.

"If I have correctly predicted the weather," Mycroft concluded, rising, "I might have correctly gauged your position as well. Oh, and a dab of Indian arnica will do wonders for the arthritis in your right foot. And the wear on the welt of your left shoe indicates a standing posture that puts pressure on your little toe—too much pressure, I'd say," he concluded. "Within three years it will be an issue."

Once again, Gardner stared at Mycroft, this time as if a second head had just sprung out of his top hat, while the latter hurried off with a wave.

"Mr. Holmes!" he heard Gardner say behind him. "Your pipe!"

"A gift from me to the best future goalkeeper in Scotland!" Mycroft called back.

Scotland would tie the game, of course. Which Gardner and his teammates would see as a loss.

Mycroft felt sorry for him, for he genuinely liked Gardner. He would have felt worse, had he not believed that he'd make a better go of it by moving to the goal line.

In any event, the Queen would have her zero-sum game, and bloodshed would be avoided.

Now all he had to do was go to the station, board the Scotch Express, and return to Nickolus House, where he would persuade Sherlock to accept the dinner invitation with Dai en-Lai Lin and his marvelous sister.

He could not reveal a possible tie between Ai Lin, the older Chinese gentleman, and Cainborn. He would have to feign being smitten and ask Sherlock for a favor.

He sighed, for it was not far from the truth.

18

DOUGLAS SAT AT THE KITCHEN TABLE AND WENT THROUGH a familiar ritual of counting small but pertinent blessings whenever the world seemed completely out of sorts. His feet might have felt as broken as old pottery but they were, at last, mercifully dry. He had gotten a few hours' sleep between last night and this. And though he'd only had time to swallow a crust of bread and a slice of cheese, it was nourishment all the same. His scratched eye was beginning to heal, and the rescued bottles of liquor were safely back in the warehouse of Regent Tobaccos. He had been able to save Nickolus House from ruination.

Not to mention that he held, at long last, a steaming cup of tea in his weary hands. And that his dear friend Mycroft Holmes, freshly arrived from Scotland, was seated across from him, his own tea untouched.

"What of Charles's interment?" Mycroft asked, interrupting Douglas's musings.

"I have managed to make arrangements," Douglas

replied, "for a decent burial. A small church in Haslemere has agreed, provided I can send them his body. And provided they find no signs of foul play upon his person."

"Needle marks are no matter?" Mycroft asked, his eyebrow raised, and Douglas shook his head.

"Its use breaks no earthly laws, so the less said about it, the better, I suppose. But now tell me of the task the Queen presented you. Is it something you are able to discuss?"

"Oh yes. It has to do with the football match between England and Scotland," Mycroft said. "One that no one is to win. It was a simple matter of weighing the players' strengths and weaknesses, and attempting to make things more... equitable. I may need a favor from the Queen at some juncture, and I wish her in my debt..."

With that, Mycroft suppressed a yawn, and Douglas smiled. "But you no longer find them worthy of you," he said.

"To what are you referring?" Mycroft asked.

"The stratagems. The manipulations, if you will," Douglas clarified.

"No," Mycroft agreed, "I do not. The 'means,' which used to fascinate me, no longer do. Only the ends matter now. Whether or not I succeeded in my goal, Her Majesty shall be pleased, but it is not worth another thought, not compared to what you have endured. Tell me about these nautical addicts you discovered in Dorset...?"

Douglas nodded. "I suppose the similarities between those two sailor boys and young Charles were so striking that it seemed to presage something more sinister," he said, all the while hoping he did not sound dotty. "And although I have acquiesced to Sherlock's help in the matter of Charles," he continued, "and am grateful for it, I have as yet withheld informing him about the sailors."

"Yes, I can see why you might," Mycroft commiserated, "as my brother would *wish* it to presage something more sinister, which would be far from pleasing to either of us. But surely you are not suggesting an epidemic of drug deaths, based upon but three subjects?" Mycroft continued. "Your sailors died of exposure. And Douglas, I realize we are in a boys' school and so must maintain some decorum, but surely ten o'clock at night is a more fitting time for brandy or cognac than for tea."

"Let me see what I can ferret out," Douglas answered, rising.

In the back of a cupboard he found a bottle of inexpensive Spanish brandy. Casually wondering whose it was, and lacking proper snifters, he poured a few fingers into two water glasses and placed them on the table, trusting that Mycroft would be charitable enough not to comment.

Then he sat again and took a sip of his drink, wishing it would provide the comfort he so needed. Instead, it soured his stomach instantly. Liquor poured over precious little food and sleep was clearly no curative.

"When I made mention of something sinister, I did not intend more than a tenuous tie to *this* household," Douglas said, pushing the glass away. "But you know well what has happened in the past several years. Britain now has eighty treaty ports, involving many foreign powers, all with rights to travel and trade within China, she be willing or not. And opium has once again become such a scourge that it is alarming the very people who made great fortunes from it. We shall soon be back to the numbers of addicts that our elders saw some thirty years ago."

"Yes, Douglas, I am aware," Mycroft said. "But we cannot undermine what has been a very good source of revenue for Britain, especially now. We have fought wars over opium; wars that we decidedly won. Three formidable countries agreed with us as to our rights. Which makes the banishment of opium rather like closing the barn door after the horse has bolted.

"And even if I believed it is the scourge you seem to think it is," Mycroft continued, "may I remind you that there are addicts of *all* types, from tobacco to single malt Scotch whiskey. There are those who use too much, and those who use sparingly; surely it is a question of moderation! One cannot single out the poppy as a demon and leave the others be—not until we have proof positive that it is as deadly as you seem to think."

"'Nobody will laugh long who deals much with opium,'" Douglas said, quoting Thomas De Quincey's *Confessions of an Opium Eater*. "'Its pleasures even are of a grave and solemn complexion.'"

Mycroft took another sip of brandy and, grimacing a little, chased it down with a sip of lukewarm tea. "Please do not misunderstand," he amended. "I do not wish to return to the time when ninety percent of Chinamen under the age of forty were addicted to the opium that we imported from India; it wreaked havoc across an already beleaguered land. Given your time aboard ship and at various ports, you have surely seen many more addicts than I."

"A few," Douglas said softly.

"But still," Mycroft insisted, "commerce is commerce. Not to mention that France, Russia and the United States fought alongside Britain to gain the two treaties that forced China to also cede Hong Kong and surrounding territories to us, an unfathomable treasure. What are we to say to those partners now? 'Never mind'? Oh, I concede that it has destabilized the Qing government, but trust me, Douglas: now is not the time to lose such a mighty source of revenue. So, might we put aside our differences and return to the business at hand?"

"Only because I realize that I cannot alter your thinking as yet," Douglas replied.

"For instance," Mycroft said, "it gratifies me that you have allowed Sherlock free rein to question the boys. It must mean he comported himself like a gentleman in his care of them. He taught them well, did he?"

Into the fire, Douglas thought, for he had said not a word about Sherlock's unorthodox methods of instruction.

"Oh yes," he replied aloud. "Lessons in mathematics and chemistry I am sure they will not soon forget. I take it you have no interest in his interrogations?"

"I?" Mycroft exclaimed, gray eyes crinkling with

feigned offense. "I am as interested in the tedium of individual lives as Sherlock is in deducing whether I live on a civil servant's salary or on a king's ransom. Unless that poor boy's death has implications for Queen and country, it is no matter for me."

"Forgive me, but you have been saying that quite a bit."

"Queen and country?"

"No," Douglas said. "What I mean is, more often than not you now avoid any involvement in matters that do not pertain directly to you. It is a tendency that does you no favors, as you have a touch of the hermit crab in you…"

Mycroft laughed. "Come now, Douglas, I am not as retiring as all that!"

"These few years have created a change in you," Douglas said, refusing to be distracted from the subject. "You are no longer the carefree young man riding through London on horseback, always a hair's breadth from calamity. Now you sequester yourself within that carriage of yours, curtains drawn, nose buried in economics. I am not faulting you," he added when he saw his friend's expression darken. "But as an older ally, one who went through heartbreak at least as great as yours, I wish you were less… dour."

"I shall take your advice into consideration, Douglas. I always have and always will."

"I infer that you gain no true sense of accomplishment from solving mysteries," Douglas went on. "That you would rather use your considerable gifts to wield power, to barter it, and eventually to consolidate it."

"Well said," Mycroft declared. "And flattering."

"I am glad you find it so," Douglas said, amused. "Now as to Charles. I should very much like to speak to Beeton, the chimney sweep, as well as to Madame de Matalin. She is the rather strange but formidable woman who told me of Charles and George to begin with. I wonder if you'd care to accompany me to meet either or both?"

"Douglas, please know that your battles are mine. Of course I shall accompany you. Though I would appreciate it if you would not mention anything to Sherlock. The last thing I need is my brother poking his nose about in places where it might get cut off."

"Think no more of it," Douglas said.

"As a matter of fact," Mycroft continued, "my acquaintance Dr. Joseph Bell is in town, do you recall my mentioning him?"

"Not offhand," Douglas said.

"Oh, I must've done. He is a medical lecturer at Edinburgh and a physician to Queen Victoria. A very good man. Has the same gift for deduction that my brother and I have, though he uses his exclusively for diagnosing diseases. Might you permit me to have the boy's body sent to him? Perhaps he can determine conclusively what killed him. From there I shall pay to send the body to the cemetery in Haslemere, if that is your wish."

Douglas's first impulse was to say no. He still believed that human beings, dead or alive, deserved the respect of a burial; they were not to be gawked at and prodded. On the other hand, there was so much loose talk regarding how Charles died that perhaps a proper inspection by a noted physician would quell the rumors, at least in part.

"If your Dr. Bell can work without defiling him…" Douglas began.

"He will simply take samples of blood, and perhaps small samples of tissue. The body will be returned whole for burial, I give you my word."

As Mycroft took another sip of brandy, swallowing quickly so as not to taste it, he wondered at his reluctance to mention his own strange coincidence of Cainborn and the Han gentleman, to say nothing of the beautiful woman who was most likely his daughter. It revealed a weakness that he would have gone a long way to abolish once and for all.

Nonsense, he thought. *I shall not keep secrets from Douglas.* And so he told him all.

When he was finished, Douglas ran a hand over his dark, close-cropped hair, a small, anxious gesture that Mycroft noted solely because it was so rare. But when Douglas spoke, his comment was brief and to the point: "I trust not only your intellect but your instincts," he said. "If there is a link between the Chinese gentleman and the woman with her bodyguards, there is. If there was something off-putting about Cainborn, there was. I take it you'll make inquiries?"

Mycroft nodded. "I have put Parfitt on the job."

"Good. As for Sherlock, I agree there too: no sense in

having him suspect someone he admires until there's proper cause."

"Here is hoping there never shall be," Mycroft said, holding his glass aloft, then downing the rest of his brandy in one burning mouthful.

19

ON THE SECOND FLOOR OF NICKOLUS HOUSE, SHERLOCK was making expeditious work of questioning the residents. His fame had increased among the boys so that he was now credited with feats of otherworldly dexterity and prestidigitation, none of which had occurred. Still, it was a useful tool to have at his disposal, and he would not soon disabuse them of their notions.

A few words with each boy, and he was able to deduce who among them knew something worth knowing and who was simply bloviating in order to spend more time with him. Alvey Ducasse proved most helpful. As a veteran of the house, he was determined to defend its character from any who attempted to besmirch it, thus making him more loquacious than he otherwise would have been.

"They's a ring in the East End, guv," he confided to Sherlock, looking about as if half expecting to be snatched up and horsewhipped for breaking a confidence. "It begun in June. I never was party to it meself but I 'ear tell it's powerful. Charlie was one as gathered the code!"

"What code?" Sherlock asked.

Ducasse shrugged. "All's I know is, there's some code put up every month of a Monday. Charlie 'ad to collect fifteen of 'em, 'e did. Sometimes there were just one, sometimes two or three to get."

"Was he paid?"

"If not, why else do it?" Alvey asked, puzzled.

"Fifteen," Sherlock repeated. "You are telling me that, beginning in summer, Charles collected a code composed of fifteen… somethings."

"That's about the size of it, guv," Alvey confirmed in a raw whisper. "Georgie, 'e might know more about it. You can beat it out of 'im, though 'e's sturdier than 'e looks. So, will you be teachin' us some more maths?" he added eagerly.

After he had finished questioning Alvey, Sherlock went to George's cot. Douglas had fashioned a cloth partition between him and the rest of the boys, to allow him some privacy in his grief.

George was lying in bed with his back to the door, seemingly no longer concerned if his new belongings became wrinkled or were pilfered.

"George," Sherlock said quietly, sitting beside him on the bed. "I know about the code."

George turned over like a shot and stared at Sherlock with eyes so filled with pain that even Sherlock had to draw a breath and begin again.

"I know that your brother did not do this to himself," he said after a moment. "I can find out who did, but I will need your aid. You are a clever boy: you helped us to locate him in the first place. Now you must help us to avenge him."

He was certain that George would not know the meaning of "avenge," but he was equally certain that he could glean the intent, and know it was favorably disposed towards him and Charles.

"Is he still…" The boy pointed towards the ceiling.

"Yes," Sherlock said. "And there's a lamp next to him, and he is warm and dry. And we shall arrange for a proper burial."

The boy stifled a sob. "I ain't s'pose to tell, guv," he murmured, glancing around in fear. "Charles made me swear."

"I know, George," Sherlock replied. "But Charles is gone. And the people who did this to him must be punished."

George nodded. "All's I know is Gin…"

"Gin," Sherlock repeated. "Is Gin a man? A woman?"

"Dunno, sir. But I know Charlie give Gin wot 'e collected and Gin paid Charlie for it. And I 'eard 'im say somethin' about meetin' Gin in a mansion…"

"A mansion? You heard that word specifically?"

"Yessir."

"I see. And what of the word 'collect'? Did you come up with that, or do you recall Charles using it specifically?"

"Charlie used it, sir."

"Do you recall how many… items he was supposed to collect?"

The boy shook his head.

"That's all right, you are doing splendidly. Does 'fifteen' mean anything to you in this context?"

"No, sir, I can't even count that 'igh…" George said, his eyes wide. "Bu' Charlie could!'

"Yes, he was quite the accomplished lad." He remembered Charles's last word. "And what of the word 'baker'?"

"Baker? No, sir. Charlie an' me, we ain't acquainted wiv no bakers." He said it as if the craft of baking were loftier than his kind could possibly dream of.

"Now, each time Charles went off to collect, what time of day was it?"

"He always went of a mornin'."

"And could you smell the tanneries from where you were living?"

George nodded. "Yes, sir, somethin' awful."

"Do you recall if the nearest factory whistle had sounded?"

George nodded adamantly, his countenance brightening. "Charlie would be gone right after the whistle! He was a good worker, my Charlie!"

"I am certain of it. And when Charlie returned from collecting, did you notice anything different about him?"

"No, sir. He was just… Charlie."

George began to cry softly. He turned his back on Sherlock and lay with his knees drawn up against his chest.

"George? The sweep that you worked for, he struck you, yes?"

George nodded. "He whacked us somethin' awful," he mumbled into his pillow.

"Did he stop beating you and your brother at the same time?"

140

"Yessir."

"Was it perhaps around the time that Charles started collecting?"

The boy said nothing. He wrapped his stick-thin arms around his knees and tucked himself into a little ball.

"George, you are being ever so brave," Sherlock said in a comforting tone. "One more question, please. Do you recall the last time Charles went collecting?"

"No, sir. But the *next* time will be tomorrow, sir."

"What next time? You mean collecting?" Sherlock asked, containing his excitement. "How do you know?"

"I knows cuz 'e had 'is collectin' bag wiv 'im."

"A collecting bag? What did it look like?"

"It was soft, like."

"Soft. Padded, do you mean? Or quilted?"

George nodded. "Quilted," he said as if tasting the word. "A *quilt* it was, sir."

"About how large?"

George held his hands out to the width of a football.

"Did you ever look inside? Did it have compartments? Pockets?" he amended for clarity's sake.

"Yes, sir, little pockets, all padded like you said."

"How many pockets?"

"I don't know, sir. I can't count," George repeated patiently. "But the last time I seen Charlie 'e 'ad it wiv 'im, and we 'ad a row about it. I didn't want 'im to do it no more, an' 'e cuffed me and told me 'don't be impert'nent' an' then 'e told me 'e was sorry and it'd be the final time…" The boy fought back sobs. "If it please, sir, can we not… gab no more?"

"We are done. Thank you, George. You have been most helpful."

Sherlock rose from the bed. Then he heard the boy whisper, in a voice dripping with dread: "Sir? Will me bruvver burn in 'ell?"

Sherlock sighed and sat on the bed again. "God knows your lot," he told George. "And he well knows the hand that you've been dealt, you and your brother. Gossips will not determine the fate of Charles's immortal soul, George. Only God has the power to do that."

"You're not pullin' me leg, sir?" came George's startled reply.

"No, George, I am not. I have read it with my own eyes. Rest easy."

Sherlock patted the boy on the back, rose again and walked out slowly, shutting the dormitory door behind him.

The moment Sherlock closed the door, he sloughed off commiseration like a used cloak. His countenance lifted. All vestiges of sorrow disappeared, for he had neither the time nor the space for it. His mind was thoroughly consumed with questions.

The foremost among them being, what had become of the quilted bag?

George had seen his brother leave with it in tow; it had been the cause of their quarrel. Charles was to use it to collect… something. So, why did he and Douglas not come upon it when they rescued him?

Had Charles left the bag somewhere? Perhaps in the storehouse behind the carriage, where he may have spent the first night and may have planned to spend the second? Had the men been after that bag, and not Charles? But if so, why had he and Douglas not spied it upon *their* persons?

He bounded down the stairs two at a time to share his news with Mycroft and Douglas. But as he neared the kitchen and saw the light flicker underneath the door, and heard Mycroft laugh at something Douglas had just said, he wondered at the wisdom of revealing what he knew.

On the one hand, his brother could certainly help with the deductions. He might even come up with questions he had not thought of, for Mycroft did not lack for imagination: an essential trait in anyone who pursued the sleuthing arts.

On the other hand, he would be unlikely to permit Sherlock to go after those fifteen *somethings* Alvey had spoken of. Mycroft would think it dangerous or, worse still, useless.

No, Sherlock would have to pretend he had learned nothing from the boys. Mycroft would commend his attempt while being secretly relieved, as he was not in the least enamored with his predilection for crime. And if Douglas was disappointed that nothing had come of the questioning, he would be gratified that Mycroft's younger brother would no longer be underfoot.

Thus decided, Sherlock pivoted on his heel and tiptoed quietly back up the stairs.

20

SHERLOCK HOLMES, LITTLE MORE THAN A MONTH FROM HIS nineteenth birthday, was finally on a case, certain that it went well beyond the wretches of Nickolus House with their miserable births and bottomless needs. Ideas were coming to him almost faster than he could contain and categorize them. It was as he had always suspected: the thrill of being at the scene of the crime, of examining it and interviewing those who had tasted misfortune, was infinitely more satisfying than simply reading their piteous tales in newspapers and ferreting out an answer that did no one a jot of good. From this moment on, he would pursue mysteries that he could see, hear, touch, smell and even taste. For it was this, not armchair deduction, that made him feel alive.

And so he had quietly retreated upstairs and shut his bedroom door, only to spend the early hours wide awake and invigorated, waiting for the moment that he might get back to work. He even forsook—for the first time in months—jotting down the details of his latest spar with the twins, for another obsession had surpassed it.

If anyone had chanced to walk in, they would have seen him lying on the bed fully clothed, in utter darkness, his feet still shod and hanging off the edge of the bed, his hands folded comfortably in his lap. He could have passed for a corpse positioned just so within its coffin. But although his body was in repose, his brain was as charged as that of Mary Shelley's fabled monster.

After following a trail of speculation down one path and another, he always returned to Occam's razor, otherwise known as the law of parsimony: the simplest explanation is often the most likely.

The trick now, and one he had to perfect at all costs, was to take the solution he was not yet certain of, and work backwards, retracing each vital step.

Dawn on Friday the 29th finally broke, sodden and bleak. And when Dr. Bell's assistant arrived to take Charles's body, it was Sherlock who steadied little George's shoulders and swore to him that his brother would not be ill used.

The assistant's cart rumbled away, and the little farewell committee, which also included Douglas, Mycroft and Huan, made its way back inside. Sherlock paused, once again considering what he had learned from the boys the previous night: once a month, somewhere in London, someone put up a code that Charles, and possibly other boys, were "collecting." What could the code be? Why would it need collecting? And why fifteen?

The most obvious collection was money or drugs. But would anyone trust these young paupers with money? And if drugs, to what end? Why would skullduggery be necessary when opium and morphine were perfectly legal?

And who was Gin, to whom the collection went? And why once a month?

Here the trail, even Sherlock had to admit, immediately grew cold, as nearly anything could have a monthly schedule—even an individual might be in London but a dozen times per year.

Though it was an important clue, at the moment it was as wide as the proverbial road that led to destruction.

Luckily, there was another detail that he had not bothered to reveal to Mycroft and Douglas: that this very morning Charles had been due to go collecting.

Sherlock returned upstairs for his vielle and short staff, both of which had proved so useful to him during his stay at Nickolus House, and grudgingly picked up the shaving kit he had been forced to purchase by his brother. After a moment's pause he opened the kit, extracted the camel-bone straight razor, scissors and tweezers, and placed them in his jacket pocket; then he threw the case—which still held the strop, shaving soap, bowl and brush—underneath the bed.

Finally, he went to the boys' dormitory to deputize Alvey Ducasse and Joe McPeel, swearing them to the utmost secrecy, for he had found a use for them.

That accomplished, Sherlock sprinted out of the front

door to his first assignation, only to find Huan and Mycroft's carriage waiting.

"Your brother, he will give you a ride!" Huan said, smiling.

"Oh, no need, Huan, I am only going to Edwardes Square, to the Quinces'," Sherlock shot back. "A handful of miles, the walk shall do me good!"

"I insist," said Mycroft's voice behind him. "You must save your strength for your studies."

Sherlock did not dare look at his pocket watch and thus draw his brother's suspicions, so he glanced up at the sky, at what passed for the sun of a London November. From what George had told him, or at least what he inferred from the proximity to the tannery and Charles's departure, he would commence his rounds at nine. Sherlock had been determined to do the same, but it was already a few minutes past eight.

He'd been hoping to run to the abandoned storehouse to try to retrieve Charles's quilted bag, but there'd be no time for that now. He had a fifty-minute ride to Edwardes Square. From there, he could hightail it back on foot four miles through Kensington and across Hyde Park... Not ideal, but it would have to do, now that his brother had stepped all over his carefully wrought plan.

Mycroft sat across from his brother in the hansom cab and marveled. What was that unexpected and unaccustomed mien to Sherlock's expression? Could it possibly be *joy*? The very notion was foreign. And yet, there it was, clear as—well, as the nose on Sherlock's face.

The night before, Mycroft had tried to speak to him about dining with Ai Lin and her brother, but by the time he and Douglas had said goodnight, Sherlock's bedroom door was closed, and the room beyond silent. He was no doubt exhausted after questioning the boys about Charles's untimely death. And although nothing had come of his queries, his diligence and patience with the difficult youngsters had been impressive.

Perhaps he might go into education, Mycroft mused. Sherlock's admiration for that strange Professor Cainborn might come in handy, helping to persuade him in a career for which he had an obvious knack. Sherlock's future could thus be set, and Mycroft's two hundred pounds per annum for his schooling would have been put to good use, instead of fluttering down note upon note into a deep and dark abyss filled with smelly pipes, the screeching of cat gut, and those dreary agony columns.

"You are smiling," Sherlock said, turning towards him.

"Am I?" Mycroft said without attempting to hide it.

"Yes. Whatever about?"

"Perhaps it is because I am quite gratified."

"I take it your mission for the Queen went well?"

"Swimmingly. But I am not thinking of that. You outdid yourself at Nickolus House. That you are now permitting me to return you to your studies without protest indicates a newfound maturity on your part."

"Well. If I am the cause of your levity, I will gladly bear

the weight of it," Sherlock said. "In truth, I learnt a great deal from those poor unfortunates, having to watch that wretched boy die before my very eyes…"

"Yes, I quite forgot you were in the room when he passed," Mycroft replied. "And I in no way meant that I am gratified by his death, but for how you comported yourself throughout."

"Clearly, Mycroft. Whatever misunderstandings we may've had in the past, I do not think you ghoulish as all that. Still, the fact is, I have never seen someone expire before," he went on. "I have been rather sheltered."

"You say that as though it were a bad thing. And yes, in a sense, you have been."

"With the exception of Mother's chronic headaches," Sherlock clarified. Then he swallowed and looked away.

"Is there something you wish to tell me?" Mycroft asked.

Sherlock sighed. "Mother has grown worse," he said at last. "The years-long dependence on laudanum has now become an unquenchable desire for morphine. Father is turning a blind eye to it, as usual. He is like your friend Cyrus Douglas. If you threw him into Hades, he would be optimistic that he could climb back out, and take everyone with him!"

"It grieves me to hear about Mother, but you are being unfair to both Father *and* Douglas," Mycroft scolded. "Father always strove to keep a semblance of family for our sakes. Surely you cannot blame him. As for Douglas, it is clear you know him not at all. As a black man in white society, he has had to comport himself always in a way that is above reproach. And that means having to compromise at times."

"At *all* times, you mean."

"Again, you misread him. He is not the dupe you perceive him to be."

"Well, I have seen him do battle," Sherlock said with a shrug, "and I admit he is more than competent in *that* arena."

"When was this?" Mycroft asked, surprised.

"The men who had Charles Fowler, did he not mention it? He took them out singlehandedly. Well, practically so. I threw a punch solely because I was backed into a corner and had to swing or be murdered."

"He did not utter a word about it," Mycroft said, frowning. "He tends not to speak of anything that might cast him in a favorable light."

"Which underscores my original point…"

Mycroft sighed. "Sherlock, I cannot alter our parents' marriage or our mother's behavior," he declared. "But I promise that I shall no longer threaten you with banishment to the country."

"For which I am grateful."

Mycroft heard Huan's soft "Wooooaah," and heard his fingers knock against the carriage as it slowed, indicating they had reached their destination.

There was no clean way to segue into the subject of Ai Lin and her brother now. He would have to come out with it.

"We have been invited to dinner on Wednesday," Mycroft said.

"By whom?"

"A lad by the name of Dai en-Lai Lin is quite taken with

your boxing acumen. Do you know him?"

Sherlock shrugged. "*Of* him. He is fond of 'western style' boxing and a good enough sort. But simply *everyone* is trying to befriend him. It is considered de rigueur to have an Oriental friend, since they are still so rare in England. However did you meet him?"

"I met his sister Ai Lin at a local chemist's," he lied— for he did not wish to divulge that he had passed through the doors of a herbalist: he would never hear the end of it. "When I gave my surname to the owner," he said—another lie—"she heard it, mentioned her brother's admiration for you, and extended the invitation."

Sherlock, Mycroft knew, had not a prurient bone in his body. Relations between the stronger and fairer sex interested him solely if they were the subjects of an agony column.

"And I fear I have taken a liking to his sister," Mycroft added.

"You and an Oriental woman?" Sherlock asked. "Old Cardwell will be so pleased he will have you burned in effigy on Pall Mall."

"Will you come?"

"On one condition. I will want a detailed account of your visit to Dr. Bell, for I have a few hypotheses that need validation."

"Done," Mycroft said.

He looked out at Edwardes Square, a line of simple terraced homes built around a large central garden. The sky overhead, which had been gunmetal gray, was now thick with black clouds so low they were like the lid to a kettle, close in and claustrophobic. In that garden were Sherlock's two friends, Eli and Asa Quince, battling it out with their short staffs, their sand-colored hair plastered to their foreheads, their coats discarded on a damp patch of grass. When they heard the carriage, they both paused mid-strike and waved, and this time Mycroft was pleased to see that Sherlock waved back.

Though the two were nearly indistinguishable, Mycroft could tell them apart.

"Aside from tiny differences in their physiognomy, one of the twins is slower," Mycroft said as Sherlock was exiting the carriage. "Only by a second," he added, "but still. And see how he holds his staff? There is something uncertain in his grip, as if—"

"Quite," Sherlock said quickly, balancing vielle case and short staff, and Mycroft went silent. No doubt Sherlock had already done a thorough study of the twins; there was nothing he could say that his brother had not already noticed three times over.

"Shaving kit?" he asked instead, and Sherlock patted his jacket pocket. "If you need anything," Mycroft added, "send a note to St. John's Wood. Huan will collect them once per day."

"Thank you," Sherlock replied, "but I plan to study."

"I envy you your learning, Master Sherlock," Huan said, the perennial smile on his face masking the gravity of his words.

"Goodbye, Huan, goodbye, brother," Sherlock said.

Sherlock waved at the carriage as it departed, a display of brotherly affection and courtesy that left Mycroft deeply unsettled.

21

SHERLOCK CONTINUED TO WAVE UNTIL THE CARRIAGE WAS well out of sight. Then, rather than join his two friends waiting expectantly for him on the grass, he sprinted away from Edwardes Square as fast as his two feet could carry him. He raced through Kensington and across the wintry heart of Hyde Park, discomfited by the close call he'd endured.

How tedious family could be! The last thing he needed was Mycroft sniffing about regarding the twins. His brother was entirely too perceptive; another few minutes and he would have guessed yet another secret that Sherlock preferred to keep to himself.

On the other hand, Mycroft had a blind spot when it came to matters of the heart. This weakness was not relegated merely to the late Georgiana—although he had certainly squandered enough time and emotion there—but to family as well. Any talk of Mother, Father, or even Douglas, whom Mycroft regarded as kin, created a smokescreen that hobbled his elder brother's formidable powers of deduction.

Love is Mycroft's Achilles heel, Sherlock thought. And bringing up their mother had been a masterstroke. Though it was a bit of an emotional bloodletting, even for him, it kept his brother where he wanted him—in his pocket—as he readied for his first bona fide adventure.

Sherlock reached his first destination, the Metropolitan Railway Underground station—at the junction of Baker Street and Marylebone Road—with two minutes to spare. George had recalled the word "mansion." The entire circuit from the Moorgate stop to Mansion House yielded twenty-two stops, not counting a detour to Hammersmith. But if one simply rode from *Baker* Street—Charles's last word before his death—to Mansion House, the end of the line, then there were only sixteen stops.

Was it possible that Charles had been getting on the Tube at Baker Street and disembarking at each stop to collect whatever it was, then clambering back on board for the next?

Would someone then be waiting for Charles at Mansion House—the sixteenth stop? And would that someone be "Gin"?

Staring at the ceiling all night long, the trajectory between Baker Street and Mansion House had been his simplest guess, and one he kept returning to.

Was Baker Street particularly convenient to whoever was leaving the 'collection'? Certainly it was convenient for Charles, as he could easily reach it on foot, both from his chimney-sweep job and from the storehouse, and make the rounds from there.

Sherlock descended the broad staircase and was immediately accosted by the sepulchral chill of the Underground station platform below. It was not simply frigid but murky: a sputtering gaslight above his head was impotent against the fog of steam that permeated the tunnel like a leaden cocoon.

But the cold and dark made little difference: even under the frigid hand of winter, Baker Street Station was awash in chattering humanity, every one of them waiting for the train. It arrived with a vibration on the rail, grinding brakes, and a belch of steam, sulfur and coal dust that rose and then clung to the ceiling in diaphanous gray spider webs.

Sherlock waited patiently for the noisy group of travelers to jostle on board, from those ensconced comfortably in the gas-lit first class—where the ceilings were so tall that a six-foot man could easily stand without removing his hat—to those holding on for dear life in the open carts of third, their scarves wrapped about their mouths and noses to shield them from wind and soot.

Another vibration, another huge exhalation of steam and grit, and the train departed.

He waited to see if anyone lingered—like him, searching the platform for some ephemeral treasure—but no. There was no one. He was alone.

For the briefest moment, he had the platform to himself, though he could hear the next round of passengers chattering away at the top of the stairs like so many magpies. The weather above might be damp and threatening, but the ventilation shafts below did not prove adequate to the smoke and fumes being disgorged by train upon train. And so most people preferred to wait for the last noxious belch to dissipate before descending the dank stairs, to be forced to stand in a shivering huddle in the catacomb-like cold for the next train to arrive.

Each time, he had a few blessed moments between waves of humanity to hunt, though he had no idea what for.

The fact that Charles did his collection with a quilted cloth bag with compartments could mean there was a sequence; or it could mean that the items were fragile.

Whatever they were.

Sherlock walked the length of the platform repeatedly while observing his surroundings: paper advertisements glued to the wall, lovers' initials carved into benches, refuse in the corners… though there was a dearth of the latter. Londoners were inordinately proud of their Underground, their "train in a drain." Sherlock was not clear why scurrying like rats beneath the surface of the streets should be a boon to humankind. But people who without a thought cast refuse from windows onto a cobblestone street dating back a thousand years, seemed aggrieved to deposit so much as the ash from a pipe in the tunnels.

No, the items would not be left on the ground. Too likely that someone would sweep them up, or that some well-intentioned biddy would complain, bringing unwanted attention to the whole endeavor.

He directed his gaze upwards, to the walls and archways. Just as a new group of passengers descended the stairs for the next train, and he was making his third sweep of the platform, he spotted something. Behind the fourth bench from the entrance, three Oriental symbols had been etched into the wall. The markings were small: no more than an inch in circumference.

Sherlock drew closer and saw that there were other symbols beside those three, but they had been defaced beyond recognition.

Trying to keep his excitement in check, Sherlock ran his finger over them. In the tunnels, damp, smoke and dirt would quickly work together to dull the edges. But these cuts were clean and fresh.

Did the artist know that Charles was dead? Or were the various parties of this enterprise kept in the dark about the identity of the others?

Is someone even now waiting impatiently at Mansion House for Charles to arrive? he wondered.

Sherlock sat down on the bench, looking out casually at the clusters of passengers ready to board the next train. He had little competition for a seat. With trains arriving every few minutes at the height of traffic, there was little need. The bench was his.

He stretched out his arm along the back. Then, feigning he was holding a small knife, he mimed scratching out a symbol.

No one would notice. No one would pay it the least mind,

given a few easy stipulations. Clearly the artist was male, as any female would have called attention to herself, had she dared to drape one arm along the back of a public bench. And whoever *he* was, he would have to know the symbols well enough to be able to make them quickly, and without benefit of eyesight. Which meant he was almost certainly Oriental. But with so few Orientals in London, how many would be able and willing to take part? Who recruited them? Were the symbols to be merely looked at, or memorized? Or were they perhaps to be copied? And if to be copied, why not just create an original list and be done with it?

And how could Charles Fowler, a boy functionally illiterate, participate in any of the above tasks? And why on earth would he need a bag, much less a padded one?

It seemed laughable.

Sherlock waited for another interval when no one was watching. Then he laid his head on the bench, peering at the symbols. Growing bolder, he lit a match and looked even more closely.

Finally, utilizing the scissors from the shaving kit, he meticulously copied what he saw, scratching each little carving on the only repository he had—the back of his vielle—all the while wondering what poor sot of a detective he was to not bring along even a notebook and pen.

Vibrations under his feet alerted him to the arrival of a train, as another group of people hurried down the stairs to meet it.

He sat up, brushed the coal dust off his trousers and,

wrapping his scarf about his nose and mouth, queued up to climb aboard the third-class carriage to his next destination.

Sherlock stepped off at Edgware Road station and looked for the most likely spot for a carving: quiet but not isolated, which would draw too much attention to the artist. He almost immediately found the spot and the carvings he sought using these criteria, quietly rejoicing that his theory had proven correct thus far.

He once again transferred the carvings to his vielle and boarded a train, disembarking at the next station, Paddington. Having no roof, it was well lit and the air more agreeable. It was also busier than the previous stations. Not only were hawkers extolling their wares, but there were many more travelers coming from the main overground station. And though Sherlock quickly spotted the Oriental symbols—this time gouged into a bench itself, rather than on the wall behind it, and with older ones defaced—he could not get to them. A man of middle years in a yellow overcoat, matching cap and red cravat had his foot firmly planted not one inch away as he smoked his cigar and heartily admired the cacophony of life all around him.

Sherlock observed him, gauging the man's tension, any possible fear, any unusual alertness or wariness indicating that things were not as they seemed. Satisfied that he was an ordinary sort and not part of a heinous cabal, Sherlock ruffled his hair, tore the pocket of his coat and pulled at the lining of his left trouser leg so that it hung tattered over his shoe. He wiped soot residue from the wall on his forehead and cheekbones, and the edges of the shirt that Mycroft had given him Easter last. He tore off a few buttons while he was at it. Then he picked up the vielle and started to play a truly execrable tune, his dark eyes soft and pleading as he appealed to the crush of humanity nearby to lend him a kind ear and a generous hand.

It was as if he had detonated a small explosive in their midst. The man in the yellow overcoat did not care to be subjected to discordant beggars and could not flee for his train fast enough. A top hat wreathed in cigar smoke was the last Sherlock glimpsed of him before he boarded. As for the other passengers, anyone who had even an inkling of curiosity quickly backed away from Sherlock, lest they be compelled to toss a coin into the open instrument case at his feet, thereby tacitly approving of the squealing and grating emanating from his strange five-stringed instrument.

By the time Sherlock took a seat on the now-empty bench, he could have scratched an entire sonnet on the back of his vielle, for the mind anyone paid him.

But it was at Bayswater that Sherlock had two bits of real luck. To start with, almost no one was embarking or disembarking, giving him the run of the platform. And although he found nothing on the benches, in one of several archways, scratched just at eye level, was the next set of symbols.

Then he noticed, still attached to one of the defaced markings, a yellowish particle about the size of a seed. Making certain he was still quite alone, Sherlock carefully collected it, using the tweezers from his shaving kit, then examined it more closely. He felt around the defaced grooves of the older markings with the tweezers until they picked up another smudge of the yellowish substance—enough to discern what it was.

Wax.

At last he understood.

Charles had a padded bag with compartments. He had no need to know anything, other than how to apply a quick-drying wax to the symbols, place each wax impression in a separate compartment of the quilted bag, and be on his way.

He then brought them to "Gin," was paid his fee, and was gone.

What were they for? What did they communicate, and who was profiting? Still so much left to learn.

In the meantime, it was four stations down, eleven to go.

22

FROM EDWARDES SQUARE, MYCROFT'S CARRIAGE HEADED toward Westminster, where he was to meet Douglas. Outside the window, the gray streets and even grayer sky made him feel as if he were aboard a small, unpleasant ship. Riding in the carriage increasingly made him nauseous. Too much reading while in motion? Or perhaps Huan's muscular driving?

As they proceeded down Homer Street and its slew of grim-faced, rather shabby Georgian edifices, Mycroft spotted Douglas. It was typical of his friend to arrive first to any rendezvous: Douglas hated the thought of inconveniencing anyone. He had his hands at his sides rather than in his pockets, head slightly bowed, with his tall, athletic frame as still as church—so as to disabuse the residents that he had any but the best intentions.

The moment he spotted the carriage, Mycroft could see him relax appreciably.

Mycroft stepped out and greeted Douglas, and together

they knocked upon the door of one Joseph Beeton, chimney sweep, to ask what he knew about Charles Fowler.

"I takes awl kinds, gents, awl kinds! Boys, gulls, I ain't no ree-spekter of persons!"

Beeton turned, licked his lips, and blinked slowly at Douglas. Then he drew back his wet lips in the semblance of a smile, exposing half-rotting teeth at the graying gum line.

"I teaches 'em out of the kindness of me 'eart!" Beeton assured him and Mycroft, as they sat across from him in his stuffy little sitting room, where the smell of soot was as encompassing as incense at Mass, but not so pleasingly scented.

Beeton was a small man, which fit his occupation, but not twisted and gnarled, as Mycroft had expected him to be, and as long-time chimney sweeps often were. Instead, he seemed boneless.

If one were to pluck a turtle out of its shell, he thought, *paint him a mottled orange and wrap him in an ill-made suit, that would be Beeton.*

And, if a turtle could speak, and if its larynx had been shoved deep inside its long, wrinkled throat so that every word emerged in a hiss, it might match Beeton's voice.

Mycroft and Douglas had been his guests a good half-hour. Not only had they not been offered so much as a cup of water, they had not yet broached the subject of Charles, alive or dead. For, however improbable, Beeton seemed to love the sound of his own susurrus voice.

"Wot you 'ave to know about chimney flues," he was

declaring, "is that flues 'as several twists in 'em, cuz they's attached to *uvver* flues wot shares one openin'. An' they *shares* that openin'," he continued, "cuz of *taxes*! That's right, gents, less 'oles equals less taxes! Now. It's pitch dark in there, an 'ard to navigate. Sometimes a sweep, he'll misremember which 'ole he shimmied up, makes a bad turn, scrambles back down *anuvver* flue where they's a fire burnin' an' *poof*! Up in smoke 'e goes! Issat *my* fault, I ask? Can I 'elp it, if once in a while, I lose one or two to the fire? An' does *I* keep 'em small?" he went on. "I do, for their own benefit! When they git stuck, who 'as to unstick 'em, I ask you? *Myself*, that's who!"

He paused and crossed his arms, seeming to want applause for the great care he was taking with his charges. Douglas took the opportunity to finally get a word in edgewise.

"Mr. Smythe is curious about one particular boy," he said, "by the name of Charles Fowler. Do you recall where you picked him up?"

"A orphanage somewhere, 'im an' 'is bruvver. Government paid me five pounds, two for the bruvver. You see, gents, five pounds is a pretty penny but h'ain't much when you counts it out. As I says, I does it out of the kindness of me 'eart."

"I believe Mr. Smythe paid you six pounds per child to release them to him," Douglas said.

Beeton dismissed this with a wave of his hand and a hearty wipe of his nose. "I 'ad 'em nearly six months by then," he said defensively. "They cost somethin' in upkeep, don't they?"

Douglas assumed that if Beeton spent more than a shilling a month for both boys together, he would doubtless feel robbed.

He folded his hands to keep them from doing something untoward to their host and gave Mycroft a meaningful glance.

Mycroft picked up on the cue, for he said: "Have you been informed yet of Charles's unfortunate demise?"

Beeton's skin went immediately sallow. For a moment, Mycroft wondered if perhaps he had feelings after all. But, judging from his shrewd and calculating eyes, sentiment played no part in whatever emotion he might be feeling.

"I... knew no such thing," Beeton said. "When did the unfortunate lose 'is life?"

"Night before last," Douglas said.

"Dead," he murmured.

When Beeton did not ask the cause, Douglas volunteered it: "We believe it was from an overdose of drugs."

Both men watched Beeton's reaction carefully, but if Beeton knew anything about Charles's drug use, or cared, his expression revealed less than nothing. "I 'as to get back to work," he said, standing up. "I gots me charges to look arter..."

Mycroft and Douglas stood and bid him farewell—but had barely made it outside the front door again when they heard the sound of Beeton calling out "Boy!" and then steps hurrying from the back of the house.

Mycroft and Sherlock ducked into a nearby entryway, their eyes on Beeton's front door to see if anyone emerged.

Their diligence was rewarded when a chestnut-haired ragamuffin peeked outside. He was about Sherlock's age and height, though he outweighed him by a good stone and a half. His skin was covered with pustules, and he had

Beeton's formless body and hooded eyelids.

Ascertaining that no one was about, he bolted out the front door and lumbered off in the opposite direction.

"Too old and too well fed to be one of his sweeps," Mycroft said. "Most likely his son."

"Do we go after him?" Douglas asked.

"No. All we need know for now is that we upset the apple cart. Let us see what else we can discover."

23

PATRONESS OF FOUNDLINGS ADELE DE MATALIN LIVED IN A grand old building in Piccadilly. The interior was a vulgar declaration of wealth, with Louis XIV furniture, exquisitely thick Persian carpets, gargantuan chandeliers from the island of Murano, primitive sculptures carved out of African ivory and lined with silver, and Ming vases so large that several men could hide therein.

Mycroft and Douglas walked past a silent footman and handed their calling cards to a butler, a man of middle years as silent as the grave and just as expressionless. As they waited in the marble-tiled hall entry for their host, Mycroft whispered: "It's a wonder that Carrara has any marble left. It all seems to have been brought here."

As the clock chimed out the hour, the rain that had been threatening since dawn began to fall in torrents, and Adele de Matalin descended the staircase, leaning on the arm of her butler.

Her dyed black hair was held in a loose chignon by two

enormous ivory pins in the shape of orioles. Her dress was garishly colorful and more fitting for a girl of sixteen than a dowager of sixty.

In spite of her man's assistance, de Matalin tottered on the final step. Her seawater-blue eyes, above two rouged and powdered cheeks, were as vitreous and fixed as a doll's.

"Ah, my friends! I see you are admiring my *tenue!*" she exclaimed, indicating her dress—for indeed both Mycroft and Douglas were nearly blinded by the blazing colors. "It is all but impossible to be too brightly attired, *n'est-ce pas?* We must give the birds of the air and the lilies of the field a bit of competition, must we not? *This,*" she added, indicating the flounce on her skirt, "is *solferino!* And the underskirt is azuline, which I dare reveal only because I am a *vieille femme* and no longer a beautiful young temptress!" she concluded coquettishly. "But when I *was* young, my trousseau—*ah, mon trousseau!*—was designed by *qui d'autre* but the renown Charles Frederick Worth of Paris!"

The butler led them into the library, an enormous affair with built-in mahogany bookcases whose every inch was cluttered with Francophile curios, a desk that could have served a prime minister, and a huge hearth with a welcoming fire.

On the end of a long padded divan with a delicate gilt frame sat a bisque doll the size of a five-year-old child. Her raven-black hair and glassy blue eyes eerily matched those of de Matalin herself. The dress she wore over her soft cloth body was every bit as garish and as expensive as the Madame's, with a clash of colors that Mycroft could not even begin to name. Her bisque hands with their pink fingernails were folded daintily in her lap. On her wrist, tied with a pretty pink bow, was a small tag that Mycroft assumed bore her name.

"*Asseyez-vous!*" de Matalin commanded the two men, indicating the divan, while she sat in a nearby Louis XIV ormolu chair. "My child, my proper Parisian child!" she exclaimed with a wave of her hand. "You are not dismayed, I hope!" she said, her eyes on Douglas, who sat beside it. "She likes to be in the midst of it all... you know how young girls are."

"Not at all dismayed, Madame," Douglas said. "But they are unusual in that size, are they not?"

"I would not call them common, but neither are they rare," she corrected him. "These bisque dolls have fallen in and out of fashion for the last several years, but they are now quite de rigueur again! She is accustomed to sitting just there, you see, holding court... my orphan, my little *bijou*. I spent entirely too much money on the girl! Then again, what was once *trés chére* has become *ma trés chére*! What was for me quite dear has become quite dear to me," she translated, in case the pun was lost. "But now, Mr. Douglas, my butler said you had information for me?"

"Yes," he replied. "Madame, I am afraid we bring sad news. One of the boys that you so kindly saved from Beeton the chimney sweep and sponsored to attend Nickolus House is deceased."

"Which one?" she asked, still smiling, as if her brain

had forgotten to inform her expression of what was apropos when it came to tragic news.

"Charles Fowler," Douglas said.

Her reaction was altogether unexpected. "Oh!" de Matalin exclaimed, opening those blank eyes wide. "Oh, *mon Dieu*! I... I feel quite faint!"

She reached for a gold box beside her chair and opened it with a trembling hand. Inside were dried mint leaves, along with a striated leaf of a paler green. She picked out a mint leaf, crushed it between her fingers and placed it like smelling salts just inside her nostrils.

As she did so, the sleeve of her blouse raised up slightly. On the tender white skin of her right wrist, Mycroft noticed small, telltale puncture wounds.

"Tell me how it happened," she said, her eyes soft and sorrowful, motioning to Douglas. "For he was a favorite of mine. A clever child, was he not?"

"Yes, quite. Forgive me," Mycroft said, rising abruptly. "But I, I feel a tad unwell. I am afraid I must importune you for the use of your..."

"Oh, of course!" de Matalin said. "We do not stand on ceremony here! You will find the water closet up the stairs to your right! Shall I ask my man to accompany you?"

"That won't be necessary, Madame," Mycroft replied politely.

"Mr. Douglas, if you will, tell me the tragic story of sweet little Charles. Leave out no detail—I am not so fragile as I appear! In fact, since my dear husband died, I have become quite the woman of business! Proceed, if you would."

She snorted another bit of crushed mint and her eyes fluttered closed again.

Mycroft passed by Douglas, who gave him a curious look. *Keep her occupied*, he indicated with a small hand gesture. Douglas nodded that he understood.

Mycroft slid past the impassive butler at the door, who did not deign to give him so much as a blink or a nod.

Once upstairs, he ascertained that the corridor was free of any prying eyes but his. He reached into his pocket for his watch. Thankfully, the midmorning hour meant that the upstairs servants had completed their tasks, so he hastened down the corridor and peered into a few rooms, but none of them were the one he sought.

At the fourth door, he heard footsteps behind him, and he turned to see the white cap of a chambermaid coming up the stairs. He attempted to turn the handle, but it was locked. She had reached the landing and was coming down the corridor now, her arms so loaded down with bedding that it was a wonder she could see in front of her.

But neither could she see Mycroft—at least, not yet.

Mycroft came to the fifth door and jiggled the doorknob. Though unlocked, the knob was stuck. A good, hard twist and it gave. He slipped into a small bathroom and closed the door again behind him as softly as he could. His heart was pounding so radically that he thought for certain the maid would hear it as she trotted by, carrying her unwieldy load.

Barely breathing, he waited until he could hear no more

sounds, then tiptoed back into the corridor, trying several more doors until he found the one he sought: Madame de Matalin's bedroom. Its enormous windows had been opened slightly to let in air. And though the rain had halted as suddenly as it had begun, the weather was continuing gray and blustery, which meant a servant would likely be back at any moment to shut them.

He would have to be quick, as time was of the essence.

He glanced about. Given who she was, Madame would surely be drawn to expensive accouterments and small rituals when it came to her habit, but she seemed too far along to be completely clandestine about it. The butler had assisted her impassively, anticipating her movements, and so well knew her secret. And if he knew, then so did the housekeeper and her lady's maid. No other member of the household staff would matter, for they would not be likely to meddle into her personal effects.

On her long bureau, among countless costly knick-knacks, he spotted a small Limoges box encrusted with emeralds and aquamarine. It was the correct type: a container in which a hypodermic syringe could fit snugly, one that was "worthy" of the appeal her habit had for her; it was within easy reach, and yet did not elicit undue curiosity.

Mycroft opened the box. It was lined with green silk. Tucked inside was a glass vial filled with reddish-brown liquid, a hypodermic syringe with a spare needle, and a delicate opium pipe sculpted in ivory, in the shape of a dragon with coiled tail.

The liquid, he knew by sight: laudanum. He smelled the pipe. Given the consistency of the residue and the potency of the odor, he assumed it had been used within the last twelve to fourteen hours. He smelled the hypodermic too but picked out mostly the alcohol used to clean it, along with a hint of something he could not quite identify: the closest he could come was an alkaloid of some kind.

These all rested on a false bottom. Mycroft tapped the underside of the box, popping the panel out of the way. Hidden below it, he found a magnifying glass and six calling cards made of silk stock with a name embossed on them: *William Angel.* The cards all bore smudge marks, tiny finger marks or friction ridges; some darker, some lighter, but quite clear on each.

Mycroft turned them over, then back again. Smudged cards, however costly, were not something a lady like de Matalin would keep in a Limoges box in her boudoir, along with the tools of her habit.

The magnifying glass was as big a mystery, one he had no time for at the moment.

Another noise in the corridor gave him a start.

A moment later, he collapsed to the floor.

24

WHEN MYCROFT OPENED HIS EYES, THE ROOM WAS SPINNING around him like a demented carousel. He was nauseated and his tongue felt thick, as if he had been wandering through a desert for days without water. He planted both hands on the floor and eased himself up as quickly as he could without vomiting.

From what he could deduce, an unexpected noise had caused his heart to leap wildly in his chest, causing him to lose consciousness.

He reached into his pocket with a shaking hand and checked his watch. He had been insensate for seven minutes. He thanked Providence he had not been discovered, until a less pleasing notion came to mind: *What in heaven's name is the matter with me?*

A sudden suspicion that he was being poisoned reared up like a cobra. The tiredness, the melancholia, the too-tight shoes—were they symptoms of something he had ignored?

Now's certainly not the time to mull it over! he thought irritably as he scooped up his hat from the floor and smoothed down his clothing. Then he headed downstairs, ready to tender whatever apologies his strange and excessive absence would require.

But he found that no excuse was needed. The butler was still standing at attention at the door to the library. As for Adele de Matalin, she appeared to be deep into a monologue to Douglas about demons, and the sway they sometimes had over her. She did not acknowledge Mycroft, nor did she seem to be taking Douglas's presence into account as anything more than a sounding board as she described her travails in a fretful, childish voice: "They are malignant spirits, fierce succubi. You cannot know *quel tourment* they cause me! Demons are the shade of toadstools, do you see? Or, better, of charcoal, because of the constant scorching they are subjected to. It is only bright, shining color that keeps them at bay. *Mon Dieu*, I must be so very diligent, so very diligent…"

Mycroft, his head still spinning, was attempting in vain to make sense of it until he realized there was no sense to be made.

He had barely resumed his seat when her inscrutably wooden butler cleared his throat.

"Madame?" he said, daring to interrupt her soliloquy in a tone that would broach no objections. "It is time for your midmorning restorative."

"Ah yes!" she replied with a heartfelt sigh reserved for an angel of mercy whisking one away from a nightmare. "My restorative!"

She rose and addressed her guests with a charming smile that said all thoughts of demons had flitted away. "I am afraid I must leave," she said as the men rose in turn. "Old women have their limits, do they not?"

She seemed to be waiting for a protest of empty flattery that neither of her guests was the sort to give. Appearing less than pleased, she added: "And, Mr. Douglas? Kindly inform Mr. Smythe that if Nickolus House is so careless as to lose a child, my business with him is done and my decision irrevocable."

With that, Douglas and Mycroft were ushered out, with the footman closing the door resolutely behind them.

As they hurried down the front steps to the street, Douglas asked: "What in the world kept you? And why are you so pale?"

"She had fresh puncture marks on her wrist, Douglas," Mycroft replied. "I gather she is a habitué," he added vaguely.

"A drug addict, you mean," Douglas corrected impatiently. "No use being mealy-mouthed about it. And as to my second question…?"

"Douglas, I am perfectly well. A tad under the weather, that is all. In that box she opened in the library," he continued, "I spied kratom, a herb meant to—"

"I am familiar with it. Meant to aid opium addicts to ease off the drug. It can be quite effective, though if what you say is true, it did not work for her."

"No, it did not," Mycroft agreed. "In her bedroom I

found a recently used opium pipe, a vial of laudanum, a syringe and spare needle, and six smudged calling cards from a certain Mr. William Angel. Does the name ring any bells?"

"None at all," Douglas replied. "Smudged, you say?"

"A misleading term on my part. In fact, the friction ridges were quite clean…"

"Friction ridges?"

"All six cards had finger marks," Mycroft clarified. "Small and distinct: two thumbs on the front, two index fingers on the back."

"Mycroft, I am not following," Douglas said.

"It was as if someone had purposely placed a thumb and index finger in soot, and pinched the card once, then again. I am no expert and had little time with them—frankly, none at all—but it seemed that, on each card, both sets of ridges were identical. But those same ridges seemed different from one card to the other—though I cannot even say if they were of the left hand or of the right."

"Soot," Douglas said, apparently trying to catch up. "Fireplace soot, you mean?"

"Yes of course fireplace soot. What else could soot refer to in this particular context?"

Douglas shook his head. "Madame is not the sort who would allow young sweeps into that spotless abode unless they entered chimney-first," he said, "and left in the same manner."

"And yet, there is a connection," Mycroft sighed. "Just out of curiosity, I shall put my young assistant, Parfitt, on a quest for this Mr. Angel. If the man works in London, Parfitt should not have much trouble locating him. Let us see if a thread or two comes together. Whatever else, it pains me that you have lost a patroness."

"I cannot say the same," Douglas replied. "The entire time I was alone with her, I must admit I was unnerved. I cannot discern whether it was de Matalin herself or that oversized doll with the staring eyes…"

"No, I meant I would dearly love to have another gander at those cards!" Mycroft said, and Douglas laughed.

"I believe that ship has sailed," he retorted.

"Has it?" Mycroft asked.

"You are sounding altogether too innocent, and yes," Douglas stated in no uncertain terms, "it has. My days of breaking and entering are over. But, remaining on the subject of dolls, did I mention that I saw similar ones at the shipwreck of the *Royal Adelaide*? A half-dozen washed ashore, quite eerie."

"Now *there* is a queer coincidence," Mycroft declared. "Although, according to de Matalin, they are back in favor…"

"I cannot see why. I would think they would frighten any sensible little girl half to death."

"Was that a name card on her wrist?" Mycroft asked, smiling, and Douglas nodded.

"It seems she is called *Marguerite*."

Suddenly, Mycroft noticed a bright yellow landaulet parked nearby. At that exact moment, the driver flicked his whip and the horse threw himself forward directly into their path. He and Douglas managed to leap out of its way mere seconds before being struck. It whisked so closely by that they felt the breeze as the carriage shuddered past them, the beast neighing indignantly as it went.

Douglas caught his breath, shaken, as the two of them watched it canter away.

"I have seen that carriage before!" Douglas declared the moment he could speak again. "It was outside Nickolus House when you and Sherlock first arrived!"

Mycroft stared at him. "Why did you say nothing?"

"Why would I have?" Douglas replied, taken aback.

"No, no, you're right of course; but I too have seen it!"

"*When?*" Douglas asked.

"It belongs to that Chinese gentleman Cainborn met on Shoreditch High Street! I could have mentioned it last night, I suppose, but it seemed trifling…"

"Not so trifling now," Douglas muttered. "But what are you suggesting? That the Chinese gentleman is following you about, wanting to do mischief?"

"He was not in the carriage," Mycroft said.

"How do you know?" Douglas said incredulously. "Please do not tell me you were able to scan the interior as it barreled past us!"

"Do not be absurd, Douglas, the blinds were pulled down—how could I have? No, it was the speed at which the horse set off from a dead stop. The added weight of even one person in the carriage would not have permitted the beast to come at us at quite that velocity. Further, the back wheels were weaving somewhat. The weight was all at the front, where the driver sat. It carried no one.

"Of course, the last time I could not see him at all," Mycroft continued, "for the carriage was heading in the opposite direction. But this time, I saw a well-proportioned, mustached, bearded man, a hat drawn over his eyes so that it is a wonder he could see the road, his hands gloved when none of his ilk would steer a carriage with gloved hands..."

"But he did not even draw rein!" Douglas said, baffled. "How could you notice all that in the five seconds it took for him to very nearly put us under his wheels? I for one was too busy trying to remain upon my feet! And if he was bearded, he could not be either of the bodyguards you saw with Ai Lin, for you described them as clean-shaven."

"I cannot know for sure," Mycroft said. "But I believe the driver was Oriental. They are not known for their fulsome beards, therefore it was likely false."

"So," Douglas said. "You are saying the driver wore a disguise. He came alone in order to spy on us. When we spotted him, or perhaps on a whim, he came at us and set about to kill us."

"I doubt that last," Mycroft replied. "For, as you mentioned, he did not draw rein, yet he handily avoided us. No, he is a terribly efficient driver, quite skilled."

"I am relieved to hear it," Douglas said. "Now I beg you, please do not tell me that we are once again to be beaten within an inch of our lives, as we were on the journey to Trinidad, without having the foggiest notion what sin we committed to provoke such treatment."

Mycroft could not help himself: he laughed.

"And may I add," Douglas said, "that before I met you, my days may've been both joyous and difficult, and upon occasion even tragic—but I cannot say that mysteries made up any part of them."

"Nor mine before you!" Mycroft declared.

"Yes, but to be fair, it was your star-crossed love that embroiled us in the last bit of bad business…"

"That I concede, but pray let us not speak of it now or in the near or far future. To my point: the driver drew as close as he could while avoiding harm to us. He *wanted* us to notice him, that was his intent."

"And in that, he succeeded," Douglas grumbled.

They heard the sound of rapidly approaching hoof beats and both turned in some alarm; only this time it was Huan at the reins of Mycroft's carriage.

"Very sorry, Mr. Mycroft!" Huan called out as he halted near them. "There was much traffic!"

"Why would that be?" Mycroft asked as he and Douglas climbed in.

"Murder!" Huan announced. "Another body found not too far from here; I passed it when I come. People all over the street, gawking! Ah, but I forget this does not interest you!"

"On the contrary," Mycroft Holmes declared, "I have become very interested indeed. Let us make our way there quickly!"

25

IT HAD TAKEN SHERLOCK UNTIL WELL PAST NOON TO travel from Baker Street to Mansion House. Sixteen stops that would have taken Charles less than two hours had taken twice that. But, carved on the back of his vielle were fifteen sets of Chinese symbols. At least, he imagined that Chinese was their pedigree, but he preferred to be certain rather than to speculate, especially with a clue as vital as this one.

He disembarked from the third-class carriage at Mansion House as grimy with soot as any common worker of coal. And he was gratified to see that, waiting there, were Alvey Ducasse, his big, ruddy face flushed even redder from excitement, and dark-haired, wolf-eyed Joe McPeel.

"'Twas as you said!" Alvey greeted Sherlock the moment the latter stepped foot off the train.

Sherlock hushed him while pulling both boys away from the other passengers.

"'Twas as you said…" Alvey repeated under his breath, his voice not much quieter for the effort. "A ginger lad waitin' 'ere since 'alf past ten! Short an' thick! Then this *uvver* boy, a big 'un, with skin like sausage innards and staring eyes, 'e come up an' whispers somethin' in 'is ear, an' they *both* runs off! But not to worry, guv! Joe 'ere give chase—"

"Did they see you?" Sherlock asked, addressing Joe McPeel.

When Joe shook his head, Alvey answered for him: "McPeel, 'e used to be a right fair barker! No one sees 'im unless 'e wants to be seen!" he added proudly.

McPeel grinned. "They both run a goodly way. I seen 'em go into a den—"

"A den?" Sherlock asked. "Do you mean an opium den?"

McPeel nodded. "That's right, guv. The one with the buggy eyes an' poxy skin, 'e come out, but the ginger, 'e stays put. I runs back 'ere to tell you…"

"You did well, Mr. McPeel," Sherlock said with enthusiasm. "How long ago was that?"

"Can't say as I knows, guv. But five trains came through while we waited!"

"Good. You'd best lead us back to this den."

McPeel's ice-blue eyes lit up mischievously. "You best try to keep up!" he said, taking off up the stairs to the street, with Alvey and Sherlock right on his heels.

Limehouse was yet another slice of what was known in common parlance as "savage" London. Far removed from the niceties of Regent Street or the grandeur of Cumberland House, and convenient perhaps to read about from the comfort of one's armchair, it was of a different grit and odor when blundering through its narrow, rutted streets.

The poor seemed to be not so much gathered under its eaves and upon its stoops as cast off like crumbs from a stale loaf. Even during this fetid gray day, when rain had already made its presence known and the air felt like an amble through coarse wet wool, being outdoors was preferable to whatever mean, soiled quarters could be found inside, where people lived, ate, slept and died twenty to a room.

To ward off the cold, children were burdened down with an array of castoff garments. These smallest residents of the East End looked like heaps of rags tramping about, or sitting at their parents' feet as if stunned that this soggy, inscrutable day was much like the one before or the one before that, and that they still had such a long way to go before their own lives were used up.

Sherlock, keeping a steady pace with his newly minted spy, Joe McPeel, had hooked his short staff into his belt like a baton and had the shaving tools in the pocket of his jacket. And though the vielle was cumbersome, it was precious, as it held the finest key to this mystery so far.

Though he could not halt, he made good use of his eagle-sharp eyes and keen sense of smell as he hurried past the closed-in buildings, their crumbling brickwork patched with plaster, like dozens upon dozens of yellowed bandages pressed upon a fighter already beaten beyond recognition.

McPeel, for his part, seemed to notice nothing save the road before him. Even winded and in need of rest, he seemed to savor the run. He had removed his shoes a mile back without breaking stride, and for convenience's sake had inserted each hand into the openings so that when his arms pumped, it appeared as if his feet were galloping in thin air.

"Beggin' leave, guv, I ain't used to 'em!" was his explanation to Sherlock, his small criticism leavened by a lopsided grin.

A pair of shoes is about as useful to a boy like that as a box of chocolates is to a cat, Sherlock thought.

Further behind them, and losing steam, was flame-haired Alvey Ducasse. Running did not appear to be second or even third nature. His ruddy forehead was beaded with sweat that trickled from underneath his flat cap. Once in a while he would muster up enough energy to swat at the bothersome trickle mere seconds before it fell into his eyes.

Nevertheless, the three kept at it until they reached the docks where the smell of mildew lingered in the air, along with the heavier aromas of raw meat and horse dung, courtesy of a butcher's shop. Beside that was a horse stall with a few ancient nags, ready for lease. Every other shop was either a cheap lodging house, or sold gear for seafaring vessels and sailors, its dirty windows crowded with brass sextants, compasses, and chronometers.

The boys were very nearly at Shadwell Basin when McPeel finally halted and pointed.

Sherlock, who had read accounts of opium lairs with a skeptical eye, half expected the wretched hole of despair described in novels; but there was nothing remotely exotic about this lair of vice, at least from the outside. If anything, it seemed rather like a proper small business that had been constrained to make do in a less than salubrious neighborhood.

The two-story edifice was squeezed in between a former grocer's and a small pub with the out-of-place name Hart & Hound, though it appeared to be closed.

The den of vice, on the other hand, seemed open to customers, judging by the many footprints in the mud that led to the door, and freshly gouged tracks of carriage wheels. Sherlock could not tell if the ruts had been made by two carriages that had come and gone, or by one that had made several trips back and forth—though he did note in passing that it was a private vehicle and not a cab, for the wheels were set further apart than the typical London hansom.

What seemed more interesting at the moment was that the establishment itself had only a discreet sign that read: THE WATER MONKEY.

Seated upon squat wooden stools on either side of the front door were two rotund Chinese women of middle age, dressed like field workers and staring straight ahead, paying the passersby no attention. Sherlock recalled from his readings that these guards of opium lairs were intent upon one thing only: to alert customers to the presence of the law in the area. The establishment might be legal, but some of the habitués less so, and would be most grateful for a tipoff and a head start.

But, although not the law, three British lads of uncertain

pedigree could not suddenly barge into an opium den without creating a small ruckus.

Sherlock ascertained that the boys were out of the women's sightline, should they deign to turn their gaze on them. He gave Alvey his vielle and short staff, which Alvey received with awe, along with Sherlock's jacket in exchange for Alvey's own, which was as rough as the hair of a wild goat, along with Alvey's sweat-soaked cap. He also borrowed Alvey's shoes, workmanlike and slightly too large for his feet, which would better fit the impression he wished to make.

Newly attired, Sherlock bid the boys wait outside. He turned up his collar, pulled Alvey's cap down over his eyes, and strutted past the guardians. As the women continued to stare straight ahead like two plaster lions, he pushed open the front door of The Water Monkey and walked inside.

26

THE FRONT ROOM OF THE DEN WAS AS ORDINARY AS THE outside. The windows had been covered over so that no natural light could enter. Three oil lamps swung from the ceiling, with two more on the wall, and all were turned down low.

There was another door besides the entryway, most likely opening onto a staircase to the upper floor. Sherlock saw a long wooden bar with the usual assortment of rum and whiskey to be found at any dockside pub. The only other furnishings consisted of three tables, with four chairs at each. Upon them sat a dozen Oriental men.

They were playing a game that utilized narrow, rectangular cards in colors of yellow, green, orange, and white. They were betting with what looked like small flat silver ingots that had been heated and marked with a mold. It seemed they had a substantial number of ingots, considering that most of the cards were still in the players' hands. From what Sherlock could tell, of the four players at each table, three held a fan of twenty cards, while one held twenty-one. It took practice to hold a fan of cards that large. These were seasoned players.

Sherlock wondered what sort of game called for so much silver already betted when no card had yet been played. From the nonchalant manner with which the men handled the ingots, the contests seemed more for amusement than for profit, though the profound silence in the room underscored the intensity and focus of their pastime.

And if there was opium use, it was nowhere in evidence, nor was there any residual smoke or odor.

Like the women at the entrance, the men made no eye contact with Sherlock or one another but kept on silently staring at their cards. Regardless, Sherlock could feel that his presence had appreciably heightened the tension in the room. He had to discern whom, of the twelve seated men, he should approach—and do so quickly.

Thankfully, exotic game notwithstanding, the men could have passed for accountants enjoying a weekly match, for they dressed in the British fashion. This meant that their rank was not hidden from him, as it would have been had they been garbed in their national dress.

He set his sights on a svelte man in his early thirties who sat at the third table, his back to the wall, eyes to the front door. Underneath the table, his shoes were more costly than those of the others, though to be fair, every shoe in the place was polished to perfection—quite a feat on such a muddy day. But while the other men's demeanor was shuttered and wary, this man sat with his knees slightly splayed, his countenance open, almost affable.

Sherlock was certain that he had found the right man.

"Beggin' pardon, sir," he said, approaching him. "I 'ear you're seekin' a lad wot knows wot."

The leader did not say a word but kept rearranging his cards. His fingernails were manicured and the skin smooth, but his dexterous hands looked as strong as vices. Arthritis had claimed the first knuckle of the right ring and little fingers. The veins and sinews on his wrists were so prominent as to seem corded. The skin of his face looked weathered, as if he had spent his youth toiling aboard ships. And his expensive shirt could not quite hide an ancient but prominent scar at the neckline, as if someone had tried and failed to separate his head from the rest of his body.

Sherlock cleared his throat. It sounded like thunder in the silent room.

He could feel the other men stiffen, twitchy to obey whatever command their leader might give. Even in the midst of his fear, Sherlock was grateful to have been proven so quickly correct.

"Charles, guv, 'im as was, 'e told me about you. Said you was a good man to 'ave a talk wiv."

The leader's eyes were still on his cards. He was twirling one of the silver ingots between the first three fingers of his left hand.

"Him as was?" the man repeated. "How do you know he is dead?" His voice had an upper-class cadence most likely learned at a public school.

"I was with 'im when 'e died, sir. I seen 'im take 'is last breath."

"I see. And where was this?"

"Nicklas 'ouse, sir. I gots me a 'prent'ship. But that ain't no life for me, sir, an' Charlie knowed it."

The man nodded thoughtfully. Placing the ingot upon the table, he said: "Let me see your arms, boy."

Sherlock was thrown by the request but was not about to show it. He dutifully set about taking off Alvey's jacket, but his slight hesitation must have been taken as a sign of disrespect because a fat man of around thirty, along with a slightly younger moon-faced man, put down their cards, rose and tore it from Sherlock's shoulders in one swift move. Grabbing one arm each, they yanked at him more than strictly necessary as they rolled up the cuffs of his shirt to the biceps.

Sherlock was gratified that he had already torn the garment in several places: the last thing he needed was to be caught wearing a pristine shirt under Alvey's shabby jacket.

The leader turned Sherlock's arms over one at a time, wrists up, and inspected them thoughtfully. Then he touched a small series of punctures above Sherlock's left elbow.

"What's this, then?" he asked, appraising him.

Sherlock did not respond.

Clutching his wrist and squeezing hard, the man looked into Sherlock's eyes—while Sherlock struggled to not be discomfited by the abyss he saw there.

"That will no longer be permitted," he murmured, indicating the injection points on Sherlock's arm. "Are we clear on that, boy?"

Sherlock mutely nodded and then swallowed hard, hoping both reactions would seem like genuine fear to the man inspecting him—for they certainly felt that way to him.

When he lowered his eyes, he noticed for the first time that the leader's shoes were not spotless after all. A few dots the size of pencil tips, dark red and in a spray pattern, colored the side of his left shoe.

"*Shòu-shòu*," murmured the fat man to his boss, who nodded.

"I will take your offer under advisement," the leader said, releasing Sherlock's wrist. "Return here on Monday, four p.m. What do we call you, boy?"

"Basil," Sherlock declared before adding, "Thank you, sir…"

The leader grinned, exposing teeth the color of copper. "You may call me Juju," he said.

Then he went back to his game, making it abundantly clear that Sherlock had been dismissed.

Trembling from cold, anxiety, and feverish elation, Sherlock lowered his shirt cuffs, slipped on Alvey's jacket, and hastened outside again.

Monday afternoon, he thought, the exhilaration of discovery quickly sweeping away all fear.

Sherlock strolled around the corner as if he had all the time in the world. He was gratified to find Alvey and Joe where he'd left them. Ducasse looked bug-eyed with news of some kind, while McPeel bounced from one bare and dirty foot to the other, his new shoes still on his hands.

"We just 'eard—" Alvey Ducasse began, but Sherlock hushed him with an upraised finger.

"Might I keep your jacket and shoes for the moment, and you take mine in exchange?"

Ducasse nodded as he returned Sherlock's short staff and vielle, while McPeel could not seem to keep still.

"We just 'eard—" Ducasse tried again, but was cut off by McPeel.

"There's been another murder on Narra Street!" Joe declared, eyes shining. "Can we have a gander, guv?"

27

HUAN DROVE MYCROFT AND DOUGLAS TO NARROW STREET: the scene of the crime. Nothing like being transported to a murder in a costly carriage pulled by a handsome beast, with a coachman of exotic extraction. Especially if the proprietor, upon alighting, is attired in hat, shoes and shirt straight from Jermyn Street, and flanked by a Negro secretary who could have put any white man to shame.

The gaping, huddled throng parted like the Red Sea all the way to the nexus: the cleaved and bleeding body. With all eyes upon him, Mycroft crouched down beside the corpse, which was lying in a substantial puddle of blood, with more blood spattered up and to the right, across the torso. Similar to the seventh victim, the man was Caucasian, and approximately thirty years of age, and had been sectioned into four parts: the head and neck had been separated from the torso, which had been cleaved right down the middle, with one arm attached to each half. The left arm was peppered from wrist to biceps with needle marks, both scabbed over and new. His lower extremities, from the hips down, formed the final section and had the indications, as clear as a road map, of a rough life: legs misshapen by malnutrition and scarred by rat bites.

Mycroft checked the punctures on the man's arm but saw nothing that he could not have inflicted upon himself. As for the cleaving, it had been well executed: the murderer had the skills and strength to make surgeon-like cuts. But though the victim's nose had been sheared off—greatly disfiguring the face and making eventual identification that much more difficult—his genitals had been left intact.

"This is an odd one," Mycroft muttered to Douglas. "Not like the others."

Douglas, standing over him, nodded.

Mycroft had not seen the first seven murder victims, other than in ghastly illustrations. Even so, it seemed obvious that all eight had utilized the same butcher: for these cuts, like those, were clean and straight, requiring deftness, a keen eye, and enormous strength.

It was also clear to Mycroft that one man alone could not have accomplished the task. Another two men would have been needed to hold down the victim when the first blow was struck. But why would the same team that so carefully followed ritual in the other murders forsake it for this one? He would have concluded that the butcher had been interrupted in his work, but for the shearing off of the nose. Genitals were always cut first, leaving the nose for last. His only explanation was that the "message" this time was for someone else entirely... though he could not guess who.

Just then, a carriage carrying several constables arrived to the scattered jeers of the crowd, who did not care for peelers in the neighborhood, however noble the cause.

Mycroft glanced at the faces of the onlookers, wondering if the perpetrators of this grotesquery might still be close by, watching for reactions. If they were, they did not give themselves away. But he did catch a glimpse of a tall, hawk-like youth pushing his way through the crowd, followed by two young scruffy urchins with self-important grins, all three of them unmindful of the onlookers' protestations and with but one goal in mind: to take in the scene of the crime.

"Sherlock!" Mycroft gasped while his brother stared down at him.

Sherlock saw Douglas pushing through the crowd. With his long reach, he snagged McPeel and Ducasse by their respective collars and tugged them through the gathering mob, all the while excoriating them on not honoring commitments, or some equally dreary bromide.

A moment later, Sherlock felt Mycroft's grip on his arm, dragging him away from the body. Mycroft's lecture had to do with duties regarding education and the evils of deception.

In truth, Sherlock was hardly listening. It was necessary that he shut out all extraneous noise so that he might better recall each tiny detail of the past hour.

He was very nearly certain who'd killed this eighth

victim—or, more accurately, who'd given the order to kill: he had just met him and his minions at The Water Monkey. The establishment fit both proximity and, given the needle marks on the victim's arm, his circle of acquaintances.

Juju the ringleader had sprinkles of blood on the side of his left shoe. These and the drops on the dead man's torso were like the flick of a painter's brush, so much in the same pattern that they might as well have been two halves of a divided canvas.

Sherlock tried in his mind's eye to place Juju at the scene of the crime. Someone must've held the man down: two men, most likely. But it was hard to believe that Juju would be one of them, and he did not have the hands of one who could deftly wield a knife. Sherlock imagined him on his feet, peering down at the prone victim from what he assumed was a safe distance—one that would allow him to witness the proceedings without staining his clothes. Was the poor drug fiend still alive at that juncture? Did Juju believe he was far enough away from the splattering blood that he had not been sullied?

If only he could have examined the incisions closer up! If Mycroft had but tarried a moment longer!

He thought back to the card players. Were there signs of bloodletting on any of them? No. But neither had they mud on their shoes or clothing—highly unlikely on a day like this. Which meant that the men had changed their clothing before they'd entered the room. The only one who had seen no need to do so had been Juju, who had doubtless ridden to and from the scene of the crime in his carriage, for it accounted for the fresh tracks in the mud outside The Water Monkey's door.

From what Sherlock recalled, the impressions of the wheels that had gone to and fro were of the same size but of diverse indentation, which meant the weight of the carriage had altered. It had been heavier in going than upon its return, and substantially heavier in the front than in the back both times.

Had Juju transported the victim to the scene of his own murder? And why was the coachman's position overly weighted?

Sherlock dearly wished he had paid more attention to the ruts at the time—though the two Chinese ladies standing at the door to The Water Monkey would not have been quite so passive, had they witnessed a strange lad closely inspecting wheel marks made by their master's carriage.

As for the card game, Sherlock's first assumption had been incorrect. The men's nonchalance about the match itself; the matter-of-factness with which they held their cards; the ease with which they'd placed their bets—all had seemed to connote a friendly, habitual game, when it had been nothing of the kind.

He now believed it had been set up for show.

How else to explain the contrast between cards played— there were undrawn piles on every table—and the bets, which appeared as if the men had been playing for a while? While it was possible that they had begun another round, the ingots had been tossed about too evenly.

There was no one with a clear advantage.

They may not have succeeded in fooling anyone who paid careful attention. But if they were expecting a visit from the police—white to a man, ignorant of the rules of the game—the ruse would have been enough.

He wished he could reveal these deductions to Mycroft, or inquire as to the particulars of slicing into a living body as opposed to one that had recently been deceased, but his brother was already angry. The last thing Sherlock was keen to tell him was that he had been nosing about for employment in an opium den.

He was fairly certain that he recognized the dead man. For the victim very much resembled the thin-haired assailant who had desired to scramble Sherlock's insides with a well-placed punch to the gut, the night that he and Douglas had rescued Charles.

Douglas might have also recognized him, but it was unlikely. It was dark, and Douglas was busy fighting three men at once. Besides, if Douglas had said as much to Mycroft, his brother would have surely brought it up by now.

Best not mention it, he thought. *Not yet.* For if he were to tie, even speculatively, this brutal murder to Charles's demise, Mycroft would view the entire undertaking as much too perilous, and that would be that.

"I shall not endeavor to ask what you were thinking, because I gather you were not thinking at all!" Mycroft was saying as he continued to manhandle Sherlock away from the scene and into the nearest pub, a grubby affair called The Bunch of Grapes. Sherlock could only assume that, abetted by a lack of windows and feeble gaslight, his brother would once again, and with a great deal more intent, lay down the law. He had to get Mycroft on his side, tell him just enough to intrigue him but not so much as to make him panic. For if his brother should prevent him from pursuing the case, Sherlock did not know if he would be able to bear it.

They took a seat across from each other and Mycroft signaled the barkeeper for two beers, then leaned towards Sherlock with his arms folded, demanding a response to a question Sherlock had failed to hear.

"Well?" Mycroft insisted as the barkeeper laid down two overfilled tankards with a clatter, their foamy heads sloshing onto the tabletop. Sherlock, feeling suddenly too warm in the low-lying air, unbuttoned his jacket, to Mycroft's continued horror.

"What is that you are wearing?" he demanded.

Sherlock took a sip of his ale and wiped his lips with the back of his hand, in keeping with the general atmosphere. Thus fortified, he reached for his vielle case, opened it, and set the instrument face down into the only feeble spot of light to be had.

It revealed the fifteen groups of symbols that had taken him the better part of the morning to collect.

"I have something to confess," he declared.

28

IN THE DIM LIGHT OF THE PUB, SHERLOCK COULD SEE Mycroft mulling things over. This was not a long process. In the time it took for his brother to order another round, he had already categorized in that ledger brain of his each tidbit of information that Sherlock had provided.

"Truly, I am livid that you kept such a potentially dangerous secret," Mycroft began. "However, I must confess you did a nice bit of work. Though the notion that Baker necessarily indicated a train station was a stretch, as it could also indicate the whole of Baker Street."

"Yes, it could," Sherlock admitted. "But not with the word 'Mansion' also in play. But, had I not located the first clue in the station, as predicted, I would have gladly traipsed the entire length and breadth of the street in search of same."

"I've no doubt," Mycroft muttered, his tone suspended between censure and admiration. "And it is equally clear, from the sample of wax you found, that Charles made impressions of those symbols to then pass along to this

'Gin.' Though I despise the fact that you put Douglas's charges in such a position, I do acknowledge the necessity of having *someone* at the final stop to gauge if your theory was correct. And that the redheaded lad *was* waiting there," he concluded, "reinforces your other theory: he had no knowledge of Charles's death."

Sherlock nodded enthusiastically. "The boys did not know about one another, nor were they meant to," he confirmed. "I am convinced of it!"

"And Gin is most likely short for 'Ginger.'"

"It certainly appears so."

"I do have a few reservations, however," Mycroft said. "The first is 'Baker.' Why would a lad who has but one breath left in him to say one word, choose *that* one? What did Charles hope to achieve? It makes logical sense but no *emotional* sense, do you see?"

"But I was proven right in my speculations," Sherlock argued.

"Yes, but if someone has just injected you with a substance that leads to your death, why not say that person's name?"

"You are saying *Baker* is a name?"

"Or a nickname," Mycroft amended. "Then, when 'Gin' ran off," he continued, "why did McPeel not immediately go after him? I had him pegged for a runner. He could have left Ducasse at the station to stand guard."

"My fault entirely; I should have given them leave to do so," Sherlock lied quickly. For of course McPeel's run had led to The Water Monkey. "In their defense, they are quite obedient. Next time, I shall give them leave to follow a trail where it leads."

"*Next* time?" Mycroft repeated. "No, no, you misunderstand. Not only is Douglas no doubt livid that you involved his charges, but *your* involvement, if there is to be any, must be severely curtailed."

Normally, Sherlock would have argued, but he managed to hold his tongue.

"As for the symbols," Mycroft said, "nearly a third of sailors on trading ships and a number of dock workers are Chinese. Douglas has acquaintances among them who might acquiesce to translate, provided the symbols are in a major dialect and not too terribly ancient..."

"Perfect!"

"Not so perfect, no, for a translator would have to assume whatever risk such revelations might generate, for it seems someone went to a great deal of trouble to keep this list a secret."

"Stating the obvious," Sherlock countered, "why not Huan?"

Mycroft shook his head. "Sadly, Huan can neither read nor write—not in Chinese, or in English. Both Douglas and I have offered to teach him, but he says that in his profession, he has no need of it."

Sherlock recalled the wistfulness in Huan's voice when he'd said, *I envy you your learning, Master Sherlock.*

"However," Mycroft went on, "I am not clear as to why you did not investigate the stations before Baker Street—

Great Portland Street, King's Cross, et cetera—to ascertain that there were no clues there."

"Time," Sherlock explained. "I had none. I knew that whoever was waiting at Mansion House would not wait forever. Then, when I found all fifteen symbols, I assumed that was it."

"And the carvings themselves?" Mycroft asked. "Were they uniform?"

"Yes, up until St. James's Park," Sherlock said. "From there to Blackfriars, they were lighter, finer. The symbols appeared to be etched by a more delicate hand."

"A woman's?" Mycroft ventured.

Sherlock shook his head. "The location of the symbols disallows that. A woman would call entirely too much attention to herself."

"A woman dressed as a man, perhaps," Mycroft suggested.

Sherlock was ashamed to note that the thought had never crossed his mind. "What of the latest murder?" he asked, hoping to glean just enough information from his brother without having to reveal any of his own. "In the others, beyond quartering the body and cutting off the nose, the killers—for surely such an endeavor requires more than one—seemed rather fixated on draining the corpse of blood, and on excising the genitals."

"You are asking my opinion?" Mycroft was surprised.

"Well, no need to bloviate," Sherlock replied. "But it does seem ritualistic, and they are most definitely Oriental. And are you not always keen to acquaint yourself with rituals and customs, given the whole—" he waved his hand as if shooing a fly "—*assistant to the War Office* aspect?"

"Special consul to the Secretary of State for War," Mycroft corrected. "And yes, there *is* a reason. It is a Chinese way of shaming a man in death."

"Ah, because murdering the poor beggar in the first place is not shame enough?" Sherlock quipped.

"In Yì," Mycroft began, apparently ignoring this last, "the nose is severed. In Gōng, the reproductive organs are removed. There is also Mò, where the face is tattooed with indelible ink; and Yuè, where a foot is cut off, sometimes both."

"What you are saying is that thus far, the killers selected Yì and Gōng," Sherlock interjected. "But could they not have decided, on this go round, to choose only Yì?"

"Yes, they could have. But once the victim has been defiled, the ritual is not ended. He is then boiled alive, beheaded, strangled, slowly sliced to death, *or* quartered. If quartered, the blood is drained."

"Always?"

"Always. Which is something you might know for yourself, if you were remotely curious about anything beyond our own shores," Mycroft concluded.

"I am not as provincial as all that," Sherlock objected. "But what is your conjecture? That they murdered the latest victim in this manner solely because they knew it would make the papers?"

"The others certainly made the papers! No, what I mean is, this latest murder seems to have been performed in haste—as if riding the coattails, as it were, of the previous murders. Of course, if one evaluates what it takes to kill and quarter a man, give the blood time to drain, then transport it in sections to a different location altogether, this one was sloppy to a fault," Mycroft replied. "And, although I am all but certain the same butcher was used, it was not intended to impart a message primarily to the Chinese community."

"What of the seafaring community?" Sherlock mused. "If many are Chinese…"

"My thought as well," Mycroft said. "Where else do Chinese intermingle freely with whites but at the docks, and aboard ship? These latest murders may be meant to warn those white sailors who would understand via such a display that the perpetrators mean business, and that Caucasians are not exempt from punishment."

Sherlock bit his tongue to stop himself from recounting the similarities between the man who lay dead in the street, his nose amputated, his body in quarters, and the scoundrel who had assailed him when he and Douglas found Charles. Or The Water Monkey where Charles once worked, and the blood he noticed on Juju's costly shoe.

But he could not. For, among other reasons, Juju had seen the marks on Sherlock's arm—and that was the last thing he wished to explain to Mycroft.

29

AFTER A VISIT TO HIS TAILOR ON JERMYN STREET TO RID his brother of his vile garments, Mycroft sat across from Sherlock in the carriage, contemplating his next move. He had to be cautious: the last thing he wished was to further entice him. Not that Sherlock needed enticement, for he was a thoroughbred at the starting line. One way or the other, he would clamber his way onto the track.

Best to control his involvement, Mycroft thought, *to give him assignments that will keep him busy but out of harm's way.*

To this end, he gave Sherlock an account of his visit to Beeton the sweep and to Madame de Matalin but omitted the meeting that he'd witnessed between Cainborn and the Chinese gentleman, or the three-time appearance of the yellow landaulet.

And, he said nothing for the moment about the calling cards or the name William Angel.

"Now. You will spend the next several days with the Quinces, perfecting your Latin—after which you will present me with a fit oration. In exchange, I shall persuade Douglas to accompany you on a hunt for a proper translator, perhaps as soon as Monday morning."

"Fair deal!" Sherlock grinned.

"But, the moment you are lax in your studies," Mycroft warned, "all this 'sleuthing' ceases immediately. Are we clear?"

"Why ever do you say 'sleuthing' as if you were handling week-old liver?" his brother asked, a smile lighting up his very nearly handsome face. "Do you despise it as much as all that?"

"Yes."

Sherlock leaned over and opened the trap. "Huan?" he called.

"Yes, Master Sherlock!" came the reply, Huan's voice battling to carry over the wind's caterwauling, for it was a blustery day.

"Would you happen to know what *shòu-shòu* means?"

"Of course!" Huan replied jovially. "We say it in Port of Spain! Means *thin-thin!*"

"Wherever did you hear that phrase?" Mycroft asked his brother.

"A coolie with a rucksack spit it my way," Sherlock said, shutting the trap. "I am fairly certain it was not meant as a compliment; nevertheless, I was curious."

Thin-thin, Mycroft thought, frowning. *Well, Sherlock is certainly that.*

But again, something was not right. A random insult from a stranger would not ruffle Sherlock's feathers in the least; he had been teased unmercifully by classmates as a child, for he did nothing to try to fit in with the crowd. And though he could still recall each raillery with painful precision, he was very nearly inured against verbal torment.

No, Sherlock had brought it up for a reason. He was continuing to keep a secret or three, Mycroft could have sworn to it. But at the moment, there was nothing he could do. Best to see how it all played out.

"Now. What say we try to locate that quilted bag, eh?" Mycroft asked, and Sherlock's smile grew even brighter.

Huan stopped the carriage at the crumbling building the color of pitch that Sherlock had recalled perfectly. Since it was not yet dark, there was no sleeping rag-and-bone man to block the door to the small warehouse. When Mycroft opened it, its hinges squealed like a piglet chasing after its mother. With Huan acting as bodyguard in case of mischief, they entered.

The room beyond was as George had described: a miserable hole infested with vermin but sound enough to impede wind and rain. The ancient newspapers that the boys had used as bedding were scattered about, and beside an old bucket, which most likely served as a makeshift latrine, was the quilted bag they sought.

Sherlock snatched it up and felt inside, but it was empty. He counted the compartments within: twenty, and arranged in circles. This made it cumbersome to place the symbols therein in some particular order, though it could not yet be discounted.

Prize in hand, he and Mycroft returned to the carriage.

Mycroft frowned at the quilted bag on the seat beside Sherlock.

"Why did Charles not take the bag with him?" Mycroft asked. "He could have slipped it underneath his jacket. Why bother to stash it here? And why, when Douglas interviewed him at Nickolus House, did he say that he was 'saving up' for a good used watch? Gin was paying him something. Else, why do it? And used watches are not so dear that he could not have purchased one by now."

"Unless he was using the money to procure his own drugs," Sherlock said.

"Did you not say that the lashes on Charles's back, and on his brother's, were approximately of the same 'vintage,' as it were? Perhaps he was giving Beeton money to stop hurting George," Mycroft posited.

"It was Madame de Matalin who sent the boys to Nickolus House and who had offered to pay for their room and board there. But how did she learn of the boys to begin with?" Sherlock wondered. "It's a bit much to think that, since they were both drug addicts, they knew each other. If that were the case, the good Madame would be acquainted with a third of London!"

"Exaggeration to make a point is not helpful in this case, Sherlock," Mycroft said. "So to summarize, it may be that Charles himself was protected from Beeton by his employer, but George was not, and so Beeton had to be paid off with his earnings. At some point, Charles must've grown weary of the arrangement. Perhaps he asked Madame de Matalin for assistance…"

"…and de Matalin contacted Nickolus House," Sherlock concluded, "providing both boys with a way out."

Sherlock mulled over this newest information. The pockmarked boy that Mycroft and Douglas had seen hurrying away from Beeton's was possibly the same lad who went to inform Gin of Charles's demise, thereby unknowingly leading McPeel and Ducasse to The Water Monkey.

And Madame de Matalin's could have been Charles's destination, and where Sherlock himself might go, if Juju saw fit to employ him.

Thin-thin, Juju's rotund henchman had called him.

A compliment perfect for the work at hand, if Sherlock's suppositions proved accurate.

30

SCOTTISH SURGEON JOSEPH BELL WAS TEN YEARS OLDER than Mycroft, yet he seemed to him infinitely wiser as he listened to Mycroft's heart, paused a moment, then listened again.

"Inherited susceptibility," Bell muttered, which struck Mycroft as ironic, given the circumstances.

"I *have* been under pressure lately," he ventured, "that can certainly be labeled 'inherited.' My brother Sherlock is often more than I can manage…"

It was a joke, and a weak one at that. But there were not even signs of polite amusement on Bell's face. He simply lifted the cold stethoscope from Mycroft's chest and bid him wait a moment before putting his shirt back on.

Bell had a military bearing, a high forehead, a strong jawline, and features that just skirted handsomeness, given a slightly hooked nose. And although his light-colored eyes were kind, he was rather inscrutable, even for a formidable appraiser like Mycroft Holmes. He suspected that Bell had taken some pains to become so, most likely as protection against nosy patients.

"Is there something the matter with my heart?" Mycroft asked pointedly.

Dr. Bell removed his spectacles and rubbed the bridge of his nose. He took Mycroft's pulse, as he had already done a half-dozen times, dropped Mycroft's arm, waited five seconds, then lifted it once more.

"What is this about?" Mycroft inquired, unnerved.

"The pulse. It has twelve variables of rhythm, each one distinct, each forecasting a different outcome. And yes," he said as he pressed his thumb into Mycroft's wrist before releasing it one last time. "There *is* something wrong with your heart."

Mycroft thought back to the physical examination he'd endured a few years previous with the Methuselah of doctors, "physician to Prince Albert" Sir James Clark, and what Clark had said upon examining his heart: *Not a pleasant sound at all—like water sloshing in there, Mr. Holmes.*

Was it within the realm of the feasible that both he and Douglas suffered from some ailment of the heart? Douglas due to those small but potent bullets lodged nearby, and he from… he had no notion. In any event, Bell was taking a Saturday morning not only to discuss Charles Fowler, but also to put Mycroft under the stethoscope. For it was Bell who had commanded him to lie down the moment he'd laid eyes on him.

"With the stethoscope, I hear what is called a 'friction rub,' lower left sternal border," Bell was saying in his light Scottish brogue. "From other sounds, as well as symptoms you have mentioned and I've observed, including the slight swelling in your feet, the left ventricle of your heart is enlarged, and you have a murmur. The murmur is light and intermittent, yet it is there all the same, rather stubbornly so. Childhood illnesses?"

"Rheumatic fever, aged three," Mycroft replied.

"Ah. Well then, these issues have likely been present for many years, nothing to do about it. Unfortunately, the already weakened muscle has been badly compromised."

"By what? A poison of some kind?" Mycroft blurted out.

"Poison?" Dr. Bell responded, eyes widening. "Whatever gave you that idea? No. A bout of untreated malaria."

Mycroft was speechless. He looked around the examination room in which he sat, trying to collect his thoughts. There were but two chairs, one for the patient and one for Bell, and a clean white counter upon which rested the most basic physicians' implements: a microscope, a thermometer, an ophthalmoscope, a kymograph, alcohol, hydrogen peroxide, carbolic acid, and an assortment of unguents and astringents.

The counter also held a handful of books: among which was the one Mycroft had seen at the chemist's, the *Shen-nung Pen Ts'ao Ching.*

Mycroft latched upon it so as to focus his floundering brain. "What do you think of that?" he inquired.

"Well, roughly translated it is 'Divine Husbandman's *Materia Medica,*'" Dr. Bell replied. "A foundational book for Chinese medicine, from what I glean."

"And do you? *Glean* from it?" Mycroft asked.

"Not a word," Bell admitted. "But I find it fascinating nonetheless. Since I am in London but a few days a month, I share the facilities with four other physicians, one of whom speaks a bit of Mandarin. As he explained it, there are three hundred and sixty-five treatments, with an emphasis on grass and roots, some of which we use with great success in our own medicine. You've been to the tropics, I take it?" he said, returning to the unpleasant subject at hand.

"Yes," Mycroft stuttered, despising the sudden tremor in his voice. "Trinidad, two years ago."

"Ah."

Dr. Bell examined Mycroft's eyes, stretching each one open with a thumb and forefinger. "Well," he said at last. "No signs of gaze palsy or cerebral malaria." He prepared a hypodermic and inserted it into Mycroft's arm.

"Before you left for Trinidad, were you not given an antimalarial drug?" he asked as he drew blood. "They are absurdly easy to procure. There," he said upon completion. "Now you may put on your shirt."

Mycroft shamefacedly recalled that Sir James Clark had offered it, but that he had declined, thinking it the precautions of a doddering relic.

"And for the past two years you have had symptoms," Dr. Bell scolded. "You told me so yourself. Did they not warn you that something was amiss?"

"I chalked it up to general fatigue."

"No such thing," Dr. Bell said. "The enlargement and

the murmur—those, you could not help. But this newest damage is of your own doing."

"Is it too late to repent?" Mycroft asked, trying to make light of a bad situation. But when Dr. Bell said nothing, he added peevishly: "I would say that a blood-sucker had *something* to do with it, so there is blame enough to go around. In any event, what can be done about it now?"

"Now? Now there is nothing *to* do. Not until we discover ways of repairing the heart muscle without destroying the patient. No, though the infection might depart, the damage has been done. To tax your heart at all is suicide."

"What do you suggest? That I wait to die?" Mycroft asked, hoping he did not sound as nonplussed as he felt.

"We are all waiting to die, Mr. Holmes. Except for the dead, of course. *Their* wait is over. Speaking of which, you came here to find out about young Charles Fowler, did you not?"

Charles Fowler's naked body was as purple as the purple marble slab on which he lay. He had been placed in a room the size of a small pantry, next to a miniscule kitchen that had been gutted of everything save a wood-burning stove and specially built ice well, which was keenly unpleasant in the dead of winter but essential to preserve the occasional corpse longer than two days.

Dr. Bell explained. "A goodly number of my patients are alive at the time of my visit, though *this* particular corpse holds a few intriguing mysteries…"

Along with the numerous needle marks, both old and those newly created in Bell's extractions of blood, Charles bore the signs of incisions where the doctor had taken small samples of flesh.

"In terms of substances," Dr. Bell said, "morphine, opium, even tincture of opium. This is rare, as young addicts on the needle tend to become connoisseurs, one might say, of one drug or the other—rather than a variety. Then of course there is the difficulty of ensuring 'standard' dosages of *any* injectable drug. I at first assumed your boy here died of an accidental overdose. Now I am no longer certain."

"What other possibilities are there?" Mycroft inquired, surprised. "He did not do himself in, surely? Nor was he murdered…"

Though why anything should have surprised him at this juncture was truly the question.

"I do not believe in either scenario," Dr. Bell clarified. "But I discovered a compound I cannot place."

"Are you saying he injected himself, or was injected, with some foreign substance?"

"Aye, so it seems. I am willing to wager that is what killed him: a foreign substance whose potency or effect may not have been fully known or understood, thus the overdose. Simply put, it sent fluid into the alveoli—the air pockets in the lungs—thereby reducing the oxygen absorption, and he ceased to breathe. You said he was being chased?"

"Yes."

"There's the culprit. When one is injected with a

powerful narcotic, one should not stress the body after." Dr. Bell sighed. "I promised your friend Cyrus Douglas that the boy would be left intact, and so he is. I might have learned more, had I been allowed to cut more deeply, but never mind. Time for someone to come and take him off my hands before putrefaction begins in earnest."

With that, Dr. Bell took up a sheet that lay crumpled on the slab at Charles's feet and covered the body.

"One moment, if I may," Mycroft said as he uncovered Charles's right hand.

"What are you seeking?"

"I realize it is odd, but I would like to make a copy of the ridges in the thumb and forefinger of both hands."

"Truly? I have just the thing!" Dr. Bell said with more enthusiasm than Mycroft had witnessed up to that point.

Bell walked out of the makeshift morgue and back in again with a long strip of white fabric with some concoction slathered on it. "Invented by a fellow surgeon!" he said brightly. "A touch elaborate, I must admit…"

"Is that India rubber?" Mycroft asked, inspecting it.

"Yes, it is."

"And… turpentine. Pine gum, litharge, and whatever is this last?" He smelled it, rubbed it between his fingers. "Cayenne pepper?" he hazarded.

Dr. Bell nodded. "Extract of. The entire assemblage does a formidable job of holding wounds together. And if you press the boy's fingers to it, you will find it makes a fair if sticky copy. You can cover it with a bit of parchment to protect it," he added. "I have some here someplace…"

It took practice, but within minutes, Mycroft had two clean sets of Charles's finger ridges, one from the left hand and one from the right.

Dr. Bell led Mycroft to the front door. Mycroft paused on the step.

"I realize there is no need to mention this," he said, "but not a word to anyone of my condition. Especially to Cyrus Douglas or my brother, should you have occasion to see either."

"Of course," Dr. Bell replied. "Though I ache to think either might find you deceased and have no worldly notion why."

"Though I do not believe 'cause of death' has ever assuaged anyone's sorrow," Mycroft said, smiling wanly, "were I to drop dead, pray do not let my secret die with me."

Mycroft lifted his collar against the rain. He wished, more than anything, to walk in it, to be drenched and somehow cleansed by it.

But Huan and the carriage awaited. Whatever happened from now on, Mycroft would exhibit no signs of distress.

"Where to, Mr. Mycroft?" Huan asked, opening the trap as Mycroft clambered aboard.

"Nickolus House," Mycroft said. Though he could not share the news of his heart ailment with Douglas, still he craved his friend's companionship. Not to mention that he had that favor to ask. It was time to start fitting together the pieces of this strange little puzzle.

As the carriage juddered into motion, Mycroft opened the trap again. "Huan?"

"Yes, Mr. Mycroft?"

"Let us first make a detour to The Golden Bottle."

And after that, to his solicitor's office, for it was time for him to make his will.

Upon first blush, he'd considered dividing his fortune equally between Douglas and Sherlock, but he realized that would never do. Sherlock would not have the feeblest notion of how to manage it. No, better to leave it all to Douglas, with a generous monthly allowance for—

He heard the trap open again.

"Yes, Huan?" he said.

Please let me not hear of yet another murder, I cannot bear it!

"Sorry, Mr. Mycroft," he heard Huan say, his voice all apologies. "The bank is not open, for it is Saturday."

Oh for pity's sake! Mycroft thought. *I really* have *gone round the bend!*

"Right you are, Huan," he said in a tone as jovial as he could muster. "To Nickolus House, then!"

"Right away, Mr. Mycroft!"

He heard the whip crack smartly in the air, and they were off.

Of all the times to die, thought Mycroft crossly, *this is by far the most inopportune.*

31

THERE WAS SOMETHING DEEPLY COMFORTING ABOUT THE homely little kitchen with its rectangular wooden table. Though made to fit four, it did no such thing. But for two, with the kettle whistling on the ancient stove, and the rain tapping in rhythm against the windows, it was nigh-on perfect, better even in some ways than the leather armchairs and Armagnac at Regent Tobaccos.

For there was no striving here, no sense that life was somehow more than its most basic necessities: a hot cup of strong tea, shelter from the storm, and conversation with an old and trusted friend. Who could wish for more?

I for one, Mycroft thought grumpily.

He wished he did not have a faulty heart. He wished he could dream of a future that included wife and children. He wished he could keep the anxiety from his brain and the stentorian tone out of his voice, for he was sounding as gloomy and one-note as the rain outside.

"Should you ever come into money, Douglas," he was

lecturing his friend, "I pray I've impressed upon you the need to invest in gold. Especially in the next ten years or so."

Douglas rose to pull the spitting kettle off the stove. "You have impressed it upon me several times this evening," he said. Douglas's tone was patient and soothing. It was the sort of tone, Mycroft thought, one would utilize on a frightened child.

"I am simply asking you to remember *gold*," Mycroft pressed. "Gold can make all the difference. This country has become fat and irresponsible. British industry is lagging, small businesses have not bothered to keep up with the times or create any incentive to push our goods abroad. We are headed for economic disaster, and no one seems remotely alarmed."

"What can be done?" Douglas asked. "In this 'free trade' era, businesses have no fiscal protection. No protective tariffs, no special rates for transport. Who would risk moving their merchandise abroad, except for mad people such as I? You saw what transpired at Chesil Beach—I very nearly lost it all!"

"But that is what I mean! Certain laws have to be changed," Mycroft continued, his fingertips drumming the table. "Demonetization of silver, protective tariffs, foreign competition, throwing money senselessly at the railroads, unproductive foreign loans and investments, antiquated factories. We are being overtaken by Germany and the United States, Douglas! *Overtaken!*"

"Yes, yes, all right…" Douglas said as he poured water from the kettle into a teapot and waited for the tea leaves to steep. "You make it sound like Attila and his Huns are even now crossing the Channel."

"The poor understand ups and downs, for they live them every day," Mycroft went on. "But the rich? The powers that be in this country? They will keep on dancing on this sinking ship until..."

"Mycroft? You said you came here to ask a favor. I certainly hope it is not to hear you bemoan the weakening of Britain's international economic position, for there is little I can do about it tonight."

Mycroft sighed. "Forgive me, but you are the only person with whom I can discuss this with any degree of comprehension," he said as Douglas poured the tea. "Oh, there shall be economic upticks, but they will be short-lived. In the meantime, the troughs will be longer and longer until the end of the century, at which point the problem shall be something else entirely, one that I cannot as yet predict."

"No? You cannot see thirty years into the future? I am chagrined," Douglas said, taking a seat opposite his friend.

"This is why gold is the key," Mycroft concluded, not yet ready to be teased out of his fretful mood.

He took a sip of his tea while Douglas appraised him.

"You are as wound up as a mechanical monkey," Douglas told him. "A spot of brandy? There are dregs in the bottle, I am sure..." he added, rising again.

"Thank you, no," Mycroft said with a shudder, recalling the last time.

"Then kindly tell me what you are really about," Douglas said, resuming his seat.

The trickle of fear Mycroft had felt when predicting

Britain's impending economic sorrows had grown into a tsunami, but enough of that. "It is of no consequence, Douglas," he replied, changing course. "How are your boys? McPeel and Ducasse. They all right?"

"I had to tell them in no uncertain terms that their tenure depended on following the rules of Nickolus House to the letter. I doubt I put fear of God into them but I *am* hoping that the fear of Smythe will keep them reasonably compliant for a while."

"I am dismayed that my brother is the cause of any troubles that have come your way," Mycroft said. "But I do have some news in that regard."

He proceeded to share with Douglas all that Sherlock had discovered, at least insofar as he had been told… for he continued to have the niggling suspicion that he'd not been told it all.

"Did you perhaps recognize the corpse on Narrow Street as being one of the men who assaulted Charles?" Mycroft asked when he was done.

"Not at all," Douglas admitted. "The night was dark as pitch, and I do not have the cat eyes your brother seems to possess. Besides, I rather flew over him too quickly: I was more intent on nabbing the blackguard who had Charles by the arm. Why, did Sherlock identify him as such?"

"No, he did not."

"Well then, it seems rather a leap, does it not?" Douglas said.

"Possibly not. I saw something in my brother's eyes

when I caught him staring at the body, in that half-second before he noticed me. Recognition has its own expression, after all, and it did not alter one iota from the dead man to me; it was the same look of surprised familiarity."

"But if he recognized the body," Douglas protested, "surely he would have told you, for it is a matter of some import!"

"Indeed. And were I to wonder if this last death had something to do with Charles," Mycroft added, "might you accuse me of entirely too much imagination?"

"Perhaps we have been associates for too long," Douglas replied. "For I too felt some link between Charles and the dead body. After all, here is a boy who traipses about in a blighted neighborhood in brand-new garb—a mark for thieves if ever there was one—yet goes blithely along. It is not out of the realm of the possible that young Charles was being protected, that he knew he was, and so did George, but that his assailants were not aware of the fact until they found out the hard way."

"Yes," Mycroft said. "The man who died was of no account. His was a body long used to neglect. But if his murder was meant to impart a lesson, then why are not all three men dead who assaulted you?"

"More tea?" Douglas inquired.

"Please," Mycroft said, finishing the last of his cup.

Douglas rose, picked up the tongs to move the glowing cinders about, and set the kettle once more upon the stove.

"When Sherlock and I came upon them," he said to Mycroft, "Sherlock's assailant was third in line, thereby assuming the least risk. Yet, he was certainly the most fierce. When first I landed in their midst, the two in front glanced quickly *behind* them, a foolish move unless one is awaiting orders."

"But you gave them no time to rally," Mycroft guessed.

"No, the element of surprise being a powerful weapon in itself. In any event, I marked him the leader of his small crew of miscreants."

Mycroft joined his hands, tapping his index fingers together. "And naturally my mind went immediately to Beeton the chimney sweep."

"Ah. Now *there*, I do not follow. Why would that be?" Douglas asked.

"At a certain point, that nasty little man stopped beating both Charles and George. Sherlock and I guessed that Charles's money might have gone in part to protect his little brother, but now I wonder if Charles's newfound affiliation made him untouchable, in that he was now the 'property' of someone else."

"Knowing the streets, that would be the most likely scenario," Douglas said, nodding. "Then bruises on the boy would no doubt be inconvenient."

"Precisely," Mycroft said. "Let us continue to suppose that Charles was being utilized to test the strength of new batches of drugs for upper-crust users such as Madame de Matalin, to ensure the poor old dear would not suffer an overdose. We'd then surmise that a client of that caliber would not want to see a boy purple with welts and contusions from a beating.

It is a matter of aesthetics! But, bad as it may be, I am hard pressed to think what any of it has to do with us."

The kettle whistled again.

Douglas stared into his cup, the second round of tea already forming an oily ring of brown against the white porcelain. Tiny fragments of leaves, not properly strained, created a smudge at the bottom, and he wondered what a gypsy might read in the patterns they made.

"This house, named after my son, takes in some of the poorest, most unfortunate creatures that ever walked the earth," he said softly. "It offers them safety and security for the first time in their lives. Now someone has murdered or was responsible for the death of one of the creatures in my charge. Last night, I held a sobbing eleven-year-old boy in my arms, and I expect to do so again tonight and every night until his sorrow abates so that he can get a decent night's sleep. Now, to hear you and Sherlock tell it, his brother was being used in the most appalling way—"

"Again, we are speculating—"

"Even so, it has much to do with me. But I am not equipped to tackle it alone. I would be unmoored. And so, though I do not yet know what favor you are to ask of me, I ask one of you. I would dearly appreciate whatever continued assistance you can give me."

"Of course," Mycroft said. "No need to even ask. What say we start with the symbols? Might you have them translated? I could do so through the War Office, but not without raising eyebrows…"

"No need. I believe I can get it done."

"As soon as Monday, perhaps? For if Sherlock is correct and they are collected once per month, we haven't much time to get to the bottom of this."

"I have a handful of contacts I can get in touch with to see if any are amenable," Douglas said. "We are at full staff here again; I can most likely be spared."

"Wonderful. And you will allow Sherlock to accompany you?"

Douglas looked at Mycroft askance. "I feel as if I have been led into a trap by the nose. May I ask why?"

"Because we will need him," Mycroft said. "And not only for the fact that he beat us to the punch, but also because I cannot take away from him what he has already discovered… though I shall do my utmost to keep him from danger."

"We might well be battling people who would sacrifice a child in order to sell their product to a wealthy addict," Douglas reminded him.

"He returns to Cambridge on Friday. I shall have Huan accompany him on the train, remain with him while he presents his orals, then escort him back to London."

"So you are determined to tell him the whole truth?" Douglas asked.

"What about?" Mycroft shot back.

"The Chinese gentleman?" Douglas said, puzzled by Mycroft's reaction. "Cainborn? The landaulet?"

"Ah. Not yet, but possibly as the links grow stronger."

"And so 'the fates lead the willing, and drag the unwilling,'" Douglas said.

"You needn't sound so sour about it," Mycroft remonstrated. "Have some faith in us. For *I* do. 'There is a tide in the affairs of men, which, taken at the flood, leads on to fortune,'" he quoted.

"Well. If you are to parry Seneca with *Julius Caesar*," Douglas replied, "then pray recall the rest of the verse: 'Omitted, all the voyage of their life is bound in shallows and in miseries—'"

"But we *have* the tide!" Mycroft protested.

"'On such a full sea are we now afloat,'" Douglas continued, smiling sardonically, at which point the two completed the quote together: "'And we must take the current when it serves, or lose our ventures!'"

With that, they clasped hands—and it seemed to Douglas much too late to turn back.

32

AFTER TAKING TEA WITH DOUGLAS, MYCROFT RETURNED TO
St. John's Wood where he gave the household staff twenty-
four hours' leave. He retired to his spare but elegant bedroom,
with its small, comfortable bed, fireplace and padded chair.
On either side of the bed were two mahogany end tables,
each with a gaslight on the wall above it. He planned to
burrow underneath the covers, shut his eyes, and sleep most
of the Sunday away—and the night too, for that matter.

He was so damnably tired. With everyone out of the
house or retired to their own rooms, he would not be
disturbed until Monday morning. At which point, he would
stand on the pavement as always, smelling the incipient rain
and waiting for Huan and the carriage to come. He would
greet his neighbor, who had reconciled with his wife.

Lovely day, is it not, Mr. Holmes? the neighbor would
proclaim, though it would be nothing of the sort. Then his
carriage would pull up, with Huan at the reins waving like
a child on a carousel, and Sherlock sullen but determined

in the back. Mycroft would grill his brother, deposit him wherever he and Douglas had arranged to meet—at the docks most likely—and then be off again for his bank, and then to his solicitor, where his last will and testament could finally be put to paper.

For now, he thought, burrowing further under the bedclothes, *what I need is sleep… just a touch of sleep.*

And yet, sleep would not come. Those calling cards in Madame de Matalin's boudoir floated before him, black with finger ridges, like a parlor trick at a séance.

What were those purposeful soot stains meant to reveal?

Mycroft, images dancing before his eyes, sat up in bed, reached over in the darkened room and turned on one of the gaslights in the hopes that it would impart figurative as well as literal clarity. It hissed to life but merely illuminated the space around him.

He opened the watch winder on the end table, checked the time and found it to be well past midnight.

Perhaps a stroll, he thought. *To Piccadilly.*

Why not? It was less than three miles. Walking might even prove bracing on a chilly, bone-dry night like this.

But once there, what would he do? Bang insistently upon the Madame's door until her cadaverous butler opened it, and demand to inspect the good woman's boudoir? Perhaps he could crawl up the side of de Matalin's house like a spider, pry open her window, tiptoe to the bureau where her bejeweled box of paraphernalia lay and help himself to its contents while she blissfully slept.

Nonsense, all of it. Why could he not let it go?

Because in his mind's eye he could see her window, open just enough to be accessible. When he and Douglas had visited, in spite of the prohibitive weather, it had been left ajar. And though Mycroft had assumed that a servant would surely close it, no one ever did—not while he lay insensate upon her floor, and not later, while she was recounting her many fears. For her chamber windows were directly above the library and were heavy and large. If they had been closed while he and Douglas were still there, surely he would have heard the sound.

Drug addicts were often contrary in nature, he knew: abusing questionable substances while loudly proclaiming the health benefits of damp or frigid air from open windows, immersions in scalding hot baths, or diets consisting principally of carrots.

Whatever the reason, the open window continued to beckon him.

He was about to extinguish the light and attempt to sleep when he was startled by a knock upon his front door, followed by a ring of the bell. Mycroft threw on a robe and slippers and padded downstairs to see who it could be.

Through the front door glass, he was surprised to see Huan's concerned face.

"Why are you about?" Mycroft asked as he opened the door.

"Why do you have your light on, Mr. Mycroft?" Huan returned accusingly. "I am thinking perhaps you need me."

"It is past midnight. You are not in bed?"

"Bed? No, no!" Huan replied in an offended tone. "I passed by, I saw your light, I must know if you are well. It is my job to protect you, Mr. Mycroft! I must do my job, no?"

Mycroft shook his head, awed. "You truly are a wonder. Come in, Huan, come in, for I can surely use your help," he concluded before he could talk himself out of it.

With that, he hurried back upstairs to change.

From the street, Mycroft could see de Matalin's second-floor window. Just as he suspected, it was slightly ajar; unreachable from where he stood but perfectly accessible if one were to park one's carriage as close to the wall as possible, climb up to the top of the vehicle and then reach up the entirety of one's height, from tiptoes to fingertips.

Provided, of course, that one was at least six feet tall.

It had taken some doing to persuade Huan that he would remain the driver and Mycroft the climber. Given Huan's dexterousness, he likely could have scaled the wall from the street with nothing but a running start. With this fact on his side, Huan had not given up easily.

Mycroft had finally been forced to remind him who paid whose keep.

They had timed the route of the single constable whose beat included the Madame's street: Mycroft had eight minutes in which to squeeze through the window, find the paraphernalia box in the dark, '*tief*' the cards, as Huan put it, then climb back out and be on his way. He had racked his brain, trying to come up with a more effective plan than simple purloining, but with limited time and resources, he could think of no other solution.

Standing on the carriage, Mycroft stretched up towards the window ledge, his height a quarter-inch shy of ideal. As his arms, toes and fingertips stretched to their limit, he spurred himself on with the thought that he had just found another sector in which to deposit his money. If he was not shot this night or dead of heart failure, perhaps he would live long enough to see an invention that could quickly replicate a document, and that could fit inside one's waistcoat pocket!

Mycroft finally managed to get a hold of the blasted ledge and pull himself up until his knees were resting on the jutting strip of wood.

As the carriage underneath him rolled away, he waited a moment, allowing his combative heart to slow, and then furtively pushed the window open far enough to clamber inside.

The scene in the darkened boudoir was very nearly as he had imagined it: he could hear de Matalin's steady inhale, followed by a noisier, more boisterous exhale. Thanking his keen memory, he walked directly to her bureau and laid a hand on the small Limoges box, with its telltale encrusted stones. He moved aside the vial, the syringe, the needle and the pipe, and dislodged the false bottom, which made a slight cracking sound—causing de Matalin's breath to catch and his own to halt for a second or two. Once she began to breathe normally again, he lifted out the cards and placed them in his jacket pocket.

Then, on impulse, he pilfered the magnifying glass as well, shut the box, and bolted out of the window with a few moments to spare.

He hung by his fingertips, suspended between heaven and earth, waiting for Huan to appear before the constable did, listening for the sound of hooves and wheels coming around the corner. If someone were to spot him now, he was done for.

Just as his fingertips were cramping and about to cede, the carriage passed underneath him. He released his hold, then balanced atop as Huan drove them away from the scene of his crime.

From there, he lowered himself back into the seat through the carriage's open window as if carriages were built for nothing but this.

"You found what you were after?" he heard Huan say through the trap.

"Yes, Huan, and I could not have done it without you," Mycroft replied. "Now, pray you, drive slowly," he added, "and watch for pits in the road."

As the carriage turned the corner past the policeman making his rounds, Mycroft pulled the cards and magnifying glass from his jacket pocket, his hands shaking. By the light of the small lantern that swung from the ceiling of the cab, he took the beaker with Charles's fingerprints out of the brass vase-holder on the door where he had placed it. Keeping the cards in their original order, he attempted to match Charles's finger marks to the smudges on the first card and was pleased with a quick reward.

Mycroft knew that each Saturday night, Douglas stayed over at Nickolus House, for his mythical Mr. Smythe had charged him with accompanying the boys to church each Sunday. Douglas would therefore not find it the least bit odd to be roused from sleep by the occasional childish bickering, the indignant retorts of aggrieved adolescence. But surely he did not expect Mycroft and Huan at his door at three in the morning.

Mycroft could read it in his friend's expression as he led them inside.

Huan let out a yawn and stretched his arms out. "Now you are safe," he said as Douglas wordlessly led them towards the kitchen, "perhaps I have a little lie-down, yes?"

"The guest room is yours," Douglas said, pointing to the second floor, even though there was no need, for Huan knew the way.

As Huan took the stairs, Douglas turned to Mycroft, eyebrow upraised. "'*Now* you are safe'?" he asked.

"I was never in danger," Mycroft replied, "strictly speaking." This caused Douglas's eyebrow to rise even further.

They walked down the hall to the kitchen and sat across from each other at the table, Douglas looking about as spent as the fire.

"Chilly in here," Mycroft said.

"Drafty old building," Douglas replied, making no move to remedy it.

Mycroft reached into his jacket pocket and did as his brother had: he led with the evidence.

"Do not reprimand me for stealing," Mycroft begged as he did so. "Rather, look through the lens and compare the calling card on top with the prints in the beaker."

Douglas hesitated, then said: "You went through her window, I assume?"

"With a bit of assistance from Huan and the carriage," Mycroft confessed.

Douglas made a disapproving noise in his throat, but at last picked up the magnifying glass.

"Naturally there is no 'science' to finger ridges," Mycroft admitted as Douglas peered through it, comparing prints. "We cannot know, for example, if finger marks are unique to the individual or alter over the course of time, or are altered by specific events or even after death, for there has been precious little experimentation done on them. Charles's fingers, for example, were grossly swollen by pooled blood. A few more hours, and the skin would have begun to split, rendering them all but useless…"

He would have said more but for Douglas's pained expression.

"The point is, his prints in death match those of the top card, would you not agree?"

"They are identical," Douglas said quietly.

"I therefore posit the following scenario," Mycroft said, keeping his voice low. "This man, William Angel, is a trusted confidante of Madame de Matalin's, or he is a procurer of street urchins, or both. For the moment, what they are to each other is less intriguing than what they are not."

"And why would that be?" Douglas asked.

"Why a card?" Mycroft said in response. "If he has a willing, capable boy, why not simply appear at her doorstep and say, 'Here is your willing, capable boy!' But he does not."

"Perhaps he does not wish the close association," Douglas surmised.

"Perhaps. But the boy has that association with de Matalin, he sees her manservant, he knows her quarters. Why would Angel protect *himself* so assiduously, but not his 'client'? No, there must be a better reason. Let us suppose she wishes to inject various substances into her veins," Mycroft continued, "but she does not wish to keel over dead because the potency of the latest batch has altered, or because the drug itself is one for which she has developed no tolerance. Street urchins may be expendable and drugs legal, but using a child as a human pincushion is still the sort of shenanigans that would be highly frowned upon in polite society."

"One can only hope," Douglas replied.

"That said," Mycroft went on, "Angel still has to ensure that the boy is willing and able, and that he can keep such an odious secret. So he hires the boy but does not bring him directly, for reasons yet unknown. The boy appears at her door, feigning to look for work as a sweep or anything else. In his pocket, he carries Angel's calling card with the finger marks—the first step in assuring the boy's legitimacy. De Matalin, or more likely her butler, then observes as the lad makes a new set of prints beside the old."

"But wouldn't any specified object or code word do as well?" Douglas objected.

"No. An object can be appropriated, a code word overheard. But there is no disguising finger marks. Both sets are inspected, and if a match, everyone is off to the races."

"Reasonable *and* horrific," Douglas replied. "But what happens tomorrow, when she opens her box and finds the cards gone, along with her magnifying glass?"

"They were under a false bottom. She will not be putting anything in, or taking anything out, until a new boy is found for her. Charles has been dead less than four days. And Angel must procure another lad that, albeit a drug user, is willing to forsake his own habit, has a strong constitution, can be trusted to keep a secret that practically invites blackmail, and is personable besides."

Douglas nodded. "And let us not forget is small enough, or thin enough, that he is a match for de Matalin—for it would do no good to have a big, burly lad with a voracious appetite for narcotics as her laboratory specimen. Still," Douglas continued, "if she finds that the cards have been purloined, along with the glass…"

"Then perhaps she will have the fright of her life and cease these horrendous activities," Mycroft replied. "I would cry no tears over *that*. Oh, and I was careful to remove the cards from her box in the same order in which she placed them. The most common placement of a series is oldest at bottom, newest on top. I believe Charles was boy number six: the last of the lads who acted as her taster… and who may've died of it."

Douglas sighed and shook his head. "Six boys? Are you speculating that *all* died?" he asked.

"I have no evidence," Mycroft replied, "merely conjecture. One does not 'retire' from this sort of work. I suppose one can outgrow it, if he lives that long. Like the chimney sweeps, he becomes too big to be of use. But even then, allowing such a one to keep secrets for a lifetime seems the height of recklessness."

"But what manner of people are these, who can do such ghastly things?"

"A question like that from you?" Mycroft countered. "After all the evil you have witnessed in your lifetime?"

"I pray that it always catches me unawares. For the moment I am too tempered, too seasoned to it… I am lost."

33

SUNDAY 1 DECEMBER PASSED WITHOUT INCIDENT AND NARY a drizzle. The morning papers revealed that Saturday's football match between Scotland and England had resulted in a disappointing zero-all tie. Douglas smiled and lifted a victorious fist for his friend Mycroft's behind-the-scenes triumph. After that, in the name of the sickly but pious Mr. Smythe, Douglas escorted his young charges to church, then back home to Nickolus House for a hale breakfast. After which, bellies filled, he watched them play a rousing game of football in the chill winter air.

In terms of rules, the match was haphazard at best, and altogether too vocal, but the players seemed merry. One contingent was England, the other Scotland, for every player in Britain worth his salt was set to putting right the previous day's wrong via a neighborhood match.

Towards evening, Douglas planned to visit the docks and secure a translator for Sherlock. He knew Sherlock was staying at Edwardes Square and would get word to him about a place and time to meet. But for the moment, he invested what he could in the children's game and for a time managed to forget all about Madame de Matalin and chimney sweeps and finger ridges and yellow landaulets and murder.

He was doubly grateful when George, however tentatively, kicked the ball around. And he marveled, not for the first time, at the stubborn resilience of children.

Sherlock, in residence on Edwardes Square, made the best of his temporary lot in life. The house was commodious, albeit with that too-new sterility that made every room seem all corners and sharp edges. The twins' father, Mr. Quince, a barrister whom Sherlock had never met, was once again away on business, though he made his presence known from a side table by the sofa. In a silver frame atop an embroidered doily sat the photograph of a long, pale, balding figure with an equally pale mustache and goatee, who stared out into the room like a man doing his utmost to appear austere, but who succeeded only in looking bewildered. Eli and Asa hardly spoke of him—a pity, Sherlock thought, as he had always been keen to learn more about the man—and he wondered how much time the twins had spent in his company.

As for Mrs. Quince, she was as wan and spectral as her boys. Sherlock was hard pressed to believe she even cast a shadow. He and the twins saw her only at dinner, when her few whispery words addressed the flavor, consistency and relative portions of the meal at hand, which she usually greeted with something akin to resigned disapproval.

Sherlock concluded that he had never met anyone as quiet, as downright sepulchral, as Mrs. Quince and her boys.

All in all, they should have been a brilliant study of "nature versus nurture." Though anthropologist Francis Galton, Charles Darwin's cousin, had coined the term of late, the concept had obsessed philosophers for eons. Plato was convinced that Nature determined what personality traits one possessed, whereas Aristotle was certain that environment and experiences defined and directed one's actions and world view.

Sherlock had hoped that observing the twins would lead to more grounded theories about the mind: whether it held a primacy of inherited or learned behavior. But although he saw physical similarities between Eli, Asa and their mother, and certain movements and expressions were surely the same, nothing tipped the scale of one path over the other.

In any event, Latin had temporarily subsumed everything else. Though he would have to meet Mycroft's exacting standards, he found that, with incentive, it became very nearly tolerable. It simply needed context. And that context had nothing whatever to do with ancient, musty texts that spoke of Caesars long gone and that served no purpose... and everything to do with his desire to get on with the business of sleuthing.

Monday morning came to pass just as Mycroft had predicted it would, with one notable exception. When Mycroft's carriage arrived at Edwardes Square, Sherlock was ready and waiting. He was less sullen than Mycroft had assumed and his Latin a good deal better than he had hoped.

"Now tell me what Dr. Bell said of Charles's demise, along with any other pertinent information you might have for me," Sherlock said when he was done reciting.

Mycroft dutifully filled him in—though he did not mention that he had entered through de Matalin's window and stolen from her, or that he had made copies of Charles's fingerprints, for he had not yet informed Sherlock about William Angel or his cards.

As Mycroft's carriage reached the docks, Sherlock repeated Dr. Bell's phrase: "He said physicians found 'a compound of unknown origin' in Charles?" he asked. "You are certain that is what he said?"

"Sherlock, please," Mycroft said with an exasperated sigh as Sherlock opened the carriage door. "Now. When you spend time with Douglas, give him his due as having lived longer. Take his lead. Your belief that he is simply a good-natured sot with a proclivity for hand-to-hand combat is not only regrettable but damaging, for you do not yet see the use he can be to you."

But he knew that Sherlock was not really listening, that his mind was already on what he referred to, in street parlance, as "the case."

And he had to admit to himself, if to no one else, that it was beginning to consume him too.

34

THE LONDON DOCKS WERE AN ENORMOUS EXPANSE THAT went from the Ratcliffe Highway to the River Thames, where they boasted three entrances: Hermitage, Wapping, and Shadwell. Sherlock, walking about, was conscious of what a small portion he had run past a few days before. Seeing it in its immensity was a whole other proposition. Just one dock had enough width, length and breadth to comfortably host some five hundred ships. Between dockworkers and their bosses, he estimated more than three thousand men were employed here, with another few thousand desperate souls clamoring for whatever scraps of labor were left. The din of mechanism and human toil—the clang of steel, whistles, rattling chains, snapping ropes, commands and curses, loading and unloading—was deafening.

The air smelled of fog and soot: here and there a ship's engines would roar to life, its smokestack coughing up plumes of black smoke.

As he walked by the cacophonous bustle, Sherlock could

taste the fumes at the back of his throat. He placed his scarf over his nose and mouth but moments later thought better of it. That small act had attracted a passel of ne'er-do-wells like sharks to blood. With impure motives—most likely having to do with his wallet or pocket watch—a half-dozen scoundrels began to follow him.

Sherlock was not keen to engage in fisticuffs with six strangers, mostly because he wished to reach Douglas in one piece, and with his wits still firmly planted in his head. He wrapped the scarf around his neck once more, then hunched his shoulders and dug his hands into his pockets. Best to simply hold his breath and continue on to Shadwell Dock, where he would try to locate Douglas as quickly as possible.

Shadwell boasted only fifty ships—a pittance, in comparison to its bigger brothers. But its warehouses were immense, with the largest more than seven hundred feet long. Bustling through and amongst the men, and looking self-important, were customs officers, whose job seemed to Sherlock both thankless and endless, for there were too many shipments for a mere army of men to plow through.

In the cacophony of Shadwell Dock Stairs, in a light but persistent drizzle as the fog turned wet, Sherlock attempted to maintain an air of calm indifference while walking ever faster.

Finally—when the sound of his pursuers' feet was so close that he could hear the syncopated rhythm of their steps—he spotted Douglas. He was conversing with a short, burly Chinese dockworker who looked something like Huan, but who was as dark-browed and circumspect as Huan was sunny and expansive.

"Ah, there you are, Sherlock," Douglas said as their eyes met. "You brought company." Douglas's gaze shifted impassively from Sherlock to his retinue of malefactors. Sherlock barely had to look behind him to know that that one look had dissolved them like a foul mist into the surging crowd. Was it simply that Douglas was a tall, imposing Negro with a no-nonsense demeanor? Or had one or more known him by reputation and decided the game was not worth that particular candle?

"Sherlock Holmes, may I present my friend Ahn Zhang," Douglas said, his expression growing equitable again.

Zhang put out his hand, which Sherlock accepted.

"Mr. Zhang is here to look at your incisions," Douglas continued.

"My what?" Sherlock bleated, suddenly alarmed.

"The symbols," Douglas clarified.

"Oh. Certainly," Sherlock replied and began to pull his vielle out of its case.

"Not here. Ahn? Whenever you are ready…"

Zhang said nothing but began walking briskly from the dock onto a nearby quay, with Douglas behind him, and Sherlock third in line, laying the vielle back into its case as he went.

In the distance, the ships and their masts rocked in the wind. Zhang, eyeing them, turned and glanced at Douglas.

"Home for you, yes?" he said, indicating the ships.

"Oh yes," Douglas responded with a wistful smile. He pointed. "You see that clipper, first in line, wooden planking over an iron shell? That's *The Ambassador*. Full of herself, cranky and overmasted. Took us one hundred and fifteen days to get to Foochow. I have never been so glad to touch solid earth in my life. Even so, she's a lovely old girl. Sixth from her is the *Fiery Cross*, you see there? The one with but a single topsail. Did well in light breezes but could not utilize the Cape. A shame, for it put her out of the running as a merchant vessel, which she most certainly is. And that pretty one beside her is the *Flying Spur*, all teak and greenheart…"

"How can you tell one from the other from here?" Sherlock asked, as they appeared to him splotches in the distance, topped with various flags flapping in the sodden air.

Douglas laughed. "I take it you see no purpose to them, or you would know the answer immediately. And you?" he asked Zhang. "Have you sailed much?"

Zhang shook his head, his expression moving from closed to impenetrable. "Sail once, Shanghai to London. Never again."

At last they came to a small ship so weathered that Sherlock was surprised she could stay upright. She sat high in the water, her green copper sheathing very nearly level with the waterline, which indicated she was empty of goods.

They clambered aboard and then below into her musty belly, where Zhang lit a match and set it to a copper lantern so tarnished that it glowed mint green. As the men's long shadows were cast across the bare, warehouse-like room, Zhang sat down on the dirt-encrusted floor, and Douglas joined him.

Sherlock crouched beside them and was opening the vielle case again when Douglas stopped him.

"What now?" Sherlock asked with some impatience.

"In Chinese calligraphy," Douglas explained, "a tiny fraction of a squiggle can change the meaning substantially. If Zhang does not think you can copy adequately, the entire exercise is useless."

Zhang mimed a squiggle in the air, and another that looked exactly like the first. "That," he said, "and that. Different word."

Lantern in hand, Zhang scratched a symbol into the dirty floor before him, then passed the light to Sherlock. Sherlock eyed the design and copied it. Zhang stared at Sherlock's handiwork, then drew another symbol beside it, more complex than the first.

Zhang followed every stroke that Sherlock made and nodded approvingly. "Good eye, steady hand," he said.

Douglas smiled. "Show him," he said to Sherlock, indicating the vielle case.

Sherlock pulled out the instrument and handed it to Zhang, who studied it carefully, while Sherlock and Douglas watched him with equal intent.

"These are *flowers*," he said at last.

"Flowers?" Douglas asked. "What sorts of flowers?"

Zhang shrugged. "*Flower* flowers. *Méiguī*. Rose," he said, pointing to various groupings of symbols. "*Yùjīnxiāng*. Tulip. This one, don't know name in English. It orange."

"Orange?" Douglas repeated. "There are many orange flowers, I'm afraid…"

"Don't know name in English," Zhang insisted. "That one *da-li-hua*…" he said, sounding out the Chinese pronunciation.

"Dahlia?" Douglas volunteered.

Zhang nodded. "That one *zǐsè*. Violet. This others, only know name in Chinese. *Lǎbā shuǐxiān*," he said, indicating one.

"But how does that help us?" Sherlock interrupted. "If you cannot translate the names into English, what use are you?"

"I say what I know!" Zhang replied, agitated. "That one, rose! That one, violet! That one, tulip! That one, dolly-ah! This, I know only in Chinese!"

"Tell us in Chinese, then!" Sherlock fumed.

"You write down?"

"No! Just… say them. Speak them out. I can remember."

"All of them? See how many!" Zhang protested, indicating the vielle case.

"Then say them slowly!" Sherlock declared. "And for pity's sake, enunciate, for I cannot be expected to reproduce the yowling sounds of such a language unless I am—"

"Sherlock!" Douglas warned, but it was too late. Zhang rose to his feet. Douglas did the same, and shook his hand. "Thank you, my friend. You have been invaluable to us."

Zhang brushed the dirt from his trouser legs.

"You crazy boy!" he announced to Sherlock before disappearing up the ladder.

Sherlock watched him go. "How," he demanded, incensed, "has he been 'invaluable'? *Flowers?* And not even in English. I did not mean to be rude——"

"Certainly you did," Douglas interjected. "For you are surely clever enough to hold your tongue when necessity warrants. Or perhaps," he added acerbically, "you have not yet learned the phrase *Humilitas occidit superbiam*?"

"'Humility kills pride'?" Sherlock responded, barely able to contain his disdain. "This had nothing to do with either pride *or* humility. I was simply trying to get on with the task at hand, and to not waste any more of our valuable time!"

"Nearly everything has to do with pride or humility when a human being is involved. You and I——for better or worse——are invested in this madness. Therefore, the only one who truly gave up 'valuable time,' for no other reason than to help, was Zhang. Ahn Zhang could have been a handy resource, had you simply been polite."

"Had he simply done as I directed..." Sherlock replied.

Douglas inhaled deeply. "Sherlock. Listen to me. The Chinese landed in Liverpool in 1834, when the first vessels from China docked there to trade in cotton and silk."

"I am aware——"

"No, you most certainly are not. For you are as interested in Chinese culture as I in knitting. My point is this. That was less than forty years ago. Which means the most recent laborers, those who came in the late 1860s to work the Blue Funnel Line..."

"Probably all know one another," Sherlock concluded glumly.

"Perhaps you might practice, instead of sullen stubbornness, a certain detached amusement," Douglas went on. "The two perspectives are related, in that they both think less of other human beings than might be warranted. But, whereas detached amusement is tolerable, sullen stubbornness is not. Oh, people will still find you arrogant, but they will not be quite so insulted from the start, and some might even be strangely charmed."

"You are intimating that my reputation with the Chinese population is now sealed?"

"I am not *intimating* anything. I am saying it direct. Within an hour everyone will know of the ungrateful *gweilo.*"

"*Gweilo?*"

"Ghost man. White man. You."

As they climbed back up to the deck, everything seemed to Sherlock a personal affront: the gunmetal sky; the endless stream of bodies jostling his shoulder as they hurried past; the incessant smell of mold; the wind whipping his hair and provoking little tremors of cold that seemed an outward manifestation of his inward misery.

The work he had done to gather the symbols! Completing each little jot and tittle to perfection, rushing from one station to the next, and for what?

For nothing.

Douglas must have noticed his anguish, for he said: "All is not lost. You accurately copied what you saw. That is no small feat. As Ahn Zhang said, 'steady hand, good eye.'"

Sherlock was not fond of this compliment. He regarded it a rather pedestrian talent for the sort of vocation he wished to pursue. But he also thought it best to engage. After all, he had already soured one connection; he did not wish to make it two.

"My great-uncle, on my mother's side, was Horace Vernet," he replied.

"The French painter?" Douglas exclaimed as they reached the quay. "Mycroft never mentioned it!"

"No. He would not have. Mycroft does not wish to be reminded that a few drops of French blood are skulking about our veins like cat burglars, waiting for the opportune time to—well, to do something *French*, I suppose. In any event, neither the steadiness of my hand, the keenness of my eye nor my pedigree does me much good at present."

"Not so," Douglas corrected. "Thanks to your abilities, we now know that the symbols are flowers, and we have the names of four: rose, violet, tulip, and dahlia."

"And *lǎbā shuǐxiān*," Sherlock repeated dully.

"Daffodil," Douglas replied.

This took Sherlock by surprise. "How do you know?" he asked.

Douglas paused a moment, then said, "They were my wife's favorite. I brought back bulbs from one of my voyages. She tried to grow them on our windowsill, to no avail. And so, I began to search them out for her at the Chinese market in Port of Spain. The Chinese farmers knew how to give them their proper cooling times. They grew to be as big as kittens," Douglas said with a smile.

"We have five now," Sherlock mused, surprised that this small victory breathed a bit of life into him again.

"As for the other symbols," Douglas went on, "I will scout out someone else to translate, though I shall have to do so without your assistance."

Sherlock agreed. "And quickly," he added as he handed Douglas his vielle case. "For how long will this list be valid? Surely they have some other trusted 'someone' to collect in Charles's stead two weeks from now.

"You must promise to apprise me of whatever Mycroft has discovered," Sherlock concluded, and Douglas turned back and smiled.

"I promise that Mycroft will apprise you of whatever he deems fit, and that you are surely a vital part of this endeavor. And I promise that I shall not ask for promises from you in return, as you are not yet ready to grant them."

With that, Douglas nodded his goodbye and walked off.

Sherlock, watching him go, wondered at such an unusual man, one whose fundamental right-mindedness was not merely unnerving but impossibly naive.

Ah, well. Douglas's life and livelihood were none of his affair.

Five symbols translated, ten to go, he thought. And that very afternoon, he would pay another visit to The Water Monkey to see what else he might discover.

35

WHILE SHERLOCK AND DOUGLAS WERE AT THE DOCKS, Mycroft finally paid a visit to his solicitor, where he made quick work of his will. Upon his demise, the entirety of his worldly goods were to be left to Cyrus Douglas to manage as he saw fit. Sherlock's education would be paid for, and he would receive a stipend of one hundred pounds per annum, enough to get by but not enough to fritter away, until he turned twenty-five. From there, the sum in question would increase as variables did, such as marriage, children, et cetera.

Children.

The loss of children in his future was what Mycroft mourned the most. Those ghosts: a little boy with gray eyes like his father, a little girl with blue, like her mother.

Or perhaps ebony-haired children, with eyes the color of tourmaline, a warm brown with golden flecks...

But never mind, he reprimanded himself. It was too late for him. He would never marry. It would not be fair to a future bride to make her so soon a widow.

That done, he walked down Fleet Street, into rain so fine that it felt like the spray from a faraway ocean, and was immediately assailed by the bustle of enterprise.

No one strolled down Fleet Street. The district's many denizens all seemed to possess direction and purpose. Its bankers, accountants, barristers, newspapermen and tavern keepers were the embodiment of England's burgeoning middle class, and proudly so. No paltry, half-hearted soaking could quell the confident hum of this busy thoroughfare. Mycroft had hoped that its hive-like vitality would energize him, put a spring back into his step.

Unfortunately, the opposite was true. He felt lost. What good was all this damnable gumption? To what end was industry if one was to remain so painfully, so irrevocably alone?

Mycroft was deep in these morose thoughts when he spotted a familiar figure under an umbrella so wide it looked like a great black octopus. Charles Parfitt was holding onto it with both hands; his cheeks were two red flames of embarrassment that began at his neckline, and rose and spread from there into his temples and beyond, for the enormous parapluie was taking up the whole of the pavement. So engrossed was he with apologizing to inconvenienced passersby that he was all but spinning in place. Mycroft hurried over to him.

"Parfitt! What is that thing you are wielding?" he asked, laughing.

Parfitt looked extremely relieved to see him. He extended

his arms so that the contraption was now fully shielding Mycroft, while he himself stood in the drenching rain.

"Parfitt, for the love of heaven," Mycroft added, "move closer, as there is shelter enough for the whole of London!"

"At the office, I noticed you were not carrying an umb— an um—"

"An umbrella?" Mycroft finished for him.

Parfitt nodded. "And I recalled that my aunt had this— sorry!" This last apology was to a corpulent gentleman struggling to get around them without stumbling off the pavement into the muddy street. "She sends her regards!"

"Which I return," Mycroft said. "Now, let us go," he urged amidst sour looks, "before someone takes a notion to have us both hung by our heels from this thing."

With no more incidents, and blessedly dry, the two made their way across the street to a small nearby pub, Ye Olde Cock Tavern. Its narrow frontage was crowded between two more prominent buildings, yet it rose up proud and flinty, and its triangular Tudor roofline seemed to pierce the mist.

Mycroft was drawn to the fact that Douglas's favorite author, the recently deceased Charles Dickens, had often dined there. It made it strangely cheerful, as if frequented by benevolent ghosts.

Inside, men were taking their repast. The ink and print stains on their fingers and coats, the pallor of their skin, and the querulous nature of their arguments marked them as newspapermen.

Like the rest of the country, they were discussing

Saturday's Scotland/England game in boisterous, combative voices that each proclaimed he knew best:

"If the Scotch had had but Tailyour and Kinnaird…"

"…and if me granny'd had wheels, she'd be a carriage…"

"And why was the match delayed a full twenty minutes…"

"Gardner had a brilliant run…"

"…for all the good it did him!"

Mycroft sat down at a table with a satisfied sigh, the earlier blue funk dissipated. He had altered a game that had resulted in front-page news. He had saved the Queen a good deal of political trouble. He may have even preserved a life or two, for riots often ended in bloodshed. Yet none of those men, for all of their fabled reporter's noses, had sniffed him out.

He wondered if Sherlock would enjoy working in such anonymity, for that was what Mycroft liked best. If he could not marry, then as long as there was breath in him, these behind-the-scenes machinations for the common good would remain his highest calling.

As the rain continued to beat down with newfound fury, streaking the pub's frosted windows, a beckoning fire blazed in the small hearth, and Parfitt and Mycroft dug into their beef pies and drank their ale as Parfitt shared what he had discovered about the Chinese gentleman and his possible ties to Professor Cainborn.

"You compared the records very carefully?" Mycroft asked when he'd heard it all, though he knew it was a question uttered mostly for the sake of protocol, for Parfitt was nothing if not conscientious.

Parfitt had just swallowed too big a bite of pastry, which he quickly washed down with a gulp of beer. "Oh yessir, Mr. Holmes, most carefully indeed," he mumbled.

"Splendid," Mycroft replied, meaning it. "What you have unearthed is quite valuable. As always, I am grateful."

"And I to you," Parfitt responded quietly. "For all you have done for me and my—"

But Mycroft, having heard what he needed, was already on his feet and paying the bill. The last thing he wanted was to give in to some maudlin emotion, especially since he seemed so close to the edge of that lately.

Parfitt's news had only resulted in a heightened sense of... what was it? Destiny? The sense of being entangled in a tattered quagmire that he did not seek out, but that Providence had laid in his path because he was the only one who could mend it?

Sooner or later, instead of arriving to a mystery kicking and screaming, would he feel a calling to search it out, to unearth evil at its foundations?

Doubtful. He would not live that long.

As Parfitt quickly gulped down the remainder of his meal and set about gathering umbrella and coats, Mycroft glanced down at Parfitt's boots. He had noticed them earlier, of course. Only this time, the wistfulness he felt upon seeing them was almost too much to bear.

Destiny indeed.

It seemed that, these days, he was destined to run from one treacly sensation smack dab into another.

"If you came by omnibus," he said casually, "I will gladly recompense you."

"Oh no, sir. It's been a good long while since I have needed it. Not since you gave me Abie, sir."

"Abie is nearby, then?" Mycroft said, pleased to know he had guessed correctly.

"Oh yessir. He is well cared for at the mews, for I know the lad what—that works there…"

As Parfitt helped him on with his overcoat, Mycroft smiled. "My hunch is, you know 'the lad what works' at just about every mews in London. For I have rarely met a kinder, more resourceful fellow as you. May I see him?"

"Now, sir?" Parfitt said, already blushing scarlet from the unexpected compliment. "Yessir, Abie would be t-tickled, sir!"

"Not nearly so much as I," Mycroft said, stepping through the door that Parfitt held open for him.

Abie the Hanoverian had always been a well-proportioned fellow, his fine reddish blond coat shiny with meticulous grooming. He turned towards the sound of footsteps with his usual equanim-ity of temper, for he was not one to startle easily. Though if horses could execute a double-take, Mycroft would have sworn that he did so the moment he laid eyes on his former master.

"Good lad," Mycroft said, approaching him, his tone gentle and beckoning. "Such a fine lad."

Abie nickered a greeting of his own, moved sideways towards Mycroft to indicate friendship and trust, and flicked his tail. Then he lowered his head so that Mycroft could scratch his brow. As Mycroft did so, he recalled Georgiana's words when she'd first laid eyes on the gelding: *Ah, what a handsome lad! Dark blond hair, a good, strong chest, a keen and brilliant eye, and a steady disposition, much like its owner!*

Abie had hardly altered in the ensuing two years. His former proprietor, on the other hand, had changed very much indeed.

Before he could stop himself, Mycroft turned to Parfitt, who stood like a proud father at the entry to the mews. "Can he still do a short run today, d'you think?"

"Oh yessir. He is as able as any horse! He has good wind, and recovers quickly!"

"Would it be all right if I borrowed him for a short ride? I promise to return him to the office before your work day is over. I realize it is awfully wet outside, and I would undo all your efforts with that blasted umbrella."

"Oh no, Mr. Holmes! I shall come retrieve him, just say where! For we would both be honored!" Parfitt added, grinning from ear to ear.

It was a two-mile canter from Fleet Street to Regent Street, where Mycroft was to meet Douglas. And even with passersby blinded by umbrellas and hats who stepped blithely in the way of Abie's hooves, and with drovers, ox carts, carriages and omnibuses carrying on as always (for London did not halt at a mere drenching), Mycroft and Abie still managed to circumvent each obstacle, and reached their destination in fifteen minutes flat.

Mycroft Holmes was sodden, his overcoat wringing wet, jacket, shirt and trousers clinging against his skin. His blond hair, which he had thus far neglected to trim, was plastered to his cheeks and forehead. His heart was pounding in his chest most unbecomingly. Even his costly hat was ruined.

Yet, he could not recall the last time he had felt so carefree.

He led Abie by the reins underneath an overhang where he would be safe from the storm. Then he paid a local lad tuppence to watch over him until Parfitt arrived to retrieve him.

"Good lad, Abie," he whispered.

Abie returned the compliment by blowing softly through his nose, then nuzzling against Mycroft's arm. As Mycroft stroked his head, it was all he could do to stop the tears.

Though in the rain, who would notice?

36

IT HAD BEEN SEVERAL MONTHS SINCE MYCROFT HAD SET foot inside Regent Tobaccos, a place that had been for him haven and respite. But Douglas was nearly always at Nickolus House these days. And of late Mycroft found himself craving a fine steak more often than a fine cigar. Nonetheless, it felt good to be back, good to have ridden here on horseback, rather than being shuttled about in a carriage like some invalid.

Feeling more fit than he had in a while, he hurried up the steps and opened the shop door, with barely the time to inhale the bewitching aroma of rare tobaccos intermingled with fine old whiskeys when he was undone by the small whirling dervish that was Mr. Pennywhistle.

"Ooh, but it appears to me, yes it does, that you are soaked to the gills, Mr. Holmes!" Mr. P. boomed as he trotted over, peering up at Mycroft through his spectacles, his small face crumpled with the effort of it. "And me here, with nothing for you to change yourself into!" he fretted.

Mycroft wondered what he could possibly "change himself into." A raptor, perhaps? One with a faulty ticker?

"Cyrus awaits by the fire," he continued, taking Mycroft's wet coat and hanging it on the rack by the door, "which I built high, for I had an inkling that on a day like this…"

"Holmes!" he heard Douglas's voice call out, then amend: "Mycroft!"

"I am coming!" Mycroft called back before Mr. P. could articulate one more thought.

The blaze in the inner room was indeed impressive. His back to the door, Douglas turned at the sound of Mycroft's footsteps.

"Good God! You are drenched to the skin!" he declared, rising.

"I rode here on Abie," Mycroft announced happily.

"Well done!" Douglas commended. "But now, take my chair, for it is closer to the fire and I can do without an inferno at my elbow. Here," he added, moving a Punch Habana cigar and cutter from the arm of one chair to the one he had just vacated. "From your box of five hundred. How's about a glass of very nice cognac, my treat, to make up for the swill I gave you at Nickolus House?"

"The cigar will do for now," Mycroft replied, "for I consumed an ale or two with Parfitt. And you? Will you not indulge? Surely one smoke every blue moon can do you no harm!"

"Get thee behind me, Satan," Douglas said, smiling. "For I well know my habit of old: one smoke would surely turn into two, then three, then ten. Besides, I rather enjoy my reputation as the peculiar tobacco purveyor who will not consume his own product."

They heard the front doorbell tinkle and the voices of two customers joining Mr. P.'s in the shop.

"He has been instructed to keep business relegated to the front of house until we depart," Douglas explained to Mycroft. "So freely tell all."

Mycroft cut the tip off the Habana. "I have real news, Douglas: a theory based on something that Parfitt discovered. But first, you have news of your own, have you not? Though I assume it did not go well, that my brother created an obstruction or two, and that you had to set about finding an alternate translator."

"It did not, he did, and I did," Douglas said ruefully. "But, out of sheer, mindless curiosity…"

Mycroft lit his Habana and took his first pull. "An easy deduction," he said on the exhale. "The symbols form a very important clue, yet you did not hurry to tell me your news. The most obvious reason is because the conclusion was not satisfying; and second, because you would have had to disparage my brother in order to recount it properly. Sherlock's vielle case lies there, in the corner," he said, indicating it with his chin. "He would not have parted with that case for love or money, unless he was forced to. So, unless you wrenched it out of his hand and ran, the most obvious reason you are in possession of it is that you are to continue this portion of the mission without him. My best guess as to why? You and he had dealings with people from a culture where diplomacy is paramount. And, Sherlock being Sherlock, I assume he created some sort of ruckus that cut short the session and truncated any possibility of success. So. What *did* you find out?" Mycroft asked in conclusion.

"Flowers," Douglas said after a pause.

"Flowers?" Mycroft repeated. "What, all fifteen?"

"It appears that way."

"But that elucidates nothing!" Mycroft declared.

Douglas nodded again, and shrugged. "It was not all Sherlock's fault. Indeed, it was mostly mine. Our translator knew the English names of but four: rose, violet, dahlia, tulip. A fifth turned out to be daffodil."

"Your wife's favorite flower," Mycroft noted.

Douglas nodded. "I was so set on finding a reader—and Ahn Zhang has knowledge of a dozen written dialects—that it never occurred to me the names in Chinese might prove difficult to then convert into *English*."

"But surely you could have muddled through?" Mycroft asked. "Describing colors and shapes and so forth?"

When Douglas did not respond, Mycroft sat back. "Ah. And that is where my brother could not successfully hold his tongue. So. Who is this new person you found?"

"How do you know I found someone?"

"Because otherwise we would not be sitting here. You would have hustled us back to the docks to ferret out another linguist!"

Douglas laughed. "Yes, I would have. I do not know him

personally," he continued, "but he was recommended by an acquaintance, a customs officer at St. Katharine Docks who will give me name and assignation this evening. Might I persuade you to come?"

"You could not keep me away. When Huan comes to fetch me, he can take us there."

"Now, what information did Parfitt discover?" Douglas asked. "I pray it is more enlightening than mine."

"I believe so, although first I suppose I should enumerate the points that are not enlightening in the least. Professor John Cainborn, aged forty-five, middle name Aloysius. Five years ago he purchased a pied-à-terre in Shoreditch. For, besides teaching at Cambridge, he conducts chemical research at St. Mary's in Westminster. Oh, and he banks at a new bank on Gracechurch Street, the Standard Chartered."

"Fascinating," Douglas said drolly.

"Not in the least. And so the trail ends there. But the Chinese gentleman I saw with him, now he is more intriguing. His name is Deshi Hai Lin. His immigration papers state that he is a widower with two children, a son and a daughter."

"From where does he hail?"

"The papers say Shanghai."

Douglas smiled. "The *boat* is more like to have come from Shanghai than he."

"That is what I assumed as well, unless every immigrant who has ever set foot on British soil hails from Shanghai. In any event, the son's birth date conforms to Dai en-Lai Lin's current age of eighteen, and the daughter's birth date to Ai

Lin, the woman I spoke to at the herbalist's. Further, a bit of news meant for the Chinese market describes Lin as 'a man of means, sole proprietor of four steamers based in the East End of London, with routes to India and China.' Three of the steamers are at the Royal Victoria: *The Latitude*, *The Maritime*, and *The Royal Richard*; while *Orion's Belt* is docked at St. Katharine Docks and the only one currently on native soil. Are any familiar?"

Douglas shook his head. "But my not knowing his ships simply means that they are recent acquisitions," he clarified, "and therefore after my time; or that they do not transport tobacco or spirits. Were you informed as to what they *do* carry?"

"What would be your best guess?" Mycroft asked.

Douglas shrugged. "Small to mid-range steamers with that trajectory? Tea. Or poppy derivatives, or both."

Mycroft nodded. "Parfitt checked with customs, and yes, those seem to be their staples. Lin is also a silent partner in another ship. Parfitt attempted to get more information on her, but there was nothing, at least thus far."

"I cannot comprehend it," Douglas said. "You saw this Mr. Lin board a yellow landaulet. I saw the same contraption at Nickolus House. Then we both saw it barreling at us. The question remains: what interest would a wealthy ship owner or his minions have in mowing us down or, as you seem to think, in warning us?"

Mycroft shrugged. "It is all quite strange," he replied, "but fascinating. For at my request Parfitt also researched the economy of the poppy trade, something I must say I know little of, as it does not fall into any category that piques my interest. In any event, opium has remained steady at a few shillings short of twenty-two per pound. The India–China trade is flourishing."

They heard retreating footsteps coming from the shop, and the doorbell tinkling once again. Then all was quiet.

"Did Parfitt happen to find out how much is coming into the country, all told?" Douglas asked.

Mycroft was lifting the cigar to his lips again when he thought better of it, for the smoke was making him queasy. "Yes, and here is the crux," he said, holding the cigar aloft. "The volume held at one hundred and ten thousand pounds until twelve years ago, 1860," he said. "At which point it *tripled*. In the last few years, adjusting for growth in population, personal use of opium has grown seventy percent in this country."

Douglas whistled softly. "The customers are there," he said.

Mycroft nodded. "Not surprising in the least. For the whole of this island is a laudanum-taking, absinthe-drinking, coca-chewing, opium-smoking, morphine-injecting morass. That said, we are back to the same dilemma: transporting drugs is commonplace. What need would there be to smuggle? I could understand if this were a few decades ago when tariffs were high. But now? With duties so low? What would be the point?"

Douglas leaned away from the fire and wiped a small

bead of sweat on his brow. "I can think of but one possibility: the new Pharmacy Act. Now that sale of opiates has been limited to pharmacists and registered chemists, the question for consumers and dealers alike becomes 'What shall the *next* constraint be?' Perhaps moving merchandise on the hidden market simply ensures that there will never be disruptions."

"Or perhaps what they are moving is not legal, or is certain to draw interest."

Just then, Mr. P. appeared, shushing himself as he entered, as if chastising his mouth for insubordination.

"Don't mean to interrupt, but, Cyrus? Thought you'd be pleased that the customer what just left bought three cases of Glenlivet! And not just any Glenlivet! Mr. George Smith's himself, may God rest his immortal soul!"

"Well played, Mr. P.," Douglas said, though Mycroft could see that his attention was still fully on their conversation.

"Nice spoken," Mr. P. went on, oblivious, "though he was Oriental! I helped put the spirits into 'is carriage, a fine landaulet of the most unusual hue! Bright yellow, it was!"

37

DOUGLAS GALLOPED OUT THE FRONT DOOR AND DOWN THE steps. Mycroft, reeling from the effects of the Punch Habana and lack of sleep, chose to remain and interrogate their only witness, though he was fairly certain it would come to naught, given that Mr. P. could hardly see past the length of his own arm.

Once Mr. P. had reiterated the catch-all word 'Oriental,' and clarified that the man had good manners, he had nothing to add but instead stared baffled at Mycroft, as if he could not imagine what more anyone could possibly require.

"Could you say how old he was, or how he was garbed?" Mycroft attempted.

"Oh, I can't never judge age, you ask the missus if that in't so, especially when they are not, well, like us, you see. Mrs. P., she believes she can tell," he added, lowering his booming voice a notch. "Says the Chinamen always look younger. Or perhaps older."

"Well? Did he look younger or older?"

Mr. P. shrugged. "I'd say younger than me and older than you!" he replied brightly.

Mycroft attempted to piece it together. A man associated with Deshi Hai Lin had come into Regent Tobaccos—that was no coincidence. He knew beyond the shadow of a doubt that there was a connection between Beeton and Madame de Matalin through Charles—Madame was the boys' sponsor, and she "rescued" the brothers from Beeton. Further, there was a connection from de Matalin to William Angel, whoever he was. And there was yet another link between Deshi Hai Lin and Cainborn, though Mycroft was still in the dark as to what that could be.

And, given his brother's expression when he'd laid eyes upon the dead body, Mycroft was nearly certain that there was a link between the latest copycat murder and Charles.

Moments later, Douglas re-entered, nearly as soaked as Mycroft had been. He had not even succeeded in getting a glimpse of the landaulet, for the heavy rain had created a curtain of water that impeded his view.

"Did this man come to cause mischief?" Mr. P. asked, noting Douglas's distress. "Should I not have sold him the Glenlivet? He paid with good money!"

"No, Mr. P., you did your job to perfection," Douglas replied. "But if he should come back at any point, whether I am here or not, you must get word to me immediately."

"Did he leave a note or word for either of us?" Mycroft asked Mr. P.

"No, nothing like," Mr. P. responded, puzzled.

"And how did he pay?" Mycroft asked.

"Sovereigns. Fine caliber gentleman, as I say!" Mr. P. added, a trifle defensively.

"May I see the coins?" Mycroft inquired.

Mr. P. looked to Douglas, who nodded approval. As he unlocked the strongbox, he muttered, "'Tis a working man's nine-months wage," in case anyone present was not cognizant of the price of a case of Glenlivet, multiplied by three.

"Just count out a dozen," Mycroft said.

Mr. P. carefully did so and put them in Mycroft's hand. Mycroft turned them over, then back again, comparing one to the next. "Australian," he muttered.

"We are permitted to take Australian coin, are we not?" Mr. P. interjected nervously, as if the law had perhaps altered from one moment to the next.

"Of course, Mr. P. Australia is part of the Empire, perfectly acceptable," Douglas assured him. "They are counterfeit?" he asked Mycroft.

"No, no, quite sound," Mycroft replied. "But they *are* unique, and rather rare. They happen to be from a mint that was established in Sydney in 1855… May I see the others?" he asked without looking up. Mr. P. dutifully counted out the remaining coins. "As I suspected, they are all of the same mint," Mycroft declared upon examining the rest. "1857— and in that, quite special."

"Why?" Douglas asked.

"That year, Australians got a bit… saucy. Have a look at the Queen's head."

"Ah. No black ribbon," Douglas said. "It has been replaced by a sprig of… something."

Mycroft nodded. "A sprig of banksia. Stunningly, no one noticed until last year when the design was unceremoniously revoked, the banksia removed, and the ribbon returned."

"These with the banksia were taken out of circulation, then?" Douglas asked.

"Yes," Mycroft replied. "However many could be found."

"But they are still good?" Mr. P. fretted.

"Oh yes," Mycroft murmured. "Quite good."

"And what is a banksia?" Mr. P. asked.

"An Australian wildflower," Mycroft responded, continuing to stare down at the face of the coin as if the answer to this mystery might be imbedded somewhere in its design.

"Not a pleasing name for a flower," Mr. P. said, disapproving.

"No. It is meant to honor botanist Sir Joseph Banks," Mycroft replied. "He collected the first specimens during Captain James Cook's expedition in 1770. The question is, why?"

"Why what?" Mr. P. asked.

"Sorry," Mycroft replied. "I have returned in my mind to the man who came to visit. He knew this to be your establishment, Douglas. Yet, if he wished to do us ill, he could have come into the back room and attempted it. Instead, he bought expensive whiskey and left Australian sovereigns of a very specific vintage, hoping you would discover... what, exactly?"

"No clue," Douglas said, "for surely I do not have a reputation as a numismatist!"

"Nor do I!" Mr. P. chimed in. "For I do not even know what that is!"

"Someone who makes a study of coins," Douglas explained.

"Strange..." Mycroft muttered, his focus still solidly on the coins.

"What now?" Douglas said.

"The dies they used in Sydney were of a slightly different makeup than those used at the newest mint in Melbourne."

"Different how?" Douglas asked.

"All the coins minted in Sydney between 1855 and 1870 had a greater variation in color than the ones minted in Melbourne. In other words, the Melbourne coins, like those minted here in England, tend to be more uniform. But look at these," Mycroft said, holding them out. "This one, versus this? Or this?"

He placed three coins in succession into Douglas's hand, while Mr. P. put his head as close as he could manage without resting his nose upon them.

"Do you notice a difference in hue?" Mycroft asked.

"I am embarrassed to say I do not," Douglas replied.

"Nor do I!" Mr. P. proclaimed.

"Because it is not there," Mycroft murmured. "And yet should be."

"You're saying these sovereigns, though dated 1857, are more compatible with coins minted in the last two years?" Douglas asked, so as to clarify.

Mycroft nodded distractedly. "Remember when I mentioned that Deshi Hai Lin has a half interest in a ship, that he is a silent partner, but that Parfitt could not track it down?"

"Seeing as how you mentioned it not ten minutes ago?" Douglas parried. "Yes. Yes, I do."

"What happens when a ship runs aground?" Mycroft went on. "In terms of contracts and the like? I seem to recall that all legal matters, including passenger names, are removed from public view until owners and surviving passengers can be apprised of their losses, is that not so?"

"Often enough, yes," Douglas replied. "As a courtesy. To preserve the privacy of those most aggrieved. But what made you think of the *Royal Adelaide*?"

"The coins. Australia. The *Royal Adelaide* had a route there, yes? And recently ran aground. Her links to proprietors and shipments were thus removed until interested parties could be fully apprised of their loss, which can account for Parfitt's inability to glean information. I realize there are thousands of ships in our ports, but thankfully few have been shipwrecked in the last month, with loss of life and goods…"

"I am acquainted with the ship's master," Douglas said. "His name is William Hunter. We are familiar enough that, having a feasible reason to do so, he would provide me with the proprietor's name."

"Splendid. Kindly do so. And how quickly can ships

travel from London to the Orient these days?" Mycroft asked.

"It depends upon the ship," Douglas replied. "Sail-powered ships have a harder time of it. But steamships have become much faster. By the turn of the century, I am convinced they will make the run in under five days. But in the past year or so, by utilizing the Suez Canal, they can complete one leg in between twenty and thirty days…"

Suddenly Mycroft was no longer even fully cognizant of the coins in his hands. He was completely focused on Charles's "once a month."

Four ships, each possibly making a staggered run so that each month, one would be in port and ready to disembark her wares?

It made all the sense in the world.

38

AT PRECISELY 3:55 P.M., SHERLOCK STOOD OUTSIDE THE Water Monkey, trying to contain his excitement. The morning at the docks had not gone well, but he had to lay all of that aside and concentrate on what came next. His aim was to show himself as good a lad as Charles, maybe better, so that he could quickly assume the dead boy's duties and responsibilities. He would have to be streetwise but personable, intelligent but not so much that he was likely to cause trouble, and just educated enough to do the work at hand without interfering with the higher-ups or making them suspicious.

Thankfully, he had managed to hold on to Alvey Ducasse's jacket and shoes solely because he had persuaded Mycroft that he would return them personally, with his sincerest apologies. As for his torn shirt, he had hoped to retain it even while being fitted for another. But Mycroft's tailor had deemed it irreparable and, with Mycroft's blessing, had quickly tossed it into the nearest bin, which had also contained the remnants of the man's lunch. Each time Sherlock had tried to retrieve it, he'd had to contend with Mycroft's eagle eye, or with the tailor's measuring tape snapping this way and that as he worked.

"He has grown longer in the past several months! Longer torso! Longer arms! Longer neck! But still impossibly thin!" the little tailor had lamented, his bald pate perspiring. "Perhaps he fills out as he grows older, eh?" he added.

"Perhaps," Mycroft had replied, sounding dubious.

The tailor was calculating the final measurements for two brand-new shirts and a jacket, and Mycroft was selecting two ready-made shirts that would "have to serve" until the bespoke clothes were delivered, when Sherlock saw his opportunity.

Plunging his hand into the bin, he dug out the old shirt and stashed it down the back of his trousers before his brother turned around.

Later, in the carriage, he'd had to convince Mycroft that he could not smell the faint but persistent odor of pig's trotters and potatoes.

The two rotund Chinese women still sat on their wooden stools on either side of the entryway, silently staring straight ahead. In full view of them—for this time he had been beckoned and was therefore legitimate—Sherlock stamped his feet, patted his arms, and blew on his fingers as if he were impatient and cold. For Basil, the character he was inhabiting, would not keep his emotions perfectly in check at a time like this; surely fear and exhilaration would surface!

Sherlock was also keen to discover whether the women

had any purpose other than to alert patrons inside that the law might be about. As he continued to fidget, the one on the right turned and looked directly at him, her irises enlarging, like those of a hooded snake.

She blinked once, slowly; then again.

"Basil. You go in now," she commanded with a forward sweep of her hand.

Then she turned and her gaze went blank again.

Inside, the bar still displayed its limited array of spirits, but the tables and the men playing cards were gone. The room was bare, and Sherlock was alone. He stood there, barely breathing. He could feel his short staff pressing against his ribs. He listened for sounds from the floor above but heard nothing at all. A gas lamp hissing on the wall was the only sign that, whatever else, he had been expected.

Two sets of footsteps came traipsing down the unseen stairs and he knew, before anyone was yet visible, that neither would be Juju, for he was too light and nimble to make such sounds. Whoever was coming to meet him was heavy and flat-footed, with a weakened right side. The stairwell door opened, and he had surmised correctly.

The first to step through was the redheaded lad known as Gin. Though Sherlock had never laid eyes on him, he was exactly as McPeel and Ducasse had described him. His thick thatch of hair grew low on his forehead, and his blue eyes were bright as a child's.

On his heels was a pockmarked hulk with a bovine expression. From the descriptions that Sherlock had filed away, this had to be Beeton's son, name as yet unknown.

Neither looked surprised to see him. Both assumed a wide-legged stance as if ready to do battle, though Gin was clearly the leader. They glared at Sherlock as a matter of course.

"Wot's your business 'ere, boy?" Gin demanded.

"I was summoned," Sherlock replied.

"By who?" Gin asked with a snarl.

Sherlock took a moment. He could not be seen as weak, but neither could he be thought too dominant, and therefore hard to manage.

"Called 'isself Juju," Sherlock replied, swallowing.

Gin turned to the pockmarked boy. "You seen 'is mug before, Ned?" he asked.

"Never in me life," Ned replied sourly. "Where you from, boy?"

"Old Pye," Sherlock replied.

"Nicklas 'ouse," Gin clarified, and Ned nodded.

"'Oo be your mates?" Ned asked, challenging.

"I got me lotsa mates," Sherlock replied. "McPeel, Ducasse, Jackie Baldwin…"

"Never 'eard of 'em!" Gin said triumphantly.

"…Reg Carter, Billy Bishop, Miles Duchamp…" Sherlock went on, with boys whose names he had memorized for an entirely different purpose. He watched recognition flood Ned's homely face as he reluctantly admitted that he knew two or three.

"Charlie was like a bruvver to me," Sherlock concluded defiantly.

"But where do you *'ail* from?" Ned demanded.

"Dover," Sherlock replied without batting an eye—for he assumed they had never been more than a mile outside London proper and could therefore make no queries about it.

"Dover?" Ned repeated but then said nothing else. With Gin keeping an eye on Sherlock, he walked past and out through the front door.

As he did so, Sherlock confirmed what he had realized on the stairs: Ned's right side was weaker than the left, from a lazy eye to a slight drooping of the mouth.

Just then, the front door opened again, and in walked Juju, followed by two of his henchmen, the roly-poly man who had referred to Sherlock as shòu-shòu, and the younger, moon-faced man who had been seated to Juju's left at the card game.

So Roly-Poly and Moon Face were Juju's steady companions! It explained why the carriage wheels had been overly weighted at the front. Moon Face had been driving, judging from the calluses on his fingers, while Roly-Poly sat next to him on the bench, leaving Juju inside with his victim.

Ned did not re-enter, and Gin quickly disappeared back up the stairs, closing the stairwell door behind him. Even so, Sherlock assumed both were standing at their respective posts, ready to assist if needed.

"It appears you overcame our first hurdle," Juju said, smiling benignly.

"And 'ow might that be, guv?" Sherlock said, smiling back, giving "Basil" a touch of bravado.

"Gin and Ned confirmed your residence at Nickolus House," Juju said.

"Pleased to 'ear it," Sherlock responded, for indeed he was.

"If we were to take you on," Juju continued, "you and they would have no dealings unless I order it, is that understood?"

"Not to worry! There be nothin' between me an' *them* two!"

"Good. Now tell me, Basil. Did Charles describe the nature of the work to you?"

"In a manner of speakin'..."

"Explain what you know of it, then, for I am all ears."

Sherlock was suddenly very thirsty. It felt as if every drop of moisture in his mouth had dissipated, and he wondered if he hadn't walked into a trap. Should he mention the symbols and the quilted bag? If he said too little, that would not do at all. But so much as an extra word might prove deadly.

"He din't, to tell the truth, guv," Sherlock said. "But Charlie knowed me, and 'e knowed I'd take to it, as it be somethin' I does regardless, if you catches my meanin'. He said I 'ad the correct con... con..."

"Constitution? Or perhaps construction?" Juju offered helpfully.

"Somethin' like, guv!" Sherlock responded brightly.

"I see. But here is what puzzles me, Basil. The first is that Charles never mentioned you to me. Do you not think that highly unusual?"

With that, the two henchmen made a move for Sherlock, snatching him up by the arms. As they did so, his short staff clattered to the floor and rolled towards Juju's feet.

Juju raised an eyebrow, leaned down and picked it up.

"Well, what have we here? You were not armed the last time we met."

"Nossir, guv," Sherlock said, swallowing hard. "Nor this time, neither, as I 'ad no bad intents with it, I swear!"

"Then why have it with you now, Basil?" Juju inquired. "And pray make it the truth. Or I will use this little staff of yours to splatter your brain matter all over this room. For we do not take kindly to liars and infiltrators in our midst."

Sherlock considered his options. He might be quick enough to grab the short staff out of Juju's hands, and he could probably attack one of the two henchman and sail out the door, but what then? Surely Ned was standing outside. And even though the right side of his body was weak, the left looked hale enough, and Sherlock would still be outnumbered three to one—four to one, if Gin made it down the stairs in time. Possibly even six, if the women could do battle—and he did not doubt they could.

No, overpowering them would not do, and neither would flight. As with the lads at Nickolus House, he would simply have to outsmart them.

"Guv, last time I 'ad two mates wiv me," he said desperately, "you can ask them old women if I din't! One mate were keepin' it for me, but they's not 'ere now, is they, guv? I ain't bricky," he added, indicating his own body with his chin. "You can see 'ow it is with your own peepers! What do I protect meself wiv, then, if not that?"

"Yes, I do see. But here is another point that puzzles

me," Juju said, slapping the short staff on his open palm with an unpleasant thwack. "Before Charles perished so unexpectedly, and of course so tragically, I did not *need* another boy. I did not *desire* another boy. And so Charles would have been alerting you to a position that did not exist, and that would have left him quite without employment..."

Juju's henchmen seemed to be breathing inside Sherlock's eardrums in unison.

"I see 'ow that could give you pause, guv," Sherlock responded, staring into Juju's malicious and unsparing eyes, and struggling to stay focused. "But does you know Georgie, guv?"

"The brother," Juju said flatly. "What about him?"

"Well now, guv, if you knowed Charlie, then you knowed Charlie 'ad a big 'eart for little Georgie. And 'e knowed 'is bruvver was 'appy at Nicklas 'ouse. So 'e was torn, you see? He'd got 'im outta Beeton's, an' now they was safe, but Georgie, 'e knowed that if old Smythe got wind of what Charles did for a livin', they'd both be out on their ears! And so Charlie swore to Georgie 'e was done wiv it. I don't know if 'e was or wasn't, but when Charlie died, I thought about wot 'e said, and so I come 'ere to see about work! I din't mean nothin' by it! Please don't beat me brains in, guv!"

Juju stepped back. "Remove his jacket and roll up his shirt cuffs," he ordered his henchmen.

They did so, and Roly-Poly inspected the needle marks. "Old," he said to his employer. "Weeks. Maybe months."

Moon Face pulled a morocco case out of his pocket,

and from it a hypodermic syringe. Within its opaque glass was a substance that looked brownish in color.

Sherlock assumed that either they would kill him immediately, or that he had passed the latest test. Juju's next statement seemed to indicate the latter: "One final examination, young Basil. This is the newest concoction. I would be gratified to hear your thoughts."

With Roly-Poly holding Sherlock's right arm, Moon Face expertly felt for a vein in the crook of his arm. Having apparently found one that met his specifications, he removed his tie from his neck, tied it firmly above the point of entry he had found, tapped the desired vein to make it stand out, and inserted the needle.

When a droplet of blood rose into the barrel, he pressed down upon the piston.

Sherlock felt burning. He began to count and reached seven before he experienced a euphoria like a wind rushing through him. He lost all presence of mind to continue his counting but knew only a feeling of ecstasy and peace, and a moment after that of falling forever into a dark, bottomless abyss that brought to his wavering consciousness Alice's adventures through the looking glass, or what he had seen when looking into Juju's eyes...

And after that, nothing.

39

AT FOUR P.M., VIELLE CASE IN TOW, MYCROFT AND DOUGLAS made their way through the noisy, bustling walkways of the St. Katharine Docks, which lay on the north side of the Thames and downstream from London Bridge and the Tower of London. Unable to accommodate more sizable crafts, St. Katharine's nevertheless had its share of activity with midsized vessels, for the lock had been sunk so deep that ships up to seven hundred tons' burden could enter at any point of the tide, with warehouses built on the quayside and the latest hydraulics, so that merchandise could be loaded and unloaded directly onto the vessels.

"They have accidentally created the perfect location for contraband," Douglas said.

"Or deliberately," Mycroft replied.

As a fine mist of rain continued unabated, porters with fraying jackets and holes in the knees of their trousers grunted and strained under gargantuan traveling bags, while beside them bowler-hatted gentlemen in tailored suits wielded nothing weightier than an umbrella.

Like every other dock that Mycroft had ever set foot on, it was a smelly, egregious affair. Worse still, St. Katharine's specially fitted steam engines—meant to keep the water level at approximately four feet above the tidal river—were not functioning to capacity. Water sloshed onto the walkways, so that the mere act of walking became treacherous.

Even so, Douglas took it all in fondly, every so often calling out the names of ships he recognized or upon which he had sailed, until he walked into the customs office, with Mycroft following.

The head officer, Martin McMullah, was a sour sort, with rheumy eyes and a good-sized paunch. He located the volumes of public records on the ships coming into port and scanned the entries until he found Deshi Hai Lin's steamship, *Orion's Belt.*

"There be nothin' out of sorts," McMullah said, volume open to *Orion's Belt*'s arrivals and departures. "Except she come into port ten days ago but is not yet at quayside," he added.

"But that is not illegal," Douglas muttered as Mycroft scanned the crew list.

"'T'isn't," McMullah agreed. "They can sit at dockside until they rot; ain't none of our affair 'til they unloads."

"Anything else you can tell us about her?" Mycroft asked.

"Pays her fees on time," McMullah said with a shrug. "No accidents at dock, the rest ain't my business. When you're finished with the logs, I've arranged for you to see a man by the name of Kang Chen. Boatswain on *The Temptress*. Like you, Cyrus, he worked the ships from a tyke, 'ceptin' he's a Chinaman. Speaks like a grandee, but a good sort. No one'll be botherin' you there, not on a heavin' day like this."

On their way to *The Temptress*, Mycroft and Douglas paused some hundred yards from *Orion's Belt*, still heavy in her slip. They had no way to draw nearer without provoking undue attention—for a ship filled with cargo was well guarded by men who tended to be suspicious of onlookers. Even as they tried to sidle closer, a rumble of thunder let them know that heavier rain was soon to come, creating yet another obstacle in an already tenuous situation.

"Does she look the sort," Mycroft asked, peering through the mist and the drizzle, "to reach Shanghai in thirty days at most?"

"Not easy to make out, but I would say so. She appears to be sleek and well cared for."

"Let us fathom a connection between Mr. Lin, the symbols, and Charles's death," Mycroft continued. "Let us say the symbols are meant to reveal *which* items will be unpacked. Is it then conceivable that the entire operation is shut down over the death of one boy?"

"Highly doubtful," Douglas replied.

Mycroft nodded. "So, what would cause someone to allow their contraband—if indeed that is what it is—to remain aboard ship for ten days? Mutiny, perhaps?"

Douglas shrugged. "If there is malfeasance," he replied, "if the crew is creating a stir or being disruptive, the owner might cease all labors until he ferrets out the malcontents, for any weakness could eventually bring down the whole affair. But he could only do so if the cargo has no expiry or fixed delivery date. Otherwise, the loss would not be worth the discovery."

"The driver of the landaulet works for Deshi Hai Lin. I believe he was trying to warn us. Might he be a malcontent?" Mycroft suggested.

"He might be, but he is not crew," Douglas protested. "He would not be privy to his employer's business aboard ship."

"But in this case, the driver would have to know only the *nature* of the contraband, how and where it is hidden, and how it is removed."

"Is that all?" Douglas teased.

"It *is* a bit much," Mycroft admitted.

With no more to discover about *Orion's Belt*, he followed Douglas along a makeshift walkway towards *The Temptress*, as the temporary walkway buckled and rolled beneath them. The whole venture was proving more treacherous by the moment.

"When we return to terra firma," Mycroft said, "might I borrow a dozen of those sovereigns? I should like to have them tested."

"I thought you said they were not counterfeit," Douglas replied.

"No, I said they were *good*, meaning I believe they are worth what they say they are worth," Mycroft corrected.

"What troubles you, then?" Douglas asked.

"Their perfection," Mycroft replied. "It bothers me a great deal."

By the time Mycroft and Douglas climbed aboard *The Temptress*, the rain had begun to fall so hard that sky and sea had blended into one. Lanterns swayed in the gale, illumining the downpour with an eerie yellow cast. Douglas had the vielle case hidden in his overcoat as they gave their names to an inscrutable Chinese guard stationed on the bridge and made their way to the dining hall.

Even had the day been splendid, there was little tempting about *The Temptress*. She was certainly not the *Sultana*, the large steamer that had transported them to Trinidad, with its stately saloon, fine linen and china, soft upholstered chairs and softer lighting. *The Temptress* was a working cargo ship that ferried few passengers, none of whom expected, or received, first class accommodation. The room they entered had more the look of a military mess hall, with a low ceiling and a few paltry wall lamps putting out more smoke than light, thereby adding to the sense of claustrophobia.

Thankfully their contact, Kang Chen, was already waiting, and he rose to his feet to greet them. Smiling, hand extended, he was a slight man in his late thirties or early forties, with a shaved head and a graceful bearing. And although he wore British-made apparel, he did not have the nonchalance that Western clothes could sometimes impart but seemed self-contained, almost constricted—as if freedom were not something he took lightly. When he walked, he shuffled his feet along the ground, as if shod in slippers and not hard-soled shoes.

When he drew closer, the dim light revealed a rather prominent scar across his neck that even a good-sized cravat could not hide.

"Mr. Chen," Douglas said, taking his hand. "I am Cyrus Douglas, and this is my associate and friend, Mycroft Holmes."

"Mr. Douglas. Mr. Holmes. Our mutual friend told me that this was a delicate matter," Kang said in fine, lightly accented English, "and so I thought a meeting here would be best, for we are quite alone. Please, have a seat, won't you?"

Mycroft and Douglas took a seat across from him at one end of the long, bare dining table.

"We are very grateful to you," Douglas said as he pulled the vielle case out from under his coat. "Our mutual friend assured me that you are quite skilled."

"Ah, he is too kind. I am your humble servant," Kang Chen said, bowing slightly, his smile intact. He reached into his jacket pocket and removed a pair of blued steel wire spectacles with lacquered ends. Putting them on carefully, he peered at the markings on the instrument.

At first, he seemed to not comprehend what he was seeing. With the tiniest hesitation, he leaned in closer, and every bit of color drained from his already sallow cheeks.

"Mr. Chen," Mycroft said gently. "Are these copies of what you drew in the Underground stations?"

Mr. Chen rose abruptly, as did Douglas, who was every bit as surprised as Chen but prepared to block his escape, if need be.

"That won't be necessary, Douglas," Mycroft said, holding up his hand. "Please sit, Mr. Chen, if you would be so kind, for we wish you no harm."

Chen sat reluctantly, as did Douglas.

Mr. Chen stared at Mycroft with haunted eyes.

"It was your expression, Mr. Chen. Too much, for symbols that denote nothing more dire than common flowers. Or for an unfamiliar instrument covered in marks clearly made by a *laowai*. No, you reacted because you created the originals. At least half, for your touch is light. There are small stains on your fingernails made by calligraphy ink. You have calluses on the thumb, index and middle finger of your right hand from holding a brush for too many hours at a time. They give you away as the artist you are, as do your spectacles. I recognize the brand: specially made in Venice, prized by artists because the lenses magnify with little distortion, and they have no shading that can interfere with the ability to discern color."

"I compliment you on your knowledge of art and artists," Chen said, licking his lips. "But I still do not comprehend—"

"Do not fret, Mr. Chen," Mycroft interrupted. "For we are not here to foment trouble, neither are we the law. Indeed we did not know until this very moment that you had any information for us, other than to translate what we brought. And so, whatever your involvement was or has been regarding the symbols, we shall leave that alone, and ask that you merely reveal to us what they mean in English."

Mycroft ignored the rather pointed look that Douglas sent his way, along with a baffled one from Kang Chen.

A moment later, Chen sighed, and his shoulders slumped. He removed his jacket a bit stiffly, revealing sweat stains on his shirt.

"I can translate for you, Mr. Holmes," he said, "but even if I wished to, I could not tell you what purpose they serve, for I do not know."

"You are quite gracious, Mr. Chen," Mycroft said, "and we are much appreciative."

Chen took a deep breath, as if diving underwater, and began. "Rose," he said dully, pointing to the symbols. "Dahlia, lily, myrtle, anise. Underneath that is amaryllis, that one is… aster, then at the end of that row we have sage, holly, violet, tulip, poppy, tansy, rue, and finally… daffodil."

"Ah, so not simply flowers, then, but also herbs?" Douglas inquired.

"Flowers and herbs, yes," Mr. Chen said, sounding as exhausted as if he had run a marathon. "I can repeat them if you wish…"

"No need," Mycroft responded.

"As you like," Chen said, eyeing Mycroft. "And I have helped you, yes?"

"You have indeed," Mycroft replied.

"Good. Please hear me now. Whatever your purpose, I will say in my defense that I did only what I had to do so as to protect a beloved mentor. And that, whatever else you unearth, and regardless of what anyone tells you, he is a good and kind man."

"Did he know what you were doing?"

"I do not believe so," Chen replied. "I was hired by someone who wished him ill…"

"I take it he was fair to his workers on *Orion's Belt*?" Mycroft asked.

"Ah, so you know that too…" Mr. Chen rose to his feet. This time, his sigh sounded like a death rattle. "Yes, he was more than fair to us," he added. "I am alive because of him. And now you will depart, as promised?"

"Of course," Mycroft said, rising. "As I said, we are accusing no one of perpetrating evil."

"Oh, do not misunderstand, Mr. Holmes," Chen interrupted. "There is *great* evil being perpetrated. I mean only that he is not the source." He shook his head. "Goodbye, Mr. Douglas, Mr. Holmes. I pray you will not be offended if I say I hope to never see you again."

40

DOUGLAS AND MYCROFT CAREFULLY WALKED DOWN THE gangway back to the dock, where they could just make out the silhouette of the carriage and of Huan, patiently waiting under a pounding deluge. Mycroft turned up the collar of his overcoat while inwardly cursing his lack of umbrella. *So much for my infallible sense of smell*, he berated himself as the sky opened up even more, seemingly out of spite.

"Well, Douglas, we unmasked one of the two artists. And, he used to work—most likely still works—for Deshi Hai Lin!"

"I give you that," Douglas said, somewhat coldly.

"What troubles you?" Mycroft inquired.

Douglas sighed. "I realize no one makes deductions as rapidly as you, least of all I—but I must insist you not make unilateral decisions without consulting me."

"Such as?" Mycroft asked.

"Such as? Such as not letting Kang Chen get off scot free, for surely there was more there to discover!" Douglas exclaimed.

"Yes, forgive me for that," Mycroft replied. "However, in my defense: his ankles had been weakened from months of being bound; he had been caned repeatedly on the bottoms of his feet; he has a vertical gash across his back that has never properly healed, and quite possibly a broken vertebra, for which he must still wear a truss."

"However did you see a gash on his *back?*"

"When he rose to his feet, frightened and indignant, his shoulders did not pull back as yours or mine would. Then, when he turned, his shirt was damp at the scapula, no doubt oozing pus. And earlier, when I shook his hand, there was a rather foul-smelling odor emanating through the jacket…"

"And yet, I noticed *none* of that," Douglas said with some chagrin.

"But you must have noticed that the thumb of his left hand was mangled, that he had what looked like a burn mark around the base of it. But that his right thumb was spared, notably because whoever held him captive was taking advantage of his artistic skills and so would not damage his right hand. He is used to torture, Douglas," Mycroft went on. "And since we would have employed nothing of the kind, he would have *revealed* nothing. Besides, I believed him: he made the markings on the wall for Deshi Hai Lin's sake, and has no notion what they mean.

"One positive conclusion," Mycroft added. "Deshi Hai Lin, whatever else he has done, was not responsible for torturing and nearly garroting Kang Chen—though I *am* curious as to who was."

"And the other artist? He is not important, I take it?" Douglas asked, clearly not giving up.

"No, he is not. He would know no more than Chen did, and quite possibly less."

"Mycroft," Douglas said, still somewhat testily, "you may wish to revisit your notions of accountability."

"Whatever do you mean?"

"If someone is hurt, regardless of whether the perpetrator is a middleman or at the bottom of the rung, he is still culpable. Hierarchy, like ignorance, is no excuse."

"I am not interested in those who take orders," Mycroft protested, "but in those who give them! Beyond that, what I told Chen is true: we are not gendarmes, Douglas! We do not go about putting people in fetters! Do you not believe that my brain is my most powerful weapon?"

"Obviously," Douglas grumbled.

"Then is it not best used to its full capacity, rather than wasted on small fry like Chen or even someone as loathsome as Beeton? The pertinent questions are these: who is managing this affair? To what purpose? And how do we stop him not once—so he can scurry off and do it again elsewhere—but once and for all?"

"You know, Mycroft," Douglas said, his tone so soft that Mycroft struggled to hear him over the merciless rain, "even the so-called 'little people' have to be given the dignity of accountability. They are still living beings that can learn, and grow, and come to the light…"

"Ah, now you are speaking of the nature of God and of

our ultimate purpose on earth! I vow that we can have all the philosophical arguments you desire, but at present, we have more mundane concerns, would you not agree?"

They had arrived at the carriage. Mycroft opened the door and both men all but hurled themselves inside. At the same instant, a flash of lightning illuminated the murky water of the docks, with rumblings of thunder close behind.

The two sloughed off their wet overcoats, laid them on the floor at their feet, and sat back. As the carriage lurched into motion, Douglas patted his friend on the shoulder.

"A few deep breaths," Douglas said, eyeing him with concern, "for you sound like a scythe whistling through the air."

"Rue," Mycroft began after a pause. "Tansy, dahlia, rose, lily, myrtle, anise, amaryllis, aster, sage, holly, violet, tulip, poppy, and daffodil. Do those suggest anything to you?"

Douglas shrugged. "You mean, other than they are all women's names?"

"Dear God," Mycroft muttered. "That is what I have been pondering since I heard the first five! And I admit to Rose, Aster, Lily, Violet, Dahlia, Myrtle, Holly, Amaryllis, and heaven help us, Tulip. I even grant you Poppy. But Tansy? Daffodil? Sage? Rue? Or what proper little girl would wish to be named Anise? What else but a child would be saddled with a name like that?"

"Dolls, perhaps?" Douglas ventured. "Those child-sized bisque and cloth dolls… or are we becoming too fantastical?"

"No, Douglas, not a bit," Mycroft replied. "Intelligent

imagination is vital to this sort of deduction! Dolls. However improbable a hypothesis, it cannot be discarded. For dolls like that can be containers for many things. And curse this old bachelor for not thinking of it first."

"You are far from an 'old bachelor,' and to be fair, you have seen only one, whereas I spotted a half-dozen sinking in the foam at the wreck of the *Royal Adelaide*..."

"*Sinking* in the foam, you say?"

"Yes, it was only the choppy waves and rather shallow water that allowed me to see them at all."

"But bisque and cloth would have floated longer, no?"

"Never occurred to me at the time, but most likely."

"So, let us suppose the ships transport dolls," Mycroft said. "And inside those dolls is contraband of some kind."

"Could they be using dolls to transport sovereigns?" Douglas asked. "Could it be that Deshi Hai Lin's driver brought us the contraband?"

Mycroft shook his head. "To begin with, I would have to ask, 'Why us?' Secondly, it seems an impractical way to move either dolls *or* coins. But, for the sake of argument: we know a sovereign weighs point-two-eight-one-seven..."

"Might we say point-two-eight ounces?" Douglas suggested.

"Fine. Let us suppose, then," Mycroft went on, "that the cloth body of each doll is now a repository for a thousand sovereigns apiece. It would weigh a tad over one-point-two stone, still easy to move about. A doll of that height, weighing in at just over one stone, would not raise suspicions.

But if the names of the flowers and herbs indicate dolls in a shipment, and there are fifteen, that still adds up to a mere fifteen thousand sovereigns per docking."

"Yes," Douglas said. "It is too elaborate a ruse for such a paltry payoff. And more weight would surely come to the attention of customs agents."

"And drugs…? Yes, but again, why? Why the cloak and dagger? There has to be more to it," Mycroft said, shaking his head as if hoping to dislodge something from it. "We seem to always be short an essential piece."

They heard the soft knocking on the carriage roof, along with Huan's "Whoa!" that said they were back at Nickolus House.

Douglas retrieved his wet coat, opened the carriage door, and got out.

"Douglas?" Mycroft queried, leaning out through the open door after him. "Do we bring Sherlock in? Or leave him in relative ignorance until after his exams? I must confess we could use an extra brain—no offense…"

"None taken," Douglas said, smiling.

"But that would force us to reveal Deshi Hai Lin's link to Cainborn, for it is now impossible to believe that Lin is not somehow involved."

"What would be the worst-case scenario if we were to tell him?"

Mycroft, feeling suddenly miserable, shrugged. "Sherlock has never expressed admiration for anyone besides Cainborn, and he is more sensitive than he seems. Linking the man, however innocently, to a potentially shady character like Lin would bother Sherlock a great deal, possibly sidetracking his exams. Getting him to study in the first place has been a Sisyphean chore. He cannot fail, Douglas, for I sincerely do not think I could ever persuade him to repeat the term. And if he does not, if he should abort his education, what in the world will become of him?"

"He has you," Douglas said. "And he still has time to grow up."

He may not have me for long, Mycroft thought—though what he said was, "He is very nearly nineteen!"

"People do change, you know! And you needn't make the decision this moment," Douglas exclaimed as he hurried towards the front door of Nickolus House. "Sleep on it. Tomorrow will bring new clarity, you will see!"

"Besides," Mycroft called back with a final wave, "what harm could one more night of Latin possibly do?"

41

SHERLOCK KEPT OPENING HIS EYES AND THEN CLOSING them again, for keeping them open seemed an inconceivable chore, as did lifting his head or his limbs. His brain felt like a ball of wool. His head ached, his fingertips were numbed. As for his feet, he could not feel them at all.

During a brief moment when his eyes were open, he noticed that the ceiling above his head was much lower than he recalled. It began to dawn on him that he was no longer on the ground floor of The Water Monkey, that he had most likely been carried, insentient, to the floor above.

As he became more cognizant of his situation, it also occurred to him that no one knew where he was: not his brother or Douglas, not Huan, not Ducasse or McPeel; not even the twins, whose nearly pathological lack of curiosity could usually be counted upon as an asset.

There was no one to come to his aid.

Given that sobering realization, he did not attempt to move his body one inch more, but mimicked the slow rolling motion of the eyes that connoted—he hoped—a dreamlike state. As he scanned his surroundings he saw that along the wall were unpadded wooden berths, while towards the center of the room where he lay, other cots had been set up with straw mattresses, their beige blankets stained the color of tobacco by too much human sweat.

Most of the cots were unoccupied, but here and there a few shadowy figures had taken up residence, curled atop them like so many overgrown fetuses.

It appeared that the windows had been boarded over, making it all but impossible to guess night from day. The only sources of light were little circles that appeared and disappeared like flaming red cicadas, or perhaps like devil eyes winking here and there. It made Sherlock wonder, in a rather detached manner: should a blaze consume the building, with but one narrow doorway leading downstairs, would anyone get out alive?

As his senses became more attuned to his surroundings, he began to hear breathing that sounded like myriad sighs, along with the hum of voices lifting and falling, though he could not make out the words. But all these rustles, whispers and murmurs were having a soporific effect, and Sherlock very nearly dozed off again until one word caused him to start.

"'E's a right proper baker," a man's voice was saying to an unseen companion in a bass so low that Sherlock could feel it vibrate inside his chest. "Best I ever come across…"

In his muddled state, and before he could stop himself, Sherlock was sitting up, peering into the darkness for the source.

As he did so, he felt a movement beside him and turned just in time to see his nemesis holding a hypodermic syringe high in the air and sporting a grin.

"Night-night, Basil," Moon Face said before grabbing Sherlock's arm and plunging the needle into his vein.

Early on Tuesday morning, as an occasional hint of sun broke through the clouds, Mycroft had Huan drive him to The Golden Bottle. In business long before London's roadways had numbers, Mycroft's bank was known less by its name, C. Hoare & Co., and more by a gilded leather bottle that hung outside the edifice. The Golden Bottle had helped Mycroft grow the bulk of his now ten-million-pound fortune, and he was nothing if not faithful. As he sat across from the bank's manager, Carl Dalrymple, Mycroft silently informed his quickening heart and sweaty palms that now was not the time to misbehave. He stretched his tingling fingers and drew a few deep breaths that caused Dalrymple to look up from his labors, his great caterpillar eyebrows lifting in concern.

Dalrymple's hair was combed forward upon his head so that it formed a frizzy Roman helmet that sat just above a set of even frizzier mutton chops, while a slug of a mustache curled over lips so thin they seemed composed of one line apiece.

In spite of this heinous appearance, Dalrymple was a keen manager of money, and he had a fine eye for detail, melded with what could only be described as a spaniel-like desire to please.

"Are you quite all right, Mr. Holmes?" he asked, a question that Mycroft had been hearing more and more, to his chagrin.

"Forgive me," Mycroft replied. "I tossed and turned a good deal last night."

"As did I," Dalrymple seconded. "Have been for months. England's economic forecast seems to me rather grim, and no one is lifting a finger!"

Mycroft, thankful not to be—for once—the only prophet of doom, nodded his full agreement. "Until the Queen and the PM are convinced, you and I, and a few others like us, can but watch the avalanche as it approaches," Mycroft grumbled.

"And invest in gold!" Dalrymple added.

On his desk were the dozen Australian sovereigns from Regent Tobaccos, side by side with another dozen from the C. Hoare & Co. vault. At his elbow was a dropper of nitric acid and a small tool that resembled a crochet hook, and before him was a troy weight scale and a glass of water.

Dalrymple made a series of miniscule scratches on the surface of each coin with the hook, then placed a drop of nitric acid on the abrasion. That done, he deposited each into the glass of water and watched as it sank to the bottom. He weighted them one by one upon the troy weight scale; and finally, with a magnifying glass, he diligently appraised them all again.

"Is it as I suspected?" Mycroft asked by rote, indicating

the sovereigns he had brought. "Are they worth their weight in gold?"

"They certainly seem to be, Mr. Holmes," Dalrymple replied, frowning. "And I am aggrieved to say I cannot explain the discrepancy of their colorations, in spite of the year and the location where they were minted."

"The *purported* year," Mycroft amended. "Yes, neither can I."

"*Purported* year?" Dalrymple repeated. "Mr. Holmes, while I admit they must be melted down to ascertain their exact percentages of silver and copper, I can assure you that the gold is very much real and of the correct gauge, point-two-eight-one-seven——"

"I realize this is far-fetched, Mr. Dalrymple," Mycroft said by way of response, "but if corrupt individuals had somehow got a hold of the precise balance of gold to copper and silver, could not metallurgists press counterfeit coins to look identical?"

Dalrymple coughed, for he was too gracious to do otherwise. "It is feasible," he said, "but it makes no sense, you see. I have heard of and even seen outlandish forgeries. But their gold content is negligible—that is the point. It is trading the lesser for the better. What would be the purpose of trading same for same?"

"Kindly follow me on this," Mycroft said. "Given that they are quite perfect, too perfect, in fact, would they raise suspicions?"

"I wish with all my heart that I could say yes, but the

answer is most likely no, not remotely. Bank clerks and merchants would not know the difference, and numismatists would not be on the lookout for such an unusual problem!"

"Now let us suppose," Mycroft pressed on, "that someone was conducting illegal ventures for which they were being paid in gold. A lot of gold, much more than they could adequately hide…"

This notion seemed to have caught Dalrymple so unawares that he shot out of his chair like a jack-in-the-box and set about pacing the room. "What you are intimating is that, rather than *hide* quantities of gold until such a time as it can be eked out without arousing suspicion, someone is minting 'coins of the realm' that can be used immediately? As native currency? And distributed freely throughout the Empire?"

"That sums it up," Mycroft said. "Given Britain's hefty stamp upon the world—its countries, protectorates, dominions, and so forth—there would be no possibility of tracking down these forgeries, even if someone were aware of them. Even were they to amount to millions of pounds. The Empire's vast holdings ensure that those millions would be but a drop in the ocean. Merchants in India, for example, are not losing sleep, wondering if they have seen one too many Australian sovereigns with a banksia instead of a ribbon!"

"But… such a thing is *monstrous*!" Dalrymple cried indignantly.

"Yes," Mycroft said. "I thought so too."

Mr. Dalrymple ceased pacing. "But then, if one goes to all the trouble to mint *this* particular Australian coin of *this* particular year, why not build in the variation? Why risk *any* exposure, however improbable?"

"Yes, I wondered that. And I realize that the difference in the Sydney hues was an anomaly, an error. So, one guess is that, even had the forgers known about it, they may not have wished to attempt it and thereby make a mess of it. Best to follow a known formula. As for why this particular coin: the banksia in Queen Victoria's hair is so unique that it allows forgers to put their coins into circulation and never retrieve them by mistake," Mycroft explained. "And, because it is an embarrassment to the Crown, the moment one *does* rise to the surface, the Crown itself removes it."

"What you are saying is that our own diligence is aiding and abetting the forgers, albeit without intent."

"Unfortunately, yes," Mycroft replied. "Though I needed someone of your stature to confirm that it was conceivable."

"I will gladly help in any way I can," Mr. Dalrymple said after a moment's hesitation.

"What is it, Mr. Dalrymple? For if I cannot fully convince you, how can I hope to convince the Queen or anyone else?"

"Though I am in scandalized agreement that it is possible, Mr. Holmes, I continue to wonder why they did not at least *attempt* to vary the hues. For, while it is true that their chances of being found out were quite slim, yet here we are," he concluded, gesturing to the coins on his desk.

"Perhaps they did attempt it. Perhaps they tried and failed. Or perhaps they could not attempt it, for they did not know. But if they did not know…"

"Then the ringleader of this enterprise may not be a coin historian at all!" Mr. Dalrymple said, finishing Mycroft's conjecture. "But then what could he possibly be, Mr. Holmes?"

"That is the question, is it not, Mr. Dalrymple?" Mycroft said.

42

WHEN SHERLOCK AGAIN OPENED HIS EYES, HE WAS NO longer in the upper chamber but back on the ground floor of The Water Monkey. Though the gaslights on the wall were dim by normal standards, the room was still so much brighter than what he'd grown accustomed to that he could feel the sting of it.

Tears began to roll down his cheeks.

He blinked and looked about, as if peering at the world through the wrong end of a telescope.

On the opposite side of the room he could see the door that led to the street, and to freedom. But between him and it stood two tables, and around those tables sat eight Oriental men in business attire.

The men were playing cards; he recognized them from the previous game, but not one showed any cognizance that he existed, so that for a moment he wondered if he truly did.

What he knew for certain was that this match, unlike the former, was real. Though the players were still throwing about silver ingots as if they were ha'pennies, the pile of face-down cards was smaller, and the winnings not so evenly distributed. They also had libations of various kinds, something he had not witnessed in the faux game. And their concentration was wholly on the hands they held.

It also occurred to him, however belatedly, that he was no longer lying down but standing upright.

This unusual state of affairs was not of his volition: rather, two men were propping him up by the armpits.

"Ah. So you awake," the man on his right uttered. "Good. You pass your final test."

With that, his two erstwhile assistants began to drag him towards the entry in an awkward *pas de trois*, wherein Sherlock could do little more than watch his feet shuffle lamely across the floor.

Still holding on to him, the man on the left opened the door as the other one muttered: "Go. Twenty-four hours, you return. If you return, you ours."

Thereupon, he released him, giving him a small but definitive shove out the door.

Blinded by the milky daylight, Sherlock staggered on his sea legs and would surely have stumbled into the mud of the street, had not the two women on stools reached out to steady him. He did not look at them, for the light was too bright and he was too disoriented, but their hawk-like grasp felt strangely comforting.

He lost track of time as he stood there, suspended, until one of them murmured, as if she were speaking to him from far away: "You go now."

It was a tone that would broach no objection.

When Sherlock next awoke, he was seated in an alleyway, his back against a rough and thoroughly unpleasant wall. His head was aching so badly that it felt like someone had been using it as a snare drum. He touched it, convinced he would feel blood; but all he felt was hair matted into a rat's nest between crown and nape. He let his hand fall upon the ground again, only to realize he had just missed a small puddle of vomitus: his own, he assumed.

Whatever else, the poppy was not the drug for him.

Shading his eyes and blinking furiously, he stared up at a hazy sun and calculated that it must be nearly four in the afternoon—though of what day, he could not be certain.

Shakily, he rose to his feet, trying to recall where he was. Then he remembered that he was in Limehouse, that it was not safe there for the likes of him, and that he should most definitely try to make his way out of the East End before dark.

But first things first.

Leaning against the wall and struggling to remain erect, he awkwardly removed his jacket, draped it over one shoulder and rolled up his cuffs.

One, two, three, four, five, six...

Six new puncture marks.

He had to shake off the fog and the wooziness so as to recall how each and every injection felt—for there was something terribly familiar about them all.

Then there was the comment in the opium den, the one that had shaken him out of his delirium: *'E's a right proper baker, best I ever come across.*

Almost instantly he recalled Mycroft's words: *Why would a lad about to die, who has but one breath left in him to say one word, choose* that *one? What did Charles hope to achieve? It makes logical sense but no* emotional *sense, do you see?*

Sherlock understood that now.

He began to shiver uncontrollably.

As he lowered his cuffs and struggled to put on the jacket, he heard a high-pitched whistle, then another one— the sort that thieves make when they lay their eyes upon an easy target. But when he looked about, he saw no one.

He took a reckoning of his belongings. He had Alvey Ducasse's shoes upon his feet. He had stashed his new shirt in a convenient hole, though where that might be, he could not recall at the moment. He still wore the torn, smelly one, with Alvey's itchy jacket over that, and his trousers were frayed. He had nothing at all worth stealing.

He breathed a sigh of relief until he heard a more harrowing sound: feet running towards him, two pairs in fact, the noise of leather slapping cobblestones reverberating off the looming buildings.

He had no one to protect him and could not have thrown a punch for the literal life of him.

He slid back down the wall, curled up into a ball, and hoped the punishment would be brief.

A moment later, he felt a hand on his shoulder, shaking him.

"Guv! Guv! It's us, McPeel and Ducasse!"

He lifted his head from the crook of his elbow and squinted into the light. Sure enough, there stood Joe McPeel and Alvey Ducasse, staring down at him, their expressions a cross between bewildered and victorious.

"How... how did you find me?" Sherlock asked.

"We din't! *Them's* the ones," Ducasse said, pointing upwards.

Sherlock followed the trajectory of Ducasse's thumb to a darkened second-floor window across the alleyway, where a shadow appeared briefly from a back window, waved, and then was gone.

"We put out word that you'd gone missin'," McPeel explained.

"And what made you do *that?*" Sherlock asked, for he had told no one where he was going.

"Douglas said you was comin' to Nicklas to switch!" Ducasse explained, modeling Sherlock's jacket, which fit him quite nicely, as did Sherlock's shoes. "When you din't show, I fetched McPeel an' we runs to the last place we seen you! Been on the 'unt ever since!"

"Beggin' pardon, guv, but that puddle stinks to 'igh 'eaven," McPeel added, indicating the vomitus. "How's about we 'elp you to your feet?"

"What day is this?" Sherlock asked as he took a hold of their outstretched hands.

"Wensdy!" Ducasse announced brightly.

Fighting nausea and the pounding in his head, Sherlock released himself from their hands and took a few tottering steps. "Wednesday," he repeated. "Two hours to find my good shirt, sober up, tidy up, and get myself to a dinner party. Might the two of you assist me in this endeavor?"

"We'd consider it a right honor, guv," McPeel said proudly.

43

TAKING ADVANTAGE OF THE BALMY EVENING, MYCROFT paced just outside the Lin residence on Kenilworth Street in Pimlico. He was smoking a Partagás to keep his temperamental nerves at bay as he waited for Sherlock to arrive. What was it about this dinner that put him so much on edge? He had been invited here as a guest, yet he was curious about Deshi Hai Lin and his business, and he was determined to ferret out a bit more information than was strictly appropriate for a dinner gathering… which made him wonder if he was suffering a pang of guilt.

But no. What Mycroft felt in the pit of his stomach were butterflies.

You cannot be carrying a torch for this girl, a girl you have met but once… and Oriental to boot! he scolded himself.

He looked to heaven, hoping to find a spark of commiseration there, but a sliver of a moon lay horizontal in the black sky, like a smile.

Even the moon seemed to be laughing at him.

Patrolling the street were the two bodyguards whom Mycroft recognized from the herbalist's shop. But when they passed, acknowledging him with a small nod of the head, it simply reaffirmed that neither man had been the mysterious driver of the landaulet.

Huan had parked Mycroft's carriage down the street, with an unobstructed view of the building. He and Douglas were to linger outside, coachman and "bodyguard," as Mycroft and Sherlock went in to dine… provided Sherlock managed to show.

This doubt had just planted itself and taken root, causing Mycroft's anxiety to grow by leaps and bounds, when he spotted his brother in the distance, arriving at a run.

"Hurry!" Mycroft exclaimed by way of greeting, putting out his Partagás and staring sternly his way—an attitude that was not entirely fair, given that Sherlock was not late.

"Taking up smoking again?" Sherlock responded jovially. "You have not done that in a—"

"What has happened to your jacket?" Mycroft demanded, alarmed. "It looks as if you've slept in it! And why is your shirt not pressed?"

"As long as your mouth is open, Mycroft, is there anything else you would care to criticize?" Sherlock replied.

"For pity's sake," Mycroft said with a sigh.

While he set about tugging on Sherlock's jacket and smoothing out the shoulders to adjust the fit, Sherlock looked about with distaste, as if he had suddenly taken notice of their location.

"I was under the impression that the family has means, so why Pimlico?"

"You know perfectly well why," Mycroft snapped, tugging on Sherlock's collar to make it stand up properly, and fixing his tie. "Stop asking foolish questions."

"It is a cut above Chelsea, I suppose, but I thought he was a wealthy owner of steamships! This is more suited to the distant relatives of minor nobility…"

"Because *this* owner of steamships is Chinese!" Mycroft reminded him. "Better neighborhoods are closed to him. And if he wishes to be accepted even in these lesser neighborhoods, he will have to keep his wits about him and not call too much attention to himself."

"And why is Douglas here?" Sherlock continued accusingly. "Is he to stand guard at the door all night like some gilded blackamoor? Surely you are not expecting trouble?" he added as Mycroft hustled him up the front steps to the Lins' residence. "And what are we to do about dinner? I am not hungry in the least! And even if I were, you know I have no taste for exotic food—"

"Sherlock, do not embarrass me—"

"—and what of the symbols?" Sherlock interrupted, restraining Mycroft as the latter reached for the bell. "What did you discover? I have a right to know!"

"Stop it!" Mycroft replied. "Why are you blathering on? And why are your eyes so bright?"

Sherlock lowered his voice. "I have slept poorly the last several days due to the studying, so I indulged in a bit of Vin Mariani."

"What is 'a bit'?"

Sherlock shrugged noncommittally. "One, perhaps two glasses…"

"Two glasses! Sherlock! That is nearly ninety milligrams of cocaine!" Mycroft scolded. "What were you thinking? Calm yourself! Breathe! Try to maintain some decorum, for the love of heaven!" He turned the bell.

The door opened and a tall, impeccably coiffed and liveried Mandarin held out a silver platter, on which Mycroft and Sherlock dutifully placed their calling cards. Though the man was clean-shaven with short, well-coiffed hair, Mycroft recognized him immediately.

At last, the driver of the landaulet!

No doubt it was he who had visited Regent Tobaccos and so impressed Mr. Pennywhistle with his gentlemanly ways; he who had paid for the Glenlivet in Australian coin. He who had worn false beard and gloves, to practically run them over outside of Madame de Matalin's!

The butler did not make eye contact or intimate that he knew Mycroft at all. As he escorted them to the drawing room, Mycroft kept his wits about him and took stock of the layout of the house.

Mycroft was well aware that Orientals could be, indeed were *expected* to be, in the ship trade. Deshi Hai Lin would not have to pretend, as Douglas did, that he was an employee rather than an employer. But still, he had to beware of jealousy or animosity from native-born citizens. The plain, unassuming house was the embodiment of caution. It had a well-bred economy, with the goal of drawing no undue attention to itself or to its owner. Yet, here and there Mycroft spotted touches of affluence. As they passed the library, glass-fronted bookshelves held several first editions of fourteenth-century works, including *The Canterbury Tales* and Dante Alighieri's *Trilogy*, the ceiling boasted a spring-loaded chandelier, and on the wall were gas brackets in lieu of traditional sconces, a definite modern and costly touch. Below their feet were several thick Moroccan and Turkish rugs.

It did, however, make him wonder again about the canary-yellow landaulet, since Deshi Hai Lin had taken such care to be discreet in his own home. What on earth had possessed him to make such an ostentatious purchase?

At that moment Mycroft noticed, through a partially open door, an alcove with a pretty little window seat. On it sat a very large bisque doll with black hair and Oriental features. He turned to see if Sherlock had noticed, but his brother was looking straight ahead while lifting his knees as he walked, like a badly strung marionette.

The butler led the two brothers into the drawing room. Ai Lin and her brother were there to greet them. She was dressed in traditional garb. Her skirt, over-blouse and Qing jacket were in emerald green this time, her coal-black hair swept up into one large chignon, a corona of holly flowers surrounding it.

"Please forgive my father's absence," she said with a

small bow. "An unforeseen circumstance having to do with his work. He assured me he would join us for pudding."

Mycroft attempted to muster up some disappointment at this—after all, poor Douglas was cooling his heels outside so that he could learn something about the patriarch, not the son or the daughter!—but he simply could not manage it.

As for her brother, Dai en-Lai Lin, he stood by her side with a smile so wide it could have put Huan's to shame. He seemed, all told, exactly what Sherlock had described: "a good enough sort" of average height and weight, with a pleasing if not handsome face, and a dusting of a mustache over his top lip. Unlike his sister, he was dressed in Western attire. And, although unfailingly polite to Mycroft, it was clear that his interest lay solely in Sherlock. Within moments after they entered, the two lads were in a conclave at the far end of the room, chattering on about the miseries of university and exams, along with the joys of self-defense.

Sherlock was as agreeable as Mycroft had ever seen him. And when, to Dai en-Lai's delight, he demonstrated one or two boxing maneuvers, Mycroft whispered a silent thank-you to Angelo Mariani and his coca-laced tonic.

As they waited to be summoned to dinner, Mycroft and Ai Lin observed their excited banter with some amusement, and she thanked him for bringing his brother.

"Dai has been counting the hours," she told him. "He could not be happier, and therefore neither could I. The flowers, in fact, are in your honor, you see?"

Mycroft startled at the word "flowers," but Ai Lin turned

so that he might better observe the garland that encircled her hair—though there was no need, for he had noticed it immediately.

"'Holme,' from what I was told, means 'one who resides near a holly tree'!" she announced.

Mycroft laughed. "I was told that as well, though I fear we are Norsemen, from the old Norse 'Holmr,' which I believe means 'small patch of land in a river'—not quite so charming."

Ai Lin raised her perfect brows. "You were told? You do not know?"

"I do not. I am woefully ignorant of our ancestry beyond a few paltry generations."

"Purposely so?" she asked, tilting her head like a curious bird.

"I assume you are acquainted with all your ancestors," Mycroft said.

"Oh yes. For fourteen generations. But of course, we revere them, and they purportedly return the favor by looking after us."

"'Purportedly'?" he inquired, smiling.

"Please do not assume I am being flippant, Mr. Holmes," Ai Lin replied. "It is merely an acknowledgment of my mortality and all that I cannot know for certain about what is to come."

Just then, the butler entered. "Dinner is served," he announced, his tone strong but pleasing.

"Thank you, William," Ai Lin said. "Might you do me the honor of escorting me, Mr. Holmes?" she asked, then amended: "You seem a bit flushed…"

William! Mycroft was thinking. *Of course!*

"Forgive me," he said, offering her his arm. "It is just that… your man is impressive, is he not?" he added as they followed William down the hall towards the dining room. "And it is so difficult to find a good manservant nowadays…"

"Indeed, he is a treasure," she said proudly. "He has been with our family since I was five. He began as postilion and is quite the horseman still. To be frank, I prefer him to our coachman and so does my father, and he is kind enough to indulge us!"

"Was he born here? Given his Christian name, I mean."

"In Canton. His real name is Wei Wing Zheping. But I was just learning English and took a liking to the name 'William.' To my ears it sounded like Wei Wing. And so, with the brashness of children, I renamed him."

"I see," Mycroft replied. "So you baptized him, as it were. Did you give him a surname as well? Or perhaps at age five you did not yet know what a surname was—"

"Of course I did! Because I adored him, I gave him one that would fit his nature: 'Angel.'"

"Ah. And are you the only one who calls him thus?" Mycroft asked.

"On the contrary. William Angel he became, and William Angel he remained!" she said as Angel himself opened the dining-room door.

So that is why Madame de Matalin could not socialize with him, Mycroft thought. *Because William Angel is Chinese, and a mere butler.*

44

ONE END OF THE LONG DINING-ROOM TABLE HAD BEEN SET with the snowiest of linens. Atop it were Georgian glasses, their round funnels engraved with an image of Britannia holding a sprig of olive, and surrounded by foliage and flowers. The plain white china that accompanied it was so delicate as to be very near transparent, the George Adams silverware shined to a fare-thee-well. Behind each setting sat a silk card bearing each of their names and written in the finest hand.

It was of the same make and fabric as William Angel's calling cards in Madame de Matalin's paraphernalia box.

At the head of the table an empty chair awaited Deshi Hai Lin. Mycroft, as the elder brother, was seated to the missing patriarch's right, with Ai Lin beside him. Sherlock was to the left, Dai en-Lai at his side.

The repast, though well executed, consisted of nothing more exotic than savory soup, roast pork, potatoes and vegetables: a meal carefully chosen to not give offense.

As they ate, Ai Lin asked about Mycroft's work and

interests, and he told her what he could. They spoke of his passion for inventions, and Dai en-Lai and Sherlock joined in for a while. Sherlock was especially delighted with the notion of an electric typewriter recently perfected by Edison.

"Soon, we shall have no need for handwritten missives!" he crowed, for his penmanship was every bit as illegible as Queen Victoria's.

"A pity," Mycroft said, "as there is much one can glean from the graphs that a human hand forms."

He turned back to Ai Lin. "And you have a keen interest in herbs," he said.

"It is an interest by default," she replied as the lads resumed their discussion on the fighting arts. "What truly fascinates me is systematic investigation into medicine; its frontiers, you might say. The work of Louis Pasteur, for example. Do you know of him?"

Mycroft nodded. "Some years ago, Pasteur suggested that microorganisms might be the cause of disease in animals and humans," he said, "and more and more evidence points us in that strange but fascinating direction."

"Ah, so you do know!" she exclaimed, her eyes shining. "I thought you might."

"But if the frontiers of medicine call to you," Mycroft asked, "then can you not pursue them even as a sort of pastime?"

Ai Lin laughed. "Mr. Holmes, that is no sort of 'pastime' for a Han woman!"

"But you are of the Hakka subset, are you not?" he argued. "Which values education even for women. I have a friend, Dr. Joseph Bell, whom I greatly admire, and who is quite open-minded. I am certain he would be only too happy to—"

"Oh, Mr. Holmes, no!" Ai Lin exclaimed as if he had just offered to apprentice her in the nearest brothel. "I could never become a *real* physician. Ever. It would shame my family. No, the Hakka value a woman's ability at music and languages. And even if that were not the case, our family is still bound to our more encompassing Han tradition. An exemplary Han woman is put on earth to give her husband good advice, to be heroic, and to sacrifice herself for her family. Not to play about with creatures that cannot be seen with the naked eye."

"But surely times are changing even in China," Mycroft persisted, sounding, even to himself, slightly pitiable. Was he truly expecting to change the course of tradition with one paltry meal? Would she see the light and leap into his waiting arms? And what of the sinister William Angel? Would he join their happy family as butler, coachman, and procurer of young boys as human pincushions for drug addicts?

"Perhaps for my grandchildren," Ai Lin was saying. "But not for me. Our stories are filled with cautionary tales about ambitious, manipulative women who create only chaos and destruction. We are taught to study the seven virtues appropriate to women." She counted them on her lovely fingers: "Humility, resignation, subservience, self-abasement, obedience, cleanliness, and industry. 'Medicine' is not among them."

Mycroft smiled sadly. "And how are you faring with those virtues?"

"I lack several, as you may have guessed," she replied. "That said, do not be fooled, for I am modern only in words, and then only when my father is not present."

Indeed, when her father entered the room moments later, the atmosphere took a definite turn. Deshi Hai Lin was some fifty years of age, and about Mycroft's height. He wore a *tángzhuāng* of silk, plain but very well made. There was no doubt he was the gentleman that Mycroft had spotted little more than a week before with Cainborn—although this night he seemed tired to the point of debility.

Deshi Hai Lin apologized for his lateness. From the moment he sat down, his children's eyes were on him. Dai en-Lai was deferential, Ai Lin solicitous. And Mycroft realized immediately that neither was doing so out of fear or even familial reverence. These children loved their father.

Sherlock, for his part, seemed to have lost interest in the proceedings. No longer basking in Dai en-Lai's undivided attention, he fidgeted in his seat, left his pudding untouched, and took to squinting into his dessert wine as if it were a crystal ball.

As Mycroft dug into his apple charlotte, he tried to engage the elder Lin in conversation, casually asking about his background.

"I am from Canton, Mr. Holmes," was all Deshi Hai

Lin offered, smiling slightly but staring off into the middle distance. "My children were young when I left, and I… younger than I am now."

"What year was that?" Mycroft asked.

"1859," he replied.

"Ah," Mycroft said. "A difficult year for Canton."

"Very difficult, yes," Deshi Hai Lin said, glancing down at his dessert.

"Papa is invested in the coolie trade in reverse," Ai Lin said. "He aims to eradicate it in his lifetime."

Deshi Hai Lin cut off a portion of apple charlotte, his fork hovering in midair. "I am afraid my daughter thinks too highly of me," he said with a sigh. "She will not boast about herself but will boast about me to whoever will listen."

"But what she said is true, Papa!" Dai en-Lai countered.

"And my son takes after my daughter," Deshi Hai Lin quipped before adding, "I confess that I inquired of Ai Lin just whom we were permitting into our home in such haste. And I discovered that you are special consul to the Secretary of State for War. So you must be aware what a scourge the so-named *coolie* trade is."

"I am, yes," Mycroft said.

Sherlock suppressed a yawn. "What are we talking about?" he asked in a tone so laconic it was a wonder he did not lay his head upon the table and drift off.

The Vin Mariani had lost its hold, and Sherlock was clearly experiencing the reverse: a nettled sort of dispiritedness. Mycroft could only thank Providence that this downturn in humor and stamina had deigned to wait until the final course.

"Foreign vessels arrive in Canton and Whampoa," he explained to Sherlock, "where they feign to employ emigrant laborers when instead they are in cahoots with Chinese crimps—kidnappers—who collect thirty U.S. dollars for every human delivery they put on board. Then in Havana, this chattel is resold for four hundred a head, never to be heard from again. Thanks to Britain's efforts and the United States', the trade has abated, but it is far from eradicated."

Deshi Hai Lin nodded. "Even with proof of the crime," he volunteered bitterly, "nothing is done: their lives matter to no one. But they matter to me, Mr. Holmes. And I will go a long way to prevent it from happening. A very long way indeed!"

"Papa purchased individual workers in Cuba and sent them to work aboard his ships as free men," Ai Lin explained.

"Why, that is commendable!" Mycroft said.

"Yes. Over the past few years several have risen through the ranks to positions of authority aboard the ships. One is now in charge of the welfare of all the others…"

Deshi Hai Lin suddenly grasped the edges of the table as if he were in danger of falling. "A bargain with the devil! A *dozen* devils!" he amended. "But I will teach them! I will let my ships rot in the docks before I—"

"Papa!" Ai Lin exclaimed.

"Papa, that is enough!" Dai en-Lai joined in. "You are upsetting yourself!"

Deshi Hai Lin drew a deep breath. "I am afraid my son is correct, Mr. Holmes," he murmured after a moment. "William?" he said to the butler. "Perhaps it is time to retire to the library."

Angel bowed slightly. "Of course, sir. Our latest procurement is a very fine single-malt Scotch, Smith's Glenlivet, if you and your guests would care to indulge…"

Mycroft glanced at Ai Lin, whose nerves seemed on edge. "It sounds delightful, but I would be sorry to leave such fine company…" Mycroft began.

"No fear, Mr. Holmes," she replied. "We break with tradition in that my father allows me access to the men's after-dinner conversation, as well as their libations…"

But Deshi Hai Lin sprang abruptly to his feet. "I am not feeling… quite myself," he stammered. "If you will please excuse me."

"By all means!" Mycroft said, rising as well, while silently urging Sherlock to do the same.

Ai Lin rose too, placing her napkin on the table. "Father," she said calmly, "may I accompany you to your chamber?" Without waiting for a reply, she smiled wanly at her guests and added, "Mr. Holmes, Master Sherlock, please do not begrudge us this infelicitous evening. I shall importune you with another invitation at a more auspicious time. William? Dai en-Lai? Kindly see to the comfort of our guests."

With that, she took her father's arm, and together they

made their way out of the dining room.

As Dai en-Lai looked sheepishly from one Holmes to the other, Mycroft came to the rescue. "I admire your taste in spirits, Mr. Angel," he said. "Would you consider a quick tour of your wine cellar?"

"It would be my privilege, Mr. Holmes," Angel said with a bow.

"Master Dai en-Lai, might you entertain Sherlock another few minutes?" Mycroft added.

Dai en-Lai looked relieved, while Sherlock pursed his lips to intimate that he was more than done with the entire affair.

45

WILLIAM ANGEL LED MYCROFT DOWN A SET OF STONE STEPS
to the cellar. It was narrow and cool, its contents sorted
in a hundred open boxes stacked one atop the other, with
a pyramid of bottles on the inside of each, marked by a
rectangular tin tag held in place by wire. On the tag, the
contents were written in chalk: *Chambertin, Clos de Bèze, Île-
de-France*, and so forth. They were dusty wares of adequate
but unexceptional vintage, along with port and dessert fare:
a further indication that Deshi Hai Lin had no passion for
spirits, and that the three cases of Smith's Glenlivet were
bought to be noticed and not as a matter of course.

As Angel lit a lamp, Mycroft edged up to a box, slipped a
bottle out and sequestered it behind his back. In his present
physical state, should Angel strike, he feared he would not
be able to defend himself without a weapon at the ready.

"It was you at the reins when your employer met
with Professor Cainborn outside the National Standard
Theatre," Mycroft began. "You and Mr. Lin who followed

us to Nickolus House; you who nearly put us under the wheels outside Madame de Matalin's abode; you who left the Australian sovereigns at Regent Tobaccos—"

"Yes, Mr. Holmes," Angel replied quietly, turning to him. "From the moment I realized who you were, I knew I had to try and gain your notice. But as you can plainly see, I could not leave my name, nor meet with you in person without arousing suspicion."

"And why should you wish to gain my notice?"

"Because of your brilliance," Angel said. "Your coachman Huan speaks of you fondly. He recounted your Trinidadian exploits to perhaps one or two people, but our Chinese community is miniscule, and word travels like wildfire."

He stepped closer to Mycroft, who tightened his grip around the neck of the bottle.

"What do you know of Professor John Cainborn?" Mycroft asked.

"Mr. Holmes," Angel replied softly. "May I remind you that I am the butler of this household, and not peer or confidante? I do not wish to disappoint you, but I know nothing of my employer's meetings, other than I am called upon to drive occasionally."

"Did you hear their conversation?"

"No, nor would I have, if given the chance to do so," Angel said with a tremulous look at the half-open door at the top of the cellar stairs. "All I can tell you," he added in an urgent half-whisper, "is that something untoward is destroying the peace of this household!"

"Mr. Angel," Mycroft said somewhat impatiently. "Whether or not I *will* help you, I cannot do so unless you tell me plainly what the matter is."

William Angel drew a breath. "One of the men my employer rescued has now stolen the reins of power—"

"Stop there. Rescued from what, specifically? Are we talking still of men he purchased in Cuba to work aboard ship?"

"In 1859 in Canton, two brothers were falsely accused of kidnapping native-born men and selling them into slavery. They were thrown into prison to stand trial, but a raging mob dragged them out and was about to behead them when my Mr. Lin rescued them! One now shows his gratitude by turning his best men against him... forcing my employer's hand with the export of a new and very powerful drug..."

"The *export*, you say? Not the import?"

Angel shook his head. "It is manufactured here in England and then sold abroad, mostly in China."

"For gold?"

"Yes. Users in other countries make their first purchase on the recommendation of wealthy users here."

"Such as Madame de Matalin," Mycroft said softly.

At that, Angel's eyes filled with tears. "Yes," he stammered.

"And how did you find the boys who were used to test this powerful new drug?" Mycroft demanded.

"I? No. I had nothing to do with procuring them!"

"Then who did?"

"I wish I knew, Mr. Holmes!" Angel whispered, shaking his head. "My task was merely to introduce them to the Madame, for she trusted me. When told to, I went for them at The Water Monkey, a local opium den."

"And how did you come to be part of this?"

"Madame de Matalin and I were both addicted to *papaver somniferum*," Angel explained. "When her butler began to procure for her, he came to me, for we were in the same profession, and he knew my habit to be as voracious as hers. She wished to meet me and took an instant liking to me… typical of drug users with the same habit, I must say. I became the only person she truly trusted when it came to… our habit, and so I *had* to be brought into the mix, regardless of anyone's feelings about it, including mine."

"And what is this 'new drug'?"

Angel sighed deeply. "Again, Mr. Holmes, I cannot tell you. I have borne a terrible secret for a very long time, and it has led me down many dark paths. My Mr. Lin is convinced that the sleep-inducing poppy ruined Chinese society. Had he known of my use, he would have fired me long ago, and that would have been the end of me. A year ago, Ai Lin discovered my secret and began to treat me with *kratom* and other herbs. She saved my life *and* my career. I have not had any altering substances in more than six months."

"So the new drug was first exported in summer…" Mycroft murmured.

"I believe so, yes," Angel said.

"In dolls?"

❦

Angel shook his head helplessly. "Again, I…"

The front doorbell rang upstairs, and Angel cast a worried glance up at the cellar door.

"What of the gold?" Mycroft persisted. "Why bring it to me?"

"I know only that there is something unique about it and that it causes my employer much heartache. I was charged with disposing of it—spending it—for goods that would not draw undue attention."

"These two men, the ones who were nearly beheaded, the ones Mr. Lin saved. Have you ever met them?"

"No. But as I said, our community is miniscule, and scars such as theirs are difficult to hide. I believe them to be Kang Chen and his brother, Ju-long Chen. Kang works the ships. Ju-long is the proprietor of the opium den near Shadwell Docks that I spoke of, The Water Monkey."

They heard the soft padding of feet at the top of the stairs, and then Ai Lin's strained voice: "Mr. Holmes? I have been called away; it is rather an emergency, I am afraid. William? Might you drive me?"

"Of course, miss!" he replied. "The carriage shall be ready forthwith!"

Her footsteps retreated, William Angel turned to put out the light, and Mycroft returned the wine bottle to its slot.

"Please. Find out what you can of my employer's business dealings. And come to his aid, I beg you," Angel said as he snuffed out the flame.

At the front door, Dai en-Lai Lin let Sherlock go only after several assurances that they would not lose touch. That settled, he and Mycroft were just stepping out when Ai Lin, in a traveling cloak, rushed up to them and pressed something into Mycroft's hand, looking up at him with those tourmaline-colored eyes.

"Thank you," she said before hurrying off.

It was only when she was out of his sight that Mycroft realized what he was holding: a small square tin, along with a note.

As the front door shut behind them, and Sherlock waved impatiently for the carriage, Mycroft opened the tin to find two small sacks of herbs. He licked a finger and tasted both. The first was green tea. The second was a mixture of hawthorn, St. John's Wort, and garlic.

Ai Lin's beautifully written note said only:

One teaspoon in the tea twice per day.
For your heart.
AL

Mycroft recalled Georgiana's anguished face, her words moments before she died: *Dearest*, she had cried out. *Guard your heart!*

Another woman, he thought, *with the same advice!*

"What is that?" Sherlock asked with a sidelong glance and a distinct lack of interest.

"For headaches," Mycroft replied, refolding the note.

"Since when are you plagued with headaches? You are not mimicking Mother, I hope! Oh, and by the by, I know her doll's name."

"Mother's?" Mycroft inquired absently.

"*Mother's* doll? Have you gone completely daft? Ai Lin's doll!"

"You noticed Ai Lin's doll?" Mycroft asked, eyeing him open-mouthed.

"Well naturally I noticed it! That abomination nearly made me jump out of my skin! I asked Dai en-Lai if the thing had a name, and he told me 'Jacinthe.' Their father gave it to her a year or so ago. Quite the coincidence, would you not agree? What with the symbols being names of flowers?"

"Flowers and *herbs*," Mycroft corrected, his voice raw.

Is it possible, he asked himself, *that Ai Lin is somehow complicit?*

"Flowers and herbs?" Sherlock repeated, but he ceased speaking when the front door behind them opened and William Angel stepped out, the color drained from his face.

"Our carriage departs in a few moments," he said, looking directly at Mycroft. "You will recognize it. I would be obliged if you would follow."

With that, Angel turned and was about to enter again when Mycroft called to him.

"Mr. Angel! Will your bodyguards be accompanying you?"

"Yes, Mr. Holmes, they must. They are charged to follow the mistress wherever she goes."

"What of your employer? Can no one remain with

him? He may be in danger. He is having troubles with his employees, that we know. There is a struggle for power. Perhaps Ai Lin was called away on a ruse, to rid the house of her, of you, and of the bodyguards."

William Angel eyed him sorrowfully.

"Mr. Holmes, I pray it has not yet come to that. But if it has, those two bodyguards would not be able to assist him. I beg you again to do what you can to save him."

With that, he stepped inside, shutting the door behind him, as Huan pulled up with the carriage.

46

WITH ANGEL'S REQUEST STILL RINGING IN HIS EARS, another piece of the puzzle had fallen into place. Mycroft had to shut out all extraneous sounds and concentrate on what he knew and what he had seen, for the yellow landaulet was sure to appear at any moment, and he hadn't much time. Unfortunately, his heart was beating erratically.

Douglas stepped off the carriage. "We saw de Matalin's butler at the door," he said. "Anxious and in quite the rush."

Mycroft drew a breath to steady himself and turned to Sherlock, for it was time his brother proved his mettle. "Deshi Hai Lin," he said. "What did you notice?"

"Flowers and herbs," Sherlock replied.

"Sherlock, we are past all that——" Mycroft began.

"*Flowers and herbs,*" he insisted.

Mycroft sighed deeply and rattled off: "Rose, dahlia, lily, myrtle, anise, amaryllis, aster, holly, violet, tulip, poppy, sage, tansy, rue, and daffodil."

"Ah! So, the names of females! No, not females. I would

say dolls—that appalling 'Jacinthe' for example—"

"Sherlock!" Mycroft scolded. "Now, please!"

Sherlock rolled his eyes. "Fine. A spot of mud on the heel of his right shoe, wrong consistency for the docks, or for Pimlico on a night like this. Two marks on his left shirt cuff, barely discernible, the size of a man's rather oily thumb, with another point of contact, forefinger and middle, on the inside. A row of fingernail marks in the palm of his right hand."

"Thoughts?"

"He was in a lower caste neighborhood. He turned to leave when some person with oily fingers on his right made a move to detain him. Lin ripped his hand away and started once more to go, only to be grabbed again, this time by another person on his left as he swung back his hand, though he was almost instantly released."

"He did not pull away?" Mycroft asked, eyeing the street and listening for the sounds of carriage wheels.

"Stains were intact, not feathered. And light. Which means the minion to his left had barely touched him when he was ordered to unhand him. Lin has a skin infection above the nape of his neck, slightly visible underneath his hair, one small vertical crimson line, freshly disturbed, its detritus under the nails of his right hand: he had been scratching at it earlier, which means these were people he was familiar with, for one does not scratch at one's head while speaking to strangers, or in a formal setting. His mouth was dry even after a few sips of dessert wine. He had chewed at his bottom lip, and had no appetite—so nerves, nerves, and more nerves. And when he spoke of the coolie trade, his primary emotion was not the frosty anger one displays over a battle fought for years, but fresh rage, barely suppressed.

"Whoever molested his peace is someone he knows well, who wields power over him and who frightens him," Sherlock went on. "'A devil' might not be overstating it from his point of view, as his pupils were dilated in fear. I am assuming Lin is second in command, but something happened this night to disturb that balance of power. 'A dozen devils' no doubt refers to those who have now turned their backs on him. He is just coming to terms with it, thus the loss of equilibrium as the magnitude of the betrayal settles in. His daughter was clearly worried for him because 'coolies' is not a subject one brings up in polite dinner conversation, but she was desperate to discern how her father was faring, which she felt she could gauge solely via his immediate and unfiltered response. Had he had a chance to consider, he would have lied to protect her."

"Yes," Mycroft said, exhaling—for he realized he had been holding his breath, hoping Sherlock would get it right. "One revision however. Lin is not the second in command, but the first, with the second now trying to wrest power."

With that, he turned to Douglas. "I see you have brought your pistol, for you are protective of your left breast pocket—"

"Not as impressive as what Sherlock just pulled off," Douglas chided.

"Then let me raise the stakes," Mycroft said. "The patriarch of this family may be in jeopardy. His daughter may have been called away legitimately, but the timing is odd.

There is but one entry into the house, and it is through that door. Might you and Huan continue your watch? For there is no one else who has a chance against what is coming."

"What is coming?" Huan asked, climbing out of the driver's seat, his tone more curious than fearful.

"You had a few hours to assess the two bodyguards," Mycroft said. "How many men could they take on?"

"If their opponents are not professional combatants? I would say five altogether, as they are more brawn than brain," Douglas replied, and Huan nodded in agreement.

"Then you might expect more than five," Mycroft said. "And if they carry weapons, they'll be of a sort that is quickly hidden or disposed of."

"Ah, so foreigners! Asian, perhaps!" Huan exclaimed. Then he glanced at Douglas and shrugged. "Better. We know how they fight."

Huan looked pensive. Then he patted the horse on his muzzle affectionately and raked his fingers several times through the beast's luxurious mane.

"We have located the yellow landaulet's mysterious driver," Mycroft added. "I am to follow him, and Sherlock will accompany me."

"Not unless you fill me in thoroughly," Sherlock complained.

"'*Eis qui sine peccato est vestrum primus in illam lapidem mittat!*'" Mycroft shot back, his eyes narrowed.

It took Sherlock less than five seconds to scramble up next to Mycroft in the driver's seat.

A moment after that, the canary-yellow landaulet came careening around the corner and took off in all haste down the street.

The landaulet sped down Wilton Road to Vauxhall Bridge Road, past the Royal Standard and Buckingham Palace. St. James's Palace seemed to float in the background, its lanterns creating an eerie glow as the mild night gave way to long, gossamer strands of fog that began to settle across the city streets and then join into a mantle that grew thicker and thicker and dropped lower and lower as they went.

In the near half hour it took to travel between Pimlico and their destination, Mycroft did his best to elucidate Sherlock as to the mysterious appearances of the vehicle they were following, the calling cards bearing Angel's name, the finger ridges made of soot, Charles's matching prints, and the sovereigns.

He held back Cainborn's assignation with Deshi Hai Lin, for after a week's investigating, he had no more than one seemingly heated tête-à-tête outside the National Standard Theatre to report. There was nothing that tied Sherlock's professor to contraband, whether drugs or gold, much less to murder.

But it left Mycroft in the unenviable position of having to manufacture for Sherlock a connection that led from de Matalin to Deshi Hai Lin. And frankly, he was not up to it.

"Once we realized that Angel was Lin's butler, we knew

we would have to investigate both," Mycroft declared.

"And how did you come to realize that, when 'William Angel' is not his real name?" Sherlock inquired.

"Parfitt," Mycroft lied quickly. "He is a miracle worker."

"To find a nonexistent name in public records?" Sherlock said, his doubting eyebrow at full mast. "He must be a bloody Merlin."

"*Language*, Sherlock—"

"Why you must keep secrets…" Sherlock began, but the quotation in Latin that "let him who is without sin cast the first stone" must have still been fresh in his mind, for he did not pursue it further.

Unfortunately, it confirmed to Mycroft that his brother was continuing to keep secrets as well. He could only hope none was dangerous.

The landaulet turned onto Piccadilly, and after a moment they'd reached the noble residences overlooking the park.

It slowed in front of Madame de Matalin's grand old building. It was still early enough that traffic, even in this residential portion of the street, was brisk. No one would notice the comings and goings of servants or visitors to the house.

As Mycroft halted the carriage, he watched Ai Lin emerge from her own vehicle, her bodyguards in tow and a key in her hand. Concentrated fully on the task before her, she crossed to the pavement as William Angel disembarked and hurried over to Mycroft.

"I will see to your carriage," Angel announced, holding out his hand for the reins.

Mycroft leaned in, whispering through his teeth: "I don't give two figs for my carriage, only for my brother's life. If this is a trap, I will find ways to hound you to the ends of the earth, do I make myself clear?"

Without awaiting reply, Mycroft gave him the reins and jumped down, with Sherlock behind him. The two caught up with Ai Lin as she reached the front door.

"How do you know Madame de Matalin?" Mycroft demanded.

Ai Lin glanced up, surprised but unruffled. "I would ask the same of you, Mr. Holmes. Though now is not really the time…"

Mycroft paused then said, "Send your bodyguards back to your father's house." When she hesitated, he added, "Your father was badly shaken. I believe he could be in danger—they might save his life. My friend is there, Cyrus Douglas, a tall black man. Have them do whatever he says."

Ai Lin looked back at her bodyguards. "Mr. Angel will wait with Mr. Holmes's carriage," she said. "You will do as Mr. Holmes has said."

She turned the key, and pushed open the door.

47

WITH AI LIN IN THE LEAD, THE THREE HURRIED DOWN THE hall. Thick Persian carpets still covered the floor and African silver and ivory sculptures still stood mute and regal. But the house was empty.

"Where are the servants?" Sherlock whispered as Ai Lin paused to listen.

"Gone," she declared.

She seemed suddenly shaky on her feet. Mycroft reached out a hand to steady her, but she steeled herself and approached the library door. Mycroft pushed it open and the three entered.

A welcoming fire burned in the enormous hearth. Every chandelier and lamp had been lit. At the far end of the gilt-framed divan sat the child-sized bisque doll, Marguerite, her glassy eyes staring straight ahead.

On the nearer end of the divan, closer to the door, sat the Madame.

She was still dressed in the garish attire that gave the

birds of the air and lilies of the field a run for their money. Her knees were splayed open and her right sleeve had been unceremoniously rolled up to the biceps, exposing skin as lined and thin as used wax paper. She had a fresh puncture wound at the crook of her left elbow, a loosened foulard draped just above it, a syringe dangling between the fingers of her right hand. Her eyes were open, as was her crimson-tinted mouth, set in a grimace that seemed to Mycroft a cross between a laugh and a scream, every trace of life extinct.

"Quite dead," Sherlock proclaimed, his voice reverberating through the enormous room.

Mycroft stole a glance at the empty Louis XIV ormolu chair, where the Madame had sat at their previous meeting.

"Yes, Mr. Holmes," Ai Lin said, following his gaze, her voice breaking. "That is her favorite chair. That is where we would have found her, had this been a simple overdose…"

Mycroft nodded. "It has been staged, and not well," he replied, eyeing the syringe in de Matalin's hand, with a little half-filled vial of brownish liquid on the table, should anyone miss the implication. Neither syringe nor vial matched the ones he had found in her Limoges box upstairs.

He tasted the liquid. "Morphine," he announced to no one's surprise.

Ai Lin removed her cloak, set it upon the ormolu chair and approached de Matalin's body. She eyed the syringe, then placed it upon the table. She took the old woman's hand in hers, palpated her neck, jaw and shoulders, and inspected her fingernails and eyes.

"This was done with a practiced hand," Sherlock volunteered, eyeing the syringe.

"Too much so," Ai Lin responded. "The Madame was a bit of a novice with the needle; others always did it for her. I doubt she would have found a vein so accurately, or inserted so cleanly."

"How did you come to know her?" Mycroft asked.

"Through William Angel," Ai Lin said. "She and he were both addicts. William prided himself on his taste in opium: I am told he purchased only the best. When the Madame's butler was scouting around for sources, he found William. Then, when William lost his taste for it, he introduced me to the Madame, hoping I could help her as well. I managed to save one, but apparently not the other."

From an emerald reticule at her hip she extracted a thermometer, two small, sheathed knives, and a handkerchief. Laying the thermometer and the knives upon the table, she palpated de Matalin's abdomen with her fingers before settling at her upper stomach.

"I have read accounts of postmortems, of course," Sherlock said, drawing closer and with entirely too much enthusiasm, "but this is the first one I have witnessed—"

"Sherlock…" Mycroft warned.

"No, it is quite all right, Mr. Holmes. Madame de Matalin was not much use in life. Perhaps in death, she can be more helpful. I have faith that Master Sherlock will put whatever knowledge he has to good use. You must have learned," she said to Sherlock, "that there are three preliminary indications of death: *algor mortis*, *rigor mortis* and *livor mortis*. *Algor* refers to the temperature of the body."

"I read that the body loses, on average, one-point-five degrees per hour," he replied.

"Simplistic *and* deceptive," she countered, "for the weight of the body matters, as does the thickness of clothing, the ambient temperature, the age of the deceased—and those are just a handful of factors. There are others."

Unsheathing the larger knife, which looked the sort that could cut a pig's throat clean through, Ai Lin followed the lining of de Matalin's dress at the ribs, ripping through the costly material.

"Children and the elderly," she continued, "tend to lose heat more quickly. There is a diurnal difference, and of course a baseline difference, which varies from person to person. But, because I had been working with Madame, I know her baseline temperature, which ran cooler than most, ninety-eight on the nose."

"How long since you last treated her?" Mycroft asked.

"Six months or more," Ai Lin declared sadly. Using the extremely sharp tip of the knife and some pressure, she made a gash in de Matalin's corset over her upper stomach. "The fire, for example, would keep her warm longer," she said as she laid the first deadly implement aside and unsheathed the smaller knife, which looked to Mycroft like a surgeon's scalpel. She inspected it as if meditating upon it, then deftly jabbed it through the gash in the corset into de Matalin's abdomen just beneath the diaphragm.

So efficient was its violence that Mycroft and Sherlock drew a collective breath.

As Sherlock leaned in, fascinated, Ai Lin extracted the bloody knife, placed it on the handkerchief, and quickly inserted the thermometer into the wound she had just created.

"There are two locations where the temperature of a corpse is to be taken, for in death the mouth is no longer a reliable indicator," Ai Lin explained. "The first is… rather intimate. The second is in the tissue of the liver. So we have her baseline temperature of ninety-eight. Let us return to her one point for diurnal and ambient, minus one point five per hour…"

She pulled out the thermometer, wiped the blood on the handkerchief, then squinted at the mercury. Sherlock's head was now very near her own.

"Ninety-six point seven!" he announced. "She has been dead an hour and a half!"

Ai Lin nodded. "Approximately, and confirmed by the beginnings of *rigor mortis*."

"The small muscles in her face and neck would already be rather rigid to the touch, though not fully so," Sherlock said. "Is that correct?"

"Touch her and see," Ai Lin said.

Sherlock placed his fingers upon de Matalin's cheekbones.

"Her arms and shoulders have not yet begun to harden, for *rigor* moves from small muscles to greater," Ai Lin went on. "Some forty-eight hours later, the process is reversed: great to small, until the corpse slackens completely. And *livor mortis*—the pooling of the blood within thirty minutes of the last heartbeat—further testifies to us its own truth," she declared. "Here is the pooling of blood in her hands, which were laid upon the divan. But oh!" she exclaimed, as if hearing her own voice for the first time. "Perhaps I should not be speaking thus! Whatever must you think of me?" she added, looking at Mycroft.

That you are the most stunning creature I have ever laid eyes upon, Mycroft thought but thankfully did not say.

What he did say was: "Sherlock, upstairs in her bedroom was once a bejeweled Limoges box. I doubt it is there still, but do check."

"I might also see if there is anything unusual or out of place," Sherlock offered excitedly.

"Yes, but do not be lax about it," Mycroft responded. "Hurry."

As Sherlock bolted out of the room, Mycroft indicated their surroundings. "The lights are for show," he said to Ai Lin, "for they were not nearly so bright when I was last here. The fire's detritus, given the flames' height, plus the flickering of the gas lamps, based on their activity since we first walked in, disclose the time the last living being fled this house—I would say some forty-five minutes ago. By now they will have contacted the local coroner, for whom they staged this macabre little scene. Is there anything here, anything at all, that can be tied to you?" he asked her.

"The tin on her end table, the one with the *kratom*—but that can be had at any chemist."

"Her man came to your house, distraught, to tell you she had died. Her other servants are mercenary types, are they not? Faithful enough to de Matalin, but not so keen on trouble?"

"Yes, Mr. Holmes. She preferred former felons. It ensured their loyalty."

Sherlock burst back into the room. "No box!" he announced. "But heel marks across her bedroom carpet and down the stairs, her bed recently sat on, then realigned. *That* is where she overdosed," he added, pointing up. "On the edge of her bed. They dragged her down a corpse!"

"You are saying her servants did not merely flee when they realized she was dead—but they were the ones who *staged* this?" Ai Lin asked.

"Madame is addicted to some new concoction, which costs a great deal and is unknown by the general public as of yet," Mycroft explained. "I would say her butler injected her, not meaning to overdose her. When she lost consciousness, he ordered she be removed from her bedchamber."

"Whatever for?" Ai Lin asked.

"He knew her. He suspected that, like most addicts, she put aside a portion of her drugs 'for a rainy day.' Such a cache would likely be in her bedroom, not in a public room like the library—"

"—and he did not wish the police or anyone else to come upon this unknown compound," Ai Lin said, completing Mycroft's thought. "For it might rouse questions that they were unprepared to answer."

Mycroft walked over to the doll and removed its shoe.

Taking Ai Lin's larger knife in hand, he ripped away the stocking and used the handle to chip off half the foot. Then he turned the doll around, tore away the back of its dress, ran his finger over the seam of its cloth body and showed the seam to Ai Lin.

"Does your doll bear this same stitch?" he asked.

"No," she said softly.

Mycroft threw Sherlock the doll's foot, which he caught mid-flight.

"Kaolin, mostly," Sherlock declared. "Not French, then. Chinese."

"It cannot be!" Ai Lin protested. "They do not make bisque dolls of this sort in China. It is why mine, with the Chinese features, is so unusual!"

"The coroner could be here any moment," Mycroft declared. "He will most likely declare it an overdose and close the case, unless of course he finds us here. We must go."

"Miss Lin," Mycroft said. "Did Madame de Matalin's butler ask you to come here? Or know that you would?"

"Oh no, Mr. Holmes, he neither asked nor suspected I would. He does not know me as well as all that; at least, not enough to know I can be a tad compulsive. I believe the poor man was simply distraught, and he knew I cared for her…"

Ai Lin drew a breath and gathered her instruments. She went over to Madame de Matalin, pressed the old woman's knees together and smoothed her skirt.

"I had wished better for you, Madame," she said. "Farewell."

48

WISPY GRAY RIBBONS OF FOG HAD MUTATED INTO A COLD, wet, punishing soup that obliterated the horizontal crescent of the moon. Pimlico had no streetlights to keep away the night. The darkness and the damp had emptied the street on which Deshi Hai Lin and his family lived.

But it was not altogether deserted.

Douglas and Huan were on opposite sides of the front door, hidden from view. The element of surprise was theirs, enhanced by Douglas's race and height, as well as by their style of fighting—for capoeira was little known outside of Brazil and Trinidad and its blows thus difficult to counter.

He and Huan had been sparring nearly every day for a year or more and were as coordinated and familiar with one another's movements as two dancers in a minuet. Since children, they had worked their neck muscles to withstand blows; they knew how to avoid a punch to the head or, as a last resort, to brace for impact.

And both had, in the past, taken on four fighters apiece.

But four against one meant battling at full force from the first instant, keeping nothing in reserve, fighting to exhaustion. One more opponent, held at the ready and fresh for battle, could easily dispatch them. They would have to create enough chaos that not one of them would think to hold back.

If there happened to be more than eight, all Douglas and Huan could hope to do was to delay the inevitable. And though his Smith & Wesson was a cartridge-firing revolver and so not as laborious and victim to weather as a black powder cap and ball, Douglas would not draw unless necessary. For he believed in shoot-to-kill, and only as a last resort. Besides, he was no expert shot. In the fog, he could only hit one or at most two living targets before the rest would come after him with a vengeance.

He and Huan had been waiting nearly an hour, battling the chill by keeping loose and focused, when their long-expected antagonists approached on foot.

At first, they could see but three.

Douglas felt a slight pull on the little finger of his right hand. In order to remain hidden, he and Huan were communicating via the hair that Huan had raked from his horse's mane and then had braided together to form one long multi-threaded strand between them.

Now? Huan's tug demanded.

Douglas tugged back once. *No.*

He felt more were coming.

And indeed, another three materialized almost immediately.

Another tug, another *no* as Douglas appraised the half-dozen men on the pavement.

A moment later, three more appeared. They were all Chinese but dressed in Western clothing. They had not come expecting a fight—at least, one they could not handle. Their movements revealed them to be cannier combatants than the mangy, half-starved malefactors who had taken Charles.

Nine, a lucky number in Douglas's native Trinidad, did not seem so lucky at the moment.

Now? Huan's tug demanded.

Douglas tugged back twice: *Countdown.*

He rose from his crouched position, shook out his limbs, breaking the strand that attached him to Huan, cracked his neck, rolled up his shirtsleeve and raked his left forearm against the rough wall. He squeezed the abrasion to draw out the blood and smeared it like war paint across his cheeks and underneath his eyes.

Capoeira taught that cunning was better than strength.

What good was the element of surprise without the corresponding elements of fear and perplexity?

Four of the men paused on the pavement at the bottom of the steps, two per side, while the other five made their stealthy way to the front door.

Douglas charged out of his hiding place. Huan was less than a second behind him, his face blooded too, his forearms naked—for they'd used the same strategies.

Douglas and Huan ran like savages, teeth bared. Their

windmill kicks caught the first two men by surprise as heels hit temporal bones. The force of the blows propelled the men's collapsing bodies onto their startled associates, who tried to maintain equilibrium while also deflecting two well-timed elbows to the chin, served up at an angle where they could do the most damage. Douglas could hear his victim's jaw dislocating, could see two heads move backwards in unison then rotate forward as brains bounced mercilessly against skulls.

And down they went.

The other five came barreling down the steps. It was they whom Douglas feared the most, for they were fresh, alert, and above all, enraged.

Train slowly, the saying went, *for anger will give you speed in the fight.*

The first man to lunge at him attempted a roundhouse kick, but Douglas grabbed his leg by the ankle and flipped him sideways. He fell back against the stairs with a loud crack that did not bode well for his spine. Two more men jumped over their comrade and came at him, with the final two flying at Huan. It was now a matter of trying to remain upright, for the moment he or Huan fell, they were done for.

As the men attacked with kicks and punches, he and Huan remained chins down, arms up and fluid. They did not permit their opponents to reach for their pockets—in case they held weapons—and avoided hits to the temple, heart, or the back of the head. Instead, they goaded them into striking less vulnerable parts—forearms, legs, abdomen, even the crown—hoping to wear them out before rising to the offensive again.

But their opponents were not so quickly drained. The luck of the draw had given Huan two of the best fighters, and he was being pummeled, while Douglas was forced to focus on deflecting blows to his chest, given the bullet fragments lodged therein. And though he and Huan were still on their feet, they were starting to fade, missing those split-second moves that could extinguish their assailants once and for all.

In the surrounding buildings, curtains were drawn and windows slammed shut, like so many winking eyes. There would be no neighborly rush to their aid.

Suddenly, Douglas heard the indignant scrape of braking wheels, the yellow landaulet screeching to a halt in front of the house.

Ai Lin's two bodyguards bounded out of the box seat and into the fray.

One of the four remaining assailants turned and gave a bodyguard a vicious headbutt to the bridge of his nose that dropped him to his knees, but the other bodyguard was throwing half-blind punches, and one or two landed. And though he too went down, they provided enough distraction that Huan and Douglas were able to draw a breath and take to the offense once more.

Huan executed a perfectly aimed armada kick, his body winding up from the torso like a top, his hands floating gently at his side, his leg utilizing momentum to rise up until his right heel was even with one tormenter's left ear. The force of the impact sent him reeling into Douglas's opponent—whereupon Douglas finished him off with a *chapa* move, spinning away as if fleeing, then dropping onto his hands and executing a deft kick to his throat that sent him staggering backwards, cranium skidding against pavement.

Now clearly losing, the two men still standing gathered their wits about them in an attempt to flee, but Huan, enraged by the blows he had suffered, catapulted himself towards his other tormenter, wrapping his legs like a vice around his neck.

He would have shattered the man's windpipe had Douglas not yelled out: "No!"

Huan released him, then backed away, wiping at the blood that was oozing from an ugly cut underneath his eye.

Utilizing every bit of fortitude left in him, Douglas drew out his pistol and pulled back the hammer. "Should you choose to return," he announced, pointing it at each man in turn, "we shall be more than ready to welcome you."

Then he stood still as death, gun drawn, until the men who could stand helped their fallen comrades. Some limping, some being carried, the lot of them hobbled away.

They might well be back, Douglas thought as he watched them go, *and forewarned is forearmed.*

But for this night, at least, it was over.

49

AS MYCROFT'S CARRIAGE HEADED BACK TOWARDS PIMLICO, the fog that had been chasing them down finally overtook them. It wrapped itself about the carriage, smothering sound until all was silent. Even the horse's hooves seemed swathed in cotton. William Angel, at the reins, was conducting with more finesse than did Huan, so that all of them seemed to be floating in a cloudy limbo.

Sherlock and Mycroft sat across from a subdued but attentive Ai Lin. Mycroft was elucidating what he could while trying mightily not to implicate Ai Lin's beloved butler in any of the more sinister goings-on.

Clearly William Angel the drug abuser had made deals to gratify his own needs. Then—when he was no longer using—he'd made more deals to preserve his sordid secret and his employment. But whatever else he was or had been, he posed no danger to Ai Lin or her family. His involvement in the whole imbroglio was as an intermediary at best. He was not running the show.

But Sherlock, listening, was well aware who was. Was it stubbornness or pride that kept him from telling Mycroft? He could have used Mycroft's counsel.

Did he wish so badly to solve the case on his own merit that he was refusing to divulge what he knew? Or was it that he could not bear the look of recrimination—possibly even loathing—that was certain to come his way the moment Mycroft learned the truth?

The Water Monkey would expect him to report for duty on the morrow. He could still go to see what else he could unearth—though it seemed to him he had already catapulted past all that...

"De Matalin's doll Marguerite was created to be a drug doll," Mycroft was explaining to Ai Lin, "to carry this as-yet-unnamed substance so it would not fall under the eyes of customs inspectors. Manufactured in China to appear French, then cut open for her wares. But de Matalin fell in love with her. After the drug was extracted, she sent her to Paris to be rebuilt 'properly.'"

"So that is why her stitching is different from Jacinthe's," Ai Lin said.

Mycroft nodded. "It is also why, when I met her, de Matalin mentioned several times how much her 'Parisian child' had cost her—because she had it shipped to Paris and back so as to make her whole again!"

"But you said the drug was being *ex*ported," Ai Lin countered.

"The *drug*, yes," Mycroft said. "But the *dolls* were made

in China, brought here, filled, then sent back to sellers in the East, to be paid for in gold."

"What of the expense?" Sherlock interjected. "Surely it would have been cheaper to make counterfeit dolls in England."

"Not at all," Ai Lin replied. "The ships' routes were already established, the dolls were little extra weight, manufacture is cheaper in China than it is in England, and frankly a secret is much easier to keep!" Turning to Mycroft, she said, "I take it the symbols at the train stations signified which of the dolls held more than stuffing."

"So the symbols never did have to be translated into English," Sherlock said.

"No. The dolls were shipped with name tags at their wrists just as French dolls are," Mycroft declared. "The translation was from French to Chinese. For of course Jacinthe means 'Hyacinth,' and Marguerite is French for 'Daisy.'"

"But I still do not understand why a doll, and not simply the drug, was brought to the Madame," Ai Lin said.

"Because she was not solely a customer. She was a principal in this affair, an investor," Mycroft explained. "Before the sellers began exporting in earnest, they brought her a doll to show her how the scheme would work."

"She always did pride herself on her savvy business sense," Ai Lin murmured.

"Yes, she said as much to Douglas and me," Mycroft confirmed. "I wish I had known then what she meant."

Sherlock continued to listen, but he was becoming

distracted; for he did not merely know the principal players, he also knew well the drug that was hidden inside the dolls.

He had suspected it at The Water Monkey when he'd felt it coursing through his veins. But then, in de Matalin's bedroom, he wondered where an addict would keep a stash of drugs that would be both safe and near at hand. He found a vial that de Matalin had secreted underneath her pillow, and he had tasted it… That taste, so familiar to him, had set a trembling in his bones that he had been struggling for the better part of thirty minutes to quell.

"Master Sherlock?"

"Yes?" he said, hoping she had not called out his name more than once.

"How did you know the doll hailed from China?" she asked.

"Because Chinese bisque and French bisque differ," he replied. "Kaolinite, feldspar and quartz, or other forms of silica, are the base ingredients for most European hard-paste porcelains, whereas China uses more kaolin to form the bones of the paste. Not that it matters, but English bone china is two parts bone-ash, one part kaolin, one part china stone."

"My goodness!" she exclaimed. "How do you come to know so much about bisque dolls?"

"Not dolls," he replied. "Porcelain. Our mother is, or was, a collector."

He gave Mycroft a sidelong glance, but Mycroft avoided his gaze. Mother was no doubt the last subject on his agenda.

"Ah. So my doll too must have been a… a 'sample' doll," Ai Lin murmured. "My father had it made for me along with the others…"

She did not say it, but Sherlock saw it written on her face: *How could he do something so perfectly vile?*

"I imagine that yours was never filled with anything but cloth," Mycroft offered. "Perhaps he wished to give you a doll that bore your likeness, and had it made for that reason alone."

"But that was barely a year ago, Mr. Holmes. I was not a child. I thought it a very strange present then, and I struggle to understand it now. Or perhaps to forgive."

"Miss Lin," Mycroft replied, "I was told your father is a good man by someone who had no reason either to give me that information or to flatter him. Your own William Angel is quite devoted. Both those sources further stated that your father has enemies who wish to do him harm. At dinner, he acted more a victim than a perpetrator. It is possible—and perhaps likely—that he was pressured or even blackmailed into this line of work. Beyond which, there is nothing illegal in the *transportation* of narcotics. It seems to me he provided the ships and little else."

"But that is enough, is it not?" she responded bitterly. With that, she placed her fingers upon her lips as if to avoid saying anything more. She moved the curtain aside and looked out of the window at nothing, while Mycroft stared at the ground.

A moment later, Mycroft broke the impasse. "Miss Lin,"

he said, looking up. "With all the care your father takes to blend in, to not give offense, why a canary-yellow landaulet?"

Ai Lin sighed. "When we lived in Canton," she said, "my mother and father often dreamt of England—a beautiful but impossible dream, for he could barely afford to put food on the table, much less transport a young family nearly six thousand miles from home.

"One day, she spied from our window an English landaulet, 'the color of a sunbird.' Yellow is an auspicious color in our culture, Mr. Holmes. It is esteemed, for it represents freedom from worldly cares. Though my mother never saw it again, it became emblematic of something she longed for, a joyous sort of life in the West where freedoms, rather than duties and ancient traditions, were prized. Before my father's fortunes turned, she died. He bought it to honor her. And to remember."

Sherlock noticed that Ai Lin's expression had softened, and wondered if Mycroft had inquired about the landaulet so as to alter the mood, to leave Ai Lin with a positive image of her father as a counterweight to what she had just learned.

It was a thoughtful gesture, though perfectly useless. And once again Sherlock thanked whatever divine powers there might be that he was not the sort to be so bamboozled by sentiment.

Mycroft's carriage arrived at the Lins' to find Douglas, Huan and Ai Lin's bodyguards seated on the front steps, much worse for the wear. One bodyguard had a broken nose and the other nursed a mangled right arm. Huan's left eye was swollen, he and Douglas had stripes of dried blood across their cheeks and under their eyes, and all four were covered in cuts and contusions.

Still, they are alive, Mycroft thought, greatly relieved.

As usual, Huan smiled and waved as if they had just returned from high tea.

"How many were there?" Sherlock asked, wide-eyed as he bounded out of the carriage.

"Nine," Douglas replied wearily. "Able fighters all."

"But trained in China! So, we knew their tricks in this Year of the Monkey, yes?" Huan exclaimed jovially.

Mycroft emerged from the carriage, then turned and waited for Ai Lin, as William Angel lent her a hand to disembark.

"Nine men were sent to dispatch a man of middle years, a boy, and two dullards?" Sherlock muttered to his brother. "Quite the show of force."

"Or of loyalty," Mycroft opined quietly. "Someone wanted to show Lin that men who worked for him, that he counted on, are now solidly on the opposing side. Your father shall need more than two bodyguards that he shares reluctantly with you!" he added full-voiced to Ai Lin as she joined them. "I would hire them this very night, four at least."

"Thank you, Mr. Holmes, but my father would never allow it," she replied. "He would rather die than show weakness, which is how he would perceive that sort of protection. Bodyguards are to protect a woman's honor; they are not for strong, capable men."

The "strong, capable" men on the steps rose to their rather wobbly feet as she made her way to them.

"I do not know how I can ever repay any of you for keeping my father alive this night," she told them. "Mr. Douglas, Mr. Huan, if you are ever in need, if there is anything I can do, please know that I am now and forever in your debt."

"And I in yours, Mr. Holmes," Angel whispered to Mycroft before returning to her side.

With a small bow of farewell, Ai Lin hastened up the steps. At the top, she waved to Mycroft and Sherlock, then stepped through the door that Angel held open for her, the two bodyguards shuffling painfully behind.

"It is a death sentence for Lin," Douglas said, his voice hoarse.

"Yes," Mycroft said. "Unless we can track down the head villain before his minions have a chance to heal. Douglas, I believe Nickolus House is the closest to us. Might you consider three bedraggled guests?"

"Of course," he replied.

"*Two* bedraggled guests," Sherlock declared, "for I shall go to the Quinces'. They are expecting me and besides, it is a fine night for a stroll."

"It is no such thing, and no," Mycroft told him. "I shall send Mrs. Quince a note that you are safe and will see the boys back in Cambridge."

With that, he pointed to the carriage, with Sherlock sighing like a martyr as he climbed back inside.

Mycroft was certain that Nickolus House would be best, for the quicker Douglas and Huan could get to bed and recover, the better off they would be. Besides, he wanted to keep an eye on his brother. Soon Sherlock would be escorted back to Cambridge under Huan's scrutiny, there to remain until this whole "sordid affair," as Mycroft had first referred to it, was over.

"One thing I find curious," he muttered to Douglas, who was about to embark.

"Only one?" Douglas said with a sardonic smile, his fingers on the door handle.

"Deshi Hai Lin said there were a 'dozen' devils against him. So where were the other three…?"

"Mycroft, there is such a thing as overthinking," Douglas muttered back.

"Huan?" Mycroft called out as his coachman hobbled past them towards the box seat. "Might you allow me to take the reins so you can rest?"

"Oh no!" Huan exclaimed, offended. "Mr. Mycroft will not do my work, I shall do my own work, thank you!" He hobbled off.

Douglas pulled the door open and stepped into the carriage, only to announce in alarm: "Sherlock is gone!"

50

SHERLOCK HAD SPIRITED HIMSELF AWAY, AND THERE WAS nothing anyone could do. Huan and Douglas could not go gallivanting after him, for both had already taxed their poor, beaten bodies to the limit; and Mycroft with his skipping heart and uncertain breath was an abysmal third candidate, particularly since Sherlock had a few minutes' head start, and would be hidden by the fog and the darkness.

Having lost that battle before it had begun, Mycroft did the only thing he could. He went back to Nickolus House, waited until his friends were sound asleep, then purloined his own carriage and crept off like a thief in the night to try to find his brother—for if Douglas or Huan had awakened, they would have insisted on accompanying him. And, since trying to find Sherlock when he did not wish to be found was a fool's errand, Mycroft preferred to be alone in playing the fool.

His first stop was the Quinces' residence. As her sons peered around her back like two whey-faced specters, their whey-faced mother let him know that no, Sherlock was certainly *not* there, and that in fact she and her boys had seen neither hide nor hair of him since early Monday morning.

As he wondered where Sherlock could have bedded down for two nights running, Mycroft traversed Baker Street and environs, though it was an act borne of desperation, for he could not imagine what his brother would have yet to find there. He even went to the National Standard Theatre, scouting Shoreditch High Street multiple times, as he recalled Parfitt's research and the rooms that Professor Cainborn had kept there for the past five years. Mycroft would not put it past Sherlock to visit John Cainborn to discuss "the case" and have him render an opinion.

Cainborn.

The name continued to plague him.

In the twilight before dawn of Thursday, Mycroft and the horse, both ragged from wear, returned to St. John's Wood— the animal for hay, water and rest, Mycroft for a nice hot bath, a change of garments, and perhaps a few hours' sleep.

The objective was to calm his frayed nerves and rid himself of the fear that something untoward had happened to his brother; and, in case it had not, the impulse to strangle him with his own two hands.

He found a note from Parfitt sticking out of his letterbox. Edward Cardwell had come down with a miserable cold… as Mycroft had predicted he would from the moment he'd noticed Cardwell's scarf draped across his coat rack.

With Cardwell indisposed, Mycroft could go to the office unhindered, and peruse tomes of various and sundry businesses that had been established in Britain during the past five years—tomes too jumbled for even Parfitt to decipher. Perhaps Cainborn had made investments that would not jibe with his rather pitiable salary as a university professor.

Just like that, the idea of a few hours' slumber went gamboling off. In lieu of sleep, he would make himself a cup of tea. He briefly considered stirring in a pinch of Ai Lin's herbs… but perhaps not yet.

He dug his hand into his overcoat pocket and clutched the little tin like a lifeline.

Sherlock's plan for escape from Mycroft's well-meaning but ill-timed clutches had been executed even more quickly than he had conceived of it. In a move purloined from the *commedia dell'arte*, it had been in one door, out the other.

He blamed this impulsivity at least in part on the after-effects of the Vin Mariani, which had made him irritable. Yes, there would be hell to pay when he saw Mycroft again, but he could not think of that now.

He knew where Cainborn's pied-à-terre was located, though he had never been invited there: for no matter how often or how well they had worked together, Cainborn had always kept their burgeoning friendship at arm's length. Sherlock had not resented that divide between student and teacher; he had always understood and honored it.

But now, it was proving sinister indeed.

Sherlock knew Cainborn was at home, for he had seen the good professor enter his lodgings a few moments before midnight. Twice he had almost knocked upon his door. Twice he'd had to duck out of sight as Mycroft had swung around the corner like a keen young lion stalking his prey… provided said lion were outfitted in Savile Row finery and driving a hansom.

By the time Sherlock was ready to knock upon Cainborn's door a third time, the chimes of the bell tower were sounding one in the morning, the streets were emptying, and Sherlock was feeling drained, weak, and irritated.

He thought perhaps it might be best to wait until light, when the narcotics were fully out of his system and his wits had returned in full force. But a lad of his age and status could not very well loiter on the corner without drawing the wrong sort of attention.

He placed a protective hand over the pocket of his jacket, for that was where he had hidden Madame de Matalin's "rainy day" cache, and made his way back to the National Standard Theatre. He had attended several performances there with Mycroft and had noticed the transom window that led directly into the theatre's storeroom.

It could come in handy at a time like this.

At Cumberland House, Mycroft had set Parfitt on the hunt for details of an uprising in Canton in 1859: ten volumes marked *China Extraterritorialities and Treaties 1857–1860*.

As Mycroft scanned his *Business Archives 1860–1870* he spotted something of note. One John Aloysius Cainborn, aged forty-three, had a one-third interest in a fledgling company that sought and promoted medical discoveries. Not yet profitable, and indeed a losing proposition, it had been christened *Mundi Morphi*, adulterated Latin for "the world of dreams"...

"Mr. Holmes? I found him!"

Mycroft marked his place and hurried over to Parfitt.

"The first part is n-nothing you are not aware of, Mr. Holmes..."

"Then kindly sum it up," Mycroft replied.

"Yessir." He cleared his throat. "After many years of the Cantonese suffering under the c-coolie trade, it is noted here that in 1859 several kidnappers were caught, thrown into prison and w-would be made to stand trial. But then some of the local populace broke into the prison and took the k-kidnappers hostage. Eighteen were beheaded in a single d-d-day..."

"Breathe, Parfitt, this is not an extreme unction."

Parfitt nodded, drew a breath and continued: "A woman who was said to be in l-league with them, with the kidnappers I mean, was dragged from her home into a public square and there m-mutilated. It documents here that her nose and f-female parts were excised."

Parfitt ran a finger underneath the offending line for seeming reassurance that it was indeed the book and not he that had broached the subject of female anatomy.

Mycroft leaned his elbow against the desk and squinted down at the line in question. "I would say 'excised' is rather feeble, Parfitt. She was kept alive while her nose and breasts were sliced off."

"Yessir," Parfitt agreed, swallowing loudly. "And several of the beheadings, as well as the s-slicing, were carried out... well, sir, you see there?" He pointed to another line in the open book. "Here they only identify the ring leader as 'a chief officer.' But then in *this* one, if you'll p-pardon me, sir," he added as he reached past Mycroft's elbow to a second book, "it says '*first mate* of the commercial steamer *Rivalry*'! But 'chief officer' and 'first mate' are alternate titles for the same p-position, are they not? And so then, in this *third* book," Parfitt went on, fumbling for it, "is written that in 1859, the chief o-officer of the *Rivalry* was Deshi Hai Lin, aged forty-one. That is one of the names you seek, is it not, sir?" Parfitt asked, staring up at him.

Mycroft sprinted out of the office without another word.

The old rag-picker had eyebrows made of mouse fur. His cheeks were streaked like a drunkard's, thanks to a bit of Spanish wool dragged across the skin. The veins on his neck stuck out purple and blue. A bit more lead paint sprinkled on his occipital bones had caused his eyes and nose to redden appreciably. A topcoat so rough that it could have been woven together from the hides of gutter rats covered the newly formed hump on his back. A wig of spare gray hair and a green felt hat completed the overall impression of penury and dissipation.

The rag-picker appeared to be shaking off a night wasted in carousing and drink when the good professor passed him on his way to the omnibus. Sherlock saw Cainborn check his watch as he went, more likely out of habit than hurry, for the nearest church bell had just sounded eight a.m., and the omnibus was not due for ten minutes.

With Cainborn waiting at the stop, the rag-picker had time to enter Cainborn's lodgings, look about for anything of interest, and then catch up with him again before he was left behind.

51

AT NINE A.M., MYCROFT CAME CALLING TO PIMLICO, AND was ushered into the Lins' drawing room. He well knew what he had to communicate to Deshi Hai Lin and (if the patriarch wished it) to his family. But he was not certain how best to go about it. His heart had been pounding furiously since he had left Cumberland House in Pall Mall, and the two-mile ride had seemed to take an eternity.

What did Ai, or her brother Dai en-Lai, for that matter, know of their father's past? Would they be able to comprehend and eventually justify his actions, or had he crossed a line too egregious even for those who adored him?

Deshi Hai Lin appeared less agitated than the night before, though not so much calmer as resigned.

"Thank you for seeing me," Mycroft began.

"Mr. Holmes," Lin replied, bowing slightly. "My daughter told me of your bravery on our behalf last night."

"There was no bravery on my part, Mr. Lin," Mycroft protested. "It was my driver, along with my dearest friend, who ensured your safety, and that of your son."

"Please sit, for you are forever welcome here," Lin replied, indicating a chair. "But I would be remiss if I did not warn you that this abode is not particularly safe. You see that my children are absent, for I cannot place them in additional jeopardy…"

Mycroft, whose heartbeat was sounding like a dissonant gong in his eardrums, very nearly sank into the proffered chair.

"You did well to send your children away," he said, straightening his spine and catching his breath as Lin pulled up a chair beside him. For, as gratified as he would have been to see Ai Lin again, he was even more grateful that she was safe.

"I know of your past in Canton in 1859," Mycroft said the moment that the older man was settled. "That, in your zeal to eradicate the coolie trade once and for all, you took several lives."

Lin did not even raise an eyebrow in surprise. It was as if he had been waiting to be caught, and now there it was.

"More than several, Mr. Holmes," he confessed sadly, joining his hands and wringing them as if he were washing something away. "One a woman, whom I tortured to death. Had it surfaced when I made my way to this country, I never could have emigrated at all."

"I understand there are two brothers, Kang Chen and Ju-long Chen, who emigrated with you, whose lives you spared."

"Yes. They were innocent of any wrongdoing, and I knew they were. I would not permit them to be beheaded with the rest. Kang Chen is a good sort. But his brother Juju is another matter. For a long while I trusted him, and he was my second in command. Then he began to spend more time at his place of business in Limehouse…"

"The opium den," Mycroft said. "The Water Monkey."

"Yes," Lin confirmed, "although it has never drawn the negative scrutiny that others of that sort have—mostly, it is a spot for immigrants to play *si se pai*. I did not know that behind the scenes he was recruiting my best workers! Enslaving some with the poppy, bribing others…"

"At first, you believed them to be importing dolls?"

"Yes, feigning they were French and not Chinese. Though less than honorable, I mistakenly justified it as a small, meaningless deception. I even had one made for my daughter. After all, these were men who had been enslaved! They deserved to make a living! But then Ju-long Chen, one of the two brothers I saved from beheading, concocted a scheme to export a new sort of powerful narcotic inside the dolls," he said. "He found a partner and sold it in exchange for gold, which he had made into sovereigns, to spend whenever he pleased! I was given some of the money in return for the use of my ships. To my undying shame, I capitulated. From there, I was quickly marginalized to the point where now I do not even recognize my own crew!"

"Threats of exposure kept you silent?"

He nodded. "And the killings. They began several months ago; no doubt you have read of them. Ritual killings meant to keep Chinese dockworkers and seamen quiet about what they know… but mostly to keep *me* quiet. It is a constant reminder of my shame in Canton, and a warning of what they will do to me and to my children if I do not cooperate fully with their schemes."

"*Their* schemes?" Mycroft asked.

Lin frowned. "Juju Chen is bright, but he is unlearned. He is not capable of this level of machination. But now they have pushed me too far! I am prepared to tell all, even if it costs me my children's respect!" He rose to his feet, agitated, for clearly it was this consequence that he dreaded the most.

"Mr. Lin," Mycroft said, looking up at him, "I am certain any official testimony coming from you will be invaluable. But first, is the name of the man who came up with these 'machinations'—the formula for the new drug, the composition of the sovereigns—Professor John Cainborn?"

Lin peered about as though seeing ghosts.

Then he sat again, undone.

"When Cainborn went looking for a partner to sell his drug," he explained, "he visited opium dens for possible associates and found one in Juju Chen. I tried to push Cainborn away from us but at that point, I had no more leverage."

"And Cainborn's company, Mundi Morphi? What do you know of it?"

"Nothing. That is, very little. I heard of it but once, and that only two weeks ago," Lin said softly. "For that is when I first learned that Cainborn was planning to leave the country for Sydney, Australia! Ah, but I have had my little revenge! It is why those men came to intimidate me! These thirteen days, I have forbidden my men to unload the goods from my ship, *Orion's Belt*! Cainborn and Juju cannot fill the dolls! They cannot send more of their poison to China!"

Ignoring the booming in his chest and ears, Mycroft stood to his feet. "How long will it take to unload the cargo and fill the dolls?"

"Less than one day, but—"

"Mr. Lin, you must grant them immediate permission to do so. Let them believe their threats worked. Give them no reason to doubt you."

"But then the ship will set sail with that poison in its belly!"

"Promise me you will give the order today! Now!" Mycroft insisted. Then, having received the promise from his startled host, Mycroft hurried to the front door.

52

SHERLOCK HAD NEVER ATTEMPTED TO PICK A LOCK BEFORE.
He had merely read about it, and not attentively. Thankfully,
he had on hand the tools he needed, and it seemed a
stunningly simple proposition.

From his jacket pocket, he pulled out the scissors of his
shaving kit and broke them in half, keeping one blade intact
and forcing the other against the door until the metal bent
like a hook. He inserted the point of the unbent blade into
the keyway, feeling for the plate behind the bolt stump, then
jerking the point upwards to release the bolt. With his other
hand, he inserted the bent blade into one of the grooves,
then turned and pushed out exactly as a key would.

The handle lifted and he walked in.

Four minutes gone.

Cainborn's pied-à-terre was hardly worthy of the name,
being only a small room with a bed, bathtub, sofa, chair, and
desk, along with a small hearth and one window where a few
strands of morning light peeked meekly through the curtains.

Sherlock's spider-like fingers felt along the walls, but there were no secret compartments that he could discern. The decrepit old desk was covered with papers, mostly a jumble of old bills, too many even for him to peruse in the time he had left.

Cainborn either had no secrets, or no one from which he needed to hide them. In fact, Sherlock found only one item worth noting: an expired one-way ship's pass to Sydney, Australia. Cainborn had been scheduled to leave on the *Royal Adelaide* on the morning of Saturday 23 November.

Had he departed, he would have been shipwrecked on Chesil Beach in Dorset two days later. Why had he not left?

Then Sherlock remembered what day that had been, and he felt a chill go through him.

He placed the ticket in his jacket pocket and bolted out of Cainborn's lodgings.

He hurried down the street but had to stop short, for Cainborn was waiting at the bus stop. He turned and looked right at Sherlock but did not seem to recognize him. When the crowded omnibus arrived, Cainborn stepped aboard; then a moment later stepped off again. Several minutes later he boarded the next omnibus, and this time remained inside.

Sherlock caught it just as it was departing. He could see Cainborn wedged in the crush of passengers, as if pinned like so many boutonnières against the blue velvet seats. Moving much more quickly than a rag-picker of his advanced age should, he scurried up to the upper deck, where he took a seat amongst those willing to brave the weather in exchange for fresher air. Cainborn would not be able to disembark from the omnibus without Sherlock seeing him.

Where are you off to, you old traitor? he thought to himself bitterly.

By the time Mycroft barged in on Dalrymple at The Golden Bottle, he must have looked ghastly, for the bank manager stared at him in alarm and called for water, which not one or two but three junior clerks rushed out to fetch.

"You are to send telegrams to banks in Antwerp, Hong Kong, Paris, Istanbul, Bombay and Sydney," Mycroft declared in a staccato delivery as he laid his hands flat on Dalrymple's desk to keep the pesky room from spinning. He drew another ragged breath. "You must inform them that they are to do no business with an outfit called Mundi Morphi. And, as a 'concerned colleague'—thank you," he added to the first junior clerk who had ventured back with a glass of water, which Mycroft gulped down in one long swallow.

"As a 'concerned colleague,' I was saying, one who has been in the banking business for some time, you must send an equally urgent message to the Standard Chartered Bank on Gracechurch Street that the Crown is set to investigate them for fraud and money laundering!"

"It is?" Mr. Dalrymple exclaimed, his eyes growing larger than Mycroft thought possible.

A second glass of water arrived, borne by another alarmed-looking little clerk. Mycroft snatched it from him.

"Yes it is, if I have anything to say about it!" he declared, wiping his lips before hastening out.

53

GAINING AN AUDIENCE WITH THE QUEEN AT BUCKINGHAM Palace without an appointment required running a gauntlet manned not by warriors but by pen-wielding bureaucrats whose sole job it was to make life easier for the monarch and excruciating for everybody else.

Mycroft was assured with barely contained condescension that Her Majesty would not see him... until, to their infinite chagrin, she did.

In truth, the Queen did not seem terribly pleased. Perhaps it was too great a breach of protocol, his asking for an emergency audience a too-obvious reward for recent favors executed. Or perhaps she feared he would assail her again with dire talk about impending economic catastrophes.

"Five minutes," she told him icily after he had bowed. "Commencing now."

As if flicking something off her finger, she dismissed her attendant so that they were alone.

"Your Majesty, you must send agents to the Standard

Chartered Bank on Gracechurch Street. There they will find a great cache of sovereigns dated 1857 and minted in Sydney…"

"Mr. Holmes, surely this is a matter for the Treasury…"

"Ma'am, the sovereigns bear your likeness, but with a sprig of banksia in your hair."

Queen Victoria sighed. "We are aware of those coins, Mr. Holmes. And though we are not pleased with that particular… *rendition* of ourselves, we cannot simply remove legal tender from a legitimate bank."

"They are *forgeries*, ma'am."

"You can *prove* that, Mr. Holmes?" she asked.

"No," Mycroft admitted. "That is, my proof would take some study, for it is too subtle to pass muster as expeditiously as we would need it. And Standard Chartered shall argue vociferously to have the money returned—"

"Well then we cannot see how—"

"—but no one will ever pursue it," Mycroft said, daring to interrupt the Queen. "Their doors will be closed within forty-eight hours. For they have one principal client, and…"

Mycroft stopped to draw a breath, and the Queen's eyebrows seemed to draw together into a line of severe judgment.

"You are quite pale, Mr. Holmes. We have never seen you so undone. And the story sounds nearly as undone as you appear to be. Perhaps, like the Apostle Paul, your great learning is driving you mad?"

"Ah, but Paul was *not* mad, ma'am!" Mycroft protested. "His story to Festus and King Agrippa was true! All I have told you thus far can be verified by Mr. Dalrymple, the manager of The Golden— that is, C. Hoare & Co."

"Yes, Mr. Holmes, we too refer to it as The Golden Bottle; we are not so cut off as all that."

"By tonight, the ship *Orion's Belt* will set sail to Shanghai with contraband and counterfeit sovereigns. It must be stopped and searched. The owner is prepared to testify to the scheme. Aboard you will also find a man named Ju-long Chen. He will be making final inspection. He and his two associates must be arrested before disembarking. He is personally responsible for several killings in the poorer parts of the city."

"The Savage Gardens Murders," she said rather archly. "We see. Anything else?"

"Yes. A man by the name of John Cainborn has no doubt bought a one-way ticket for Australia, to depart at the end of the week. He is the principal in all of this, and he too must be stopped. Ma'am, if you have *ever* trusted my judgment…"

"Mr. Holmes," the Queen declared. "Begging does not become you. Neither does waving your laurels about. We shall confirm what we can and decide what to do from there."

"I pray you do so quickly—"

"*Mr.* Holmes…" she said again, her tone a warning.

"Thank you, Your Majesty," Mycroft said with a bow.

Mycroft was given an escort out so that he might not loiter one second longer than permitted. Little did his superfluous companions know how desperately he wished to depart and to be seated again, for remaining upright was proving more and more difficult.

Reins in hand, he was about to climb into the box seat, and gratefully so, when he noticed that the horse seemed enervated. He no doubt needed more respite than he had been permitted in the last several days.

There was a public mews close by. Mycroft could leave the horse there to recover, then hail a cab for himself back to Nickolus House.

It meant effort on his part—effort he was not certain he could exert.

Sighing, he rubbed a hand over the gelding's soft muzzle and patted his forehead. The elegant, dutiful Irish Cob had been with him a year and had not yet been named.

"Forgive me," Mycroft murmured, pressing his forehead against the beast's long silky nose. "You deserve better."

The horse huffed as if he understood, and forgave.

Mycroft led him to the mews to rest. Then, with shallow breaths and halting steps, he returned to the street to hail a cab.

54

AT THE STOP NEAREST THE WATERFRONT, CAINBORN STEPPED off the omnibus. As did Sherlock, though he waited until it was well in motion again before disembarking, at which point he catapulted down the ladder, jumped into the road and sprinted to keep his feet well underneath him, where they belonged.

It would not be a calamity if Cainborn were to spot him, for Sherlock was prepared, at any given juncture, to confront his teacher. But he was curious as to where Cainborn might be headed, and preferred to remain unseen. He slowed to a walk, keeping an eye on Cainborn from a small distance away, following his rather serpentine route and shedding his rag-picker disguise as he went.

A few minutes later, they reached malodorous and bustling St. Katharine Docks. Sherlock watched Cainborn push his way through the crowds less than successfully, for the professor was small, with a face like a groundhog peeking out of its den. Unless one knew him by reputation, he was not the sort of presence for whom most people made room.

Though Sherlock could only witness it from behind, the simple effort of jostling past strangers whose gazes were all but fixed above his head seemed to provoke in Cainborn a tension bordering on rage. His shoulders hunched. His neck stiffened and pushed forward, so that he seemed to be leading the rest of his body with his forehead. And Sherlock realized what he feared he should have gleaned all along: Cainborn despised being overlooked, both figuratively and literally. The admiration and fear that his students provided him in abundance, he craved from the world at large.

For he was a magician after all, was he not?

"The manufacture of any narcotic: the isolation of morphine from opium for example, or opium from the poppy," he had once told a group of rapt students, "is modern-day alchemy. One transforms worthless organic matter into an essence worth more than gold."

Sherlock was still a milksop then, who had only just arrived at Cambridge University. Yet he had dared to quote Robert Boyle's *The Sceptical Chymist*: that modern chemistry was not alchemy at all, in that alchemy was haphazard.

"Alchemists are frauds," Sherlock had declared. "Confined to hell by Dante; whereas chemists look for cause and effect. If one relies on the scientific method, one is a scientist, not a magician."

Sherlock had irked every professor he had ever come across and expected no better in this case. But Cainborn had simply smiled.

In fact, that small dispute had provoked his attention, and eventually his admiration. And Cainborn's allowance of alchemy—the happy accident—into the cauldron of science had in turn broadened Sherlock's imagination, until Sherlock had become his most devoted acolyte.

He watched Cainborn pause on the street, pull out his briar pipe, fill it and light it.

Sherlock paused as well, pulled out *his* briar pipe, stuffed it and lit it. Teacher and student were now walking a hundred paces apart, furiously smoking.

"Perhaps I shall be henceforth known as 'baker,'" Cainborn had replied upon that first meeting. "Less lofty than 'alchemist' and more apropos," he had added, to the students' amusement.

Cainborn halted on a small promontory, where he stared intently out at the water. Sherlock followed his gaze. A steamship was navigating from mooring to quayside where a large warehouse was just opening its doors to accommodate her goods.

The name on her bow was *Orion's Belt*.

Sherlock made his move.

"Is that where the dolls are kept?" he whispered in Cainborn's ear, making the professor turn with a start. "Do they hold my concoction in their Oriental bellies?" he added, his voice awash with recrimination.

This significant moment, one which he had so long imagined, did not go precisely as planned. Firstly, the emotional toll of such a thorough betrayal proved much greater than he had anticipated. And secondly, the guilty party, instead of muttering a confession, simply glanced behind him.

"Drown him," he said.

Mere seconds later, his briar pipe sent flying, Sherlock found himself surrounded by Juju's two henchmen, Moon Face and Roly-Poly, along with Ned and Gin. He wondered why and how they were there—might Cainborn have recognized him at the omnibus stop? Might he have alerted someone? But there was not much time for speculation. That he would be thrown into the filthy water was not in question, but he could not permit his captors to dictate the location of his prospective drowning. He would have to somehow influence their actions.

It was a precarious balance: to alert all bystanders within hailing distance that he was being carted off by force, yet without causing so much of a hubbub that his captors lost patience and drowned him in the nearest puddle. Despite his cries, no one intervened. To a man they looked the other way and pretended things were business as usual. It did not pass Sherlock's notice that many were Oriental. *Gweilo*, their expressions declared. *Ghost.*

"Wish you had a needle for him," Roly-Poly said to Moon Face, as Gin planted a large, salty hand over Sherlock's mouth while Roly-Poly delivered a rather vicious blow to the back of his head. It seemed that Cainborn's command had caught them unprepared.

As advantages went, it was trifling, but Sherlock would take what he could get.

Douglas awakened to a timid but insistent knocking upon his bedroom door. His room was bright as day, though it could not be thus, for he could have sworn it was the middle of the night. He reached for his pocket watch on the bedside table, and indeed he and it were of one mind, for it read two a.m.

He glared at the impertinent light streaming in through the window before realizing that it was indeed the sun, and that his watch was agreeing solely because it was not ticking, for he had neglected to wind it.

"Yes, yes, I am coming," he muttered, stumbling from his bed to the door. He could only thank Providence that he had fallen asleep in his clothes, as he did not think himself yet capable of putting on trousers without falling headlong.

The housekeeper, a good soul of older years named Nora, whose face reminded him of a potato on which eyes, mouth, nose and ears had been haphazardly appended, was staring at him askance.

"Douglas?" she inquired—for she did not realize that it was he who paid her salary—"I was tole by Mr. Capps not to bother if y'ez sleepin', but a Chinaman is below, wantin' to speak to you…"

Douglas shook the cobwebs from his mind. "What time is it?"

"Ten in the mornin'."

He had never in his lifetime slept so late. It seemed indecent. No wonder that Nora was eyeing him as if he were naked!

Thrusting his feet into slippers, he padded to the landing and peered downstairs to see Ahn Zhang peering up at him, breathing hard.

"Douglas!" Zhang called up to him. "Your friend, *gweilo*, crazy boy, he about to die!"

Mycroft, very nearly spent with exhaustion, had made it back to Nickolus House and was just placing one shaky foot out of his cab when he saw three men hastening out of the front door: Douglas, Huan and a sour-faced Chinese man whom he did not recognize.

Douglas waved at him not to disembark. As Huan and the Chinese man climbed into the carriage beside him, Douglas ran up to the driver and climbed into the seat next to the man.

"St. Katharine Docks!" he said. "And hurry!"

55

STRUGGLING FIERCELY BUT WITH INTENT, SHERLOCK DRAGGED his four captors as far from Central Dock as he could manage, and close to the center of West Dock. He had almost cajoled them to the desired location when they spotted two customs agents in the distance, having a smoke by the water.

His kidnappers stopped short.

"Good here," Moon Face opined.

Sherlock dared to look around and indeed, they had reached an area where the water was deep enough, passersby were few, and the murder of an anonymous eighteen-year-old boy was not likely to attract much notice. No matter how much he flailed, they would go no further.

Roly-Poly pulled some twine from his pocket and tied Sherlock's legs together at the ankles with a prowess and speed that said he had done this before, while Moon Face gathered large handfuls of pebbles which he deposited none too gently into Sherlock's trouser pockets.

Ideal or not, this was the place. Although Sherlock's

ankles were bound and his legs weighted, it was time to act. He bit the briny hand that had been pressed down upon his lips. This he executed with less finesse and more beastly force than was perhaps warranted, for Gin pulled away, shrieking, so that Sherlock was forced to spit out a small but noticeable chunk of the boy's right palm.

On his left, Ned tried to tug him off his feet, but Sherlock was too firmly planted. Even with his ankles bound, Sherlock had enough ballast to take full advantage of Ned's weak right flank, landing his knuckles square on the underside of his tormentor's tender jaw. Ned went down, though by that time Gin was coming back at him, filled with a homicidal fury over his gnawed hand, but Moon Face and Roly-Poly had apparently had enough. They each took Sherlock by an armpit, as they had at The Water Monkey, and shoved him to his knees so that his face dangled over the edge of the quay, the water perilously close below.

Sherlock was not keen on this plan, so he lunged forward and hurled himself into the drink. But with his ankles tied and his pockets filled with rocks, he could not manage to swim off quickly enough. Moon Face hurled himself upon the dock, reached down and grabbed him by the hair as Roly-Poly knelt beside his fellow, and both on their knees laid a hand upon his head as if performing a baptism.

"Goodbye, Basil," Sherlock heard Moon Face say just before his ears went under. He had but one escape route, and that was to use their expectations against them. Very nearly out of breath, he allowed a few little air bubbles to escape his lips and rise to the surface, and then he went limp.

His lungs were screaming for relief, but he held on until he felt their hands loosen their grip on his hair, testing to see if he would sink. At that exact instant he arched himself up, took one long breath, and as they cursed and forced him back down again, he used their momentum combined with the weight of the rocks in his pockets to propel himself deeper into the water and out of their reach.

As their hands flailed above him, trying to snatch him back, he struggled against the weight of his sodden clothes and propelled himself away from them.

There was no breath left in him to try to loosen his bonds underwater. In the murky depths, Sherlock discarded his shoes and looked around, trying to keep panic at bay. At two arms' lengths, he spied a corroded old ladder, attached to a concrete block too deep in the water to be helpful. He hurled himself at the ladder, grabbed onto it and with excruciating effort pulled himself up one rung at a time, while his saturated clothes fought against him every step.

He managed to lift himself out of the water just enough to draw a cleansing breath when a wave hit him. It was small, but it was enough: water shot up his nose and he began to gasp, while more water filled his mouth.

Even with his nostrils a few inches above the waterline, he was drowning.

Mycroft's rented carriage had barely arrived at the docks when Douglas and Huan opened the doors and bolted out. Mycroft attempted to follow but made it only as far as the street before his legs collapsed out from under him. If it had not been for Ahn Zhang supporting him, he would have fallen.

He saw Douglas look back almost by instinct. "Stay where you are!" he called. "We will get him back!"

For once—and given that he had absolutely no choice in the matter—Mycroft did as he was told, for he knew he would do naught but hinder a search for his brother.

Zhang helped him back into the carriage. On the journey Mycroft had learned that it was Zhang who had witnessed Sherlock's kidnapping; Zhang who had run without stopping from St. Katharine Docks to Nickolus House, a distance of more than three miles. The same Ahn Zhang whom Sherlock had disparaged.

"Thank you for what you did for my brother," Mycroft said. "Neither he nor I deserve such kindness from a stranger."

"Do not thank," Zhang said in a tone that was both conciliatory and practical, "for he most likely dead now."

With a nod of commiseration and goodbye, Zhang closed the carriage door.

St. Katharine's was as familiar to Douglas and Huan as their own sitting rooms. They well knew all the places where water was deep enough for a ship, and where those with bad intent could be sure that a weighted-down body would sink to the bottom.

Sprinting to the location where Ahn Zhang had seen Sherlock last, it did not take them long to follow the most obvious path to such a place, and then to spot unusual behavior in the midst of the usual business of the docks—two Chinese and two Caucasian men were standing stock still and peering over the quayside, seemingly at nothing.

Douglas did not know the others, but he instantly recognized one of the white men: the hulking, pockmarked lad he had seen scurrying out of Beeton's abode, the lad he and Mycroft had assumed was the master chimney sweep's son.

"Sherlock is down there!" he said to Huan, indicating the water.

"You go!" Huan replied. "I will take care of them!"

"All four?" Douglas wondered skeptically, all too aware of what they had been through the night before.

Huan snapped his fingers dismissively. "Two are boys! And I slept good last night, ate plenty of bread and dripping this morning. Go now! Go go!"

Douglas removed his jacket and shoes and dove into the water, while Huan strolled silently but purposefully towards four men whose backs were turned to him.

For he, like Douglas, was an avid believer in the element of surprise.

Douglas was a powerful swimmer. But by the time he'd reached Sherlock and wrapped an arm about his chest, the latter was very nearly unconscious—though what little consciousness remained was as stubborn as a mule. At first, Douglas assumed that Sherlock either did not recognize him, or that he did not comprehend that he was trying to help: for the more Douglas tried to extricate him from the rusty ladder, the harder Sherlock held on.

"Let go!" Douglas shouted, but Sherlock's fingers were all but welded to it, so that Douglas was forced to pry them loose. The moment he did so, and in spite of Douglas's sustaining arm, Sherlock began to sink, and Douglas realized that he weighed a third again what he should.

"Breathe!" he commanded, and this time Sherlock tentatively obeyed, though Douglas could see that he was afraid.

While keeping the boy slightly raised so that his nose and mouth remained above the waterline, Douglas eased himself down into the murky water. He began to undo the twine about Sherlock's ankles and emptied handfuls of pebbles from his pockets. Then he swam with his much lighter charge towards the shore.

Douglas pulled Sherlock onto dry land and looked around for Huan. Three men were down but the fourth one, a moon-faced Chinese man, was giving Huan trouble. He seemed quite strong and, above all, precise, which made Douglas wonder if it had been he who had made all those barbarous cuts to the Savage Gardens bodies.

Huan went down, and Douglas felt desperate. Even if he'd had the energy to throw himself into the fray, which he doubted, he could not leave Sherlock alone.

Then he saw two men running towards the skirmish. A moment before he panicked, thinking Huan was really done for, he realized who they were.

Customs agents.

Good, honest men who knew him, and by extension his friend Huan, very well.

The moon-faced man began to fight them by instinct until he too realized who they were, at which point he tried to flee. But they grabbed him and held him fast while Huan rose to his feet with his usual grin, looked around, and then waved to Douglas who—mightily relieved—waved back.

From the window of the carriage, Mycroft saw a lovely sight: Huan and a sopping-wet Douglas escorting a sopping-wet Sherlock to safety. Energized by the sheer joy and relief of it, Mycroft stumbled out of the open door, removed his jacket and put it about his brother's shoulders. By way of thanks, Sherlock gave him a look of recrimination: *I do hope my kidnapping did not inconvenience you overly much*, it said as clearly as if he had spoken it aloud.

"Who did this?" Mycroft asked as he and Douglas helped Sherlock back into the carriage.

"Cainborn," Sherlock croaked. "It was Cainborn all along."

56

DURING THE TWO DAYS OF HIS CONVALESCENCE, IN THE room at Nickolus House that was becoming his by default, Sherlock entertained a parade of visitors, including McPeel and Ducasse, who crept in to inquire about his health. So relieved were they that he was on the mend that they spread the news to the other boys. They arrived en masse to Mr. Capps' office, beseeching him that Sherlock—*please, sir!*—teach them again.

"Not in my near lifetime!" was Sherlock's only response.

Mr. and Mrs. P. arrived with sausages, sweetmeats and other delicacies, while Parfitt and his aunt Mrs. Hudson brought baked goods and all the latest newspapers, freshly pressed. The twins, Asa and Eli Quince, brought nothing and said less, but stood like two sentinels at the foot of his bed, staring, until Sherlock shooed them away with a rather brusque, "Thank you for coming."

Little George Fowler arrived with a statement he had prepared himself and delivered like a proclamation, so that

Mycroft half expected it to lead with a hearty *Hear ye, Hear ye!* and end with a *So Say We All.*

"Thank you for wot you done for myself an' for my bruvver Charles," he declared, his somber little face nearly crushed with the weight of it. "If you ever needs anythin' from me, alls you gots to do is ask."

Even Mr. Capps came to wish Sherlock well, doffing his cap while his hair stood at attention.

Meanwhile Mycroft, aided by Douglas and a good pair of binoculars, had witnessed from a promontory the seizure of *Orion's Belt* and all her cargo, along with the arrest of Ju-long Chen, known as Juju. Customs officers—acquaintances of Douglas—had then allowed him and Mycroft to board the *Orion*, where they found nearly a million pounds' worth of Australian sovereigns, all dated 1857, and fifteen bisque dolls stuffed with "a narcotic of unknown compound."

There would be no shortage of witnesses against the accused. The moment the head of the snake was cut off, they came scurrying out of their burrows like so many grateful rodents.

That same day, a message from an equerry to the Queen informed Mycroft that Professor John Cainborn had been arrested at his pied-à-terre, in the act of packing for a voyage to Sydney. Unfortunately for the good professor, 'banksia' sovereigns from 1857 had been found on his person.

That evening, Ai Lin sent a note, brought to Mycroft at

Nickolus House by none other than William Angel:

You have restored the dignity of our family,
and our love and devotion for one another.
My gratitude, Mr. Holmes, is boundless.
AL

Angel informed him that Ai Lin and her brother were on their way to Canton, there to remain with family until after Deshi Hai Lin had testified and their tormenters were put away once and for all.

It was for the best, Mycroft decided. He would not mourn. He would simply continue to be relieved for her, and grateful that he had been able to come to her aid.

Sherlock revealed his portion of the story at the close of those two days of respite. He was seated on the bed, appearing to Mycroft as if he dreaded even speaking of it, while Mycroft sat on the chair, feeling that perhaps he dreaded it more.

The year before, Sherlock had passed a rather brutal summer at home in the country with their parents, which was where he began his story: "Mother was weeping because of her terrible headaches, Father and I were not getting a wink of sleep; we were at the end of our tethers—"

"What about her laudanum?" Mycroft interrupted. "Was she not using it? And did you not tell me she had escalated to morphine?"

Again, he thought but did not say.

"Yes," Sherlock replied, "but the relief was short-lived, and the headaches were of a potency and duration that not even morphine could touch. She was not pretending. She truly was in agony. After all this time, I can tell the difference."

Mycroft sighed. He well knew the scenario. He heard in his head a child's plaintive voice: *Mama, do not die! Please, Mama! Do not die!*

How long ago that had been.

Mycroft could not have been more than six years of age, as Sherlock had not yet been born. He could still see in his mind's eye his mother's nightdress lifted most unbecomingly.

Her stomach, filled to bursting with his future sibling, was the color of monkfish, as was her staring face. She lay on the floor, bubbles of spit forming in one corner of her lips, one of his father's cravats wound tightly about her left arm, a rivulet of blood trailing from the crook of her elbow.

Papa! Papa!

It was nearly impossible for Mycroft to recall for certain if he had cried out, or if his father had simply appeared in the doorway, his face a mask of grief, one that would be chiseled in Mycroft's memory, and then mirrored in his own face and that of his brother, for as long as they all drew breath.

He encouraged Sherlock with a nod to go on.

"I was already experimenting on my own with concoctions and so forth," Sherlock explained, "but there was so much I could not do, simply because I did not have the proper equipment. So by the autumn I took full advantage of the Cambridge laboratories, which were Cainborn's domain. I can only say in my defense that I did not yet understand the complexities of addiction. I was simply attempting to cure Mother's migraines and was rather enjoying the experiments."

"Of what did they consist?"

"Oh, this and that, mixing morphine with various acids," Sherlock hedged.

"Sherlock…" Mycroft said, his tone a warning.

"Very well, but you will not approve," his brother said with stunning understatement. "I tried all sorts of combinations," he explained. "And then at last I boiled acetic anhydride with anhydrous morphine alkaloid for several hours. It produced a more potent, acetylated form of morphine."

"How do you know?" Mycroft asked.

"Because I injected it into my own arm," Sherlock replied quietly. "No need for that face, Mycroft. I am given neither to morphine, nor to opium. And I would prefer that my using myself as a laboratory specimen remain between the two of us. But an experiment is an experiment, after all…"

Sherlock had no name for the resulting compound, but he knew it by look, taste and effect. More importantly, he was certain he could replicate it.

"It cured Mother's headaches instantaneously. It had a much faster absorption rate and lasted nearly twice as long as the morphine. I was beside myself with relief: for her, for me, for Father, even for you, if you were ever to come around to visit…"

"And you shared your discovery with Cainborn," Mycroft interrupted.

"Yes. But then very quickly, things at home deteriorated. Father was nearly mad with worry, for Mother had become hopelessly addicted. And I knew I had done that to her, I had made her worse. I told Cainborn of my findings, of course. I gave him the formula, thinking that he and I could attempt to come up with a concoction that would have the same efficacy but not be so addictive. When he said he would work on it, I believed him.

"Then at The Water Monkey, when I was forcibly injected, I thought I recognized the sensation, but I dismissed it. Perhaps someone had done what I had done, spent weeks and weeks in a laboratory, attempting all sorts of combinations until they hit upon the right one. I simply did not wish to believe I had been so betrayed. For here I was, hunting for a formula that would prove as powerful but less addictive, only to realize that for Cainborn, strength was but half the equation. The other half *was* the addiction! In any event, on Friday 22 November, I thought I had found the key. I did not wish to have more signs of usage on my arms, for I had already scarred myself in the former experiments, so I injected between my toes. It was then that I realized I had succeeded only in formulating an even stronger concoction. I was heartsick. I sent a note to Cainborn, informing him of my desire to destroy the experiment and any traces thereof. But he insisted on meeting me the following day at the laboratory. He persuaded me to take him through the steps of the newest compound. That is why he did not leave for Sydney that day! He knew I'd made something even more powerful, and he wished to possess it!"

"You were experimenting on one of the twins..." Mycroft said.

"I assumed you would notice," Sherlock replied. "Asa was already addicted to morphine. I was simply trying to provide him the same effect while lowering the addiction and symptoms of withdrawal. I was unsuccessful. Alas, Mycroft, much as I would wish it, I am no scientist."

"I am not certain at the moment *what* you are, Sherlock," Mycroft said softly. "I do know you have a rather careless way with human beings."

"As do you, brother," Sherlock said in a tone that was almost gentle. Then suddenly his eyes were swimming in tears. "Why did you not come to my aid, Mycroft? You are the strongest swimmer I know. Why send Douglas to do what you could have so easily done?"

Mycroft's heart was beginning to pound again, so loudly that he was afraid Sherlock would hear it. *Say nothing!* Mycroft warned himself. *If you tell him, you are simply adding to his burden!*

"Sherlock," he said. "You are going to have to believe that I love you. Most often in the absence of concrete proof."

With that, he rose from the chair and left the room.

As he closed the door, he could hear Sherlock beginning to sob, a rare sound indeed.

Mycroft made his slow but steady way down the stairs to the kitchen of Nickolus House. Douglas was already abed, a well-deserved rest—as was Huan, and the boys and the servants, all asleep.

Soon Sherlock too would drift off, cradled in his own misery and, one would hope, repentance.

Mycroft would be the only one awake.

England was about to be shaken. He knew it. And he insisted to his poor, broken body that it must remain alive to try to prevent that earthquake from doing inestimable damage to all the proverbial and literal sleepers, especially those for whom he cared so much.

Eventually, most likely sooner rather than later, he would have to resign his post as special consul, if for no other reason than it would be unfair to be marked as a successor, only to drop dead before the Honorable Edward Cardwell had even left office.

But for tonight, the stove was on and the kettle was boiling. And Mycroft would sit alone at the table for four and stretch out his legs and drink his strong, hot tea, along with the herbs that Ai Lin had put in his hand, and he would taste the bittersweet comfort of having a place and a purpose in the world.

ACKNOWLEDGMENTS

THE AUTHORS WISH TO ACKNOWLEDGE TWO INTREPID women whose invaluable help brought this work to fruition:

Deborah Morales, part cheerleader, part den mother, irrepressible and irreplaceable manager and friend; and Miranda Jewess, our brilliant editor who cleans up after us, instructs and admonishes us, and makes us sound much smarter than we deserve.

We would also like to thank the always-professional and talented Titan team, whom we've come to rely on: Nick Landau, Vivian Cheung, Laura Price, Sam Matthews, Julia Lloyd, Paul Gill, Chris McLane, Lydia Gittins, Philippa Ward, and the lovely Katharine Carroll.

KAREEM ABDUL-JABBAR

AT 7' 2" TALL, KAREEM ABDUL-JABBAR IS A HUGE HOLMESIAN in every way. An English and History graduate of UCLA, he first read the Doyle stories early in his basketball career, and adapted Holmes's powers of observation to the game in order to gain an edge over his opponents. His first novel featuring Mycroft Holmes was published in 2015; it received multiple starred reviews and was lauded as a story that "rivals Conan Doyle himself" by the *New York Times* and a "triumphant adult fiction debut" by *Publishers Weekly*.

He played basketball for the Milwaukee Bucks (1969–1975) and the Los Angeles Lakers (1975–1989), scoring 38,387 points to become the National Basketball Association's all-time leading scorer. Kareem was inducted into the Basketball Hall of Fame in 1995. Since retiring, he has been an actor, a producer, a coach, an international speaker, and a *New York Times* best-selling author with writings focused on history. His previous books include *Coach Wooden and Me—Our Fifty Year Friendship*, *Becoming Kareem—Growing*

Up On and Off the Court, Writings on the Wall—Searching for A New Equality, Beyond Black and White, Giant Steps, Kareem, Black Profiles in Courage, A Season on the Reservation, Brothers in Arms, and *On the Shoulders of Giants—My Journey Through the Harlem Renaissance.* His children's books include *Streetball Crew—Sasquatch in the Paint, Stealing the Game,* and *What Color is My World?—The Lost History of African-American Inventors,* which won the NAACP Award for "Best Children's Book." In 2016 he was awarded the Presidential Medal of Freedom, the USA's highest civilian honor, by former President Barack Obama. Currently he is Chairman of the Skyhook Foundation and a columnist for the *Guardian* newspaper as well as a cultural critic for the *Hollywood Reporter.*

ANNA WATERHOUSE

A PROFESSIONAL SCREENWRITER AND SCRIPT CONSULTANT, Anna Waterhouse has worked alongside such legends as Robert Towne, Tom Cruise, and producer Paula Wagner. She has consulted for premium cable miniseries and basic cable series, and co-produced a feature-length documentary for HBO. She was supervising producer and co-writer (with Kareem Abdul-Jabbar) of the critically acclaimed feature-length documentary *On the Shoulders of Giants* (Netflix and Showtime), which won Best Documentary NAACP Image Award and two Telly awards. She is currently writing and co-producing a limited eight-part TV series alongside multiple-Oscar winners Robert Towne, Mike Medavoy, and Mel Gibson. She has written several how-to screenwriting seminars for *Writer's Digest* and has taught screenwriting at both Chapman University in Orange, California, and at the University of Southern California.